MAGWAVE

BOOK 2

THE RORSCHACH EXPLORER MISSIONS

A NOVEL BY

K. PATRICK DONOGHUE

Published by Leaping Leopard Enterprises, LLC

This book is a work of fiction. All the characters, incidents and dialogue are drawn from the author's imagination or are used fictitiously. Any resemblance to actual locations, events or persons, living or dead, is entirely coincidental.

DEDICATION

To my brother, Brendan, and my sister, Patricia.

It has been a long time since we transformed bunk beds and boxes into boats, airplanes and spaceships for all sorts of imagined adventures, but a brother couldn't have asked for better crewmates, back then and now.

CONTENTS

ACKNOWLEDGMENTS

I am fortunate and grateful to have received some amazing support from a number of people in the creation of *Magwave*.

This includes David Gatewood, my editor, and a number of expert volunteers who helped vet the story's physics, medical and radio-related content. While I bent (or ignored) reality in a number of spots when crafting the story, I tried to incorporate their guidance and suggestions in many other places. For their help in this regard, I'd like to thank the following people for their contributions: retired electrical engineer Collin Matheny, retired vascular trauma surgeon Christopher Morin, physics professor Alex Small, amateur radio enthusiast Karl Bridges and mechanical engineer Brian Fentress.

Separately, I owe thanks to science fiction fan Jeff Baker, as well as proofreaders Lisa Weinberg, Paulette Jones and Cheryl Hollenbeck. Beyond their review of spelling, punctuation and grammar, each provided valuable suggestions that improved the storyline.

A thank you is also due to illustrator and computer graphics designer, Keith Draws, who turned my descriptions of the *Rorschach Explorer* into stunning CGI images that can be viewed on my website at kpatrickdonoghue.com. Speaking of that website, I'd also like to thank my web designers, James Lee and Kevin Maines, for continually improving the site as I add more titles.

Last, but in no way least, I would like to thank my wife, Bryson, and my sons, Michael and Stephen, for their continued support. During the writing of *Magwave*, there was a lot going on in our immediate and extended family that made the last seven months challenging for all of us, but we weathered the challenges together. As always, Bryson, Michael and Stephen exhibited the essence of being good to one another throughout it all.

NOTES TO READERS

Greetings, friends, fans and new readers! Thank you in advance for choosing to read *Magwave*, book 2 in my new sci-fi thriller series, the Rorschach Explorer Missions.

For those of you already familiar with the series, you will find *Magwave* is a continuation of the storyline first hatched in the series novella prequel, *UMO*, and further explored in book 1 of the series, *Skywave*. Hard science fiction fans among you will hopefully enjoy the blend of adventure/fantasy and science, but a word of caution — you'll need to suspend your disbelief to fully enjoy *Magwave*. While I endeavored to bolster the science in the story by soliciting feedback/incorporating suggestions from volunteer scientific experts/enthusiasts, it's still fiction and many of the elements of the story bend, stretch or ignore reality.

If you are new to the series and haven't read *UMO* and *Skywave*, not to worry. I've incorporated enough background from the previous two stories to allow *Magwave* to be read as a stand-alone story. However, to fully appreciate the storyline and character relationships, I'd strongly recommend at least reading *Skywave* prior to starting *Magwave*.

As a heads up to both sets of readers, I've created a few reference tools to aid in your enjoyment of *Magwave*. First and foremost, with the help of a skilled CGI designer, we created a dozen different angle depictions of the *Rorschach Explorer* spacecraft that can be viewed by visiting my author website at www.kpatrickdonoghue.com. From the main navigation bar, select the "Series" link and click on the Rorschach Explorer Missions option. From the Rorschach series page, you'll click another link that will take you to the image gallery page. Once you've arrived on the *Rorschach Explorer* gallery page, just click on any of the thumbnails to view and cycle through larger-sized images. You may find these images useful to visualize the ship since a significant portion of the story takes place on *Rorschach*.

In addition, I've included two appendices at the end of *Magwave*. One is an illustration that depicts the crested head of a Parasaur dinosaur, a proxy for the appearance of the crested head of the aliens identified in the story as Callistons in some spots, and the Suhkai in others. The second appendix is a glossary of terms and acronyms that appear in the story and their associated meanings.

Finally, a separate heads up for those of you familiar with my other series, the Anlon Cully Chronicles. You will be happy to learn there are expanded cameo appearances by four characters from that series in *Magwave*: Anlon Cully, Pebbles McCarver, Jennifer Stevens and Antonio Wallace.

To all readers, I hope you enjoy the space exploration adventure presented in *Magwave* and look forward to the next story in the series, *Dynewave*.

PREMONITION

SET OF *IN THE SPOTLIGHT*
BCON STUDIOS
NEW YORK, NEW YORK
JULY 1, 2019

The television camera zoomed in on Carlton Rawlings. "It's a mistake, I tell you. A horrible mistake that will end in tragedy."

"Why?" asked Nigel Ewing, the British host of *In the Spotlight*. "Why are you so convinced?"

The ninety-two-year-old retired astronaut waved off the question. "What's the point of rehashing it again? Amato won't listen. He's launching his bird next week come hell or high tide."

"Don't you think it's important to go on record?" Ewing asked. "Not for your colleagues, not for Amato. But for people all over the world who've fallen under his spell. They haven't heard from you. They don't know the significant issues you've raised."

A smirk formed on Rawlings' face. "The average person doesn't care about the risks, Nigel. To Joe Billy Bob, this mission's a made-for-TV drama about space bees and giant lizard men."

"That may be true for some, but not for our viewers. They want more than fairy tales. They want facts. That's why millions tune into my show." Ewing explained that many of his viewers had expressed reservations about Augustus Amato's decision to accelerate the launch of his state-of-the-art spacecraft, the *Rorschach Explorer**. "They agree with you, Colonel. They think Amato's change in plan is reckless."

---

* To see CGI images of the *Rorschach Explorer*, visit the author's website, www. kpatrickdonoghue.com.

Rawlings frowned and lowered his gaze. "It's just so stupid. I can't understand why he would push up the launch window, or why NASA would support his decision."

"Some have suggested NASA is reluctant to appear uncooperative after Amato exposed their cover-up of the *Cetus Prime* mission and the existence of UMOs."

"Would not surprise me one iota."

"Others believe Amato's sincere, that he really believes the recent activity of UMOs on Callisto signals the return of the Callistons, your so called lizard-men."

"Whether he's right or wrong doesn't matter," Rawlings said. "What matters is creating a mission plan that gives you the best chance of success and sticking to it. That's where Amato's gone off the rails."

The host paused to adjust his cufflinks, allowing Rawlings' comment to linger before he shifted the focus of the interview. "You don't think much of the *Rorschach Explorer* crew, do you?"

"No. I do not." The former Apollo astronaut, a man who'd walked on the Moon, stared at Ewing. "They're beaks and talons, Nigel. A crew of misfits."

The camera switched to a close-up of Ewing, listening to Rawlings with studious intensity. "Many don't share your views about the crew," Ewing said. "Take Colonel Morgan, for instance. A lot of people, both inside and outside of NASA, respect his experience and leadership."

Zooming out, the camera brought both men into view. Rawlings leaned forward and laughed. "The man's in his mid-sixties, Nigel! He hasn't been into space since the late 1980s. Look, I know Paul Morgan's a legend inside the halls of NASA, and I know he was close to the *Cetus Prime* crew, but that doesn't make him the right man to lead *this* mission. Let's face it, his selection is more sentimental than it is rational."

The camera didn't pick up the thin smile on Ewing's face. Instead it zeroed in on the ranting astronaut.

"The same goes for his co-pilot, Julia Carillo. Her last shuttle mission was the same one that put Morgan behind a desk for the last fifteen years of his NASA career. Truth be told, a lot of my fellow astronauts blame her for the disaster that cost both of them their wings. Hell, nowadays she spends her days teaching teenagers to build toy spaceships. Why on Earth would Amato pair the two together? Why didn't he select active-duty astronauts? Ones with long-duration mission experience on ISS? I'm told Amato was offered carte blanche to select any astronauts he wanted from NASA's roster. He didn't pick a single one of them."

Ewing held up his hand. "That's not entirely accurate, is it? Dr. Shilling's an active NASA employee."

"The beekeeper?" Rawlings laughed. "Bob Shilling's an animal behavior researcher, not an astronaut. Though, I will concede, he's the most qualified scientist Amato could have chosen to join the mission."

Ewing looked over the astronaut's shoulder to see his director smiling. He winked at her before lobbing his next softball. "But he's never been into space, isn't that right?"

"That's absolutely true," Rawlings said with a nod. "And sooner or later, that will pose problems."

Ewing transitioned to his next question. "So that means three of the five crew members are still in their nappies. Neither Dr. Walsh nor Mr. Joshi have been into space either. True?"

Rawlings gritted his teeth. "Don't get me started on those two. A JPL washout and an amateur astronomer. They're completely unqualified."

"I'm shocked you think so little of Dr. Walsh. She designed *Rorschach's* unique engines and radiation shield. Amato has said she knows more about the ship's systems than anyone other than the mission director, Dr. Fulton."

Rawlings pounced. "She's also a hothead who quit NASA's *Juno* team because she didn't get her way. Answer me this, Nigel. Would you want that kind of temperament in your flight engineer when things go sideways on them?"

"The way you say that, you seem convinced the mission *will* go sideways."

"Oh, it will. Mark my words. I've been around the space program for too long. No NASA mission has *ever* gone according to plan. And when Amato's mission starts to fall apart, Miss Walsh is going to curl up in a ball and suck her thumb. Just watch."

"And Mr. Joshi? You feel he's unqualified as well?"

"Ha!" Rawlings pounded the arm of his chair. "He's less qualified to be part of *Rorschach*'s crew than a C-minus high school physics student."

"That's a bit harsh," Ewing said. "After all, Mr. Joshi was the one who first noticed the radio signals that led Amato's probes to Callisto. He's the one who deduced where to look on the moon to find *Cetus Prime*. Amato has stated numerous times that he considers Ajay the person most responsible for all of the discoveries they made on Callisto."

"All true." Rawlings nodded. "But how does that qualify young Mr. Joshi to serve as communications officer for *Rorschach*? This is the big leagues. He doesn't belong. Even more so now that Amato's cut their training to push up the launch."

Ewing's mouth opened to ask another question, but this time Rawlings needed no prodding. The astronaut looked into the camera, his eyes black and his stare cold. "They're going to die out there."

CHAPTER 1

BUMPS AND BURSTS

D r. Kiera Walsh shielded her eyes and took in one last view of Earth. The twinkling light was barely perceptible through the halo of the Sun's rays, but she could just pick it out to the right of the fiery orb.

While her shipmates lingered at the flight deck window to wave final goodbyes, Kiera turned away and walked to her station. Strapping into her safety harness, she checked the mission clock on her console monitor. T+49. That meant another one hundred days of space travel to Callisto, and for the next seventy of them, the only vista they would see from the flight deck would be an endless black filled with stars.

As awe-inspiring as that view had been to Kiera during the first few weeks of their journey, it had lost its magic by week five. And now there would be nothing to break the visual monotony until Jupiter began to morph from a dot of light into a planet at around T+120.

That hadn't been the initial plan. Originally, when they expected to launch in January 2020, their flight plan included a slingshot around Mars on their way to the Jupiter system. But once the launch date was moved up, Mars' orbital position put it well out of reach.

There was still a chance *Rorschach* might cross paths with the dwarf planet Ceres as they exited the asteroid belt, but only if they sped up to make up for the time lost during these idiotic loops to catch glimpses of Earth.

Though Kiera knew the real purpose of the loops was to perform shake-out testing on the fleet management system, she couldn't help but view them as sightseeing interludes for the benefit of Ajay Joshi and Dante

Fulton. Dante, back at Mission Control, wanted to capture video footage for the *Expedition to Callisto* television show chronicling their mission. Ajay wanted them because, well, he was a goofball.

As if to prove her point, Ajay currently had his hand pressed against a pane of the flight deck windows, fingers spread to mimic the letter V. "Live long and prosper, fellow Earthlings," he said.

Kiera rolled her eyes. "Colonel, can we just get on with the test, please?"

Colonel Paul Morgan slid into his seat at the commander's station directly in front of Kiera's post. "Yeah, I guess it's time to get back on track." He turned to the co-pilot, Major Julia Carillo. "Prepare to swing the fleet around, Julia."

"Roger that," Carillo said.

"Unpucker from the window and buckle in, Ajay," said Kiera.

Ajay turned and saluted. "Roger dodger."

As he took his seat at the communications station behind Carillo, he turned to Dr. Robert Shilling, who occupied the center post in the second row of flight deck stations, between Kiera and Ajay. "Do you think our UMOs miss Earth?"

"I doubt they have emotions," Shilling said. "If they do, they haven't shown them to me."

Another eye roll from Kiera. Geez, the way Shilling talked about the UMOs —electromagnetic balls of light known to some as unidentified magnetic objects and to others as space bees — you'd think he had a direct line to God.

Kiera shook off the scientist's sanctimony and cycled through the ship's cameras on her console monitor until she hit upon the feed from Cam-8. The rear-view video image showed thousands of golf-ball sized lights flitting around in space aft of *Rorschach*. "Looks to me like they're hungry."

"They *always* seem to be hungry," said Shilling.

Kiera felt the familiar urge to walk over to Shilling's station and slap him across the face. *No shit, Sherlock. That's why I pointed it out.*

"Colonel," she said, "I think we should feed them before we resume our heading."

"No, no, no. I don't think so," said Shilling. "Remember, we don't want the tail to wag the dog, now do we?"

Words balanced on the tip of Kiera's tongue: *If it'll bat your pampered ass out into space, I'm all for a wagging tail.*

Her mental image of Shilling tumbling into space was disrupted by the colonel. "You still think we should finish the loop before we feed them?"

"Yes," said Shilling. "If Dr. Walsh has properly addressed her software bug, we shouldn't have any more problems."

The problem isn't my software. It's the damn UMOs.

Kiera had heard enough. "Listen, if you had properly trained your little space bees, limp dick, I wouldn't have needed to reprogram the fleet software."

A smirking Shilling turned to face her. "How charming."

"All right, you two, knock it off. That's an order," Morgan said.

At issue was the recent behavior of the UMOs accompanying the *Rorschach Explorer* and its fleet of sixteen unmanned probes. Before Kiera met Shilling — before she knew what he was really like — she had been in support of Augustus Amato's decision to include a colony of the electromagnetic aliens as part of *Rorschach*'s fleet.

The aliens were strongly attracted to the stream of ions ejected by *Rorschach*'s engines, as well as to the very-low-frequency radio waves in the engine's output. As a consequence, when the engines were active, the UMOs formed into a swirling ball aft of the spacecraft and absorbed the propulsion system's byproducts. In so doing, they created a magnetic bubble that exhibited unusual properties, including a bow-shock-like push against *Rorschach* and its probes that resulted in a dramatic boost in spacecraft acceleration. In addition, the magnetic bubble appeared to largely neutralize the g-forces associated with dramatic changes in speed. It was almost as if the UMO bubble was somehow capable of nullifying the fleet's mass, making it possible for the spacecraft to accelerate to mind-boggling speeds without experiencing the g-forces that would normally rip the ship apart and kill the crew.

By luring this UMO colony, trained by Shilling, to accompany the *Rorschach Explorer*, Amato had hoped to shave months off the travel time to Callisto ... if, that was, Shilling could manipulate the UMOs to behave as desired.

And therein was the problem.

Shilling's primary experience training UMOs had centered on keeping them away from high-value satellites in Earth's orbit. Using Pavlovian conditioning techniques, he'd trained the honeybee-like aliens to gather and feed at designated ion-pod satellites instead of aggregating around the International Space Station, military payloads, or crucial scientific or commercial satellites. But Shilling was learning on the fly how to adapt that experience and his conditioning techniques to gain the UMOs' assistance in propelling *Rorschach*.

In the earliest stages of the mission, his techniques had worked. But the last time Morgan looped *Rorschach* around to look back at Earth, the UMOs had magnetically bumped two of the probes surrounding the ship, disrupting communications with the CubeSats and making the probes veer off course, nearly clipping *Rorschach*'s instrument array. If the errant probes had collided with the ship, they could have caused significant damage or destroyed the ship. Therefore, it was critical to avoid a repeat occurrence.

Shilling claimed the mishap merely demonstrated that the UMOs had learned to associate the fleet's use of maneuvering thrusters with the eventual powering up of their engines. In other words, the bumping was the UMOs' way of communicating they expected to be fed.

To solve the problem, Kiera had suggested feeding them with a short burst of the engines before using thrusters. Shilling disagreed, fearing this would cause the UMOs to associate their bumping with spot-feedings, encouraging them to employ the bumps whenever they wanted to eat instead of adhering to the feeding schedule he had established through training.

Morgan, unfortunately, had sided with limp dick. The colonel had tasked Kiera with developing a software fix to overcome the effects of the bumping on ship-to-probe communications. Though Kiera still held to her opinion, she'd followed the colonel's orders.

And now it was time to try out Kiera's patch.

"Julia, deactivate RCS auto-pilot," Morgan said.

"Aye, aye," said Carillo. "Kiera, verify fleet management is active."

Kiera responded with a half-hearted "Roger that" and checked her data screen. "Fleet program running. All probes green."

"Confirm probe RCS synced with *Rorschach*."

"Reaction control system sync is confirmed."

"Bob, keep an eye on our UMOs," said Morgan. "I want to know if they get frisky again."

"Copy that," Shilling replied.

"RCS now on manual," said Carillo. "Commencing turn."

Kiera kept her focus on the data screen showing the status of each probe as Carillo fired the maneuvering thrusters. The ship veered left, and the probes' fired their own thrusters to follow the ship's turn. Two more thruster shots by Carillo produced further synchronized reactions from the probes.

"So far, so good," Kiera said. "Probe RCS nominal."

But within seconds, Shilling piped up. "Uh … Colonel, I've got activity. The UMOs are splitting up."

Red alerts began to flash on Kiera's screen. "I have sensor faults on three Shield probes."

"I see the alerts," said Morgan. "Are they still in formation?"

Kiera darted her eyes from one set of probe data to another. "No, they're veering off course."

"Colonel, we're getting interference spikes on X-band," Ajay said.

"How long should it take for the patch to kick in?" Morgan asked Kiera.

"Should have been almost instantaneous."

"Damn. Julia, kill thrusters. Kiera, shut down the breakaways."

Carillo quickly acknowledged, but Kiera delayed acting on Morgan's command. Under her breath, she urged the probes to get back on course. "Come on, come on. Go to UHF. Pay attention to your neighbors."

"I said shut them down, Kiera."

Kiera watched the readings from the three probes begin to adjust. "Hold on. It's starting to work. They switched over to UHF. They're coming back into formation."

"I don't care. Power them off. Now."

"Just give them a little more time … the new code is working."

"Colonel," cut in Ajay, "the X-band radio interference is subsiding."

Morgan shook his head. "Shilling, update?"

"The UMOs are re-forming behind *Rorschach*."

On Kiera's screen, the sensor alerts ceased. "All probes green."

"Roger that," said Morgan. He turned around to face Kiera. "What happened? What caused the delay?"

"The cutover to UHF took too long. I'll have to re-look at the patch to figure out why."

"They're back on X-band now?"

Kiera scanned her screen. "They are."

"All right," said the colonel. "Let's not take any chances. Override X-band comms and switch fleet comms to UHF so we can finish the turn maneuver. Work on the program later."

"Roger that."

Kiera clicked a drop-down menu and changed the default comms channel to UHF. After verifying the switch by pinging all sixteen probes, she confirmed the change to Morgan. The colonel then gave Carillo the green light to resume use of *Rorschach*'s thrusters to finish the loop maneuver.

The UMOs bumped the probes again, but this time all the probes maintained their positions.

At Shilling's behest, Morgan waited thirty minutes after the turn was completed before giving the order to power up the fleet's VLF engines. Aided by the push from the feeding UMOs, the engines remained on until they had reached their targeted cruising speed, at which point Morgan ordered the engines powered off. They would proceed toward the asteroid belt on momentum.

He then dismissed everyone but Kiera from the flight deck. The look on Morgan's face told Kiera to expect another lecture about following orders.

JUNO MISSION CONTROL CENTER
NASA'S JET PROPULSION LABORATORY
PASADENA, CALIFORNIA
AUGUST 29, 2019

Project manager Ed Chen scooted his chair closer to the computer screen and shushed the other controllers gathered around his station. The next downlink from *Juno* was due to arrive within minutes, and he needed to concentrate.

The venerable Jupiter probe was in orbit around Callisto, serving now as a data relay satellite between the marooned *Cetus Prime* and NASA's Deep Space Network. Chen, like many of his *Juno* team underlings, had not been thrilled when the probe was redeployed for this seemingly mundane mission, but that opinion had changed after the JPL whiz kids discovered a way to reactivate *Cetus Prime*'s twenty-five-year-old external cameras.

While some of the ship's cameras had their views obscured by a mix of ice and dust, others did not. Two of them could still rotate, and one of them had a working zoom. And with the skill of the NASA photographic experts, *Juno* had been able to relay stunning images to JPL, including still images of the Nuada crater and the abandoned alien spaceport first discovered there by Augustus Amato's CubeSat ten months earlier.

None of the images were more remarkable than the photographs that had led Amato to accelerate the launch of the *Rorschach Explorer* — the ones that showed streaks of light melting away the ice encasing the ancient alien structure. In fact, UMOs appeared to be systematically de-icing the building from one end to the other, revealing more of the structure's features. As a result, each new batch of photos produced jaw-dropping new details.

It was Chen's job to make certain *Juno*'s relays of the downlinks were received, processed and distributed without incident. That was why he nearly soiled himself when a stream of empty files and error messages began to populate his screen.

Around him, the sound of epithets and keyboard strokes rose up in a symphony of angst. Chen's staff had seen the errors as well.

Chen scrolled through the file listing on his screen. Of the hundreds of expected files, only a handful had made it through with any data, and none were photo files, just files containing readings from *Juno*'s array of instruments.

Chen pushed back his chair and looked down the row of stations to the instruments controller, Sergei Kolov. "Sergei," he called, "you're the only one with data. Report. What do you see?"

The hulking, seven-foot Russian shook his head and mumbled something inaudible.

Chen repeated his query, this time louder. Most of the other controllers stopped what they were doing and turned toward the Russian.

"It's gone," he said. "*Juno's* fried."

OFFICE OF THE CHIEF ADMINISTRATOR
NASA HEADQUARTERS
WASHINGTON, D.C.

Dr. Helen Brock, NASA's chief administrator, hovered over the speakerphone. "You're certain? Absolutely certain?"

"Yes, Dr. Brock, there's no doubt. *Juno* is LOS," Chen said.

"Could it be an issue with DSN?"

"No. DSN passed us what they received."

"Did you try handshakes on all bands?"

"We did. No return pings on any band."

Brock slumped back in her chair and massaged her temples. "I can't believe it. I can't believe my baby's gone."

Chen remained silent as Brock absorbed the news. She had invested ten years of her career getting the *Juno* program funded and off the ground, and another ten as its internal champion as she rose through the ranks at NASA.

"What happened?" she asked at last.

"Gamma burst," said Chen. "*Juno's* GRS detected a huge spike before its electronics were cooked."

"Where did the burst originate?"

"Unknown. Our first thought was the spaceport. But if it originated from the structure, it didn't affect *Cetus Prime*. After we lost *Juno*, we pinged *Cetus Prime* directly and it answered back. None of its systems were affected, as far as we can tell. What was working before the burst is working now."

"What about the UMOs that have been de-icing the spaceport?" Brock asked. "Could they have been the source of the burst?"

"As far as I know, they've never been observed to emit gamma rays."

"True, but that doesn't mean they can't. And they've certainly been known to knock out satellites with active spectrometers like *Juno*'s GRS."

"I guess it's possible," said Chen. "But *Juno*'s been orbiting Callisto for months, Dr. Brock. Why would UMOs only take notice now? It's not like we just turned its spectrometers on."

"Well, we shouldn't discard the possibility."

"We won't discard any possibilities."

"I'm sure you won't. What other ideas do you have?"

"Well, we were thinking along the lines of a magnetar, but there aren't any known magnetars with beams in line with Callisto's current position. At least, not that we can detect from Earth."

A magnetar is a type of radio pulsar that emits powerful beams of electromagnetic radiation in the form of gamma rays. While scientists estimate there are more than thirty million magnetars in the Milky Way galaxy, a grand total of twenty-three have been observed from Earth. Not twenty-three million. Twenty-three. And many of those are located far beyond the Milky Way. The rest are either inactive or, if they are active, invisible from Earth.

Invisible because, similar to pulsars, magnetars behave like celestial lighthouses, shooting out a focused beam of magnetic radiation each time the star rotates. But the only way to detect the beam is if you're in a direct line with it. In other words, the only way to detect a magnetar's beam from Earth is if the beam is pointed directly at Earth. If the beam is aimed anywhere else, the magnetar and its gamma-ray bursts are invisible.

"A magnetar? Did Fermi detect the burst?" Brock asked.

"No. It was in use for a limited field-of-view project when it happened. Still is. We've asked to prioritize a sweep toward Callisto ASAP."

The Fermi Gamma-ray Space Telescope is a NASA space observatory in low Earth orbit. With the ability to view the vast majority of space surrounding Earth, its two gamma-ray detecting instruments have made numerous discoveries.

"And no other observatories detected it either?"

"We're still calling around, but thus far, no. It's odd. The cone of the beam would have to be crazy narrow to hit Callisto and not hit Earth."

"That is odd. And *Juno* didn't record any preceding gamma spikes?"

"Doctor, I've been part of this team for four years, and we're used to seeing background gamma radiation. I assure you, we've never picked up a spike like this."

Brock rose from her chair. Hands on her hips, she paced behind the desk. The sudden appearance of a gamma burst directed at Callisto, one that wasn't observed from Earth, suggested three possibilities.

The most obvious one was an attack on *Juno* by the UMOs residing on Callisto. Perhaps they were aided by a device in the spaceport, or perhaps this was simply an unobserved-to-date capability. Unfortunately, there was no way to investigate the possibility remotely. *Cetus Prime*'s spectrometers had been destroyed by UMOs around Mars twenty-four years ago.

Second, there was a chance a dormant magnetar somewhere in the Milky Way had woken up. While this was theoretically possible, unless the magnetar's beam was detectable from Earth, there was no way to prove or disprove this possibility remotely either. One would have to scan the heavens for follow-on gamma-ray bursts while in close proximity to Callisto's orbital position when *Juno* was knocked out.

The third, but least likely, possibility was an isolated starquake. Starquakes are earthquakes that take place on neutron stars. Magnetic forces in the crust of the star build up tension until the crust experiences a sudden shift or displacement. When that happens, the neutron star emits an intense beam of gamma-ray energy. Starquakes can occur in isolation or in bunches. When they occur in bunches, the neutron star producing the rays is considered a magnetar and, given the frequency of bursts, is easier to detect. But when starquakes happen in isolation or intermittently, they are much harder to detect.

Another beam from a starquake on a relatively stable neutron star might not shoot out for thousands of years. One might arrive tomorrow. There was no telling when or how often they would occur. And even if an isolated burst did appear, Jupiter's and Callisto's positions in their orbits might put the celestial bodies well out of reach of the beam.

However, Chen's observation about the beam hitting Callisto but missing Earth seemed to argue against either a starquake or magnetar. While gamma bursts are narrow at their points of origin, their conical beams spread out as they travel through space. The farther the beam travels, the wider the cone becomes. So unless the burst that took out *Juno* came from a previously undetected neutron star very close to the solar system, it should have been detected on Earth.

Brock's thoughts were interrupted by a comment from Chen. "I'm sorry, Ed. I missed that. What did you say?"

"I said we were thinking it might be a good idea to alert Mayaguana and have them pass the word to the *Rorschach Explorer*. If I'm not mistaken, *Rorschach* is about to enter the asteroid belt."

The loss of *Juno* had hit Brock so hard she hadn't considered the implications for Amato's mission. But she recognized them now.

"Get on it right away, Ed. I mean, like, *right now*. Get off the phone with me and call Dante Fulton. Don't stop trying until you reach him. I'll do the same with Amato."

HANGAR-1
A3ROSPACE INDUSTRIES COMMAND AND CONTROL CENTER
MAYAGUANA ISLAND, THE BAHAMAS

As the doors slid open, the climate-controlled hangar was quickly overwhelmed by the heavy push of Caribbean air. Augustus Amato dabbed his bald pate with a handkerchief and stepped out onto the launch apron.

He was pleased to see two Cargo probes had already been loaded on flatbeds and another two appeared ready for their turns with the crane. Filled with supplies and provisions for the *Rorschach Explorer*, the delivery truck–sized vessels would travel by plane to Florida where NASA would launch them into space next month.

Without a colony of UMOs to boost the speed of their VLF engines, the supply probes had no chance of catching up to *Rorschach* before it reached Callisto, but they wouldn't be needed until the return trip to Earth. There were already four identical cargo vessels in *Rorschach*'s fleet of probes, with ample provisions to supply ship and crew on the way to the Jovian moon.

Turning back toward the hangar, Amato unbuttoned the Panama suit jacket covering his prodigious belly and wiped the handkerchief across his neck. With the aid of a cane, the seventy-nine-year-old billionaire walked to the elevator inside the bay, stopping occasionally to greet workers moving in and out of the hangar.

As he neared the elevator, the doors opened and out stepped Dr. Dante Fulton, the mission director for the *Rorschach Explorer*'s expedition to Callisto. The trim, black aerospace engineer was accompanied by Dr. Dennis Pritchard, the former chief administrator for NASA and now an executive with Amato's A3rospace Industries. Joining the two men was Mark Myers, Amato's assistant.

Amato halted. It was never good news when all three came looking for him.

Dante was the first to speak. "We just got off the phone with NASA. We need to talk."

"Fine, fine," Amato said, resuming his path to the elevator. "Let's do it inside before I melt."

On the ride up to the office level of A3I's Command and Control Center, Dante filled Amato in on his conversation with Ed Chen at JPL. When he finished, Myers said, "Dr. Brock called as well. She said she needed to speak with you as soon as possible."

As the elevator doors opened, Amato nodded. "Yes, I imagine she's anxious to talk. Go on ahead and ring her back and tell her we'll call her in thirty minutes. I want to confer with Dante and Dennis first."

"She's on hold on your office line," Myers said.

"Ah. Well, go on ahead and tell her I'll be there as fast as I can shuffle."

"Yes, sir."

On the turtle-paced walk to his office suite, Amato asked Dante, "How big of an issue is it?"

"I don't think we can say yet."

"Dennis, you've been quiet," Amato said to Pritchard. "What's your view?"

Hands stuffed inside the pockets of his khakis, the bespectacled Pritchard shrugged. "Hard to know without more data, but there's a scenario where it could force us to scrub."

"I was afraid you might say that."

When they finally arrived at Amato's office, the three men gathered at the meeting table at the far end of the room. Myers followed them in and activated the conference speakerphone to connect the waiting Dr. Brock. Then Myers left the office.

Brock began the conversation by covering the same ground that Chen had discussed with Dante, but with more details than Dante had shared during the quick elevator ride. Amato listened without question or comment. He left that for Dante and Pritchard, and they did not disappoint. For fifteen minutes, they engaged the NASA chief in a robust scientific dialogue about pulsars, magnetars and gamma rays.

As the conversation turned more technical, Amato's thoughts began to drift. A magnetar … a magnetar. He imagined a twenty-kilometer-sized ball — small enough to comfortably fit on Mayaguana's northern peninsula — rotating once every second. A magnetar of such dimensions would be three times heavier than the Sun. He could envision the hypermagnetic neutron star shooting out gamma rays like a disco laser ball. Get within reach of its electromagnetic beams and you'd be cooked. Dodge them and live to explore another day.

"The first thing we need to do is isolate the source of the bursts," Dante was saying, "then find out whether we're dealing with a one-time event or one that's ongoing."

"Agreed," said Pritchard. "You're thinking of sending the Recons ahead of *Rorschach*?"

"It's the only thing we can do."

"Unfortunately, Dante's right," Brock said. "*Juno*'s last position only gives us one data point, and we don't have any other assets near Callisto. If it's an ongoing phenomenon, you're going to have to triangulate gamma readings from several spectrometers to pinpoint the source. The Recons are your best bet. You don't want to sacrifice your Shield probes."

Amato winced at the thought of sacrificing any of his CubeSats traveling with *Rorschach*, but he understood Brock's reasoning. Of the sixteen probes in *Rorschach*'s fleet, six were designated as Recon probes. These CubeSats were as long and wide as medium-sized surfboards and as thick as large roller-suitcases. Outfitted with a variety of instruments, they had originally been intended to detect anomalies in *Rorschach*'s path.

"Do we need to sacrifice them all?" Amato asked. "I'd like to hold at least two of them back with the fleet. We may need them to back up the Shields."

While *Rorschach*'s onboard radiation shield would suffice for most of the journey to Callisto, it would need an extra layer of protection when it approached Jupiter's massive magnetic field. The radiation streaming from the planet would eventually breach the ship's unique shield design unless that shield was bolstered by six Shield CubeSats. The Shields were of similar dimensions as the Recons but the makeup of their components was different given their unique mission. The Shields would use ion-projecting magnets to form an ionosphere-like bubble around *Rorschach* and its four Cargo probes. Inside the bubble, VLF radio waves ejected by the fleet's engines would bounce around, helping to block dangerous radiation.

"I don't think we have a choice," Dante said. "We have to send all six Recons ahead. Besides, we can always launch replacements."

"They'd never catch up in time," said Amato.

"Not necessarily, Augie," Pritchard said. "Until we know what caused the burst, and whether to expect further gamma bursts, it's prudent to slow the fleet down."

"That's right," Dante said. "And if need be, we can have the fleet turn back and rendezvous with the Recon replacements before resuming the mission."

The call continued for several more minutes, during which time they discussed the risks associated with scanning the spaceport and its resident colony of UMOs for signs of gamma radiation. Given the UMOs' known sensitivity to high-frequency radiation, there was a concern the UMOs would attack the probes, thereby wearing out *Rorschach*'s welcome before it arrived.

When the call ended, Dante and Pritchard left to convene the rest of the Mission Control team to craft a plan for the gamma-burst hunt.

Alone in his office, Amato loosened his tie and unbuttoned his sweat-dampened collar. Replaying the phone call in his mind, he recalled an exchange about magnetars between Brock and Pritchard. Magnetars, Brock had told them, are poorly understood. They are thought to be byproducts of supernova explosions, and most of them burned out long ago. "There are very few documented examples of spontaneous restarts and no consensus as to what triggers magnetars to wake up."

"If memory serves me," Pritchard had said, "the reigning belief is that a disturbance in a neutron star's magnetic field can reactivate a magnetar."

"Yes, but what causes the disturbance?" Brock asked. "The influence of a nearby neutron star? A gamma beam from an active magnetar or an X-ray beam from a pulsar? The pull of a black hole? The ripple of energy from a new supernova?"

"I'm sure all of those are capable of triggering magnetic instability if they're close enough and powerful enough."

"Yet none of those have been observed near a documented magnetar-restart."

Now Brock's final words on the subject echoed in Amato's mind. Leaning back in his chair, he mumbled, "Magnetar ... I wonder ... "

CHAPTER 2

STING LIKE A BEE

In the production booth, the director gave the command to queue the title sequence of *Expedition to Callisto*, the weekly broadcast chronicling the *Rorschach Explorer*'s mission to the second largest of Jupiter's moons.

Since the show's inception a month prior to the spaceship's departure from Earth, the series known colloquially among viewers as *XTC*, or ecstasy, had become the most-watched program in the history of television and the Internet, with each successive week's episode setting a new viewership record.

Jenna Toffy, the show's host, looked up from her notes to watch the familiar opening sequence on an off-camera television monitor. As the intro music played, a video of *Rorschach* flying through space appeared on the screen. Below the image, a caption read: *Episode XII — Entering the Asteroid Belt.* The voice-over announcer then teased the episode's lineup of features and guests, and a montage of video and still images cycled on the screen, including shots of *Rorschach*, its crew, the Mission Control Center and, of course, UMOs.

XTC's viewers *loved* UMOs. They found the aliens' honeybee-like behaviors fascinating. And their fascination had been rewarded with stunning clips of interactions between the UMOs, *Rorschach* and its fleet of probes during the early stage of the five-month journey to Callisto.

Now, two months into the trek, *Rorschach* had arrived at the inner boundary of the asteroid belt. Powered by the breakthrough VLF propulsion technology and an additional speed boost provided by the UMOs, the ship had traveled 225 million kilometers in record time. And with 400 million kilometers left to go, the producers of *XTC* were anxious to shift viewer attention away from the UMOs and toward the mission's ultimate goals: the exploration of the Nuada crater and the two mysteries inside, the abandoned *Cetus Prime* and an ancient spaceport built by a race of humanoid aliens that NASA had named Callistons. As such, the montage for tonight's episode included not only the CubeSat photograph of the crater, but also renderings of both the ship and spaceport created by artists from five continents.

While the director delivered last-minute instructions through her earpiece, Toffy watched the final two segments of the montage. The first was a slow-motion video clip of the three members of the *Cetus Prime* crew, Lieutenant Colonel Avery Lockett, Captain Nick Reed and Mission Specialist Christine Baker. The video was shot at a pre-launch picnic held in the crew's honor at the Johnson Space Flight Center in September 1994. Less than a year after the video was recorded, the three astronauts were marooned on Callisto after clashing twice with UMOs in orbit around Mars. With little food and water left aboard the ship, and no means by which to return to Earth, the crew abandoned their crippled vessel and left in a Calliston spacecraft they discovered in the spaceport.

That was twenty-four years ago.

While the picnic video ran, the audio of the crew's final message, recorded by Nick Reed, played in the background.

"Well, folks, this is the last you'll hear from us. Kind of sad we won't see any of you again, but excited at the same time to start our new adventure. As angry as we were about what happened to us around Mars, it's all good now. If things had gone differently, we wouldn't have connected with the UMOs, they wouldn't have led us here, we wouldn't have discovered the spaceport or found our new ride.

"It's a slick-looking ship, and it comes with our own UMO hive. They're actually useful little guys and gals, not the threats we made them out to be. So, we're off to wherever Christine's 'beekeepers' went, with our UMO hive leading the way. Not sure where that might be or how long it will take to get there, but we figured it was a better option than starving to death here.

Anyhow, 'til we meet again, love to our families and friends. Be good to one another. Cetus Prime *out."*

As the audio neared completion, the picnic video clip faded and was replaced by computer-generated simulations of a male and female Calliston, the humanoids that Nick had dubbed "beekeepers" in his final message. The side-by-side CGI headshots were based on murals photographed inside the spaceport by Christine Baker on the crew's first reconnaissance of the structure.

Toffy didn't care for the images. The studio's graphic designers had cast dark shadows on the left side of the Callistons' gray-green faces to give them a more mysterious look; Toffy thought the shadowing instead created a cold, sinister vibe that would lead their worldwide audience to believe the Callistons were evil. Better to portray them as friendly, she thought. *It'll drive better ratings.* But she'd already waged that fight with the director earlier, without success.

Shivers raced through Toffy as she stared at the lizard-like features of the Calliston faces one last time before the light atop the studio's center camera flashed red. Then Toffy turned her head toward the camera and smiled, her eyes drifting to the teleprompter display below the lens. "Good evening, ladies and gentlemen, and welcome to another edition of *Expedition to Callisto.* I'm your host, Jenna Toffy. On tonight's program ... "

While two billion people across the globe settled in front of televisions, smart devices and computers to watch Toffy deliver the latest mission updates, another two billion people congregated in bars, theaters, stadiums and other public venues to do the same.

Little did any of them know that the five crewmembers of the *Rorschach Explorer* were, at that very moment, engaged in a desperate fight for survival.

CREW READY ROOM — THE *RORSCHACH EXPLORER*
FLYING THROUGH THE ASTEROID BELT
225 MILLION KILOMETERS FROM EARTH

Colonel Paul Morgan examined the sullen faces of his crew. It had been two days since Mission Control on Mayaguana had delivered the news about *Juno* and the gamma burst. He'd done his best to focus his shipmates on executing their new instructions, but their frustration and disappointment had inevitably bubbled up. Kiera and Shilling fought like teenaged brats. Ajay moped around like someone had stolen his favorite Elroy T-shirt. Even the normally stoic Carillo exhibited signs of strain.

Morgan sympathized with all of them. There was nothing he could do to change their circumstances — at least, not until the Recons located the source of the gamma radiation — but he *could* try to change their moods.

He opened the storage container on the ready room conference table and addressed the crew. "I had hoped to save this surprise for our first night on Callisto, but I feel like we could all use a little pick-me-up now." He pulled out the first pouch, looked at the label and tossed it to Ajay. "Don't open it until I tell you."

"It's pretty light. What is it?" Ajay asked.

"You'll see."

He retrieved two more packages and slid them across the table to Kiera and Carillo.

"What are you up to, Paul?" Carillo said. "Where did the box come from? That's not Mayaguana issued."

"Never mind that." Morgan pulled the last two bags from the box and gave one to Shilling. "Bob, this one's yours."

"I'll bet it has something to do with the other boxes he took into the cargo bay this morning," Ajay said.

"What boxes?" Kiera asked.

"Boxes like that one." Ajay pointed to the empty container on the table.

Morgan removed it and sat down. He picked up the last remaining pouch, the one labeled *Skywalker*. Holding it up, he said, "Now, I want you all to return to your cabins and open up your packages. Follow the instructions inside, then meet me at the cargo bay airlock in ten minutes. Is that clear?"

Instead of a chorus of assents, the four astronauts gave Morgan the fisheye.

"Cargo bay airlock," he repeated. "Ten minutes. No exceptions. Dismissed."

Morgan completed his change of clothes in two minutes and headed for the cargo bay to make the final preparations. While his magnetic boots looked ridiculous with his Bermuda shorts and Hawaiian shirt, they did prevent him from floating away as he clanked down the magnetic flooring of *Rorschach*'s center corridor.

He ducked his way through the airlock and emerged into the cargo bay. After admiring his decorating handiwork, he turned to the intercom panel and worked his way through the touchpad menu until he located the desired option. He pressed the icon and the sounds of ukuleles began to echo in the bay. If he'd entered the command correctly, the same music could now be heard throughout the ship. A smile crossed his face as he dipped his hand in the box beneath the panel, withdrew one of the plastic flower leis, and draped it around his neck. Adorned with magnetic beads, the lei lay flat against his chest, pulled by magnetic sensors woven into the shirt.

Morgan retrieved the remaining leis and passed back through the airlock to wait for his crewmates to arrive for the party. He knew they'd be late, but that was okay. He was sure they would read and reread the handwritten notes tucked inside their party gear.

Ajay was the first to appear from the ship's center-cross-section corridor where their cabins were located. He sported a red Hawaiian shirt embellished with images of the sixties cartoon character Elroy, Ajay's alter ego. Morgan was happy to see the tailored shorts fit the string-bean thin Nepali, as the measurements had been estimated by Ajay's mother. In Ajay's hand, he clutched a dozen notes family and friends had written before they launched. He beamed as he pointed at Morgan. "You're da man, Skywalker!"

"*Mahalo,*" Morgan said with a smile and a bow. He draped a lei around Ajay's neck and invited him to join in greeting the rest of the crew.

Next to arrive was Carillo. Her Hawaiian shirt looked a little loose on her lithe frame, but the shirt's design turned out better than Morgan had expected. Against the deep blue background was a repeating pattern of images: headshots of her husband, her two teenaged daughters, the Carillos' horse, Lucy, and the family Labrador, Linus, along with pictures of the Carillo family horse farm. She didn't carry her notes, but she dabbed her eyes with a tissue as she walked down the corridor. In the tight curls of salt-and-pepper hair by her ear, she had anchored the plastic magenta orchid with bobby pins included in her pouch.

When she reached Morgan, she wrapped her arms around him. "This is too much."

He hugged her and put on her lei. As she admired the lei's matching magenta orchids, she took a closer look at Morgan's shirt and laughed out loud. "Are those lightsabers?"

Kiera and Shilling stepped into the hallway at the same time — the five-foot-three Kiera from her cabin on the starboard side of the corridor, the six-four Shilling from the port side. What an odd pairing. Kiera's sun-bleached hair and tan had faded early in the flight, but she still carried herself with beach-bum ease as she sauntered toward the cargo bay. By contrast, Shilling's skin was so pale it almost glowed, as if he'd never set foot on a beach in his life, and his posture was stiff and formal.

For the first time in three weeks, however, Morgan saw them smile at each other. He had worried one or the other wouldn't get into the spirit of the occasion, but from the looks on their faces, the tension between the two appeared to have thawed. They were even pointing to the images on each other's Hawaiian gear and chatting. Kiera's shirt was pink, with pictures of paddleboarders and beach umbrellas. Shilling's shirt had been the toughest to design, because Morgan knew so little about the man, but a consultation with the scientist's wife had resulted in the perfect solution: a baby-blue background featuring crayon artworks drawn by his five-year-old son and eight-year-old daughter.

With the last of the leis bestowed on Kiera and Shilling, Morgan invited the crew into his tiki lounge. It had taken him two hours to decorate the bay, but he was proud of the results. He had strung party lights across one section, wrapped grass skirts around the two probe docking platforms underneath the lights, and set up a makeshift bar on the top of two drone-landers stored next to the docking platforms. The drinks, delivered in pineapple-shaped bottles with capped straws, were filled with mai tais concocted according to Morgan's own recipe.

For the next hour, they chatted, danced and laughed. They shared stories about the pictures on their clothing and even had a gravity-assisted limbo contest. Ajay won. They ate freeze-dried pineapple and sampled vacuum-packed pupu platters. After yet another round of mai tais, the festivities devolved into tattoo reveals. Of course, Ajay displayed a smiling Elroy on his chest.

Carillo said teasingly to Morgan, "Word around NASA is you have lightsabers on your butt."

Morgan stroked his white, Fu Manchu mustache and winked. "If you think I'm pulling down my drawers to disprove it, Major, you've got another thing coming!"

Ajay leaned all one-hundred-fifty-two pounds of his weight against Kiera. "These are the best mai tais I've ever had."

To which Shilling quipped, "They're the *only* mai tais you've ever had!"

Kiera was the first to laugh at Shilling's joke. Mission accomplished. For sixty minutes, Morgan had made space, Callisto and their gamma troubles disappear.

As the laughing died down, Morgan said, "I have one more surprise."

He returned to the area near the airlock, opened another box, and pulled out five virtual reality headsets. After handing them out, he tapped out a set of commands on the touchpad by the intercom and motioned the crew to gather around him.

"This is pretty crazy," he said. "You might want to find a place to sit. I don't know how Augie and Dante pulled this off, but we owe them a big-ass thank-you. Put on your headsets and enjoy."

Before any pictures appeared on the screens inside their headsets, the sounds of laughter and conversation emanated from the intercom. At first the voices were indistinguishable, just random snippets of people having fun. Then the black vista began to lighten and a solitary voice rose above the others.

"*Quiet, everybody!*" the voice said. "*It's time to say hello.*"

Kiera gasped. "*Mom?*"

On the five 3D displays, a scene came into focus. The extended families of the five crewmembers stood on a sandy beach wearing the same Hawaiian outfits their astronaut loved ones wore. Spouses, children, parents, siblings and close friends smiled and waved.

In the center was Kiera's mother, Donna, and her father, Kyle. Though Morgan couldn't see Kiera with his headset on, he heard her sniffle.

Donna Walsh, the duly elected spokesperson for the crew's families, stepped forward. She wiped tears from her eyes and said, "*Hello, our heroes! We miss you so much and pray you are happy and safe!*"

Morgan slid off his headset and saw his shipmates reaching out as if trying to touch their family members. He heard the astronauts' families and friends sharing expressions of love and well wishes. When he heard his own brother's voice, he put his headset back on.

"*Thinking of you, bro!*" Jason Morgan said. "*Next round at Bennie's is on me, but you better not bring back any alien ick with you. My health insurance sucks!*"

When the video ended, the crew implored Morgan to replay it — which of course he did.

Halfway through the second showing, an alarm began to wail.

Carillo slid off her headset and turned toward the airlock. "I got this. You guys keep going. I'll be back in a few."

"Are you sure?" Morgan asked.

"Yep. If I need help, I'll call. It's probably just the UMOs bumping the Shields again. I heard the thrusters just before the alarm." To stay on course, every so often the auto-pilot guidance system fired thrusters to offset the pull of the Sun's gravity on the fleet.

Carillo hurried to the flight deck, buckled in at her co-pilot station, and pressed the blinking light on the panel of overhead buttons and switches. The alarm silenced. Then she brought up the probe status data screen on the center display of her dashboard, and a frown crossed her face.

"Hmmm ... that's odd."

She'd expected to see one or more sensor fault error messages associated with the Shields, but the sensor faults blinking on the screen were coming from one of the Recons. Hours ago, they had sent the six Recons ahead at full engine power without an escort of UMOs. It had been a tricky maneuver to pull off, requiring three attempts and two more fleet management software patches over two days to drop the Recons out of the fleet without attracting the attention of the UMOs. But they'd ultimately been successful, and *Rorschach* then fired forward thrusters, slowing the ship, along with its four Cargo probes and six Shields, to a crawl of fifty thousand kilometers per hour. The Recons were zooming ahead at three times that speed, and by now they were nearly three hundred thousand kilometers ahead of the rest of the fleet.

Carillo toggled through the data feeds available at her station and pulled up the instrumentation feed to review spectrometer data from the Recons. Was it possible they had been hit by a gamma-ray burst? Had they found a magnetar beam already? No ... the gamma spectrometer for all six showed nominal readings.

"What the hell is going on?" The alarm began to squawk again. Carillo clicked it off and grumbled, "Shut up, you hunk of junk."

Another scan of the probe data screen showed LOS error messages for two of the Recons. Loss-of-signal meant one of three things. There could be interference blocking the Recons' ability to communicate with *Rorschach*; something might have hit the probes — an asteroid or some other physical object — and damaged the probes' ability to communicate; or, the probes had been destroyed.

"That is damn peculiar," Carillo murmured.

The six Recons were deployed in a diamond formation. One probe at the tip, two more on each side of the leader, fanned out at angles to form an upside-down V, and the last probe in the slot behind the lead probe. The distance between adjacent probes in the formation was set at two hundred meters. So it was surprising to see that the LOS messages were coming from *Recon-1*, the lead probe, and *Recon-4*, the second of the two probes on the left side of the formation.

If interference had been the source of the alerts, Carillo would have expected it to affect all of the probes, or at least two probes close together. And if an object had destroyed or knocked out comms to *Recon-1*, then *Recon-6*, traveling in the slot behind *Recon-1*, would have been more likely to be hit by the debris than *Recon-4*.

Carillo pulled up the camera-feeds menu and selected the feed from *Recon-6*. The probe carried two video cameras, one on top, the other on the bottom. The standard configuration had the top camera, Cam-1, aimed forward of the probe. Cam-2 was positioned to provide a rear view.

There was a short delay in securing the feed, given the distance between the probe and *Rorschach* and the amount of video data being transmitted.

When the first images arrived, Carillo's frown deepened. *Recon-1* wasn't visible in *Recon-6*'s Cam-1 feed. Nor was there any visible debris.

She turned Cam-2 to the left to see if *Recon-2* and *Recon-4* were visible.

While she was waiting for the video images, a third alarm sounded. Another Recon was now showing LOS: *Recon-5*, the one on the far right. Carillo grumbled and shut off the annoying sound.

Morgan's voice came over the intercom. "What's going on, Julia? You need help?"

"We have a situation with the Recons. Three have gone LOS. Still trying to sort out why."

"Roger that. We're on our way."

Morgan and the others filed out of the airlock into *Rorschach*'s central corridor and plodded forward toward the flight deck. Their gaits were awkward, not because of the mai tais, but because of quirks with the ship's magnetic gravity forcefield, GEFF, pronounced "Jeff." The forcefield, designed by Dante Fulton, made it so that as long as crewmembers were wearing their magnetized flight suits and boots, they could walk, stand and sit as if they were on Earth. The forcefield also allowed other magnetized objects to stay where placed.

But Morgan and the others weren't wearing their black-and-gold flight suits, and the magnet sensors embedded in their Hawaiian gear were not as powerful as the sensors in their suits. Complicating matters, the forcefield wasn't perfect. Simultaneous use by multiple people in close proximity created unbalanced magnetic loads in the adaptive forcefield. At times, it led to intermittent floating, boots that stuck to the magnetized flooring and choppy strides. That was exactly what was happening now.

Ajay, the last to leave the airlock, watched his comrades stagger down the hallway toward the flight deck and narrated their progress. "And they're off! Skywalker takes the early lead, but wait! Here comes Walsh on the outside, churning hard along the rail while Shilling slows to a standstill on the straightaway—"

His narration came to an abrupt halt when one of his boots stuck to the floor and his foot pulled right out of it, causing his now-weightless leg to dangle in the air. "Ugh!"

Kiera turned back and laughed. "Karma, Elroy."

Unwilling to waste time retrieving the boot, Ajay pressed the GEFF icon on his smartwatch to deactivate his remaining boot and drifted up. While the others teased him, he propelled down the corridor behind them by pulling on handholds.

Ajay had nearly caught up with the group when the ship jerked upward. Ajay bounced off the floor as the others reached for handholds to steady themselves. The ship continued upward and began to spin. Morgan, Kiera and Shilling were pressed against the wall as GEFF fought to balance the gravity in the spinning corridor. *Rorschach* trembled and creaked as the forces of the new momentum took control. The auto-pilot for the reaction control system fired thrusters to fight back and reorient the ship.

Above the clamor, Morgan shouted toward the flight deck, "Turn off RCS! Quickly!"

"Roger that," came Carillo's swift reply over the corridor intercom.

Before Morgan could issue another command, something hit *Rorschach* aport, a violent jolt that sent Ajay crashing face first into the wall, then ricocheting across the corridor into the opposing wall. Like a pinball caught between bumpers, the weightless Ajay rebounded from floor to ceiling to wall.

"Ajay! Turn on your GEFF!" Kiera shouted.

But he was out cold. His body continued to bounce around as the ship careened further off course. Sizzling crackles echoed throughout the corridor as bolts of electricity leapt between metallic surfaces.

"Holy shit!" Kiera said. She craned her neck to face Shilling. "It's the UMOs!"

He nodded and called out to Carillo. "Major, are the UMOs spinning? Can you see them spinning?"

On the flight deck, Carillo's eyes darted from her dashboard computer displays to the cockpit's windows. Streaks of blue light swirled with orange, colliding here and there into brilliant flashes of white. Instrument gauges spiked with furious intensity, and multiple alarms pealed. The fleet management display showed flashing LOS emblems for multiple Shields.

Morgan shouted above the sounds of rending metal, "What's going on up there, Julia?"

"UMOs. They've gone nuts," she said. "We've lost three Shields … there goes a Cargo."

"Turn the engines on!" Kiera said. "Full power."

"Belay that." Morgan wheeled to face Kiera as more lightning arced across the corridor. "Are you nuts? We'll rip apart."

"Not *Rorschach*'s engines — the Cargos!" Kiera said. "One of them. All of them. Just do it! Now!"

Over the pops and sizzles of lightning, Morgan looked to Shilling. "Will it work?"

"I don't know. I don't have a better idea."

"Okay. Julia, light the Cargos. All of them," Morgan yelled.

"Roger that."

Within seconds, the lightning ceased. As the ship continued to spin like a football in flight, Carillo announced, "The UMOs are leaving … black sky."

"Copy," Morgan said. "Turn on RCS again. Stop the spin."

The sound of the thruster jets firing in rapid succession could be heard throughout the ship, and soon *Rorschach* leveled out.

"Helm in control," Carillo said over the speakers.

"Roger that. All stop," said Morgan. He corralled Ajay's limp, bobbing body and then turned to Kiera and Shilling. "Get up front and help Julia figure out what the hell just happened. I'll be there as soon as I can."

CHAPTER 3

INQUISITION

ugustus Amato dipped into his suit pocket for a tin of antacid tablets. He had hoped the pills wouldn't be necessary tonight, but he hadn't expected the symposium to be such a disaster. In a whisper, he said, "Am I that naïve?"

The mumbled words caught the attention of Dennis Pritchard, who set down his fork and knife and patted his friend on the back. "Don't beat yourself up, Augie. It was the right thing to do. They'll come around."

Amato had created the Gateway Symposium to assemble the various factions vying for inclusion in A3rospace Industries' space exploration projects. Ever since his team's discovery of *Cetus Prime* and the alien spaceport on Callisto, and their breaking of the fifty-year coverup shielding the existence of UMOs from the public, there had been a groundswell of interest in participating in Amato's follow-on explorations. Among those interested were scientists eager to research the UMOs, archaeologists and anthropologists with dreams of excavating the Callisto spaceport, space agencies pressing for access to A3I's breakthrough VLF engine, billionaire privateers seeking to commercialize the *Rorschach Explorer* and governments salivating about potential military applications of A3I's new technologies.

Yet the collective excitement of these parties had eventually morphed into a quagmire of paranoia and self-interests — which was precisely why Amato had called for the symposium. His aim was to lessen tensions and begin a formal dialogue with all factions represented. But the event descended into a firestorm of accusations within the first ten minutes.

"Who are you to control access to these discoveries?" one scientist railed.

"You're just lining your pockets," charged another.

"It's not fair. You are holding us all hostage!" shouted a foreign government official.

"I, for one, don't trust your intentions!" said fellow billionaire Hawkeye Huggins, his voice trembling with anger. And this from one of Amato's closest friends!

Pritchard, sharing the stage with Amato, had employed his considerable political skills to quell the animosity, but there was little he could do once a near-physical brawl erupted between rival scientists. The room soon turned into a virtual steel-caged death match between academics, bureaucrats and tycoons.

Shaking the vision of the melee from his mind, Amato said to Pritchard, "You have more faith than I do, my friend. Right now, I feel like I'm at the center of an inquisition."

"It's to be expected," Pritchard said. "Discovering proof of alien humanoids on another world? Exposing the secret about UMOs? Explosive stuff, Augie."

Dr. Antonio Wallace, technology magnate and Amato's other dining companion for the evening, chimed in. "Don't forget disruptive new tech that's damn scary to think about in the hands of the wrong people."

Chewing on the antacid, Amato nodded. "I know, I know. But I didn't expect this much hostility."

"Look, you've upset the balance of power in the world," said Pritchard, returning his attention to his veal parmigiana. "All these people's heads are swimming trying to figure out where they fit in — and *if* they fit in — in the new world. You're holding all the cards, and they don't like it. Honestly, I think the only thing preventing you from facing a *true* inquisition is the Callisto mission."

Antonio twirled pasta around his fork. "I agree. *Rorschach*'s odyssey has captured the imagination of the whole world. Folks in every country, from every walk of life, are following them to Callisto. The average person gets what you're about, what you're trying to do. Sharing the experience with them, making the crew accessible, was a great move."

"Right. It puts the people of the world on your side, even if their leaders aren't," Pritchard added.

"Well, I guess that's something." Amato checked his watch. It was almost time for Dante's segment on *XTC*. He rose from his seat and retrieved two remotes from the mantel above the dormant fireplace. With the first, he retracted a panel above the mantel, revealing a flat-screen television. With the second, he powered on the TV and tuned it to WNN.

A commercial break was in progress, giving the three diners an opportunity to position themselves to face the screen.

SET OF *EXPEDITION TO CALLISTO*
WORLD NETWORK NEWS
NEW YORK, NEW YORK

When the program returned from break, Jenna Toffy and Dr. Dante Fulton were seated on opposite sofas on a cozy, living-room-style set. After a bit of casual banter, Toffy asked Dante, "So, everyone's on pins and needles. Any new tricks from the UMOs to share tonight?"

The previous week's episode had included a recorded video clip of an experiment Dr. Shilling had conducted several days before the program aired. Three of the Shield probes were lined up in a row, and as each engine was turned on and off in increments of thirty seconds — left, middle, right — the UMOs moved to the active engine to feed on their ion outputs. Dr. Shilling went through the cycle twice — left, middle, right, left, middle, right — and then stopped. But the UMOs didn't stop. After they finished feeding on the ions from the far right engine, they moved back to the far left, expecting the engine to turn on. They'd anticipated the pattern. Shilling then altered the pattern and repeated the experiment. Again the UMOs learned the new pattern within two cycles, and again they anticipated the start of the next cycle.

Shilling then showed a slow motion, close-up video of the UMO movements from one engine to another. He pointed out that each time the group moved, the same small cluster of UMOs led the way. The experiment demonstrated that the UMOs had a hierarchy of responsibilities, just like honeybees in a colony, including UMO "foragers" that were intelligent enough to anticipate when and where food might appear. These foragers then communicated with the other UMOs to coordinate activity.

Dante tugged on his suit lapels and leaned forward. "Not this week, Jenna. There have been some new developments in the last few days. *Rorschach*'s mission is all business right now."

"The *Juno* incident?" Toffy asked.

While NASA had announced the loss of the probe, and while there had been extensive media speculation about the impact the sudden gamma burst might have on *Rorschach*'s mission, no one on Amato's team had publicly commented on the matter. Until now. Dante had been chosen by Amato to deliver A3I's official comments on the broadcast.

"Yes, that's right," he said. "We've had to reassess our near-term objectives in light of what happened to *Juno*."

He explained the concerns about gamma radiation and its potential effects on the fleet and crew. He touched on magnetars, but on advice from Toffy prior to the show, he kept his description at a high level. He finished up by describing the Recon deployment and the decision to slow down the fleet. "We just want to make sure we know what to expect before *Rorschach* gets near Callisto. We don't want to risk the crew getting hurt."

"I'm sure they appreciate your caution," Toffy said. "How long will the mission be delayed?"

"That's hard to say. We'll know more once we've located the source of the gamma burst."

"How long will that take?"

"Well, it's going to take the Recons an extra ninety days to reach Callisto without the help of UMOs. Unless they detect and zero in on the gamma source before then, we're looking at a minimum of six months."

Dante's candid assessment had been ordered by Amato. He believed it was important to be as transparent as possible with the public.

"Oh, wow," Toffy said. "I'm sure a lot of our viewers are disappointed to hear that."

Dante nodded. "None of us are happy about it, but we have to think of the crew's safety first and foremost."

"There've been some rumors over the last couple of days suggesting the mission might be scrubbed," Toffy said. "Any truth to them?"

"We hope not." Dante held up crossed fingers.

"Same here." Toffy smiled at the camera with crossed fingers raised as well. Turning back to Dante, she asked, "What will the crew be doing during the delay?"

"Good question, Jenna. We haven't ironed out those details yet. We might have the crew alter course to explore Ceres. It's a dwarf planet on the outer edge of the asteroid belt. There've also been discussions about conducting a detailed survey of the asteroid belt. Conversations are ongoing."

As Dante finished speaking he felt his cell phone vibrate in a distinctive three-buzz pattern — indicating a text from the on-duty flight director at Mission Control on Mayaguana.

While Toffy asked another question, Dante reached in his suit jacket and slid the phone out as discreetly as possible. Darting a look at the lock screen, he read the message preview box. It showed a three-digit code.

911.

AUGUSTUS AMATO'S RESIDENCE
WINTER PARK, FLORIDA

Eleven hundred miles away, the same three-buzz pattern pinged Amato's and Pritchard's cell phones. Pritchard opened the message first. "Uh-oh."

After viewing the alert, Amato turned back to the television screen. Though the show was a live broadcast, the network had built in a seven-second broadcast delay and, as a result, Dante was only just now reaching into his pocket. When Dante glanced at his phone, his head snapped up and he leaned forward to whisper to Toffy. She motioned to someone off camera, and the show quickly cut to commercial.

By then, Pritchard had already called Mission Control. He put his phone on speaker and set it on the table in front of Amato. "I've got Norris Preston on the line." Preston was acting mission director in Dante's absence.

Amato leaned over the speaker. He could hear background chatter and raised voices. "Norris, it's Mr. Amato. What's going on?"

"One second, Mr. Amato," Preston said. "Trying to patch Dr. Fulton in."

When Dante was connected into the three-way call, Preston said, "We don't know what happened yet. Everything was fine. No problems. Then, boom. Crazy town. Major sensor alarms, then LOS on more than half the probes."

Dante's voice, cool and calm, came through the speaker. "Problem with A3I-TDRS?"

"No, sir," Preston said. "The relay satellite is operating fine. Problem originated with *Rorschach* and the rest of the fleet."

"Have you pinged *Rorschach* on all bands?" Dante asked.

"Yes, sir. It's the first thing we did. But it'll be forty minutes before any return pings come back … assuming they can respond."

"What about the sensor faults? Did they happen all at once?" Pritchard asked. He turned to Amato. "If they did, could be another software glitch."

There was a pause on the line, then Preston sighed. "No. The first alerts were from the Recons, then the Shields. Sensor alerts from *Rorschach* and the Cargos started going nuts shortly after that. We're putting together a timeline right now."

"Have someone shoot me a copy of it ASAP," Dante said. "Send it to Mr. Amato and Dr. Pritchard, too."

"Roger that."

Pritchard put the phone on mute. "Sounds like UMOs to me."

"Or asteroid debris," Amato said.

Dante probed Preston with more questions. What specific sensors had sent out alerts? Were they the same from each vessel? When was the last scheduled downlink received? Was there anything amiss in the downlink data?

While Amato and Pritchard focused on Norris' answers, Antonio tapped out a series of text messages. His company, Whave Technologies, had built the drone-landers stored in *Rorschach*'s cargo bay and, earlier in the day, his technicians at Mission Control had remotely powered on the landers to uplink and test a software upgrade. He was now in the midst of trying to determine whether the landers had reported any sensor faults.

"Mr. Amato?" Dante said.

Amato unmuted the phone. "Yes?"

"I think we have to assume it's not a software glitch. The sequence and types of alerts — all communications and electrical faults, starting at the leading edge of the fleet and then moving through it — suggest Shilling's colony. Though I can't explain why they would have been out front of the fleet. We know they didn't follow the Recons when they split off on the gamma mission."

Amato reopened his antacid tin. "Were there any structural failure alarms or life support alerts from *Rorschach*?"

"No, thank goodness." Dante paused. "At least, not so far."

"Sir?" Preston said.

"Yes?" Amato and Dante answered in unison.

"Hold on!" said Norris. "We're receiving a new downlink from *Rorschach*!"

Amato exchanged a glance with Pritchard and Antonio and whispered, "Thank God."

"It's a message … from Major Carillo."

"Read it out, man!" Amato practically bellowed.

"Yes, sir," Preston said.

CCDR-TRE to MAYA-FLIGHT: Fleet attacked by UMOs. Heavy losses. All Recons LOS. Half of Shields. Three Cargos intact but AWOL. Trying to recall them. TRE okay. Mostly electrical shorts. X-band out. All other comms operational. Crew okay. UMO colony gone. Will provide full sitrep as soon as possible. CCDR-TRE out.

MEDICAL BAY — THE *RORSCHACH EXPLORER* DRIFTING AT ALL-STOP IN THE ASTEROID BELT

As Kiera and Shilling headed for the flight deck, Morgan pulled Ajay's floating body to the ship's medical bay, where he strapped the bony Nepali's body to a gurney and performed a quick triage. No broken bones or cuts, just a walnut-sized lump on the man's forehead. Most importantly, he was breathing, though his respiration was shallow.

With care, Morgan slid a silvery cap over Ajay's wild shock of black hair and fastened it beneath the scraggly patch of hair under his chin. He gently pressed Ajay's head down until it was flush against the table and flipped a switch to activate the gurney's magnetic surface. With Ajay adhered to the gurney, Morgan tilted the leg portion of the table up in order to elevate Ajay's legs and increase the blood flow returning to his heart.

"Hang in there, buddy," Morgan said, patting Ajay's shoulder.

Morgan felt a special responsibility for Ajay for a variety of reasons, none greater than the debt of gratitude he owed the amateur astronomer for discovering the radio signals that first led Augustus Amato to send a fleet of probes to Callisto. If not for the young man's love of the stars, his conviction that the radio signals were something more than electromagnetic interference and his resilience to keep searching for someone to believe him, Morgan was convinced *Cetus Prime* would never have been found.

And the discovery of the ship had lifted a burden Morgan had carried for twenty-three years. As CAPCOM for the *Cetus* mission, he had been the crew's representative in Mission Control — which, in his view, made him the person most responsible for the crew's welfare. So when *Cetus Prime* and its crew went missing, Morgan blamed himself. If he had taken a bolder stand with NASA and the Pentagon when UMOs first attacked the ship around Mars, he believed the crew would have returned safely to Earth. Ajay's discovery had given him a chance for redemption, an opportunity to determine the fate of the *Cetus Prime* astronauts, and possibly even bring them home.

Now he talked to Ajay in soothing tones until the man's eyes fluttered open. Morgan tilted the leg portion of the table back to level and retrieved a pulse oximeter and blood pressure device.

Ajay tried to sit up but found himself restrained. "What's going on?"

"Lie still, you've got a nasty lump on your head," Morgan said. "I need to check you out before you get up."

He checked Ajay's pupils and eye movements for evidence of a concussion and monitored his vital signs for several minutes. In between moaning about a headache, Ajay bitched about the restraints the whole time. Morgan ignored the complaints as he peppered Ajay with questions to test his memory.

When he was satisfied that his patient was okay, Morgan unstrapped Ajay and turned off the magnetic table. He handed Ajay some ibuprofen pills for his headache and gave him a cold pack. "Okay, Elroy, let's go find your other boot and get to the flight deck."

After taking the ibuprofen, Ajay applied the pack to his forehead. "Roger dodger."

The two men arrived at the ship's command center to find the others engrossed in a conversation, but the discussion ceased when they saw Morgan and Ajay. Their expressions were a cross between stern and glum. They perked up upon seeing Ajay was conscious and seemingly in good shape, but their raised spirits appeared to diminish quickly.

"Geez," Morgan said, "is it that bad?"

"Well, it ain't good," said Carillo.

"Give me the rundown." Morgan buckled into the commander's seat, and Ajay secured himself at the comms station.

"All the Recons are LOS — I assume they've been destroyed," Carillo said. "Same goes with three of our Shields. The others are still communicating, but they're damaged. One Cargo is LOS and the other three we used as bait served their purpose. They drew all the UMOs away. It appears they're still feeding on ions from the engines. I signaled the

Cargos to power down, but they didn't respond, and I haven't been able to gain control over their thrusters."

"You're right. That ain't good," Morgan said. He turned to Kiera. "What about *Rorschach*?"

"We were hit with a crap ton of electrical discharges. A bunch of circuit boards were cooked," she said. "We have swap-outs in the storage room for the more critical ones, but the rest are going to be a problem. Their replacements are aboard *Cargo-4*. If we can't recall it, we won't be able to swap out the others."

"Is life support okay?" Morgan asked.

"Yes."

"Comms?"

Ajay set aside the cold pack, slid on headphones and fiddled with one of the radio transmitters while Carillo provided the update. "X-band is out. We have Ku, S, UHF and HF. I sent a heads-up message to Mayaguana on all but HF about ten minutes ago. It'll get there in another ten, but the first sensor alerts would have reached them before I even sent the heads-up."

Morgan turned to Shilling. "What happened, Bob? Why did the colony attack us?"

"They didn't," Shilling said. "Matter of fact, they defended us. Bizarre as that sounds."

Ajay removed his headphones. "Defended us?"

"Yes. They defended us from another colony. There's no doubt. It's clear in both the data and video. We were just attacked by a second UMO colony."

"A second colony?" Morgan said. "Where did it come from?"

"I'm still trying to work that out," Shilling said.

"Where are our UMOs?"

"The videos of the attack show both colonies went after the Cargos."

Morgan stroked his mustache while he considered Shilling's comments. Carillo's first description of the alarms had indicated there was a situation with the Recons. "How far ahead were the Recons when the first alarm triggered?"

"Two hundred eighty-seven thousand kilometers," Carillo answered.

"And how long was it between the first Recon alarm and the attack on us?"

"I'd say twenty, twenty-five minutes. No more than that."

Morgan did the math in his head. Accounting for the fleet's speed, the distance between the Recons and the fleet, and the time lag between attacks, the second colony of UMOs would have had to travel at over six hundred thousand kilometers per hour to reach *Rorschach* in twenty-five minutes. He let out a long whistle.

"Yeah, I know," Carillo said. "They closed on us at tremendous speed."

"What set them off, Bob? The Recon VLFs?" Morgan asked.

"I know I sound like a broken record, but I don't know. I need to study the data some more," Shilling said.

"Well, study it quick. If those things come back, we're at their mercy."

"I understand that, Colonel. Believe me, I do."

Kiera jumped in. "Could they have detected our UMO colony? Could that be why they attacked?"

Shilling shrugged. "It's possible. The video of the attack did have the look of a classic hive-robbing response."

"Hive what?" Ajay asked.

"Honeybees are very aggressive when protecting their hive," Shilling explained. "If they sense a foreign group of bees trying to steal honey from the hive, they'll fight to the death. It's quite remarkable to watch."

The explanation had merit. The second colony would have viewed *Rorschach*'s UMOs as a threat to its food supply and attacked to eliminate the threat. But why, then, had they attacked the Recons? The ions and VLF radio waves emitted by their engines should have attracted the second colony to feed instead of attack. Morgan pointed this out to Shilling.

"Again, I don't yet have enough data to posit a theory one way or the other," Shilling said. "I'm just going off what I saw in the video feed. The attack looked like honeybees protecting a hive."

"How do you know it wasn't the other way around?" Kiera asked.

Shilling turned toward her. "Meaning?"

"How do you know the second colony wasn't after the ions from our engines? Isn't that sort of our colony's hive? Their honey?"

"In theory, it's possible, but I doubt it. As Colonel Morgan noted, they passed up on ions from the Recons and then attacked them. Besides, honeybees *don't* hive-rob en masse. They send scouts to get the lay of the land and test the hive's defenses before they press an attack. I think it's *far* more likely they viewed our UMOs as a threat."

With his nasal, dismissive tone, the scientist sounded to Morgan like a preppy country-club fop dressing down a caddie who'd misjudged the line of his putt. Kiera's face turned red.

So much for the thaw in tensions!

Ajay interrupted the brewing confrontation. "This reminds me of the asteroid belt attack on our CubeSats last year." He provided a brief summary of the run-in. The CubeSats had been flying through the asteroid belt, just as the fleet was now, and UMOs had appeared out of nowhere and attacked a few of the probes. "Maybe it's the same UMOs," he finished.

"Nah, can't be," said Kiera. "We entered the belt a long way from the point where our CubeSats did last year. And these UMOs look very different than the ones the Cubes ran into last time."

Morgan frowned. "Looked different? How?"

"These ones were blue lights. The ones last year were whitish," Kiera said.

"They were blue?" Morgan said. "Are you sure?"

Carillo, Kiera and Shilling all nodded.

"And you know what's weirder?" Kiera said.

"What?"

"Our UMOs turned orange when they started fighting."

After a bit more discussion, Morgan gave the crew their instructions to deal with the aftermath of the attack. He sent Kiera and Ajay to the storage room to retrieve new circuit boards and begin replacing as many of *Rorschach*'s damaged boards as they could. He asked Carillo to concentrate on recalling the Cargos, marshaling what was left of the Shields and attempting to reestablish comms with the LOS Recons. Then he tasked Shilling with developing a more refined explanation for the attack and to devise a strategy to lure back their own UMOs without attracting the second colony. Shilling questioned the feasibility of the second assignment, but as he departed for the lab compartment to re-examine the feeds of the attack, he agreed to explore options.

Morgan himself stayed with Carillo on the flight deck and prepared a more extensive update for Mission Control.

A little less than an hour later, a new alarm began to whine. This time, Morgan saw the swarm coming. A flashing blur of spinning blue lights was racing head-on toward *Rorschach*.

Carillo saw them too. "Oh, my God."

"*That* does not look good," Morgan said.

"What do we do?"

"There's not much we can do." *Rorschach* couldn't outrun them, and the ship had no weapons.

"We could turn on the Shield engines," she suggested. "See if they chase them like they did the Cargos."

"No." Morgan reached for the engine control panel and spoke into the intercom. "Hold on, people. They're back. This is going to get wild."

Carillo watched as Morgan activated *Rorschach*'s engines. "What are you doing?"

"Turn on all our lights. Landing, spotlights, everything we got," he said. He switched the reaction control system to manual and used the thrusters to initiate a spin.

"I don't understand," Carillo said.

"No time to explain. Just do it."

Carillo activated *Rorschach*'s external lights.

As the ship ramped up speed, Morgan fired the thrusters to spin the ship at a higher rate. "Activate the shortwave transmitter."

"What? Why?"

"Turn it on and start talking to them," Morgan said.

"Excuse me?"

"I don't care what you say, just say something. Anything. Sing if you want, just do it now!"

Carillo chose not to sing. Instead she shouted expletive-filled warnings at the approaching swarm over the radio transmitter.

As *Rorschach* flew toward the spinning blue mass, Morgan increased the engine power to full throttle. The ship quaked from the combination of speed and spin. Carillo gripped her armrests and shut her eyes as impact neared.

CHAPTER 4

WATCH YOUR SIX

SET OF *EXPEDITION TO CALLISTO*
WORLD NETWORK NEWS
NEW YORK, NEW YORK
SEPTEMBER 1, 2019

D ante's abrupt departure from *Expedition to Callisto* did not go unnoticed by the show's viewers. Within seconds of his walk-off, rumors began to circulate in social media groups dedicated to *XTC*. The show's social media correspondent dutifully alerted the director to the spike in chatter.

The director was already scrambling. When Dante stepped away, he'd informed the director that he'd received an important call that couldn't wait — but he'd given the impression that he would return when the call ended. Yet at the next commercial break, he was still missing from the set. The director's assistants had been calling his cell number. No answer. They'd texted and emailed him. No replies. The director had even sent a cadre of staff to search for him in the network offices, and no one could locate him. Meanwhile phone calls, texts, emails and social media posts continued to besiege the network. *Where is Dr. Fulton? Why did he leave? Is there a problem? What's going on?*

"I've never seen anything like this," the director complained to Jenna Toffy.

"Something's definitely up," she said. "He looked shaken. I don't think he's coming back."

"Okay, what do you want to do? How do you want to handle it?"

In their earpieces, a voice from the production booth said, "Back live in thirty seconds."

Toffy adjusted the fit of her suit jacket while a makeup artist performed last-second touch-ups. "I'll come up with something. But we should start working our A3I contacts now. As soon as we're off-air, I'll call Amato directly."

"Sounds like a plan."

When the show resumed, Toffy did her best to downplay Dante's departure. "Welcome back to *Expedition to Callisto*. You may have noticed our special guest for tonight's program, Dr. Dante Fulton, stepped away to attend to a matter during our last segment; a mission director's work is never done. He asked me to extend his apologies and promised to join us for a future episode. For now, we'll do our best to forge ahead without him. Next up, a prerecorded interview with Mission Specialist Ajay Joshi ... "

CREW READY ROOM — THE *RORSCHACH EXPLORER*
DRIFTING AT ALL-STOP ABOVE THE
ECLIPTIC IN THE ASTEROID BELT

Shilling stalked around the crew ready room, his fists clenched at his sides, his eyes riveted on Morgan. "Are you insane? You could have killed us all!"

Morgan stood against the wall with his lumberjack-thick forearms folded across his chest. "I did what I thought was best, Bob. We were short on options."

"This isn't some damn video game!" Shilling ranted. "We don't know *anything* about these foreign UMOs!"

"Not true, Bob," said Carillo. She, Kiera and Ajay were seated at the briefing table. "We know they don't behave like our colony. I for one am glad we didn't just wait for them to attack again. It was a good call on Paul's part."

When the blue UMOs streamed toward *Rorschach*, Morgan had known the ship wasn't capable of evading the creatures. He'd also known that playing dead hadn't worked for the crew of *Cetus Prime* twenty-four years ago. A swarm of UMOs had ravaged *Cetus'* engines, leaving her dead in space.

The only option that hadn't been tried was to confront the electromagnetic beings head-on.

So Morgan had tried his best to simulate a competing swarm of UMOs. With *Rorschach*'s engines blazing the vacuum of space with a heavy ion trail, he spun the ship with all its lights on. And for an added touch, he had Carillo activate the radio transmitter to talk to the oncoming colony. That last bit was inspired by a discovery Ajay made last year. During a CubeSat encounter with UMOs in Earth orbit, Ajay picked up the sound of UMOs communicating with each other. The chirp-like sounds went back and forth, one high tone, the other low, creating the impression of a conversation. So Morgan had Carillo "talk" to the attacking swarm with the hope the radio chatter would reinforce the ruse of a competing swarm.

The actions certainly had an effect, for the pulsing of the blue UMOs waned as it neared *Rorschach*, and groups of the light-balls scattered from the main body. These actions led Morgan to believe the swarm was unsure of its prey — which presented him the opportunity for one last element of confusion.

As the collision neared, Morgan cut the power to the engines and fired the forward thrusters. And with that, the swarm scattered altogether. From the flight deck, the UMOs looked like the glittery trails of fading fireworks.

"It was a *lucky* call," Shilling said.

"You're right," Morgan agreed. "It *was* lucky. In fact, I'm not sure it would work a second time. If they're anything like our UMOs, I have a feeling they're a little too smart to be fooled twice."

"Then what are we going to do if they come back?" Ajay asked.

"I'm hoping we can avoid another confrontation."

"How in blazes can we do that?" said Shilling. "We don't know where they came from, where they went, what attracted them or why they attacked."

"That's your job to figure out, isn't it?" Carillo said.

Shilling's face reddened.

"I'm afraid it's *all* our jobs at this point," Morgan said. "Just cross our fingers that we put enough distance between us and the UMOs to buy us the time we need to figure out our next steps."

After piercing through the dissipating swarm, Morgan had powered up the ship's engines and used thruster controls to fly *Rorschach* up and away from the ecliptic, the plane around which most objects in the solar system orbit the Sun. When he judged they had traveled a safe distance, he cut the engines and used thrusters to arrest *Rorschach*'s momentum. With the spacecraft idled, it began to drift, orbiting the Sun just like the asteroids in the belt below. Though Morgan was not happy drifting away from their intended course, it seemed the better short-term alternative to using their thrusters or engines to maintain their heading and velocity. Until they had a handle on what had precipitated the attack, he didn't want to risk the possibility of attracting the blue UMOs again by emitting a trail of electromagnetic radiation.

"Figure out our next steps?" Shilling said. "It's obvious, isn't it? Return to Earth."

The mention of Earth stirred Ajay. "We're going home? We're not going to Callisto?"

Shilling buried his face into the palm of his hand and shook his head. "Wake up, Elroy. We have no Recons to scan for gamma rays. Our Cargos are gone. So is our UMO colony. And we don't have enough Shields to protect us from Jupiter's radiation. Even if the hostile UMOs don't take another crack at us, continuing on to Callisto would be suicide."

Ajay looked to Morgan with eyes that pleaded for a different answer.

Morgan said, "I'm sorry, Ajay. I don't want to pull the plug, but I can't argue with Bob's assessment of the situation."

"We're just going to give up?" Ajay said, his anger rising. He snapped his fingers. "Just like that?"

Morgan nodded. "Nothing official's come from Mayaguana yet, but I think it's just a matter of time before they order us to scrub."

Thus far, Kiera had said nothing. In fact she seemed lost in thought, just staring at her folded hands resting on the table. But now she looked up and said, "What if we could salvage some of the CubeSats and get the Cargos back?"

"Salvage them how?" Morgan asked. "They were destroyed."

"We don't know that. We lost comms with them. It's possible one or more might be intact. Damaged, but intact."

Carillo shook her head. "I don't want to shoot you down, Kiera, but I tried multiple times to ping them … on all three of their bands."

"I understand, but I'd still like to try," Kiera said. "Your pings might have been blocked by interference from the UMOs."

Carillo frowned, shrugged, then looked to Morgan. "I guess it won't hurt to try."

"Oh, please," said Shilling. "What difference will it make?"

"It might make a huge difference," Kiera said. "If we can link with enough of them, we might be able to bring them back to *Rorschach*, fix 'em up, and redeploy 'em."

Shilling laughed. "And then what? You can't be suggesting we continue the mission."

"Why not?" Kiera asked.

Shilling threw up his hands. "You're all insane." He stormed out of the ready room.

Kiera shouted after him, "And you're a pussy!"

Morgan's rebuke was sharp and swift. "Cool it, Kiera!"

"I'm sorry, Colonel. I'm just tired of his BS. Now, do you want to try and save the mission or should we just sit here and wait for Mayaguana to scrub?"

Morgan glared at her. Kiera glared back.

"You've got two hours to work some magic, Dr. Walsh," Morgan said. "Get a move on."

The meeting ended.

Morgan returned to the flight deck and typed out a status update to send to Dante. He informed him of the second attack, the evasive actions he'd taken and their current situation. He acknowledged the likelihood of aborting the mission but appealed for Mission Control to wait until Kiera had taken another crack at reconnecting with the LOS CubeSats. He ended the message with a second appeal. *As an aside, we could use some additional perspective re: new UMOs. Shilling rattled. Concerned about his state of mind and objectivity.*

By the following morning, Dante's unexplained exit had exploded into a story big enough for the traditional news media to cover it. And the intensity of the coverage only ramped up when the public relations executive for A3rospace Industries stonewalled reporter requests for an official explanation.

Toffy, annoyed at Amato's lack of response to her repeated requests for an off-the-record conversation, left him a blistering voice message.

"I covered Dante's ass last night, and what did I get in return? I'll tell you what I got. *My* ass left out in the cold! Look, you need to understand something, Augie — we've been very accommodating, kid gloves and all that. No tough questions, no pushbacks. But that's going to end if you don't cut me in on what's going on. There's a story here, and you can't just shut me out. Everybody, and I mean *everybody*, is looking to *you*, to *me*, to *us* for answers. Going radio silent is … not … helping … matters! Now, I'm not one who normally threatens sources, but unless I hear from you by noon Eastern, I'm going full investigative reporter on the story. I'm not getting scooped on this!"

Her anger was fueled in part by leaks from "anonymous sources with intimate knowledge of the situation" that had crept out overnight — leaks fed to *other* media outlets. According to these leaks, Mission Control had lost communication with the *Rorschach Explorer*. The UMOs traveling with the fleet had attacked, wiping out most of the fleet and badly damaging *Rorschach*. Some rumors even claimed that some of the crew had been killed, that the mission had been aborted, that there was no hope of rescue for the survivors.

And no one at A3I would confirm or deny any of these rumors — not to Toffy, and not to any other reporter at WNN. That left Toffy, the show's production staff and WNN executives as easy targets for angry *Expedition to Callisto* fans, snarky media competitors and holier-than-thou journalism critics.

At noon Eastern, Amato finally released a terse statement.

Despite the irresponsible rumors that have been reported as fact, we are in contact with the Rorschach Explorer, *and all five of the crew are alive and well. There was an incident last night that caused damage to* Rorschach *and other probes in the fleet. We are still in the process of gathering information on that incident and we will release an update once our internal review is complete. Until that time, we will have no further comment. The* Rorschach *crew, mission team and I would like to thank those who've offered expressions of concern and support.*

For Toffy, the statement was a dagger. Amato could have chosen to funnel the statement through her, but he never reached out. Instead he'd distributed the statement via A3I's website, adding to the growing perception that WNN and Toffy were non-factors.

Like a shooting star fading into dark skies, so went the cozy relationship between Toffy, Amato and their counterparts.

ABOARD THE SUPERYACHT *SOL SEAKER*
PORT DENARAU, FIJI
SEPTEMBER 2, 2019

Pebbles McCarver sat in bed, her legs covered by the sheets. Television remote in hand, she muted the program and leaned toward the half-open bathroom door. "Hurry, Anlon. Antonio's about to come on."

"Buh ruh err," came the muffled reply. Dr. Anlon Cully emerged from the bathroom in boxer shorts and a T-shirt with a toothbrush wedged in his mouth. He held up his index finger. "Un secun."

"Okay, but you're gonna miss Nigel's opening."

As Anlon disappeared back into the bathroom, Pebbles unmuted the TV. It was tuned to BCON. With its lighthouse beacon logo and ubiquitous tagline, *BCONtroversial*, the network offered an array of news and entertainment programs designed to stir controversy around any and all subjects. Cynical and snarky, their programming purported to cut through all the bullshit to provide viewers with the unvarnished truth. Sometimes they tacked left on the political spectrum, other times they leaned to the right. Of course, they exhibited their own biases that were clear to see, but their burgeoning audience didn't seem to care.

Neither Pebbles nor Anlon were fans of the network, but their friend, Dr. Antonio Wallace, was scheduled to appear as a guest on *In the Spotlight,* a morning talk show dedicated to exposing incompetence and corruption wherever the show's host, Nigel Ewing, sniffed it, and this morning his prodigious schnoz was pointed at Augustus Amato and the *Rorschach Explorer*'s mission to Callisto.

Sixteen hours ahead of New York's time zone, Anlon emerged from the bathroom ready for bed and climbed under the sheets next to Pebbles. "What did I miss?"

"Same ol' crap Ewing's been shoveling for months. Augie's a greed-mongering egomaniac with mothballs for brains ... yada, yada. He just finished teasing this guy coming on now. Says the guy knows why Dante walked off *XTC* yesterday."

She turned up the volume as Ewing began to interview his first guest, Dr. Richard Collins. At the bottom of the screen, a graphic informed the audience that Collins was the chairman of an organization called Concerned Scientists for Equal Access to Space.

"*Dr. Collins, you've been a sharp critic of Augustus Amato ever since he announced his plan to send the* Rorschach Explorer *to Callisto,*" Ewing said.

The red-bearded astrophysicist shown on the split screen furrowed his brow. "*That's right. I believed it was a foolhardy idea from the start. An idea driven by ego, not by science. Now it looks like I was right.*"

"*You're referring to the rumors leaking out about last night.*"

"*Indeed I am. Something's clearly amiss. Something serious. For all Amato's openness until now, his sudden silence is telling. His ego won't allow him to admit he was wrong.*"

"*Wrong about what?*"

"*Everything. Wrong about the mission, the crew, UMOs, everything. He should have listened to the concerns of our coalition, taken our point of view more seriously.*"

"*As I recall it, Dr. Collins, you and your colleagues preferred inclusion in Amato's investigation of UMOs and the artifacts his probes photographed on Callisto.*"

"*Preferred is too mild a word, Nigel. These discoveries are simply too profound to have been exclusively entrusted to Amato and his collection of amateurs.*"

"What a douche," Pebbles said. "I hope Antonio crushes him."

"*I mean, really, who puts leadership of a mission of this import in the hands of a sixty-five-year-old retired astronaut?*" Collins continued. "*He's been flipping burgers on Kauai for the past two years, for heaven's sake. He doesn't even look the part. He ought to be riding a longboard with a doobie hanging out of his mouth, not commanding a spaceship, though I guess we should be thankful he traded his ponytail for a crew cut.*"

Fed by a series of softball questions from Ewing, Collins continued his diatribe, picking apart the qualifications of the rest of the crew. As he laid into Kiera and Ajay, Pebbles muted the television.

"What is it with Nigel? Everyone he interviews about the crew bashes them."

"A lot of people think they're unqualified," Anlon said.

"You don't think that, do you?"

Anlon shrugged. "Honestly, I don't think I would have picked them, but I understand why Augie did."

Pebbles folded her arms across her stomach. "Well, *I* think Augie made great choices."

Anlon slid his arm around her shoulder. "Now don't get all irritated. I'm not on Nigel's side. I think highly of the crew."

A photograph of *Rorschach's* last crewmember, Dr. Robert Shilling, appeared on screen. According to the bullet points next to his picture, the trim neurobiologist had been born and raised in Hong Kong by his Chinese mother and British father, and he was an accomplished triathlete and honeybee ethologist.

Pebbles unmuted the broadcast. "What the heck is a honeybee ethologist?"

"They train honeybees, teach them new behaviors," Anlon said.

"Why not call him a honeybee trainer?"

"Ethologist sounds more impressive. Now, shhh. I want to hear what Collins has to say about Shilling."

" … *if he's such an expert, where is his research? He's published no peer-reviewed articles on his work with UMOs, and his early honeybee papers were inconsequential. For all we know, he's more quack than crack scientist.*"

"*His experiments on XTC have been pretty impressive,*" Ewing said.

Collins scoffed. "*Parlor tricks compared to cutting-edge ethology. Face it, Nigel, Shilling is no different than the rest of Amato's crew. They're nothing but lightweights and has-beens. Add to that an untested spacecraft, a mission director still wet behind the ears, and Amato's inexplicable rush to launch a deep-space mission, it's no wonder they're now facing a disaster.*"

"*What kind of disaster?*"

"*A major problem with the ship. Something the crew can't handle.*"

"*You know this for a fact?*"

"*What else could it be? If it were something minor, I'm sure we would have heard something from Amato by now. I know I've said it before, but it bears repeating under the current circumstances. He really should have sent another probe fleet to Callisto before sending a manned mission. He should have sought the guidance and participation of the aerospace community instead of going off on his own.*"

"*Well-made points, Dr. Collins. Thank you. And on that note, we'll take a break. When* In the Spotlight *returns, we welcome Dr. Antonio Wallace for his take on Augustus Amato, the* Rorschach Explorer *and the rumors of an unfolding disaster aboard the ship. Stay tuned.*"

Pebbles hopped out of bed. "Time to make some popcorn!"

Antonio Wallace joined Ewing live on set in BCON's New York studio. Seated next to the pudgy show host with the bad toupee and rumpled suit, the tall, elegantly dressed billionaire looked like the television star with Ewing as his guest, not the other way around.

Of course, Antonio *was* a star. As the founder of Whave Technologies, owner of the Bay Area's professional basketball team and one of the most accomplished black entrepreneurs in the world, he appeared frequently on television. He also had quite a media following on the Internet, and a horde of paparazzi were always anxious to snap the billionaire bachelor out on the town with one starlet or another.

He was also a close friend of Anlon and Pebbles — hence Pebbles' popcorn-accompanied enthusiasm for his appearance on the show. As she snagged a fistful, she said, "Come on, Antonio. Show everyone what a phony Nigel is."

"He's got to be careful," Anlon said. "Nigel's good at getting under people's skin."

Ewing played nice for the first few exchanges of the interview, buttering Antonio up with compliments and benign questions about his basketball team and personal life. And then the moment came when it was clear that the fawning was complete.

"*Dr. Wallace, you're an engineer by training. Am I right?*"

"*That's right, Nigel.*"

"*And you've used your engineering talent to invent a host of new technologies.*"

"*Not so much my talent, Nigel. I'm not the mad scientist behind most of our inventions. Our team of engineers and scientists are the real geniuses.*"

"*Oh, come now. You're being too modest.*"

"*No, truly. I'm more of a facilitator than inventor.*"

"*I see. Just like Augustus Amato?*"

"*We are alike in many ways.*"

"*He's a friend of yours?*"

"*He is.*"

Ewing paused, waiting for his guest to elaborate. But Antonio merely sat with his hands resting atop his crossed knee, gazing back at the host with a friendly smile.

Ewing tapped a notepad on his lap with a pen. *"In fact, Amato's much more than a friend, isn't he, Dr. Wallace? You own quite a bit of A3rospace Industries' stock, don't you?"*

"Gah, what a slimeball!" Pebbles said.

Antonio smoothed his necktie. *"My company does, yes. And A3I owns shares of Whave Technologies as well."*

"You've profited handsomely from your A3I investment over the last year, have you not? Since the Callisto discoveries, A3I's shares have tripled in value."

"Anyone who's been a long-term investor with Augie has done well, Nigel. Even before Callisto."

"Yes, but other investors don't have the same vested interest in the current Callisto mission as you do."

Putting the popcorn bowl aside, Pebbles said, "Can you believe this horse crap?"

Anlon spoke to his friend on screen. "Careful, Skipper, don't let him back you in a corner."

Antonio uncrossed his legs and leaned forward. *"You're referring to our drone-landers, I assume."*

"That and other technology you sold to Amato for the Rorschach Explorer." Ewing ticked his pen on the notepad as he listed the various Whave Technologies components aboard the spacecraft — the probe docking system, the ship's landing struts, and modules incorporated into the GEFF forcefield.

"Don't forget the CubeSat thrusters, Nigel," Antonio said. *"We supplied those, too."*

Ewing frowned as he jotted down the missed component. He looked at the revised list and shook his head. *"You have a lot to lose if the mission fails, don't you, Dr. Wallace? Billions. Tens of billions. Maybe more."*

"Who said anything about the mission failing?"

"You were with Amato at his home for dinner last night when Dr. Fulton dashed off the XTC set in a panic, were you not?"

The camera zoomed in on Antonio's face. His face held a neutral expression, but there was a noticeable twitch below his right eye. *"I'm not sure how you know that, but yes, I did dine at Augie's … and I don't agree with your characterization of Dr. Fulton's actions."*

"The camera doesn't lie, Dr. Wallace." Before Antonio could retort, Ewing charged ahead. *"You are privy to the crisis facing the crew, are you not?"*

Anlon squeezed the remote. "God, I'd like to knock the smirk right off his ugly mug."

Pebbles massaged her wrists. "You'll have to get in line."

The camera was still trained on Antonio's face, showing beads of sweat appearing on his forehead. *"Nigel,"* he said, *"it's not my place to speak for Dr. Fulton or Augustus Amato, so I won't. But I will say this: despite the opinions of your previous guest, I have the utmost confidence in the abilities of Dr. Fulton, Augie, the* Rorschach *crew and everyone at A3I."*

"Is that your way of confirming there is a crisis?"

"No. I didn't say that."

The screen switched to a close-up of Ewing. *"Then how do you explain Dr. Fulton's actions? Amato's cryptic statement?"*

"As I said, it's not my place —"

Ewing interrupted. *"I have to tell you, Dr. Wallace, we've heard shocking accusations from sources in a position to know what's behind Amato's sudden lack of transparency."*

Though he was off camera, Antonio's booming voice was loud and clear. *"Bullshit."*

That spurred a fist pump from Anlon. "Let him have it, Skipper!"

A new camera angle showed the back of Ewing's head in the foreground and Antonio's snarling face in the background. *"Dr. Wallace, there's no need to be so defensive."*

"Really, Nigel? You toss a turd on the table like that and expect me to let you get away with it? You don't have any inside information. You have no idea what's going on at A3I, good or bad." Antonio stood and began to remove the mini-microphone pinned to his lapel. *"You're just trying to stir the pot, scare people and ruin the reputations of some fine individuals."*

Ewing, still seated, glanced up at Antonio and then back at his notes. In a calm tone, he said, *"I'm just asking questions, Dr. Wallace. Questions that need to be asked."*

"*Well, you can ask 'em of an empty chair.*"

Antonio dropped the microphone on the floor and walked off the set. A camera followed him as he brushed past a member of the broadcast crew.

The view then switched back to a close-up of Ewing. He looked into the camera and shrugged. "*I guess Dr. Wallace is afraid to answer tough questions ... *"

As the camera began to zoom out, Ewing balanced his notepad and pen on the armrest of his chair and stood. He walked to the center of the set and stared into the camera. "*When we return to* In the Spotlight, *we'll hear from correspondent Rita Haynes, who will share the chilling details of her talk with an insider who claims the* Rorschach Explorer *faces a dire situation.*"

CHAPTER 5

POSTMORTEM

A mato exited his office by the back door and stepped onto the catwalk above a cavernous hangar. Gripping the handrails on both sides, he slowly walked to the center of the room and gazed down at dozens of technicians in the process of installing compartment upgrades into a second *Rorschach Explorer*. The work-in-progress ship didn't have its own name yet, so for now Amato referred to it as *RE2*.

Most of *RE2*'s upgraded compartments had been built to address design flaws that had emerged during the first two months of *Rorschach's* journey to Callisto, including the balky GEFF system. Other compartments were mere duplicates of those aboard the in-flight spaceship. When *Rorschach* returned to Earth, its out-of-date compartments would be swapped out with upgrades similar to those now incorporated into *RE2*, and of course any compartments damaged during the UMO attacks would be replaced as well.

Whether those upgrades would occur sooner or later remained an open question.

Amato's knee-jerk thought after the first attack had been to scrub the mission and order the *Rorschach Explorer* to return to Earth immediately. While the abort would be embarrassing to Amato and everyone else involved in the mission, it wouldn't be the end of the world. After licking their wounds, they would try again in a year or two.

But then Kiera had reestablished communications with two of the Recons and two of the Cargos, kindling hope of a resumption of *Rorschach*'s flight to Callisto. But for now, only hope. There was still much to do. Kiera first had to guide the damaged spacecrafts back to *Rorschach* for repairs and retrofitting, and then she, Dante, and his team of Mayaguana engineers would have to stitch together a makeshift fleet capable of giving the ship adequate radiation protection and enough probes to scan for the perpetrator of the gamma burst that had ended *Juno*'s mission.

And even if those efforts proved successful, the decision to resume *Rorschach*'s mission would still hinge on estimates of their ability to avoid another UMO attack. To that end, Amato had ordered Pritchard to form a working group to examine the data from the recent attacks and put forth recommendations to help *Rorschach* steer clear of the aliens. Pritchard had been given a mere twenty-four hours to complete the analysis and present their findings. Amato couldn't let Morgan and his shipmates hang in limbo any longer than that. Every minute *Rorschach* drifted above the ecliptic waiting for a go/no-go decision risked another attack by the blue UMO colony.

Amato also owed the crew's families, the media and those who had been following *Rorschach*'s mission a fuller explanation about what had transpired over the preceding two days. And he wanted to be transparent — but early on he'd concluded he couldn't stand at a podium full of microphones until a decision to proceed to Callisto or return to Earth had been made. In his mind, half-answers would only make matters worse.

Now, however, he'd come to realize he was wrong. Silence was far worse than half-answers, for it allowed rumors and speculation to stir up a frenzy. And that, in turn, set the stage for leaks and hysteria. It frayed long-standing relationships and sowed distrust. It pummeled A3I's share price and angered investors.

There was no better example of this than Antonio Wallace's appearance on Nigel Ewing's program yesterday. Amato hadn't asked his friend to appear, and if Antonio had checked in with Amato before accepting Ewing's invitation, Amato would have suggested he decline. The outcome of the interview was entirely foreseeable: Antonio had refused to divulge any details, and Ewing had spun that in order to create suspicion of a conspiracy.

As soon as Amato finished meeting with Pritchard and Dante, he decided, he would jump on a conference call with the *Rorschach Explorer* families. Then he would call Jenna Toffy, mend fences with WNN, and provide her the opportunity to conduct an on-the-record interview.

And then he would get down on his knees and pray nothing else went wrong.

ENGINE CONTROL ROOM — THE *RORSCHACH EXPLORER*
DRIFTING AT ALL-STOP ABOVE THE
ECLIPTIC IN THE ASTEROID BELT

Flexing her shaking hands, Kiera closed her eyes and whispered, "Keep it together, girl. Focus ... focus."

It was taking too long, way too long, to guide the hobbled probes back to *Rorschach* — a fact drummed into Kiera by Shilling during his hourly visits to the engine room to check on her progress. The last of those visits had led to another shouting match but, this time, instead of detaining Kiera for a lecture, Morgan grabbed Shilling by the arm and hauled him away.

That had been satisfying.

But the feeling hadn't lasted for more than a few minutes before Kiera's thoughts once again returned to the slow pace of the probes. If only they hadn't flown quite so far away before Kiera reconnected with them, they might have already rendezvoused with *Rorschach*. But Morgan, fearful of attracting the attention of the blue UMOs, had not only ordered her to shut down the probes' VLF engines, he'd insisted she slow their momentum by firing their forward thrusters. The resulting snail's pace was agonizing.

Kiera looked up to see Carillo standing in the engine room doorway.

"Hey," Carillo said. "How's it going?"

Kiera unclenched her fists and forced a smile. "Hey there."

"You okay?"

"I'm good. You?"

"Scared shitless," Carillo said with a smile of her own. "I know it's a loaded question, but how long before they're all back?"

Kiera pointed at the estimated arrival times on the monitor in front of her. "Looks like the Cargos will be back within two hours. The Recons closer to four."

"Gotcha. Do you have the component list for the Recon swap-out yet?"

"Yep, I'll move it to your folder right now." Kiera selected the file from her folder on the shared drive and pasted it into Carillo's folder. "Okay, it's all yours."

"Great, thanks." Carillo patted Kiera on the shoulder. "You're still up to assist me with the swap-outs?"

"Roger that," Kiera said.

As soon as the Cargos arrived, they would be docked at an airlock connected to *Rorschach*'s primary storage room on the starboard side of the ship. Their supplies would be unloaded and the necessary CubeSat components retrieved, then Carillo would perform an EVA to dock the damaged Recons on platforms in the cargo bay. Once they were secured to the platforms and the cargo bay was closed and repressurized, Kiera and Carillo would take the probes apart and install new components to convert the probes to serve as Shields. Morgan would perform another EVA to undock the probes and guide them out of the bay. Finally, once they were clear of the ship, Kiera would activate their fleet management programs and the probes would take their assigned positions around *Rorschach*.

"Let's just hope we get it all done before ... you know ... "

Carillo wagged a finger at her. "Uh, uh, uh. Positive thoughts only."

"You're right. My bad," Kiera said.

"We can't afford *two* doom-and-glooms around here. Whether we scrub or continue to Callisto, we've got a *long* way to go."

"Yeah, I know. I hear ya. Speaking of our ass-hat biologist, why do you think he's upped his pucker factor?"

"He's under a lot of pressure. Everyone's looking to him for answers, but he doesn't have 'em. Not yet."

"Yeah, I get that, but he's making things worse by being such a prick."

"I know, but calling him names to his face isn't helping."

Kiera frowned. "Should I take that to mean you think I'm being an a-hole, too?"

Carillo sat down next to her. "Look, long missions are super stressful, even for the most experienced astronauts. We're cooped up together, nowhere else to go. We miss home, we get frustrated when things go wrong, we get on each other's nerves. But each of us has to work through it and remember we're a team."

Kiera felt heat rise on her neck and chest. "So I'm not being a team player. Is that it?"

"No, not at all. I'm just saying we have to keep the long game in mind when we have disagreements. Especially when we're facing a crisis like we are now. This isn't like social media, Kiera. You can't just rip off a one-liner and then shut down the account. Shilling's not going anywhere any time soon, and neither are you."

Carillo's social media comment was a reference to an exchange Kiera had had with Colonel Carlton Rawlings after he went on live television the week before launch and questioned Kiera's qualifications to be part of the crew. The quote that sent her over the edge was Rawlings' quip about the inevitability of a crisis that would cause Kiera to curl up in a ball and suck her thumb.

Kiera's social-media response had been short and to the point.

Hey grandpa, f*** u and the rocket you rode 2 the Moon! #nothumbsuckerhere

That had sparked a vicious backlash from Rawlings ... though on the bright side it had also gotten Kiera two million new followers — before Amato ordered her to shut down the account.

"Don't get me wrong," Carillo continued, "I think Bob's an a-hole too. But I'm not going to say it to his face. Scream it into your pillow, flip him the bird behind his back, but let's avoid confrontations. You need him, he needs you. We all need each other."

Just before Kiera snapped back at Carillo, Ajay floated into view in the engine room doorway, clad in sweatpants and a T-shirt featuring the smiling Elroy cartoon character.

"Greetings, Earthlings," he said with a smile. "Might I have a word?"

"Not now. We're kinda in the middle of something," Kiera said.

"It's important. Well, I think it's important."

Carillo motioned him in. "Why aren't you wearing your GEFF gear?"

Ajay twirled his body in midair. "I don't know. I feel more like an astronaut when I'm floating around."

Carillo laughed. "You crack me up."

Kiera glared at the both of them.

Ajay smiled wider as he tucked to perform a flip. "You should try it, Kiera. It's fun."

"Knock off the clown show, it's annoying," Kiera said. "Now what's so damn important?"

"Okay, okay." Ajay reached for Carillo's shoulder to steady his flip, but he missed and almost grabbed one of her breasts by mistake. "Oops, sorry about that. Navigational error."

Kiera growled and stood. She took hold of Ajay's T-shirt and pinned his weightless body upside down against the wall. "Out with it!"

Staring up at the two women, Ajay said, "I think I know where the BLUMOs came from."

"BLUMOs?" Kiera said.

"Yeah, that's what Dr. Shilling said Mayaguana is calling the colony of blue UMOs now. I suggested Bluto or Blammo, but got rejected."

"Why are you telling us about this rather than Dr. Shilling?" Carillo asked.

"He's with Skywalker in the ready room. They're yelling at each other pretty good right now. I didn't think it was a good time to interrupt."

AUGUSTUS AMATO'S OFFICE
A3ROSPACE INDUSTRIES COMMAND AND CONTROL CENTER
MAYAGUANA ISLAND, THE BAHAMAS

Amato looked from Dante to Pritchard. Both men seemed upbeat and full of energy, despite the likelihood that neither man had slept more than a few hours over the last forty-eight.

"Well, gentlemen, what's the verdict? How did your meetings go?"

"Good. Productive," Pritchard said. He turned to Dante. "Do you agree?"

"I do. Everybody came to the table with contributions."

"That's a relief. I was worried there might be some 'I told you so' energy from the NASA folks you invited into the working group," Amato said. He held up a hand toward Pritchard. "No offense, Dennis."

"None taken, Augie. I kind of expected the same. Credit Helen. I think she's trying to instill a new attitude at NASA. Plus, she's always been good in crises. She checks her ego and works the problems. It's obvious her mentality has rubbed off on her team."

"Excellent," Amato said. "So, give me the highlights."

Pritchard handed Amato a packet. "Here are the materials handed out at the meeting. I've emailed you a complete set, plus the video and data files we discussed. Short version — the first probe to be attacked was *Recon-1*, the command CubeSat in the Recon group. We think the BLUMOs were triggered by X-band comms between *Recon-1* and the other CubeSats."

"BLUMOs?" Amato asked.

"Blue UMOs," Dante said. "We kept on getting confused about which UMOs we were talking about, so I came up with the new term. Anyway, like Dennis said, we think X-band comms started the whole chain of events."

"Really? I was sure you'd say the catalyst was the gamma-ray spectrometers or the VLF engines."

Pritchard nodded. "We discussed both, but based on what happened afterward, they're less likely than X-band."

It was well known by now that UMOs were sensitive to radiation at the low and high ends of the electromagnetic spectrum. Toward the higher end, they reacted to X-rays and gamma rays, and at the lower end, to radio waves, including the super-high-frequency waves transmitted by X-band radios, high-frequency waves transmitted by shortwave radios, and the very-low-frequency waves used to agitate ions in the plasma chambers of Kiera's VLF engines.

"Elaborate," Amato said.

"Okay, let's start with the VLF engines," Dante said. "There was no data from the Recons that suggested the BLUMOs fed on ejected ions. There was no evidence of boosts in speed, no bump from a bow shock and the Recons never veered off course before they went LOS."

"And the gamma spectrometers?"

Dante deferred to Pritchard for the answer. The former NASA chief said, "Well, as you know, the spectrometers were operating, scanning for gamma bursts, when the attack occurred. But the BLUMOs didn't target the spectrometer sensors. At least, not at first. Which wasn't surprising, since gamma-ray spectrometers don't emit gamma rays. The devices detect the rays by emitting electrical pulses that interact with gamma photons captured by the spectrometer's sensor."

"Yes, I know," Amato said. "But we also know from past experience that UMOs don't like the spectrometers, nonetheless. Whether it has to do with the electrical pulses, the germanium crystals in the sensor head or background radiation leaked by the device, we don't yet know. But we do know they will attack a GRS."

"Well, they didn't this time," Pritchard said. "The first component to get zapped on all the Recons was the X-band transmitter."

Dante chimed in. "And we think the attack cascaded because *Recon-1* transmitted a sensor alarm back to *Rorschach* and to the other Recons before the BLUMOs finished it off. Those X-band signals led the BLUMOs from one probe to another and ultimately guided them back to *Rorschach*, the Shields and Cargos."

Amato had been flipping through the packet while Dante spoke, but now he paused and looked up. "But if that's the case, why didn't our UMO colony react in the same way? They've been flying with us since we left Earth. We've used X-band the entire way, ship-to-probes, fleet-to-Earth."

"Shilling says he conditioned *Rorschach*'s colony to ignore X-band signals a long time ago, so they lost whatever sensitivity that made the BLUMOs attack," Pritchard said.

Amato stood, his pot belly brushing against the conference table. He began to pace, looking down, while rubbing the smooth crown of his head. "Hmmm ... "

"What's the matter, Augie?" Pritchard said.

Amato halted and turned to face him. "Your comment about *Rorschach*'s colony. Are you certain the BLUMOs didn't attack because they detected our UMO colony?"

"Oh, everyone believes things went batshit once the two colonies became aware of each other," Dante said. "But the sequence of the attack implies they were first triggered by X-band signals."

Pritchard explained the working group's view of how the attack unfolded. After the BLUMOs attacked the Recons, they homed in on the flurry of sensor alarm pings going back and forth between the Recons and *Rorschach*. When the colony traveling with the fleet detected the BLUMO swarm, they tried to move *Rorschach*, their food source, out of harm's way and then dispersed to deal with the BLUMOs. By then, all the electromagnetic energy flying around had triggered sensor alarms on the Shields. A melee ensued.

"When the crew fired up the Cargos," Dante said, "our UMOs detected the engine ions, broke off the fight and chased after the probes. The urge to feed won out. We're not sure why. Maybe their strength was depleted from the battle. Anyway, for some reason, the BLUMOs took off after them instead of finishing off *Rorschach* and the rest of the Shields."

"Thank heaven for that." Amato resumed pacing. "Most of what you've said sounds plausible, but there is one piece that doesn't fit."

"What piece?" Pritchard asked.

"Why did the BLUMOs come back to *Rorschach* later? The ship's X-band antenna was knocked out in the first attack, so X-band comms couldn't have attracted them."

"It turns out that not *all* X-band was out," Dante said.

"I don't follow," Amato said.

"He feels bad about it, Augie. It wasn't intentional," said Pritchard.

"Who feels bad about what? What are you two talking about?"

"Antonio Wallace. Remember when we were watching *Expedition to Callisto* and he was texting?"

"What's that got to do with anything?"

"He texted his tech guys to ping his drone-landers aboard *Rorschach* to see if they were okay. They don't rely on *Rorschach*'s X-band antenna, Augie — they have their own specialized antennas. The BLUMOs must have picked up the signal and homed in on *Rorschach* again."

"Are you saying if we shut off all X-band, we shouldn't have any more problems with the BLUMOs?"

"I don't think either of us are prepared to go that far," Dante said.

"Then are you advocating we scrub?" asked Amato.

Dante exchanged a glance with Pritchard, then said, "Not yet. We think we have a solution that buys us time to assess the Callisto gamma risk without exposing *Rorschach* to another run-in with the BLUMOs."

CREW READY ROOM — THE *RORSCHACH EXPLORER*
DRIFTING AT ALL-STOP ABOVE THE
ECLIPTIC IN THE ASTEROID BELT

Facing Shilling from the opposite side of the ready room conference table, Morgan unloaded on the man. "This bullshit's gotta stop, Bob. Right here and now."

"I agree," Shilling said, just as forcefully. "We shouldn't even wait to hear from Mayaguana. Turn the ship around and let's get the hell out of here."

"That's not what I'm talking about and you know it." Morgan jabbed a finger at the UMO researcher. "You gotta stop with the condescension. Stop with the attitude. Stop with the insubordination."

Shilling's face turned purple. "Me? What about *her*?"

"Look, I realize Kiera's got a quick trigger and a sailor's mouth, but you can't let her get to you. It affects how you deal with everyone else."

"Then rein her in. I'm fed up with her questioning my manhood."

"I've talked to her. I've asked Julia to talk to her. And she's getting the same message I'm giving to you. Knock it off, get in line and keep it civil."

"Or else what? Are you going to confine me to quarters? Shoot me out the airlock?"

"Don't tempt me."

Shilling leaned over the table and sneered at the shorter Morgan. "You don't scare me, Colonel. You're a shadow of the legend that follows you around."

"This has nothing to do with legends," Morgan spat back. "It has to do with the here and now. We're up to our neck in shit. We can't afford to be at each other's throats."

"Up to our necks in shit … a perfect analogy." Shilling glared. "And guess who put us there?"

"What are you driving at?"

"You've sniffed your shit so long you can't even tell the danger you've put us in." Shilling pounded the table and kicked at a chair. "You don't have a wife and kids. *I do.* I want to see them again. More than I want to see Callisto, UMOs or anything else out here. *You*, on the other hand, are chasing ghosts. People who probably died within weeks of leaving Callisto … *twenty-four fricking years ago.* But you can't admit that to yourself. Instead, you're obsessed with 'bringing your crew home,' even if it means exposing *this* crew to unnecessary risks."

A3ROSPACE INDUSTRIES COMMAND AND CONTROL CENTER
MAYAGUANA ISLAND, THE BAHAMAS

Dante and Pritchard walked Amato through their proposed revisions to *Rorschach*'s mission. The first order of business: bolster the ship's radiation shield. This would be accomplished by retrofitting the two "rescued" Recons to serve as Shields.

"Kiera's already created a component list for the swap-out," Dante said. "Once the retrofit is complete, *Rorschach* will have a total of five Shields. We'd rather have six, but five will work."

Task two, Dante explained, involved creating new Recons out of Antonio Wallace's two drone-landers. "The landers are already outfitted with gamma spectrometers, but they only have maneuvering thrusters. They would take forever to reach Callisto. So to speed their trip, we're suggesting using the two Cargos as taxis."

The jury-rigged solution made sense to Amato. After the crew unloaded the Cargos, the empty vessels would have no purpose in the near-term. Why not take advantage of their VLF engines to transport the drone-landers? "So, you'll have *Rorschach* remotely deploy the landers to scan for gamma bursts when the Cargos reach Callisto."

"That's right," Pritchard said.

"You're not concerned BLUMOs will attack the Cargos?"

"Oh, we're concerned all right," Pritchard said. "But — knock on wood — Kiera has guided them back without incident so far."

"Yes, but that's because she's using thrusters only. What happens when they power up their VLF engines again?"

"We'll tell them to keep the Cargos well above the ecliptic until they're through the belt," said Dante. "But if the probes get attacked, we'll scrub immediately and bring *Rorschach* home."

"All right." Amato crossed his arms. "Assuming the Cargos make it to Callisto unmolested, are two landers enough to do the job? Before, you lobbied hard to have all six Recons scan for gamma radiation."

"It's less than ideal, and it'll take more time, but we think it's manageable," Dante said.

"What about *Rorschach* and the Shields? Where will they be while the Cargos are on their way to Callisto?"

"We'll have them also stay above the ecliptic until the Cargos are past the belt, then we'll send them on," Pritchard said. "They'll only be about a month behind the Cargos if all goes well."

"And once *Rorschach* nears the outer edge of the belt," Dante added, "its course will put it within a few days of Ceres. We'll divert the ship and Shields there and have them insert into orbit while the drone-landers conduct the gamma search."

The plan appealed to Amato. If the search yielded no sign of gamma radiation, *Rorschach* could proceed to Callisto, and if the landers did detect gamma bursts and the mission had to be scrubbed, there would still be the opportunity to conduct meaningful scientific research on Ceres before returning to Earth.

"Have you run your plan past Paul or Kiera?"

"Only part one, retrofitting the Recons to become Shields," Dante said. "We wanted to discuss part two with you first to make sure you were on board with repurposing the landers, using the Cargos as taxis and the idea about the Ceres diversion."

"Very well. Let's run it by both of them after they finish the refit of the Recons. I don't think we should distract them until then."

CHAPTER 6

BIRD CALLS

COMMS & INSTRUMENTATION CENTER
— THE *RORSCHACH EXPLORER*
DRIFTING AT ALL-STOP ABOVE THE
ECLIPTIC IN THE ASTEROID BELT
SEPTEMBER 3, 2019

Ajay handed headphones to Kiera and Carillo and plugged them into the ship's radio spectrum analyzer. "So, as you know, I've kept our radio receivers on throughout the trip. I like to listen to our UMO colony."

Ever since Ajay's discovery of the radio wave dialogue between groups of UMOs the prior year, he had developed a keen interest in listening to the aliens' conversations. In fact, he hoped to learn enough from observing their chirp patterns during the flight to Callisto to discern a way to directly communicate with them. To this end, he was especially interested in the sounds generated by the apparent ringleader in most UMO colony conversations — the colony queen.

He would not have known the lead chirper was most often the colony queen if not for insights provided by Dr. Anlon Cully the prior year, but once he learned of this communication characteristic, he became intent on deciphering the chirps of *Rorschach*'s UMO queen.

"Yeah," Kiera said. "So what?"

"After you listen to them long enough, they sound like birds chirping," Ajay said.

"We'll take your word for it," Kiera said. "Get to the point."

"For most of the trip, one of the UMOs has done most of the talking, er, chirping. I assume that's the queen. Every now and then you hear other chirps, though. Sort of like when you hear one bird chirp in a tree and then others chirp back."

"I get the audiovisual," Kiera said, her voice tinged with sarcasm.

"Well, I've been recording the chirp sessions, and I went back and listened to the recording on BLUMO Day. During the attack, at least until the colony split up, a different-sounding chirp appeared. A quivering kind of chirp. I don't think it was from our colony. I think it came from the queen of the BLUMOs. Put on your headphones and listen."

First Ajay played them a clip of pre-attack chirps. There were intermittent, slow bursts of the bird-like sounds. He then played a snippet of the early part of the attack, in which the chirp pattern ramped up in intensity and frequency. Finally, they listened to a clip where the quivering chirp first entered the dialogue. It was an eerie sound, more like a whistle than a chirp. A terse battle of chirps ensued until electromagnetic interference overwhelmed the rest of the recording.

Carillo removed the headphones. "Wow. That's an earful."

As Kiera removed hers, she said, "I take it you went back in time and listened for the quiver in earlier recordings."

"Yup."

"And you detected it."

"Right again."

Carillo smiled. "And you identified when it first appeared, and our exact position when that occurred."

"You guys keep going, I'll stop you if you get off track," Ajay said, leaning back in his seat and propping his feet on the console.

Kiera closed her eyes and rubbed at her temples. Then she gasped and her eyes shot open. "There's a large asteroid near where the quiver started, isn't there?"

"Don't know," Ajay said. "Outside of my wheelhouse. But it wouldn't surprise me."

"The infrared data," Carillo said to Kiera. "How wide a field did the Recons scan?"

"Pretty damn wide. Let's pull up the files and find out." She high-fived Ajay, then planted a kiss on his forehead. "Elroy to the rescue once again!"

Ajay blushed as she slid into a seat at the bank of spectrometer displays next to him. He gave her the date and time he first detected the quiver, and she searched the scan files for the period in question. There was a separate file for each of the six Recons, meaning they would have to review each individually.

"Can we divvy it up?" Carillo asked. "There's another spectrometer console in the lab compartment."

"Yeah, absolutely," Kiera said. While the two women began to discuss their plan to divide up the recordings, Ajay cleared his throat. "Um, I think I can simplify your task."

The women turned their heads in unison.

He smiled. "I think I know the direction they came from."

Carillo's mouth fell open. "You can tell that from the audio?"

Ajay shook his head.

"Then how?" Kiera asked.

"I went through the video cam files of the Shields."

"What? Why the Shields?"

"It was a hunch, really. The first time the quiver shows up on the audio, there was more than one quiver tone. One was much louder than the other. It was as loud as the chirps from our own colony."

"Okay ... so?" Carillo said.

"Our colony has been flying behind *Rorschach*, just outside our ion-shield, so if some of the quivers were just as loud as the chirps, to me that meant some of the BLUMOs must have been very close to us ... as close as our UMOs. So I wondered whether the louder quiver might be a scout calling back to the BLUMO colony. A 'Hey, look what I found!' kind of thing. Like I said, it was just a hunch."

Kiera leaned forward, her eyes widening. "Oh my God. You saw a scout party on the video. Just like the one that hit our CubeSats in the belt last year."

"Port side, *Shield-3*." Ajay smiled.

Carillo turned to leave. "I'll go pull up the video file from the lab. Kiera, you handle the infrared files."

"Hold up," Ajay said. "No need, I've already queued up the video files." He stood and stepped aside from the console.

"Files? As in plural?" Kiera asked.

"Uh-huh. They stalked us for almost twenty hours before they attacked."

Ajay, Kiera and Carillo arrived at the ready room to find the door closed and the fireworks between Morgan and Shilling still going.

Ajay turned to his shipmates. "Are you sure we should interrupt them?"

"This can't wait." Carillo stepped forward and pounded on the door.

"What?" Morgan yelled from inside.

"We need to talk with you. Both of you," Carillo said.

"Not now, Julia."

Carillo pushed open the door to find the two red-faced men glaring at each other from opposite sides of the table. She motioned for Ajay and Kiera to follow her into the room.

"I said *not now*," Morgan said.

Carillo took a seat. Ajay and Kiera joined her at the table.

"It's important," Carillo said. "It's about the BLUMO attack."

"I don't care if—"

"Ajay, set up the display," Carillo said.

Ajay opened the laptop he'd brought from the comms center. While he activated the wireless connection with the flat screen monitor on the wall behind Morgan, Carillo kicked off their presentation.

"We have something to show you that puts a whole new spin on the attack. Ajay, it was your discovery. You do the honors."

As Ajay opened his mouth to begin the briefing, Morgan turned to Shilling. "This conversation isn't finished, Doctor. Understood?"

"Good," Shilling said. "Because I have *plenty* left to say."

Just as it appeared their fight might erupt anew, Carillo tugged on Morgan's arm. "We were stalked, Paul."

"What?"

"The BLUMOs stalked us before they attacked. Go ahead, Ajay. Show them."

Ajay led Morgan and Shilling through the audio and video data. Here and there, Kiera and Carillo stopped him to add their perspectives. As Morgan's and Shilling's ire subsided, the two men took their seats at the table and focused their attention on the latest twist in UMO behavior.

When the briefing concluded, Morgan shook his head. "Unbelievable. Every time we think we've figured UMOs out, they remind us how ignorant we are."

"Agreed," Carillo said. She turned to Shilling. "Have you seen this kind of predatory behavior before?"

"With my UMOs? No. What you recorded is beyond honeybee behavior, beyond swarm and flock behavior in general. It's closer to pack hunting. Tracking us, biding their time, waiting for conditions that favored their attack."

"Pack hunting? You mean the BLUMOS are like wolves?" Ajay asked.

Shilling nodded. "In a way, it's an understandable adaptation given the scarcity of ions in the asteroid belt."

"Explain what you mean," Morgan said.

"Pack hunting is most prevalent in harsh environments. Environments where it's hard for individual animals to find food. Safaris, deserts, tundras. Those kinds of places."

"I don't understand," said Ajay. "If there isn't enough food for them, why would the BLUMOs choose to live here? Why wouldn't they go toward Jupiter? Set up their colony in its huge magnetic field?"

"That's a good question — it does seem like a strange choice. But then again we have no proof that UMOs *can* live in Jupiter's field. It might be too strong. It might be inhospitable for them. We know they don't care for X-rays, and Jupiter's field at the poles is X-ray dense."

"Oh, come on," said Kiera. "You can't be serious."

"I am being serious. They've never been observed around Jupiter. Nor, if I recall correctly, did your CubeSats encounter them in orbit around Callisto."

"There's a gigantic hive in the Calliston spaceport," Kiera countered. "If they're not feeding in Jupiter's field, where are they getting their food, Einstein?"

Shilling clenched his jaw. Before responding to Kiera, he glared at Morgan. "Tell me, Dr. Walsh, have you *seen* this gigantic hive?"

"No."

"Then how do you know it exists?"

"*Cetus Prime.* The crew. They said—"

"That was *twenty-four years* ago, Doctor."

"Fine, you want more recent proof? The NASA pictures of them de-icing the spaceport."

Shilling let out a short laugh. "That's your proof? *Rorschach*'s colony is, or was, larger than the clusters of UMOs in those pictures. Face it, Doctor, your only *proof* comes from the words of people who've probably been dead for more than two decades."

"All right, Bob. That's enough," Morgan said.

"No, it's *not*, Colonel," Shilling said. "If there's a pack of BLUMOs hunting us, this mission is definitely over." He pushed out of his seat and turned to leave the room.

"Stay here, Bob. We're not done," Morgan said.

The scientist kept walking.

Morgan roared, "Get back here, Shilling! Right now!"

Shilling paused and turned back toward Morgan. Though his face was red and his stance was rigid, his tone was calm. "Look, Colonel, based on what's in those videos, those little blue bastards are coming back, and we don't have a prayer of stopping them. We've got one choice and one choice only. Abort. Now, I'm going to the lab to write up a report to send to Mayaguana saying just that. You can try to stop me if you want, but if you value the lives of *this* crew more than those of the *Cetus Prime* crew, you won't."

Ajay raised a timid hand. "Excuse me, Dr. Shilling. How do you know they're coming back?"

"Simple. Pack hunters don't give up easily."

Morgan rose to follow Shilling, but he was dissuaded by Carillo. "Let him cool down, Paul. You're not going to make any headway until he does. Until you do, too."

Morgan halted in the doorway and bowed his head. "You're right."

Carillo turned to Kiera. "What's the ETA for the Cargos now?"

Kiera glanced at her smartwatch. "I'd say a little over thirty minutes."

"All right, then let's get a move on. The quicker we dock, unload and retrofit, the faster we can get out of here."

"And go where?" Ajay asked. "Back home?"

"I'm not ready to give up. Not yet," Carillo said. "Are you?"

"No way."

"How about you, Kiera?"

She shook her head. "No thumb-sucker here."

"Roger that." Carillo looked to Morgan. "What do you say, Skywalker? Are we gonna do this or what?"

Morgan raised his head to see the others staring at him. "You all go ahead. I'll catch up with you in a few minutes. I need to take care of something on the flight deck."

LABORATORY COMPARTMENT — THE *RORSCHACH EXPLORER*

Shilling was apparently so engrossed in composing his pack-hunting report, he didn't notice Morgan enter the lab until the commander closed and locked the door. He turned at the sound.

"Ah, Colonel. So you've come to stop me. Is that it? How are you planning to do it? Break my fingers so I can't type?"

Morgan smiled. "No, that's not my style."

"What's it going to be, then?" Shilling stood and slashed a make-believe sword through the air. "You have lightsabers in your quarters for just such an occasion?"

"No, I don't have any lightsabers." Morgan laughed and stepped closer.

Shilling balled his fists. "I'm warning you, Colonel. I will defend myself."

"Relax, Bob. I haven't come to fight you. Just to talk."

"What's the point?" Shilling said, unclenching his hands. "We'll just wrap around the same wheel again."

"Please, sit. This will just take a minute."

Morgan's matter-of-fact tone seemed to puzzle Shilling. He squinted as if trying to read his commander's thoughts. "I prefer to stand."

"Fine, have it your way." Morgan sat down at the console station next to Shilling's and looked up at him. "I've had some time to think about some of the things you said earlier. About taking unnecessary risks. About my motivation for leading this mission. I appreciate your candor. It was a good reality check, and it's good to know where you're coming from."

Shilling crossed his arms over his chest. "You almost sound sincere."

"I am sincere. Just like I'm sincere about this. It's one thing if you challenge me behind closed doors, Bob. It's another if you defy my direct orders, especially if you do it in front of the crew."

Shilling sat down and glared at Morgan. "I'm trying to *save our lives*, Colonel. If it means stepping on your authority, so be it."

Morgan shook his head and let out a long sigh. "I'm disappointed to hear you say that, Bob. I really am." He stood and turned to leave.

"That's it?" Shilling said.

"Yeah, that's it.'

"What about my report?"

"What about it?"

"I wasn't joking, Colonel. I *will* send it to Mayaguana."

"Let me know when it's ready to send. I'll be in the storage room helping to unload the Cargos."

STORAGE ROOM — THE *RORSCHACH EXPLORER*

The first Cargo to approach *Rorschach* was *Cargo-2*. Kiera activated its auto-docking system from the auxiliary flight control console in the engine room, and the system guided the probe to the rear starboard airlock. As soon as it was docked and pressurized, Kiera and the other crewmembers, sans Shilling, lined up in a chain gang to unload its storage containers. Carillo, inside the Cargo, pulled containers off shelves and passed them to Ajay, who ducked through the airlock and into *Rorschach*'s primary storage room. There he relayed the containers to Morgan, who carried them into the main corridor and lined them up against the wall for Kiera to inspect. She moved between the containers and removed the necessary replacement parts to convert the two Recons into Shields.

In all, it took them forty-five minutes to clear *Cargo-2*, pull the needed parts and stow the leftover supplies in the storage room.

When the job was finished, Kiera said, "On to *Cargo-4*. Or should we skip it for now?"

"Do we need anything from *Cargo-4* for the retrofit?" Morgan asked.

"No, but it does have circuit board replacements we need for *Rorschach*."

"All right. Go ahead and dock it, but let's not waste time unloading it now."

"Roger that."

Kiera saluted and headed for the engine room directly across the corridor to decouple *Cargo-2* and maneuver *Cargo-4* into position for its turn to dock. Morgan followed her and added, "Oh, and when you're done, send a message to Maya and let them know we're about to start prepping for Julia's EVA."

As he stepped back in the corridor, he found himself face to face with a livid Shilling. "You disabled my comms ID!"

"Hold on, Bob," Morgan said. He turned to Ajay, who was standing nearby. "Ajay, secure the storage room airlock, then help Julia move the Shield parts to the cargo bay."

"Roger dodger." Ajay disappeared into the storage room, leaving Morgan in the corridor with Shilling and Carillo.

The commander turned to face Carillo, but Shilling stepped between them. "I demand you turn my ID back on."

Morgan leaned his head around Shilling to address Carillo. "I'll see you in the cargo bay airlock in about half an hour."

Carillo bit her lower lip and left the two men alone.

"Now, what was it you were saying, Bob?" Morgan asked.

"You know very well what I was saying."

"Oh, right. The comms ID. Yeah, sorry about that, Bob. No can do."

"Is this some kind of game to you, Colonel? Our lives are at stake."

Morgan shook his head. "Nope. No game. Now, let's go take a look at the report you've written before *I* send it off to Maya."

DR. DANTE FULTON'S OFFICE
A3ROSPACE INDUSTRIES COMMAND AND CONTROL CENTER
MAYAGUANA ISLAND, THE BAHAMAS

End game.

Dante scribbled the two words on the cover page of Shilling's "pack-hunter" report. An hour ago, Morgan had transmitted the report with a short preface:

In light of the new information highlighted in the attached report, there may be a stronger case for aborting the mission. However, firmly suggest seeking second opinion of Dr. Shilling's conclusions before ordering a scrub. Concerned his personal preference for aborting shaded his conclusions. Until otherwise instructed, we are proceeding with the CubeSat refits.

Dante picked up the printout and left his office to meet with Amato. If Shilling's assessment was correct, it was just a matter of time before the crew confronted the BLUMO colony again. While Dante gave weight to Morgan's perception of Shilling's bias, he found it difficult to discount two larger points raised in the report.

First, Shilling suggested it was likely that other "packs" lurked in the asteroid belt. As basis for this claim, the researcher cited the high degree of hunting skill evident in the BLUMOs' stalking of *Rorschach's* fleet. *On Earth,* he wrote, *such well-developed pack skills are honed through competition over prey.* Shilling also pointed out that Amato's CubeSats had encountered a scouting party from a different UMO colony in the asteroid belt the previous year. *We have two instances of attacks on VLF-powered vessels with X-band radios and active spectrometers traversing two different swaths of the asteroid belt. Even if* Rorschach *successfully passes through BLUMO territory with no further losses, I believe there is a possibility we may encounter other UMO packs.*

The second point that concerned Dante had to do with the UMOs residing on Callisto. If the ship made it all the way to the Jovian moon, Shilling asked, would the aliens there consider *Rorschach* friend or foe?

In our haste to explore, we have, I'm afraid, assumed too much and proved too little about these alien beings. I am as guilty of this as anyone. In light of the varying behaviors we've now observed, how can we assume the UMOs on Callisto will welcome our arrival instead of viewing us as territorial threats — or as prey?

This very thought had been bouncing around Dante's head for the last ten months. *Cetus Prime* had landed inside the Nuada crater with the help of UMOs, but it was unclear whether the assistance had been provided by the same UMOs that had escorted the ship from Mars to Callisto, or whether the UMOs from the alien spaceport had played a role. The crew logs extracted from *Cetus'* computers shed no light on the mystery.

Those same crew logs, however, made it clear that *Cetus'* flight engineer, Nick Reed, had developed an ability to communicate with the Mars UMOs after he was electrocuted by the creatures during a spacewalk. He described the communication interaction in one log entry.

"It's a mental thing. I don't physically talk to them. They don't talk to me. But we are on the same wavelength, so to speak. I get different vibrations from them that give me a sense of what they're trying to say. I think of things I want to say to them and I guess they get vibrations back from me. It's hard to explain. It's like a dog and its person. You can't really communicate with each other, but somehow you understand each other."

The level of communication was rudimentary, but it had been effective enough for Nick to gain the UMOs' assistance to fly to Callisto, land in the crater, explore the spaceport, commandeer one of the Calliston ships docked there, and depart Callisto with their own hive of UMOs leading the way. These facts implied the Mars UMOs had either brokered an introduction to the Callisto UMOs, or Nick had been able to directly interact with both colonies.

Unfortunately, no one aboard *Rorschach* had Nick's ability to communicate with UMOs. Shilling had demonstrated an ability to train them to perform basic tasks, but that didn't involve any interactive, back-and-forth communication — just basic conditioning techniques. Do this and get fed. Dante had hoped Shilling would gain further insights along the way that might assist the crew in interacting with the Callisto UMOs when they reached the moon. But that wouldn't be possible now. *Rorschach's* trained colony was gone, and the BLUMOs who'd chased them off had demonstrated nothing but hostile intentions. At this point, Dante agreed with Shilling. It wasn't worth risking the crew and ship any further.

It was time to abort.

At the waiting room outside the door to Amato's office, Dante approached Mark Myers, Amato's assistant. "Is he available? I need to talk with him."

"He's on the phone with the *Rorschach* families right now."

"Oh, right. Please have him call me when he's free. Tell him it's about Dr. Shilling's pack report."

Myers scribbled down a note. "Is it urgent?" he asked. "He's got the interview with Jenna Toffy after finishing with the families. Then a call with Anlon Cully. But if it's urgent, I can have him reschedule."

The mention of Anlon Cully surprised Dante. Amato must have already read Shilling's report and Morgan's preface. "Yeah, it's urgent. Tell him I'd definitely like to touch base before he speaks with Dr. Cully."

"Will do."

As Myers entered the office to pass the message to Amato, Dante felt his cell phone buzz. It was a text from Dennis Pritchard.

Just received a new downlink from TRE. The first Recon has arrived.

Myers stepped out of Amato's office and gave Dante a thumbs-up. "He's wrapping up now. You're up next."

CARGO BAY AIRLOCK — THE *RORSCHACH EXPLORER*
DRIFTING AT ALL-STOP ABOVE THE
ECLIPTIC IN THE ASTEROID BELT

While Morgan held the spacesuit's lower shell, Carillo shimmied her legs inside. "How hard did you have to twist Bob's arm to get him to help?" she asked.

"It was a piece of cake," Morgan said.

"Ha! I doubt that."

"No, really. It was a quick and easy negotiation."

"Let me guess. You promised to give him back his comms access in exchange for helping us with the EVA."

Morgan smiled and winked. "Nah, it was a little more stick than carrot."

"Well, whatever you did, I'm glad you worked it out. I'll feel better out there with another pair of eyes keeping watch."

"You and me both. I really hate the idea of either of us going out alone, but we don't have a choice."

Standard procedure for an extravehicular activity dictated that a minimum of two astronauts participate in any spacewalk. That way, in the event one of the astronauts incurred an emergency, a second was available to provide immediate assistance. But in *Rorschach*'s present circumstance, standard procedure wasn't an attractive option. The only two people onboard with spacewalk experience were Morgan and Carillo; the others had only performed simulated EVAs in NASA's training pool, and that training had been truncated due to Amato's decision to move up *Rorschach*'s launch date. Morgan and Carillo agreed the tasks associated with this EVA were too important to add managing a rookie into the mix. And Morgan and Carillo couldn't perform the EVA together without delaying the redeployment of the converted probes by a full day, because of another standard procedure that called for a twenty-four hour recovery period between spacewalks by any given astronaut. This practice existed to ensure an astronaut replenished his or her blood oxygen levels after completing a spacewalk. Attempting another EVA in less than that time would increase the risk of decompression sickness-like symptoms.

Given Shilling's conviction about the likelihood of another BLUMO attack, no one aboard wanted to wait a second longer than necessary to redeploy the Shields and get *Rorschach* moving again. That meant the only realistic option was to send out one astronaut to dock the two probes, then send the other astronaut out to relaunch the probes once they were converted from Recons to Shields. Since Carillo had been trained as Kiera's primary backup to repair the fleet's CubeSats, it made the most sense for her to perform the initial spacewalk. Morgan could then begin prepping for his EVA while the two women worked on the probes.

As Morgan assisted Carillo into the top shell of the suit, he noticed she was shivering. "Cold or nervous?"

"A little of both."

"Well, not to worry. We'll have the sky covered from every angle. If any of us detects a whiff of the BLUMOs, I'll order an abort. You just make sure you get your butt inside the airlock as fast as possible. Don't delay."

"Easier said than done. I can't exactly stop in the middle of docking a probe. It could ram the ship or damage the bay."

Morgan clasped a hand on Carillo's shoulder. "Kiera can take over the probe from the engine room. You just hustle for the airlock. Understood?"

Carillo nodded.

Morgan patted her shoulder. "All right. Let's get this over with."

CHAPTER 7

HUNTERS OR FORAGERS

CETUS PRIME CALLISTO TASK FORCE
NASA'S JET PROPULSION LABORATORY
PASADENA, CALIFORNIA
SEPTEMBER 3, 2019

tanding inside the 'U' configuration made by six folding tables, Dr. Ed Chen leaned over to examine the first of the seventy-two photographs that had been laid out. The pictures, showing various sections of the Callisto spaceport, had been shot over the preceding three days by *Cetus Prime*'s cameras.

The particular photograph Chen was studying depicted a familiar scene. Streaks of light — the UMOs — were massed over an ice-covered area of the building, and chunks of fallen ice littered the floor of the crater below. For months, *Cetus Prime*'s cameras had observed the UMOs performing this ritual around the clock. Chen's team, having calculated the approximate square footage cleared over the course of each Earth day, had one of *Cetus Prime*'s two rotating cameras tracking the UMOs' progress, snapping hourly images of the de-icing. Occasionally a newly cleared section revealed an interesting feature of the building, and another of *Cetus*' cameras, one with an operational zoom, would capture a more detailed image.

Chen moved six photos down to study one such zoomed-in image. It showed what looked like a docking bay, the first one uncovered by the UMOs during their months of labor. Chen found it curious that the bay was open, for all other doors, hatches and windows they had found were fortified by coverings that reminded Chen of storm doors. And not only was the bay open, it was empty. The immediate speculation on Chen's team was unanimous: this was the first physical proof that the crew of *Cetus Prime* had successfully launched one of the Calliston ships docked in the facility.

When the photo was released to the public, Chen knew it would ramp up demands for answers to questions about the crew that had been circulating ever since Amato discovered *Cetus Prime*. Where had they gone? Were they still alive? Would they ever come home?

Chen skipped the next dozen photos, but chose to stop and study a photo he believed was destined to be the number one shared image on the Internet as soon as it was released. He marveled at the scene. If a thousand of the world's foremost photographers had all been standing on Callisto with unlimited storage space on their digital cameras, he doubted any of them would have surpassed the splendor of the image.

Twice a day, Chen's team ordered one of *Cetus'* cameras to capture a panoramic view of the four-kilometer-wide facility in order to record the UMOs' overall progress. Some of the previous shots were already worthy of magazine cover treatment. In one, sunlight coated half the facility while the other half was obscured by darkness, save for a small cluster of glittering light that looked like a Christmas tree. In another, the ice surrounding the structure sparkled so brightly it created a glow around the spaceport. Some of Chen's colleagues thought the glow gave the impression the building was floating.

But none of the panorama photos compared to the one Chen stared at now. It was shot two days ago, when Callisto was on the far side of Jupiter. With the Nuada crater facing a vista of black space, the entire image would have been dark if not for two swirling trails of light streaking up above the spaceport. To Chen, those streaks looked like rocket contrails, one arcing to the northwest of the crater, the other to the northeast. The number of UMOs in each streak must have totaled in the millions, dwarfing the small clusters previously photographed.

Where had the UMOs gone? Why did they leave? When would they return? Those would be the questions everyone would ask.

Chen scanned the remaining photos lining the tables. None of the ones taken after this one showed a single UMO. The aliens had seemingly packed up and vacated the facility, their de-icing job left unfinished.

Chen had sent Brock a digital version of the image earlier and had included a short note. *Not sure if it's a good sign or a bad sign, but recommend forwarding this to A3I ASAP.*

AUGUSTUS AMATO'S OFFICE
A3ROSPACE INDUSTRIES COMMAND AND CONTROL CENTER
MAYAGUANA ISLAND, THE BAHAMAS

Dante had been convinced Amato would support his recommendation to turn *Rorschach* around and return back to Earth. After all, his boss and mentor had been teetering on the edge of aborting the mission ever since the initial damage assessment from the first BLUMO attack.

But Amato now appeared hesitant to accept Dante's recommendation.

"Is it because of Colonel Morgan's comments?" Dante asked.

"Partially. I think his advice to seek other opinions is wise," Amato said.

"That's why you've set up the call with Anlon Cully?"

"Not just Anlon. I've also talked with Helen Brock."

"Oh? I wasn't aware NASA had sent us their analysis yet." Dante had circulated the pack-hunter report to NASA's UMO research team, but he was surprised to hear that Brock had contacted Amato instead of him with NASA's findings.

"They haven't," Amato said. "I called Helen to discuss the *Cetus Prime* image she forwarded to us. Have you seen it?"

"No, I've been focused on Shilling's report." Dante retrieved his cell phone and scrolled through his email to find the message from Brock. "What does it show?"

As Amato described the photo, Dante located the message and opened the file.

"How bizarre," he said. "And you say the UMOs haven't made an appearance since this was taken?"

"That's right," Amato said.

"What do you think it means?"

"I don't know. I thought it might be a reaction to another gamma burst. Anyway, in the course of my conversation with Helen, I asked her about their progress on the report. She said there's dissension among her team about some of Shilling's conclusions."

"They don't think it was a pack hunt?"

"No, on that point, the whole team agrees with Shilling."

"Then what's the debate?"

"The *aim* of the hunt. Some agree with Shilling, that the purpose of the hunt was to eliminate territory invaders. But others think their prey was our UMO colony."

Dante considered this alternative interpretation and quickly deduced what had led the NASA dissenters to form this opinion. Where had the *Rorschach* colony gone after the attack? Why hadn't the UMOs returned? "They think the BLUMOs killed our UMOs?"

"More like *ate* our UMOs," Amato said. "Remember, Shilling points out packs exist due to scarcity of food. Might UMOs themselves be a more attractive food option than ions from our engines?"

If this theory was correct, then *Rorschach* was never the target of the BLUMO attack, which meant another attack was less likely. But Dante saw a flaw in that logic.

"How do they explain the BLUMOs returning a second time?" he asked. "There were no UMOs around by then."

"Therein lies the debate," Amato said.

He explained the dissenters' main counter-arguments. First, if the BLUMOs viewed the fleet as a territorial threat, why did they leave some probes untouched while destroying or disabling others? And second, if the BLUMOs are such sophisticated hunters, why did they give up so easily on *Rorschach*?

Both points were valid, Dante thought. And as he pondered this UMO-eat-UMO theory further, he thought of another counter to Shilling's conclusions. The scientist had pointed to the scouting party attack on the fleet of CubeSats last year as an example of UMOs protecting territory. In that incident, the UMOs zapped some of the probes and then flew away. Shilling believed the zap-and-go encounter showed that the UMOs viewed the small contingent of probes as an insignificant threat. But if, instead, the attack had been precipitated by a search for food, the UMOs' decision to bypass the fleet after zapping a few probes might have meant they didn't find the probes appetizing.

"In any event," Amato said, "I think there's merit on both sides of the argument. Enough to pause any discussion of scrubbing until Shilling and Morgan have a chance to chew on NASA's report."

"Okay, that's fair. When does Helen expect to send over their report?"

"She didn't commit to a time, but she understands the urgency."

"I'll call her when we're done to pin down a time."

"Good," Amato said. "Meanwhile, I thought it would be of value to run Shilling's report and data by Anlon Cully."

"Makes sense. What time is the call?"

"In fifteen minutes. Will you join me?"

"Absolutely. I'd like to hear what Dr. Cully has to say. And I'm sorry to make you bump your meeting with Jenna Toffy."

"This was more important. I'll fit her in later tonight. Mark is already working to set up a new time."

"By the way, how did your conversation with the families go?"

"They were hard to read, to be honest," Amato said. "I think they were appreciative of the update, but they're apprehensive. They were quiet. They didn't ask many questions."

"Do you think they'll talk to the media?"

Amato shrugged. "I hope not, but they're the least of our problems. They don't have access to the kind of information that's been leaking out. Speaking of which, have you made any progress isolating the source of the leaks?"

"Unfortunately not. Our IT security guys are working it hard, but it's likely there are multiple leakers given the information has been popping up in multiple places. The IT guys don't think the leaks are coming from anyone at Mayaguana. Could be someone at HQ in Orlando, people from NASA or one of our other subcontractors, or all of the above."

"They shouldn't discount the possibility the leaks are coming from Mayaguana. Make sure they don't."

"Roger that." Dante shifted the conversation back to the UMO exodus photo. "I'm curious. What did Dr. Brock think of your suggestion of another gamma burst?"

"She agreed it was a possibility, but questioned why the UMOs didn't react the same way during the first burst. I suggested a potential reason for the discrepancy. She was skeptical."

Amato described his theory. The initial gamma event occurred as Callisto's orbit approached the dark side of Jupiter. But six days later — the day the exodus photo was taken — Callisto was at the midway point of its crossing of the planet's dark side. Thus the Nuada crater, and the hive of UMOs in the spaceport, had been shielded from the burst on the first occasion, but not during the second burst.

"But if Nuada was exposed to the second burst, the gamma rays would have affected *Cetus Prime*," Dante said.

"Yes, Helen pointed that out. She also questioned why the UMOs would leave the spaceport. Presumably it has adequate radiation shielding. Why not stay inside until the gamma rays dissipated?"

"Hard to argue with that logic."

"True," Amato said. "But something disruptive occurred, wouldn't you agree? The UMOs stopped in the middle of their de-icing and left. They haven't returned. Therefore, it seems reasonable to believe something caused them to flee. If it wasn't another gamma burst, then what triggered them to bug out?"

ABOARD *SOL SEAKER*
PORT DENARAU, FIJI
SEPTEMBER 3, 2019 (SEPTEMBER 4 ON FIJI)

From the upper deck of his yacht, *Sol Seaker*, Dr. Anlon Cully looked toward the marina inlet, hoping to catch a glimpse of two Jet Skis. His companion, Pebbles McCarver, and their mutual friend, Jennifer Stevens, had taken the Jet Skis out into Nadi Bay earlier in the morning. Anlon had texted Pebbles as soon as he received Amato's text requesting a phone conference, guessing both she and Jennifer would want in on the phone call.

He pulled his cell phone from his boardshorts pocket and texted Pebbles again. *Tick tock. Call starts in 10 min.*

He knew the chance of Pebbles hearing the text chime above the roar of the watercraft's engine was nil, but she was wearing her smartwatch, and hopefully she would see the message alert notification and hustle back.

After another minute of fruitless surveillance, Anlon retreated inside, descended to the main deck, and settled in at his desk in his office cabin. He put his phone on the desk pad in front of him and reopened Amato's text message.

Urgent. New developments. Need your input ASAP! When can you talk?

Anlon, Pebbles and Jennifer, like the rest of the world, were devoted viewers of *Expedition to Callisto* and had been watching the last episode when Dante abruptly departed in the middle of the show. They were well aware of the subsequent media firestorm, including Nigel Ewing's interview with Antonio. Even on Fiji, the mystery surrounding what had happened to the *Rorschach Explorer* was atop the news.

Anlon's phone buzzed. Amato. He tapped the answer icon and activated the speaker. "Anlon Cully," he said.

"Anlon! It's good to hear your voice!"

"Good to hear from you as well, Augie. It's been a while."

"Yes, I know. Too long. Where are you today?"

"We're in Fiji for a couple of weeks, then on to Auckland."

"Sounds delightful," Amato said. "My apologies for intruding on your voyage."

"It's not an intrusion at all. I would ask how *Rorschach*'s trip to Callisto is going, but I know you're dealing with some issues at the moment."

Amato's tone turned serious. "Yes, we've run into unexpected trouble."

The office door opened and Pebbles ducked her head through the gap. With a contrite expression, she whispered, "Sorry."

Anlon motioned for her to enter. "I'm sorry to hear that, Augie. How can I help?"

Pebbles tiptoed in with Jennifer on her heels, and they sat down in the guest chairs. Pebbles wore a magenta short-cut wetsuit that matched the color of her hair, with a towel wrapped around her waist, and Jennifer wore a wetsuit patterned after the *Rorschach Explorer* crew's flight suits.

"Before I get into all of it, I wanted to let you know I have Dr. Dante Fulton on the line," Amato said.

"And a heads-up in return, Augie — I have you on speaker. Pebbles is here with me, along with a friend of ours, Jennifer Stevens. She's a former police detective."

After quick pleasantries were traded, Amato said, "So, Anlon, I guess you have a sense of why I wanted to speak."

"UMOs?" Anlon asked.

"Yes, UMOs ... with a twist."

He explained the attack by the BLUMO colony, including their apparent pack-hunting behavior. Dante then provided a clipped description of the damage done in the attack and the current status of the fleet. Amato finished up by sharing the highlights of Shilling's report and the dissenting views within NASA's UMO research group. Anlon, Pebbles and Jennifer listened closely, occasionally exchanging looks of surprise and concern.

"Sounds scary," Pebbles said. "How is the crew?"

"They're working hard, doing their best in a tough situation," Dante said.

"Yes, they're a resilient bunch," said Amato. "However, there's only so much they can control. Regrettably, as much as it sickens me to say the words, we may need to scrub the mission."

"Because of the BLUMOs or because of what happened to *Juno*?" Jennifer asked.

"Ah," said Amato, sounding surprised. "I see you've kept in touch with the news during your voyage."

"Oh, believe me," Pebbles said, "Jen knows more about your mission than some of your Mission Control people. She's obsessed with it."

Jennifer smacked Pebbles' thigh and whispered, "Bitch!"

"Is that so?" Amato said. "Well, both are problems, but the more immediate of the two is the BLUMO colony. Dr. Shilling believes another attack is imminent."

Anlon noted Amato's choice of phrasing. *Dr. Shilling* believes another attack is imminent. "I take it you don't agree with Dr. Shilling."

There was a pause on the line before Dante answered. "There is a concern Dr. Shilling may be a little too close to the situation."

"And as I mentioned, we have received a difference of opinion from voices within NASA," Amato said.

Great, Anlon thought, they want *me* to be the tiebreaker. "To be candid, Augie, I don't have much experience studying pack-hunters. I can speak to their general behavioral characteristics, but I'm not an expert."

"I suspected as much, but I trust your observation skills. If you're amenable, I'd like to send you Dr. Shilling's report along with the video and audio of the BLUMO pack behaviors the crew observed, and the summary reports of the attack from an internal working group we set up. I'd like your impressions and observations. Specifically, I'd like to know whether you agree with Shilling. Was it a pack hunt? If so, should we be concerned about another attack?"

"I'm happy to take a look," Anlon said. "Out of curiosity, do the videos show the pack alpha?"

"If they do, I'm unaware of it. Dante?"

"There is a distinctive chirp that can be heard on the audio," Dante said. "I wouldn't have called it an alpha. We've been thinking in terms of queens."

"I can understand why," said Anlon. "From the description you gave of the attack, it sounds like it was a mix of conflicting behaviors. Part swarm, part pack."

"How so?" Pebbles asked.

"Swarms are generally reactionary," Anlon explained. "A threat's detected, and the swarm forms to protect the most important members of the colony. Using honeybees as a proxy for UMOs, the swarm's main purpose is to protect the queen. The swarm will attack if necessary — particularly when defending their turf — but that's typically their last line of defense. Setting aside the stalking behavior the crew observed, the description of the actual attack sounds like the BLUMOs were defending their turf.

"On the other hand, it also sounds as if they exhibited classic predatory behaviors. Track prey, stalk to detect weaklings, separate the weak from the strong during the attack and lead the weak into a kill zone. Highly coordinated behavior. Very different than swarms. Only problem is, packs typically form to hunt for food, and the crew said they ignored the ions from the fleet's engines."

"So the highly coordinated aspect makes you think there's an alpha," Pebbles said.

"Yes. In a swarm, each member of the swarm acts in response to the member closest to it, rather than by the actions or commands of a central leader. In a pack, a central leader, the alpha predator, coordinates the attack."

"The queen bee doesn't lead a swarm attack?" Jennifer asked.

"Nope," Anlon said. "She's basically pushed to the innermost spot in the swarm and told to stay put. For example, let's say the threat is coming from the left of the swarm. The bees on the swarm's outermost layer on the left side are the first to detect the threat. If the threat is avoidable, those outermost bees will turn away from it and the rest of the swarm will follow their lead, including the queen. If the threat *isn't* avoidable, the outermost bees will attack. Others will join the attack, but not all, and a contingent always stays with the queen to keep her out of harm's way. She never enters the fray."

"Can a queen act as an alpha?" Dante asked.

"In UMOs? Wouldn't dare to venture a guess," Anlon said. "But that would be contradictory behavior among most animals on Earth. That's not to say female animals can't be alphas. Take gray wolves, for instance. Their packs usually have co-leaders, an alpha male and an alpha female, and it's not uncommon for the alpha female to lead a hunt. Even in lions, where pride alphas are always male, the hunting is done by females and the hunting pack is led by a female. But the composition of a honeybee colony is very different than a predator pack."

"One queen," Pebbles said. "One breeder."

"That's right, that's the key difference," Anlon said. "Packs typically have multiple female members. If a female alpha is killed during a hunt, another of the females in the pack takes her place and the pack survives. In a honeybee colony, there is only one queen. If she's killed during a swarm, it's a serious blow to the colony."

"So you're saying the BLUMO colony may have a queen *and* an alpha?" Amato asked. "And they're two different individuals?"

"At this point, I'm just pointing out the oddities in the behaviors you've described," Anlon said. "How they're inconsistent with typical swarms and packs. I can't make any definitive judgments until I go through the data."

"Very well," said Amato. "We'll send you everything we have. How soon do you think you can get back to us? I know it's an imposition, but we're rather pressed for time."

Anlon looked to Pebbles and Jennifer as he answered Amato. "I'll get on it as soon as I receive the data. You tell me the deadline and I'll make it happen."

"What do you think, Dante?" Amato asked. "Two hours?"

"That sounds about right. We should have NASA's report by then," Dante said.

"Understood," said Anlon. "I'll get back to you faster if possible. If Shilling's right and an attack is imminent, it's a problem on two fronts."

"Oh?" Amato said.

Anlon frowned down at the phone. "If they're like pack hunters on Earth, they'll change their tactics for the next attack. They'll probably be harder to detect, and they'll wait for better conditions ... conditions that provide a higher chance of success."

There was silence over the phone for several seconds. When Amato spoke, his voice was thin. "That's sobering to hear, Anlon."

After another stretch of silence, Dante said, "Dr. Cully, you said there were two aspects that concerned you. What's the other?"

"Well, the behaviors you described suggest they're seasoned hunters," Anlon said. "If the data bears that out, you have another issue on your hands."

"There's some other kind of prey out there," Pebbles interjected, her eyes glued on Anlon. "That's what you're saying, right?"

He nodded. "They have to be eating something to survive. If they're just consuming ambient ions, there would be no need to pack-hunt, and they wouldn't have developed the behavior."

"Dr. Shilling suggested the BLUMOs' hunting skill indicates the presence of other packs," Dante said. "He says competition for food honed their skills."

"I'm sure that's a contributing factor, but … "

"But what?" Amato asked.

"I'm not sure you'll like the answer."

"I already don't like the answer and I haven't heard it yet!"

"Wolves don't form packs to hunt squirrels, Augie. Whatever these UMOs normally hunt isn't small."

After the call, Anlon tilted his seat back and ran his hands through his sandy-gray hair. "Who would have guessed such diversity lives in our solar system?"

"It's crazy," Pebbles said. "What kind of prey do you think the BLU-MOs hunt?"

"No clue. It's gotta be something electromagnetic, right? They feed on ions."

"And radio waves," said Jennifer. "Don't forget radio waves."

Anlon chuckled. "You do know your *Expedition to Callisto* episodes, don't you."

"It's a cop thing. I remember small details," she said with a smile.

Pebbles walked to the window overlooking the marina and gazed out at the tropical haven. "Oh well, Fiji will still be here tomorrow."

"Excuse me?" Anlon said.

Pebbles turned to him. "There's no chance we're playing surf and tan while you dig through the data. Right, Jen?"

Jennifer tugged off the band holding her blond ponytail. "Looks like you have some research partners, Anlon, whether you want them or not."

AUGUSTUS AMATO'S OFFICE
A3ROSPACE INDUSTRIES COMMAND AND CONTROL CENTER
MAYAGUANA ISLAND, THE BAHAMAS

Dante found it hard to concentrate. He'd gone into Amato's office determined to abort the mission in order to protect the crew, but then the conversation about NASA's dissenters had lessened his concerns about an imminent attack. Now Anlon's final comments had alarmed him enough to push him back toward aborting again.

He knew the *Rorschach* crew was already on alert for signs of a BLUMO return; they were watching and listening for the same cues that preceded the earlier attack. But now it seemed that might not be enough. They would need to broaden their detection and scrutinize any unusual phenomena, no matter how small.

And then there was Anlon's speculation about yet another electromagnetic life-form residing in the asteroid belt. Would that life-form be predatory, too? And how would the crew detect it? Using their full array of sensors to scan for other electromagnetic anomalies might attract the new life-form or, worse, attract the BLUMOs again.

Amato must have been grappling with similar concerns, for he, too, seemed lost in thought. Finally he lifted his head and said, "Is your brain spinning as fast as mine?"

"It is," Dante said. "We need to give Skywalker a heads-up about Anlon's thoughts. ASAP."

"Agreed."

Dante's cell phone buzzed with a text from Pritchard. *Another downlink just arrived from TRE. CCDR EVA to convert Cubes underway.*

In a low and drawn-out voice, Dante said, "Oh, shit."

CHAPTER 8

WOLFPACK

CARGO BAY — THE *RORSCHACH EXPLORER*
DRIFTING AT ALL-STOP ABOVE THE
ECLIPTIC IN THE ASTEROID BELT
SEPTEMBER 3, 2019

In the cargo bay on the underbelly of the ship, Major Carillo watched the doors crank open. Encased in her spacesuit and tethered to one of the walls, she was upside-down relative to the ship's orientation.

From inside the main cabin, the others monitored the space-scape around *Rorschach* for signs of BLUMOs or any other unusual activity. Morgan kept watch from the flight deck, Shilling and Ajay manned consoles in the lab compartment, and Kiera was stationed in the engine control room.

"*Recon-3* should be coming into view any moment, Julia," Kiera said through her headset.

Carillo scanned the darkness outside the bay and spotted the instrument-laden probe. "Roger that. I see it."

"Copy," Kiera said. "Transferring probe guidance control to you in five, four, three … "

Carillo swiveled the docking control system's video monitor into place. When Kiera finished her countdown, a light on the thruster control panel turned from red to green, and a split screen showed Carillo the views from the perspective of the approaching probe and from the platform. Crosshair templates overlaid both feeds.

Using the docking system thruster controls, Carillo slowed and maneuvered *Recon-3* until it hovered a few feet above the docking platform, a process that took nearly twenty minutes. When it was finally in position, she looked up to inspect the probe.

"Jesus. You guys seeing the damage on this sucker?"

The probe's X-band dish had melted into a bizarre sculpture. Several holes had pierced through *Recon-3*'s body. A number of instrument receptacles protruding from the grid atop the probe were twisted or blown apart. One of the solar panels was missing, as was the boom holding the CubeSat's gamma-ray spectrometer's sensor.

"Whoa. How in God's name did you get that junker back here, Kiera?" Morgan asked.

"Mad skills," said Ajay.

"Roger that," Kiera agreed.

Carillo interrupted the chatter. "Activating dock in five, four ... " At zero, she pressed a button on the docking control panel. The probe wobbled as the magnetized platform pulled on magnets embedded in the probe's underside. It floated down and landed. "*Recon-3* docked."

Cheers sounded through her headset.

"Proceeding to fasten safety clamps," Carillo said.

"Copy," Morgan replied.

Carillo propelled herself from the docking control station to the platform, a distance of ten feet, and hooked a second tether from her suit's utility belt onto a railing on the side of the platform's bed. Over the next thirty minutes, she anchored clamps connecting the large eyelets on the four sides of the probe to corresponding eyelets on the platform.

The process was tedious, for every step happened in the slow-motion vacuum of space. One at a time, Carillo had to remove each clamp from a storage locker beside the platform, attach it to the platform, and secure it to the probe. Then it was back to the box for another clamp, and so on. And even when this part of the process was complete, she had to move around the platform to tighten each clamp with a winch kept in the storage locker.

When at last she'd finished tightening the last clamp, she said, "*Recon-3* secured."

"Roger that," said Kiera. "Deactivating platform magnets. Powering off *Recon-3*."

"Copy."

"Platform and probe off."

"Good job, Julia. Good job, Kiera," Morgan said. "One down, one to go."

"Roger that," Carillo replied. "How am I doing on O2?"

On the flight deck, Morgan examined readings from Carillo's life support system. "Looking good. Tanks are at sixty-eight percent remaining."

Inside the lab compartment, Ajay fought to keep his eyes open as a light static through his headphones teased him to fall asleep. Shilling wasn't faring any better; his eyes had tired from darting back and forth between instrument monitors and video screens. And Kiera had turned her attention to the probe flight control system in order to position *Recon-5* for handoff to Carillo.

Thus no one detected the BLUMO scouting party.

No one, that is, but Carillo.

As she opened the storage locker to stow the winch, she felt a rattle from the connected docking platform. "What the—"

Morgan's eyes darted to the cargo bay camera feed. "What's the matter, Julia?"

"Just had a strange thing happen," she said. "I was replacing the winch and the whole platform shook."

"How can that be?" Kiera asked. "The dock is off."

"Ajay, Bob, report," Morgan said. "You picking up anything unusual?"

Before they could respond, Carillo felt another vibration, this one from the life support control module attached to the chest of her spacesuit. "Shit. That's not good." She turned away from the platform. "Paul, something's not right. I'm calling it. I'm aborting."

"Roger that," Morgan said. "I'll meet you at the—"

An anguished cry ripped through his headset. On his monitor, he saw tendrils of electricity jolting Carillo from all sides, contorting her body.

"Damn it!" he shouted. He hit the button to close the cargo bay doors. "Kiera, get up here and take the helm! Bob, Ajay, meet me at the cargo bay airlock!"

He unstrapped from the commander's seat and propelled himself from the flight deck into the main corridor. Eschewing the GEFF forcefield, he used handholds to shoot his body aft. As he passed the ready room, another scream from Carillo echoed through his headset.

"Stop!" she cried. "Leave me alone!"

"Come on, Doctor! We have to go," Ajay implored Shilling.

The scientist paid no attention. He was mesmerized by the assault on Carillo, which he was watching on a lab video monitor.

Ajay tugged on Shilling's shoulder. "Now, Doctor! To the airlock!"

Shilling didn't take his eyes from the screen, and his voice was just above a whisper. "I don't see them. Where are they?"

Giving up on Shilling, Ajay ran down the corridor in clunky strides. He reached the airlock just behind the weightless Morgan. Another scream echoed in Ajay's headset, and this one ended in a series of guttural croaks.

Kiera emerged from the engine control room. "She's not moving. What do we do?"

Morgan cranked the airlock door handle. "Ajay, as soon as I'm inside, close and lock the door immediately. Kiera, get up front and make sure the cargo doors finish closing. Make sure they seal and then start repressurizing the bay."

"Roger that," she said. "What are you going to do?"

"I'm going to get her inside the airlock as quick as I can." At that moment Shilling finally stepped into the corridor. Morgan shouted, "Bob! Get the med kit and get your ass down here!"

"But Colonel," Kiera said, "it'll take an hour to repressurize the bay."

"I know, but we don't have that kind of time," he said.

Morgan didn't even wait for the airlock door to fully open. As soon as he was able to squeeze through, he pressed his body through the gap and told Ajay to crank the door shut behind him. He raced to get into his spacesuit in the zero-gravity chamber. That was a daunting task even with help from one or two others, and harder still on one's own — worse still when under duress. It took a full fifteen minutes, and Morgan spent the entire time cursing himself for the decision to send Carillo out alone. But finally, suited up, he took in several deep breaths of pure oxygen dispensed through a mask connected to the airlock's life support system, locked his helmet into place, activated his suit's life support module, and started to crank open the outer airlock door.

This abbreviated attempt to adapt to the change between the pressurized main cabin and the now closed, but still depressurized, cargo bay was far short of the two-hour depressurization required for a normal spacewalk. When the cargo bay airlock door opened, the sudden drop in pressure would begin to create bubbles of gas inside Morgan's body — and those bubbles could kill him if he didn't return to the airlock quickly.

The situation was eerily reminiscent of his famed "Skywalker" spacewalk thirty years before — which also involved rescuing Julia Carillo from a cargo bay mishap. Only this time, he wouldn't be jetting off-structure to retrieve an unconscious Carillo as she drifted off into space. This time, he'd only have to push forward fifteen to twenty feet into the cargo bay, unhook her tether and pull her back into the airlock via his own tether.

He'd just have to do it fast and hope for the best.

Ajay and Shilling had returned to the lab to watch Morgan's rescue attempt and monitor for signs of more BLUMOs, and now Ajay was picking up a new hissing sound through his headphones. The sound was followed by a faint, quivering chirp.

"Yikes!" he said.

"What's that?" Shilling asked.

"Shhh." Ajay pressed the headphones tight against his head. A conversation had commenced between the snake-like hisser and the quiverer.

Ajay maneuvered the microphone bar of the headphones to his lips. "Colonel Morgan, I can hear them. They're talking."

From the copilot seat on the flight deck, Kiera cycled through camera feeds from the three operational Shield probes surrounding *Ror-*

schach. No BLUMOs were evident. She spoke into her headset. "I don't see 'em."

"They sound far away ... not like last time," Ajay said.

A chime signaled the arrival of a new transmission from Mission Control. On the comms station monitor, Kiera saw the message appear. *MAYA-FLIGHT to CDR-TRE: Abort EVA! Repeat, abort EVA ASAP! Await further instructions. MAYA-FLIGHT out.*

In the ice-cold cargo bay, Morgan grabbed hold of the bobbing Carillo. He didn't bother to examine her, he just unclipped her tether and attached her to one on his EMU utility belt. Pushing off the platform, he pulled on his tether, hand over hand, all the way back to the airlock. The process took an excruciating ten minutes.

As soon as they were inside, he cranked the cargo bay airlock door closed, turned the pressure equalization valve to the emergency setting, and opened the valve. Three minutes later, the airlock pressure had stabilized, and Morgan was able to turn off the life support functions on his suit, remove his helmet and gloves, and reactivate an airlock oxygen mask.

Before donning the mask, he pressed the intercom button. "Open the cabin airlock. Bring the med kit."

Fighting through dizziness, he tethered the unconscious Carillo to the airlock wall and examined her suit. At once, he saw that her life support module was inactive. "Damn it!"

He removed her helmet, applied another oxygen mask over her nose and mouth, and felt for a pulse on her neck. He detected her heartbeat and shallow breathing. Through cloudy vision, he surveyed the rest of her suit. It was covered with burn marks but he saw no punctures. "Jesus, Julia, I'm so sorry."

As his senses began to fade, he heard a cranking sound from the cabin airlock door. He lolled forward and collapsed next to Carillo, completely unaware of the blue light hovering above him. It pulsed for a few seconds and then vanished.

ABOARD *SOL SEAKER*
PORT DENARAU, FIJI

Through noise-canceling headphones, Anlon Cully listened to the sounds of the BLUMOs surveilling Amato's fleet. There were five recordings in all, and Anlon had listened to each of them several times. At present, he was replaying the third of the five clips, the one he found most interesting.

In the first two clips, the new quiver-tones seemed disconnected from the chirp-tones. There was never an exchange between quivers and chirps, just numerous back-and-forth exchanges between chirpers and a few exchanges between quiverers. In a couple of spots, the chirps and quivers overlapped each other, but the sounds struck Anlon as two groups of UMOs minding their own business. All of this suggested that the UMOs traveling with *Rorschach* had been unaware of the BLUMOs' surveillance early on.

That impression changed in the third clip. In the midst of a chirp conversation, a quiver intruded, causing the chirpers to halt their chatter. After a short bout of silence, a sharp chirp sounded out, and an equally sharp quiver answered. This loud, curt exchange bounced back and forth for a few rounds before another bout of silence. Then two more quiver-tones followed —one soft, the other loud. After that, the pattern of chirps Anlon had observed in the first two recordings resumed. There were a few more low-volume quivers, but they once again seemed disconnected from the chirps.

In his reviews of clips four and five, Anlon hadn't detected any more chirp-quiver conversations, but the frequency of the independent quivers and chirps increased. Anlon felt this signaled a building tension on the parts of both colonies, as if they both knew a conflict was brewing. That was what made clip three so interesting. It signaled a different kind of pack behavior.

Jennifer was seated to his right, watching the videos of the BLUMO attack on her laptop. Next to her was a printout of the attack chronology, prepared by Amato's BLUMO working group, and occasionally she would stop a clip to refer to the chronology, then back up and watch a scene again. When something piqued her interest, she would scribble her observations on a notepad.

Pebbles sat across the desk from the other two, arms folded, head back, staring at the beams lining the cabin ceiling. In front of her sat her copy of the chronology printout, full of highlighted passages and notes in the margins. She'd already had enough of the videos and audio clips and was now just waiting for Anlon and Jennifer to finish so they could discuss their independent observations.

"Come on, people, let's wrap it up," she said.

Jennifer looked up from the laptop. "Almost done, hold your horses."

Anlon removed the headphones and laid them on the desk. "What time is it?" he asked, looking out the window.

Jennifer glanced at her laptop. "Uh … one-forty."

"Wrong," said Pebbles. "It's time to quit looking at the damn videos!"

"Okay, okay. Relax." Jennifer halted the video and pushed her chair back from the desk.

Anlon smiled at Pebbles. "I take it you found something interesting and can't wait to share it."

"It wasn't a pack hunt," Pebbles blurted. "Well, not like you described earlier."

"Diving right in, are we?" Anlon said.

Pebbles pushed up the sleeves of the sweatshirt she'd layered over her wetsuit. "Well, you did say you wanted to get back to Augie as fast as possible, didn't you?"

"I did." Anlon turned to Jennifer. "Any opening thoughts on your end?"

"I have to agree with Pebbles," Jennifer said. "They didn't surround the fleet. They only did recon from the port side. They went after *Rorschach*, not just the probes. I saw it as more of a swarm than a pack hunt."

"That's right," Pebbles said to Anlon. "You said packs lead prey into a kill zone. That didn't happen here. You said packs go after the weak. The BLUMOs went after both weak and strong."

Anlon had been jotting down their observations as they spoke, but now he looked up. "I see what you both mean," he said, "but I don't agree.

I think it *was* a pack hunt, with part of it disguised as a swarm. A clever strategy designed by one very crafty alpha."

Pebbles frowned. "Really? For what purpose?"

"To trick the UMOs. To draw them into a fight, separate them from *Rorschach*."

"Right," Jennifer said. "They viewed *Rorschach* as a threat and attacked to eliminate it."

"Wait," said Pebbles. "Are you saying you agree with Shilling? The attack wasn't about food? What about *Rorschach*'s UMOs? Why did the BLUMOs chase them if it wasn't to feed?"

"Because the Cargos broke from the fleet," Jennifer said.

"Why would they care about that?"

"They didn't want the Cargos to escape."

"Come again?" The frown on Pebbles' face twisted into a glare.

"Think of *Rorschach* as the queen of a colony inside a swarm of escorts — the UMOs and the fleet probes," Jennifer said. "The BLUMOs detected the swarm coming into their territory. They didn't want the competition for food, so they attacked to wipe out what they saw as invaders. First order of business, get rid of the escorts to expose the queen. Make sure none of them survive. Then take out the queen."

Pebbles turned to Anlon. "Do you buy that?"

Part of Jennifer's theory aligned with Anlon's thinking. He agreed that the BLUMOs' attack was an attempt to isolate *Rorschach* from the rest of the fleet. But his view diverged with Jennifer's as to the purpose of this action. "I think the analogy fits up until the taking out the queen part," he said. "But I don't think they intended to destroy *Rorschach* once they got it alone."

"But they *did* come back and try to destroy the ship," Jennifer said. "The report says the X-band signal from Antonio's landers lured them back from chasing the Cargos and they attacked the ship."

"I don't think that's what happened," Anlon said.

Pebbles cast him a dubious look. "Are you saying the report's wrong?"

"I am. First off, I don't think the second encounter with the ship was an attack. Read the report again. They didn't zap the ship with lightning in the second encounter. They didn't bump it or otherwise impede it."

"Right, because Colonel Morgan scared them away," Pebbles said.

"No, because Colonel Morgan *confused* them," Anlon countered. "And I don't think the two groups of BLUMOs that led the first attack were the same ones that approached *Rorschach* once it was alone. I think the alpha split the pack into three groups. One to take care of the Recons, the second to deal with the UMOs and the rest of the fleet, and the third lying in wait to capture *Rorschach*."

"Capture? For what purpose?" Jennifer asked.

"It's gotta be food," Pebbles said. "*Rorschach's* VLF engines are huge compared to the probes. All those tasty ions were too hard to pass up."

"I agree that seems like the most logical answer, but there's a puzzle piece that doesn't fit," Anlon said. "According to the report, during the twenty hours the BLUMO scouting party followed the fleet, *Rorschach's* engines were idle. The first use of VLF engines the BLUMOs observed would have been the Recons after they separated from the fleet."

"Maybe they tracked the fleet longer than the crew thinks," Pebbles said.

"Maybe."

"Then you agree with me," said Jennifer. "They attacked to defend their territory."

Anlon shook his head. "I'm having trouble with that explanation too. Packs are typically ruthless when they confront territorial invaders. I can't imagine why they wouldn't have finished *Rorschach* off as fast as possible. The third group wouldn't have waited so long to go after the ship once it was isolated."

"Take a step back," Jennifer said. "How do you know the pack split into three different groups?"

"Timing." Anlon described his theory. The pack was tracking the fleet, waiting for an opportunity to pounce. That opportunity presented itself when the Recons were sent ahead, breaking the fleet into two separate chunks. "The attack happened not long after that. I think it was the opening the alpha was waiting for."

Pebbles nodded. "I see what you mean. If *Rorschach* was the target, the main pack wouldn't have left the ship just to chase after the Recons."

"That's right," Anlon said. "Also, remember the report's remarks about how ridiculously fast the BLUMOs closed in on the fleet after attacking the Recons. Doesn't it make more sense that a second group was deployed to take on the UMOs and the other fleet probes? I think the alpha sized up the opposition during the BLUMOs' surveillance and realized the full pack wasn't needed to deal with the UMOs and the probes. And, wow, was the alpha right. The UMOs were *way* overmatched. You can tell that from the audio clips alone.

"In the early recordings, the UMOs didn't even react when the quiver-tones from the BLUMOs showed up. Somehow, the UMOs didn't view the BLUMOs as threats. Normally, if forager bees from a foreign colony show up at your hive, you're going to act quickly to drive them off. You don't want them getting too close to your honeycomb. You don't want them spotting weaknesses in the hive that can be torn open, making it easier for other foreign bees to get at the honey inside. The UMOs were way too docile."

Jennifer tapped a pen on the edge of the desk. "Yeah, it does seem strange the UMOs let them get so close for so long. The UMOs should have sensed their electrical energy, right?"

"You would think so. In fact, I'm sure they sensed them. They just didn't seem to care until it was way too late."

"Why?" Jennifer asked.

"If I had to guess, I'd say it's because they had become domesticated. They were trained by Dr. Shilling to react to certain stimuli, and in the process they lost some of their instinctual behaviors. Matter of fact, I think *Rorschach*'s UMOs dumbed down so much, they didn't even notice the BLUMOs' first attempt to lure them into a fight."

Pebbles, who had been thumbing through the report again, looked up. "What first attempt?"

"On clip three," Anlon said. "The sharp interaction between the quivers and the chirps. I think the alpha tried to bait the UMOs by making itself known as a threat, expecting the UMOs to respond. The alpha probably had the BLUMO pack lying in wait, hoping to draw the UMOs away into a kill zone. But the UMOs didn't do anything but chirp back a few times. It's almost as if the UMOs closest to the BLUMOs didn't recognize the quiverer as a threat."

Jennifer frowned. "A lot of your theory makes sense. But if it's correct, why did the third group take so long to attempt to capture *Rorschach*?"

"This is pure speculation on my part," he said, "but I think the sudden departure of the Cargos surprised the third group, the alpha's group. Especially after *Rorschach's* UMOs chased after the probes. I think the alpha was surprised again by Morgan's ruse, but I'll tell you one thing: they won't be surprised like that again."

"So you do think the BLUMOs will come after *Rorschach* again," Pebbles said.

"Without a doubt," Anlon said. "And Lord help the crew when they do. This time, the whole pack will be together."

AUGUSTUS AMATO'S OFFICE
A3ROSPACE INDUSTRIES COMMAND AND CONTROL CENTER
MAYAGUANA ISLAND, THE BAHAMAS

Amato read the grim summary from Kiera:

FE-TRE to MAYA-Flight: CCDR attacked by UMOs and severely injured during EVA to repair Cubes. Multiple burns on torso, arms and upper legs. Additional symptoms consistent with decompression sickness due to life support system shutdown during EVA. Will forward CCDR bio data ASAP. CDR also injured during emergency EVA to rescue CCDR. Also exhibiting symptoms consistent with decompression sickness. Extent unknown. We've done our best to treat them but need further medical guidance ASAP. FE-TRE out.

A hot poker to the gut would have felt better than the sensation searing inside Amato's abdomen. He looked up at Dante.

The mission director turned his eyes away. "I'm sorry, Mr. Amato. It's my fault. We sent them the EVA abort message, but it didn't arrive in time. We had an uplink in progress. Even though we killed it to send the abort, enough had been transmitted to delay *Rorschach's* receipt of the abort."

The principal sacrifice in switching to UHF-band from X-band is a drop in data throughput. While radio signals of all frequencies travel through space at the same speed, the speed of light, the amount of data that can be transmitted is dependent on the frequency of waves in the transmission. At lower frequencies, less data can be transmitted. At higher frequencies, the opposite is true. For example, an SHF transmission over an X-band antenna can deliver ten times more data at one time than a UHF transmission. This means downlinks and uplinks of data via lower frequency bands can take much longer.

"It's not your fault, Dante," Amato said. "It's just bad luck."

"All the same, I feel responsible." Dante sighed, his head lowered. When he looked back up, he said, "The flight surgeon sent a list of triage questions and initial treatment suggestions to Kiera. Once we get her answers back, the doctor will provide more specific treatment options. In the meantime, I've got the team next door prepping for mission abort."

Another stab to the gut. "You're right, of course. I should have listened to you earlier."

"I could have fought harder if I felt that strongly about it. Like you said, just bad luck on our part," Dante said.

"Mark the time and send the command."

"Roger that."

As Dante stood to leave, Myers entered. "Mr. Amato, I have Dr. Cully on the line. He says he needs to speak with you urgently."

Dante looked to Amato. "You want me to stay?"

"No, go ahead and transmit the abort. If he has something important to share, I'll have Mark patch you in."

CHAPTER 9

SENTINEL

D ante stared at the blinking cursor on his computer screen as midnight came and went.

"How did everything fall apart so fast?" he muttered. Short of *Rorschach*'s engines exploding, killing everyone aboard, Dante couldn't imagine a bleaker scenario.

The fleet of support probes was scattered and disabled. *Rorschach*'s only experienced astronauts were injured, possibly incapacitated. The hobbled ship and crew were more than 200 million kilometers from Earth, being hunted by lethal aliens, with no weaponry to defend themselves, no means of escape and no ability to communicate with their attackers.

Back on Earth, despite their collective brainpower, Mission Control was powerless to do more than transmit suggestions over radio waves that took thirty minutes to reach *Rorschach*.

The adage "a day late and a dollar short" kept rattling around in Dante's head. Aborting the mission was easier said than done. And turning for home provided no guarantee the BLUMOs would call off their hunt.

Anger swelled within him. *How can we get out in front of what's happening? There has to be something we can do to buy the crew time to regroup ... some way to confuse or distract the BLUMOs.*

A knock sounded on his office door. Dennis Pritchard stood in the doorway. "Hey. *Rorschach*'s latest downlink is coming through. A couple of the files have already finished. You need to see them ... right now."

Dante sighed and looked up at the ceiling. "Jesus, what now?"

During the short walk to the Mission Control Center, Pritchard briefed him. "One of the files is a video of the attack on Major Carillo. I won't BS you, it's disturbing to watch. The other is Kiera's triage report on Julia's injuries. It's just as gruesome. But damn it, Dante, together they paint a whole different picture of what's going on up there." The news sounded awful, yet Pritchard actually seemed excited by the new information.

As they approached Pritchard's station, Norris Preston's head appeared above the console. "Just reached Dr. Brock. She received the files."

"Good. What about Augie?" Pritchard asked.

"Mr. Amato's on the phone right now, but Mark said he'd slip him a note."

"But you sent the files, right?"

"Roger that."

Pritchard gripped Dante by the shoulder. "Sorry about the breach in protocol. I know I'm ordering your people around, but this was too important to wait until I tracked you down."

"No worries, Dennis. Just tell me what you discovered."

Pritchard pressed a couple of keys on his console, and a video of the *Rorschach*'s cargo bay began to play. Carillo was floating over the CubeSat docking platform at its center. "Watch carefully," he said. "The lightning's about to start." He pressed another key, switching the video to slow-motion playback.

Dante leaned forward and strained his eyes to spot the BLUMOs. An electrical discharge spiked out of nowhere, hitting Carillo on her helmet. Even in slow motion, it was so abrupt, Dante flinched.

Carillo's body lurched forward. Another jolt sent her backward until her tether tensed. Two more shocks followed. Then another six. Dante cringed at Carillo's twisting and flailing.

Pritchard paused the video. "I muted the sound. If you want to hear it, I'll plug in my headset for you. Just don't want to freak out everybody around us."

"I'll listen to it later," Dante said. "What are you wanting me to see here? The fact that the BLUMOs aren't visible?"

"That's surely significant, but it's not the most important part. Watch again. Focus on the order of discharges and where they strike." He replayed the video.

The first jolt hit Carillo on the helmet. The second one zapped her in the chest. The next several hit her arms, legs and torso. Thank God they didn't hit her oxygen tanks, Dante thought. It was hard not to view the video as a savage attack, but on the second viewing, he began to see nuances that changed his interpretation.

Before he could share his impressions, his cell phone vibrated. As he pulled it from his pocket, Preston reappeared. "Dr. Pritchard, I've got Dr. Brock on the line."

"Can you pipe her to the conference room phone?"

"You got it."

Dante looked at his phone. It was Amato calling. "Hello, Mr. Amato?"

"Are you with Dennis?"

"I am."

"Good. I've got Anlon on the line, and I just finished watching the video Dennis sent. We need to have a group discussion right away."

"Yes, sir." Dante rose to follow Pritchard to the conference room. "Dr. Brock's called in. We're on our way to the conference room. I'll call you back from there and patch in Dr. Cully."

"Finally, a glimmer of hope," Amato said before ending the call.

As Dante raced to catch up with Pritchard, his mind grappled with the implications of the video.

The BLUMOs hadn't attacked Carillo.

They'd scanned her.

OFFICE OF THE CHIEF ADMINISTRATOR
NASA HEADQUARTERS
WASHINGTON, D.C.

Helen Brock muted the call and scribbled a list on the nearest piece of paper on her desk. Handing it to her assistant, Mary Evans, she said, "Have Houston send me these files from the *Cetus Prime* archive. Tell them I also want anything and everything they have on the UMO attack on Nick Reed, including his medical files."

"Yes, Doctor. It may be a little difficult though, given the time."

Brock looked at her watch. It was after one a.m. "So be it. And track down Dr. Mazari. Tell him to stand by for my call."

As Evans rushed out of the office, Brock unmuted the speakerphone, where the conversation had been continuing without her.

"If true, it's remarkable," Amato was saying. "Are you sure, Dennis?"

"I can't be one hundred percent certain until we compare the data with what we downlinked from *Cetus Prime*, but it looks too much alike to be a coincidence," Pritchard said.

Brock agreed. She hadn't been part of the *Cetus Prime* mission team, but she'd spearheaded NASA's internal investigation of the files Amato's team had extracted from the ship's computers the preceding November. Those files had included video footage of the UMOs' attack on flight engineer Nick Reed. He had been in the midst of a spacewalk to investigate a malfunction on the ship's girder-like pallet when a small party of the alien beings surrounded him and zapped him with electrical discharges. Those bolts of electricity had rendered him brain-dead ... or so the Mission Control flight surgeon had declared. To the surprise of his crewmates, Avery Lockett and Christine Baker, Nick awoke from a coma two days later. Their surprise turned to astonishment when they learned the encounter with the UMOs had left him with a crude ability to communicate with the aliens.

"I didn't notice the similarity at full speed," Pritchard continued, "but when I saw Kiera's diagram of the burn locations on Julia's body, it was a déjà vu moment."

Brock cut in. "Dennis, forgive me for interrupting, but didn't Avery's report indicate Nick's burns were aligned with his flight suit's sensors?" Nick had worn a flight suit beneath his EMU, with sensors sewn into the fabric to measure his pulse, respiration, circulation, body temperature, blood-oxygen saturation and other life support metrics.

"Yes, that's right, Helen. I wonder, though, if Avery might have been wrong about that. And we never had the opportunity to examine his injuries directly."

"Anlon? Are you still on the line?" Amato asked.

"Yes, I'm here."

"I sent Dr. Cully the working group report on the first BLUMO attack and Ajay's video-audio clips of the BLUMOs preceding the attack. He's reached an interesting conclusion. In light of Dennis' discovery, I think we should hear Dr. Cully's theory. Anlon, the floor is yours."

Brock only half-listened to Anlon's summary of his findings as she rewatched the video of Carillo's encounter with the BLUMOs. There was something tugging at her mind about the sequence, something beyond its similarity with the assault on Nick Reed.

She stopped the video and clicked on the file containing the drawing of Carillo's injuries. The document featured a pre-printed outline of the front and back of a female human body, on which Kiera had added small circles indicating the locations of Carillo's burns. Brock could see why this had captured Pritchard's attention. The burns clearly weren't random. Center of the torso, right and left sides of the upper chest, the undersides of both forearms and the fronts of both thighs.

If Nick's burns had been in the same locations, Brock could understand why Avery Lockett had linked this symmetrical burn pattern with the electromagnetic sensor locations in Nick's flight suit. But over the twenty-five years since *Cetus Prime* launched, flight suit technology had evolved, and so had the biometric sensors incorporated into the suits. Modern suits had more sensors, and the placements were different than they were in the 1990s. Which led Brock to the same conclusion Pritchard had reached: the burn locations had nothing to do with the suit sensors.

But there was a clear pattern — which indicated a purpose. The question was ... what was that purpose?

Anlon was just finishing his summary. "So you see, I don't think the BLUMO attacks were about territory or food. They were designed to isolate *Rorschach*. And in light of what you've said about the attack on Major Carillo, how it jibes with what happened to Nick Reed, I think I now understand the BLUMOs' purpose. They're trying to determine whether *Rorschach* is friend or foe."

"You mean they want to know if *Rorschach* is another *Cetus Prime*," Dante said.

"Yes, I guess that's a better way of putting it. You can understand the BLUMOs' confusion. *Cetus* didn't travel with a fleet of probes, and the presence of *Rorschach*'s UMO colony would only have added to that confusion."

"Because the UMOs didn't behave as the BLUMOs expected," Amato said.

"Yes, that's what it suggests to me. But I would run it by NASA's UMO research group and have their animal behaviorists review our conclusions. They may disagree."

"We will," Amato said. "But assuming you're right, then the attack on Julia was part of that assessment process. To see if she was another Nick Reed, possibly?"

Amato's question pushed an answer to the front of Brock's mind. She murmured, "No, not Nick Reed … "

"You're thinking what I'm thinking, aren't you, Helen?" Pritchard said.

Brock gazed at the diagram of Carillo's burns again. Center of the chest. And in the video, the BLUMOs had zapped Carillo's helmet, too. The discharge hadn't made it through the helmet, so she hadn't been burned … but her head had definitely been the target of their first shot. The back of her head.

"Dennis," she said, "can you remember — did the UMOs zap Nick's helmet? The back of his helmet?"

For a moment, there was silence over the speakerphone. Then Brock heard a gasp, and a female voice said, "Oh my God, Anlon. They thought she was a Calliston!"

"Bingo!" Pritchard said. "Think of the order of the discharges. Head first, chest second."

Brock recalled the murals of Callistons found inside the Nuada spaceport by the *Cetus Prime* crew. They showed aliens that had humanoid features in some respects, one head, two arms, two legs, but with several differences, none more noticeable than their elongated, crested heads. To the biologists NASA hired to study the Callistons, the cranial feature looked similar to the crest of a dinosaur known as Parasaurolophus*. And while there was no consensus

* For an illustration of the crested head and crest tubes of a Parasaurolophus dinosaur, turn to page 303.

among paleontologists as to the purpose of the Parasaur's crest, a prominent theory suggested it was a resonating chamber for producing and receiving low-frequency sounds. This theory appealed to the space agency's biologists, given the Callistons' apparent ability to communicate with UMOs. The scientists speculated the Callistons' crest tubes transmitted and received low-frequency electromagnetic radiation instead of mechanically produced sounds.

And then there was the rounded feature in the center of the Callistons' chests. Some scientists speculated that was an anatomical feature beneath the Callistons' clothing; Brock thought it looked similar to the display-and-control module attached to the chest of NASA astronauts' spacesuits. Regardless of what it was, Brock couldn't now ignore that the BLUMOs had fired their second shot at Carillo's chest, right at the spot where the Callistons had a bulge — as did the astronaut.

"I've got to admit, I think I agree," Dante said. "The video sure gives the impression the BLUMOs scanned Major Carillo. I mean, if they really meant to attack her, they could have killed her easily given the kind of damage they've inflicted on our probes."

"True," Amato said, "but why such an extensive scan?"

"If I may offer a suggestion," said Anlon, "it is not uncommon for animals to use multiple methods to distinguish friend from foe. Scents, calls, gestures. When the BLUMOs didn't get the response they expected from the first couple of jolts, they may have determined Major Carillo was not a Calliston, and then they used the follow-on discharges to figure out what *else* she might be."

"Yes, I see what you mean," Brock said. "Like another Nick Reed."

Another unidentified female voice came through the speakerphone. "Anlon, going back a sec, you mentioned calls. Do we know if the BLUMOs tried to communicate with Major Carillo before they started with the electric shocks? You know, the quiver-chirps or something like that?"

"Actually, they may have tried to communicate with her," Dante said. "While we've been on the phone, Dr. Shilling's report on the attack arrived. The report says Ajay picked up a hissing sound on the HF receiver."

"Really? Is there an audio recording?" Anlon asked.

"Hold on, let me check," Pritchard said. "Uh … nothing yet. The rest of the downlink is still in progress."

Brock frowned. HF receiver? No, that was the wrong frequency. "Excuse me, Dante, but if the BLUMOs thought Carillo was a Calliston, wouldn't they have tried to communicate with her on VLF?"

"Good point," said Dante. "You're thinking about the Callistons' head crest?"

"That, and the fact Nick Reed built a VLF antenna to communicate with the UMOs around Mars."

Amato jumped in. "*Rorschach* has a VLF antenna. Has it been deployed, Dante? If not, we should instruct the crew to deploy it immediately. The BLUMOs may be attacking because they're trying to talk with *Rorschach* and the ship's not answering."

"They have two different VLF antennas, one for receiving, the other for transmitting," Dante said. "The receiver antenna is on the instrument array but inactive. Kiera thought it would be useless when *Rorschach*'s engines were active. Same with the radiation shield. Too much interference to pick up anything from the UMOs. All they have to do is turn on the receiver in the comms center and they're in—" He paused. "Hold on."

Through the speakerphone, Brock could hear muffled conversation.

"Dante?" Amato said.

"Yes, Mr. Amato, hold on please," Dante repeated.

The muffled conversation continued. Possibly an exchange between Dante and Pritchard.

"Is something the matter, Dante?" Amato asked.

Three sharp pounding sounds came over the phone, followed by a burst of grumbled expletives. Brock wondered if there'd been another unwelcome development. She closed her eyes and prayed the BLUMOs hadn't launched another attack.

She was in mid-prayer when another possibility popped into her mind. Had Carillo or Morgan taken a turn for the worse?

"Dante, answer me. What's going on?" Amato demanded.

After a long sigh, Dante said, "As I was saying, if we want *Rorschach* to listen to the BLUMOs, all the crew needs to do is switch on their VLF receiver. There's a magnetic loop antenna already installed on the *Rorschach*'s instrument array. But if we want the crew to try communicating with the BLUMOs, we've got a problem. Deploying the transmitting antenna requires another EVA." He explained that the coiled-wire antenna was two hundred fifty meters long. An EVA would be required to carry, unfurl and install the antenna in its pre-assigned slot on the instrument array. "It's a bit higher grade than an amateur VLF setup, but not by much, and that means we may not get much out of it."

Brock understood Dante's dilemma. The length of each VLF radio wave is very long. A professional-grade VLF broadcast requires a huge antenna to output even partial wavelengths. These "electrically short" antennas are kilometers long and are therefore not practical for spacecraft. So *Rorschach* had been outfitted with a lower-quality transmitting antenna. This seemed acceptable given Nick Reed had been able to attract UMOs to *Cetus Prime* with a VLF transmitting antenna he'd scrapped together from scavenged materials aboard the ship.

"Between the watt output of the transmitter onboard *Rorschach* and the smaller antenna, any broadcast they send won't have much of a transmission range," Dante continued. "We knew that going in, so it's not a surprise, but it does mean the BLUMOs will need to be close to *Rorschach* to detect the broadcast before the VLF waves diffuse and scatter into space."

"Yeah," added Pritchard, "the short range didn't seem like such a big deal when we thought *Rorschach* might use the setup for experiments communicating with Shilling's UMO colony, but as we've seen, the BLUMOs are way more dangerous at close range."

There was a pause as everyone absorbed Dante's and Pritchard's comments.

Amato broke the silence. "Dante, can we use *Rorschach*'s VLF engines to respond to signals from the BLUMOs? Just to ping them back and let them know we're receiving their signals if they're broadcasting any."

"Maybe, but I doubt we could generate much of a message," Dante said. "The engines' VLF transmitters are broadcasting waves into their plasma chambers. There's some leakage of the waves in the engine output, but the BLUMOs would have to be bumping up against the engines to detect the signals, and I don't think we want them that close."

Brock felt the group's energy falter. There had to be something they could recommend, something Kiera could engineer to communicate with the BLUMOs. But what?

She looked at the frozen image of lightning bolts arcing toward Carillo in the cargo bay. Dante was right: an extended EVA to install the VLF transmitting antenna was impossible. Carillo was out of commission, and even if Morgan made a miraculous recovery, his body couldn't withstand another EVA without stabilizing his blood-oxygen levels for another twenty-four hours. That was too long to wait. While sending out one of the other crew members was an option, their lack of EVA experience was problematic. If they couldn't come up with another solution, Brock might recommend that, but she considered it a last resort.

Relying on the ship's engines as an alternative was even more fraught with peril. She hadn't wanted to raise it before, but she believed there was a strong possibility the BLUMOs would react with aggression to the expulsion of ions from the engines rather than pay attention to the VLF signals mixed into the output.

The conversation switched to a discussion of the flight surgeon's recommendations for Carillo's and Morgan's follow-up treatments, and Brock's eyes drifted to Carillo's tether and the CubeSat docking platform.

"Holy shit, that's it!" she exclaimed.

The flight surgeon stopped in midsentence. "Excuse me?"

"Dante, what about tethering the VLF transmitter antenna to one of the fleet probes?" Brock asked.

"I thought of that. Not feasible."

"Why?"

"Simple. Even if Kiera can salvage the one Carillo was working on, there's no practical way of running cabling from the VLF transmitter in the comms center to the antenna unless we leave the Cube docked. But that means keeping the cargo bay doors open to allow the antenna to extend outside the ship, and that scares the shit out of me."

"I wasn't thinking of the CubeSat. I was thinking of *Cargo-4*. It's still docked, right?"

"It is," Dante said.

"And there's a power conduit in the dock's airlock, correct?"

There was an extended silence before Dante spoke again. "Ahhh, I see what you're thinking. It might be doable … "

"What might be doable?" Amato asked.

"But it'll be awfully tight quarters with an EMU on," Dante continued. "And they'll have to find a way to anchor the antenna."

"And reinforce the hole," Brock added.

"Reinforce what hole? What are you two talking about?" Amato asked.

Brock and Dante took turns explaining the idea. There was a conduit in the Cargo dock airlock that fed the ship's power to the probe once it was docked. The crew could snake a spliced cable from the VLF transmitter in *Rorschach*'s comm center through the conduit and into the Cargo. Once the cable was in place, one of the crew could perform an EVA inside the depressurized Cargo to drill a hole in the probe fuselage, connect the antenna to the transmitter cable and feed the long antenna through the hole.

"The antenna will have to be anchored inside *Cargo-4*, but we'll have our engineers provide them with options," Dante said. "Once that's done, whoever performs the EVA retreats inside *Rorschach* and seals the dock airlock, and they'll have a working VLF transmitting antenna."

"There is a downside, though," Brock said. "If more supplies are needed, there's no place to dock another Cargo. They'll have to use the cargo bay."

"Hey, if this works and the BLUMOs back off, that's a tradeoff I'd make any day," Pritchard said.

"Agreed," said Amato. "Dante, looks like you've got a lot to sort out and uplink to *Rorschach*. I suggest we ring off and let you get to it."

MISSION CONTROL
A3ROSPACE INDUSTRIES COMMAND AND CONTROL CENTER
MAYAGUANA ISLAND, THE BAHAMAS

Dante marched into Mission Control and announced he wanted the abort preparations put on hold. With the team gathered around him, he relayed what was discussed during the call and divvied up new tasks. It felt exhilarating to finally have some meaningful data to share with the crew and concrete recommendations to offer.

He was in the midst of discussing the proposed VLF antenna solution when alert chimes began to ping from consoles all around.

CHAPTER 10

KILL ZONE

Kiera lay on her bunk, trying to block visions of Carillo's burns from her mind — along with the astronaut's accompanying screams. In the heat of their attempts to save Carillo and Morgan, Kiera had suppressed as much of the unpleasantness as her psyche would allow, and afterward, she'd managed to keep the memories from bubbling up while she prepared updates for Mayaguana.

But now, in the quiet of her cabin, they demanded her full attention.

Battered by shock, exhaustion and fear, Kiera draped a forearm across her eyes and negotiated with her subconscious. *I just want to sleep a little, can we do this later? Please?* But the visions would not yield. Nor would her aching muscles or growling stomach. Together they schemed to prevent her from drifting off.

"Why did I come?" she whispered. "What was I thinking?"

No answers formed, but the questions drove a wedge through the competing sleep inhibitors, and a new vision filled her mind. She was on her paddleboard looking west toward Cocoa Beach. A mix of gold, purple and orange colored the sky as the last of the sun dipped below the horizon. She could hear the sounds of the surf and her friends gabbing at their encampment on the beach. Sinking her paddle in the ocean, she rotated the board to face east where the rising Moon hung above the darkening waters. Any minute now a sparkle of light would appear low in the sky, just ahead of the Moon. Kiera kept her eyes focused on this spot as waves bobbed her board up and down.

And then Jupiter flickered into view, and Kiera heard a voice to her right. "Can you believe it? You're going there."

She smiled. "Crazy, right?"

The voice said, "It's so far away."

"Yeah, it is," Kiera answered, her smile fading.

"I'm gonna miss you."

"Gonna miss you, too." Kiera turned toward the voice as the vision faded.

Asleep at last. A dreamless sleep at the outset, dark as a bottomless pit. But then a new vision rose in the emptiness. First came the sound of crashing waves, then the sensation of being pitched to and fro. A shiver of fear, a prick of panic. Another voice. This one urgent.

"Kiera! Wake up! Wake up!"

Her eyes snapped open. Ajay hovered above her. "They're back! Hurry!" He turned and dashed out the cabin door, his boots clanking against the magnetic floor.

Kiera stumbled out of the bunk and gave chase. She ran as fast as GEFF would allow her legs to lift and plant.

Up ahead, Ajay yelled, "She's up! She's coming!"

Was Morgan awake already? Had she been asleep that long?

As she neared the flight deck, alarms met her ears. Entering through the cockpit door, she spotted Shilling in the commander's chair.

"What's happening?" she yelled above the claxons.

"Get strapped in," Shilling shouted back.

Ajay, in the co-pilot's seat, fumbling the buckle of the safety harness, stared at the computer screen full of flashing icons. "They're all around us. They're taking out the rest of the fleet."

"What are you doing?" Kiera yelled.

"Getting the hell out of here," Shilling said.

"No!" she screamed. "Don't!"

The ship lurched forward hard enough to dislodge Kiera's boots from the floor. She flew backward and crashed into the wall by the door.

"How do I turn this damn thing?" Shilling said to Ajay.

Ajay pointed at the panel separating the two stations. "Thruster control."

Though Kiera was unable to push her whole body off the wall, she did manage to tug her hands free long enough to reach her smart watch. As she deactivated her GEFF sensors, she cursed. The artificial gravity forcefield was just not effective during sudden accelerations. Free of GEFF's influence, she fought against the remaining g-force produced by the engine's thrust. Finally, she pushed off the wall and grabbed hold of the nearest seat at the comms station. She pleaded with Shilling. "Stop! Turn off the engines!"

"No way. We've got one chance to get away, and this is it!"

In his attempt to alter course, Shilling sent *Rorschach* into a spin.

Kiera gripped the seat as the ship twirled around. "Damn it, Shilling, you have no idea what you're doing! Stop before you kill us all!" The man had lost his mind.

Ajay tried to tug Shilling's hand off the thruster control joystick. "Let me do it, Doctor."

"Let go, I've got it," Shilling said.

Kiera watched Shilling and Ajay fight for control of the thrusters. For a second, she thought of joining the struggle, but she realized it would only make matters worse. There was only one way to stop this.

She pushed off the seat toward the flight deck door. Another push sent her flying down the spinning corridor.

As she passed the medical bay, Carillo and Morgan flashed into her mind. Oh, no. The spin! What's it doing to them? Though both were sedated and strapped down, Morgan in his cabin and Carillo in the medical bay, they were hooked to IVs and oxygen masks that might dislodge. But there was nothing Kiera could do for them until she stopped the ship.

The centrifugal force created by the spin was not yet intense enough to pin her to the wall, so Kiera was able to grab a handhold and shoot herself toward the engine control room. The doorway was a moving target, but she managed to hook the top of the door frame with a foot and curl her body into the cabin. Her first attempt to grab hold of the flight control station failed as the force of the spin increased its pull on her body.

Finally she snagged the side of the station seat with the crook of her arm. Steadied by the seat, she lunged forward, flicked open the cover of the emergency shutdown and smashed a closed fist on the button beneath.

The hum of the VLF engines silenced, but the spin continued. It would not stop until someone competent at working the thrusters intervened, and Kiera couldn't override Shilling's manual command of the thrusters from here. What she could do was activate the reaction control system's autopilot function. If Shilling noticed, he could disable it immediately, but in his frenzied state Kiera hoped he wouldn't detect it until the RCS eliminated the spin.

The RCS would also reorient the ship to its original heading prior to Shilling's escape attempt, but until Kiera could get back to the flight deck there would be no telling how far they'd traveled or in which direction Shilling's panic had led them.

Kiera activated the system. An instant later she heard the telltale sounds of the thrusters firing in rapid succession to right the ship. Quickly the spin began to slow.

As the g-forces also subsided, other sounds followed: the clank of rapid footsteps, a roar of expletives from Shilling, a stream of entreaties from Ajay for Shilling to calm down. As the volume of the competing noises rose, Kiera muttered, "Uh-oh. Coming my way!"

Kiera saw only two choices. Confront Shilling in the corridor, or barricade herself in the engine room and try to reason with him. She chose the latter.

She quickly closed the hatch-like door, but before she could engage the lock, Shilling wrenched the hatch's corridor-side handle and pushed open the door. "You stupid bitch! Turn the engines back on!"

Kiera began to feel her body drifting up. She toggled on her GEFF sensors and braced her body against the hatch as she fought against Shilling's effort to break into the cabin. Through the three-inch gap in the doorway, she called out, "Ajay, try and wake Skywalker!"

"Roger that," Ajay said.

"Fuck Skywalker!" Shilling bellowed. The door shuddered as he kicked it. "Turn on the goddamn engines!"

"I'm not doing shit until you calm down!"

"Listen to me! We don't have time for this! We must get away!"

Kiera closed her eyes as Shilling's blows turned more ferocious. *Come on, Ajay! Come on, Skywalker!* As the gap in the door widened, she tried again to reason with him.

"We can't outrun them. You know that."

The door flew open and the wild-eyed Shilling stormed into the room and used both hands to pin Kiera to the wall by her neck. "You skanky little fuck."

Kiera dug her fingernails into his hands and kicked at him, but her counters were ineffective. As he crushed his grip on her throat, she pleaded with him to stop.

A blur of motion behind Shilling caught Kiera's eye. She looked over his shoulder and saw Ajay floating into the room, a syringe in his hand and a snarl on his face. Before Shilling knew what was happening, Ajay plunged the syringe into the back of the man's neck.

Shilling cried out and let go of Kiera. He turned to Ajay, saw the syringe, and charged. But within two steps he faltered and slumped to the floor.

Ajay floated to Kiera. "You okay?"

Kiera wrapped her arms around him in a tight embrace.

FLIGHT DECK — THE *RORSCHACH EXPLORER*
FLYING THROUGH THE ASTEROID BELT

With the unconscious Shilling restrained and locked in the cargo bay, Kiera and Ajay checked on Carillo and Morgan. By some miracle, neither of the sedated astronauts had been further harmed during the ship's spin. Kiera and Ajay tended to both, ensuring their IVs and oxygen masks were functioning properly, then returned to the flight deck to assess their situation.

Kiera tried to make sense of what had transpired. Before she went to sleep, the three able crewmembers had agreed to one-hour rotations between short rests, so at all times someone could be keeping tabs on Carillo and Morgan and another could be manning the flight deck. Kiera had drawn the first rest period, while Ajay monitored the two astronauts and Shilling manned the flight deck.

"Tell me what happened," she said.

"About twenty minutes after you went to your cabin, Dr. Shilling called me to the flight deck," Ajay said. "He said the BLUMOs had surrounded us."

"And?"

"He showed me the cam feeds from our probes. There were BLUMOs around all of them. Thousands of BLUMOs around each."

"And that caused him to freak out?"

"Not at first." Ajay buckled in at the co-pilot's station.

Kiera looked out the flight deck windows as she strapped into the commander's seat. Pulsing blue lights filled the entire vista. "So when did things go ape?"

"First, the BLUMOs attacked the second Recon we'd hoped to repair. Then alarms on the Shields went crazy. Dr. Shilling said something about them leading us into a kill zone. He tried drawing them off like we did the first time, sending *Cargo-2* away, but it went LOS almost immediately. That's when I came to get you."

Kiera accessed the station's computer and checked the fleet probe monitoring system. All of them showed as LOS. She pulled up *Rorschach*'s camera feeds and cycled from camera to camera. There was a thick layer of pulsing blue lights everywhere. A sudden pang of regret churned in her stomach. Had Shilling been right to make a run for it?

"What do you think we should do?" Ajay asked, his gaze on the BLUMOs outside the flight deck windows.

Kiera checked to make sure the ship's radiation shield was still active. It was. She toggled the computer to check comms. No new uplinks from Mayaguana. Then she checked the navigation console on the commander's dashboard. *Rorschach* was traveling at sixty thousand kilometers per hour. The ship was still above the ecliptic, but closer to the asteroid belt than they had been when Morgan had ordered all-stop to retrieve and repair the damaged probes. The RCS autopilot had reoriented *Rorschach* toward Callisto, and it appeared the system's thrusters were guiding the ship back down into the heart of the asteroid belt to assume their original course.

A sudden urge to fire up the engines, punch through the BLUMOs and turn for Earth overtook Kiera. But then a thought occurred to her.

She turned to Ajay. "What are they waiting for?"

"Huh?"

"Why haven't they attacked us?" Kiera asked. "I mean, we're sitting ducks. They've wiped out all our probes. We're all alone. Why haven't they finished us off?"

"I dunno," Ajay said. "I don't wanna know."

The longer Kiera pondered her own question, the stranger the BLUMOs' behavior seemed. If Shilling had been right about the aliens drawing *Rorschach* into a kill zone, their pack hunt had accomplished its mission. Why hadn't they moved in for the kill? Then again, how would destroying *Rorschach* feed the BLUMOs?

It didn't take long before she conjured an answer, turning her earlier pang of regret into full-blown nausea. Had Shilling inadvertently given them what they wanted when he turned on the ship's engines? He thought he was escaping, but perhaps he was actually feeding the BLUMOs. Was that why they had surrounded the ship? Were they waiting for another crack at *Rorschach*'s electromagnetic honey?

Yet Ajay had said the BLUMOs had destroyed the Cargo Shilling had tried to use to lure them away. They could have had all the ions they wanted if they had just followed the probe like they did the first time. Even if the BLUMOs found *Cargo-2*'s ion output meager in comparison to *Rorschach*'s, why destroy it?

A ping sounded, and Ajay said, "We have an uplink coming in from Maya. Wait, there's more than one."

The first file was small and downloaded quickly. It was a message from Dante. Ajay opened and read it to Kiera. "*MAYA-FLIGHT to FE-TRE: Have detected fleet alarms. Report status ASAP. Important instructions to follow. MAYA-FLIGHT out.*"

Another short message followed. "*MAYA-FLIGHT to FE-TRE: Additional transmissions following, including (1) Maya-NASA analysis of BLUMO intentions; (2) Recommended BLUMO action plan; (3) Further medical guidance re: CDR and CCDR injuries; Review all ASAP. MAYA-FLIGHT out.*"

"Thank God someone has an action plan," Kiera said, "because we sure don't!"

While they waited for the other uplinked files, she typed out a reply to Dante's first message. *FE-TRE to MAYA-FLIGHT: TRE nominal but surrounded by large BLUMO colony. Fleet LOS. CDR, CCDR and MSRS incapacitated. FE and MSAJ unharmed. Will review Maya files and implement Maya BLUMO recommendations and med guidance ASAP. FE-TRE out."*

COLONEL PAUL MORGAN'S CABIN —
THE *RORSCHACH EXPLORER*

A voice calling his name stirred Morgan awake.

"Colonel Morgan, wake up, please."

Morgan cracked open his eyelids to see a blurry shadow looming over him.

"Colonel Morgan? It's me, Ajay. Please wake up."

Morgan squinted as he tried to adjust to the light. "Where am I? What's going on?"

A hand patted him on the shoulder. "You're in your cabin. You've been asleep."

As Morgan became more conscious of his surroundings, his memory kicked into gear. The cargo bay. Julia. "Where's Julia?"

"She's in the med bay," Kiera said.

Morgan's head turned in the direction of Kiera's voice. He blinked several times to clear his vision. In slurred speech, he said, "I feel drunk."

"Sorry. We gave you a sedative," she said. "You kept trying to pull off the oxygen mask and yank out your IV."

He began to recall details of the rescue attempt. "How long have I been out?"

"Eight hours, give or take," said Ajay.

Morgan tried to raise his head but found it difficult to move. "Julia. How is she?"

"She's still asleep," Kiera said.

"That's not an answer. What's her condition?" Morgan growled.

Kiera's voice was soft and reassuring. "She's hanging in there."

Morgan attempted to sit up but found his arms and legs restrained. "Can we lose the straps, please? I feel like I've been glued to the bed."

"Hold on, we've got you wrapped up in a thermal bag." Keira explained that the bag had been necessary because Morgan had exited the airlock so fast on his way to help Carillo, he hadn't given his spacesuit time to heat up. By the time they reached him in the airlock after he returned, his body temperature had fallen to dangerous levels.

With the straps and blanket bag removed, Morgan floated off the bed. Kiera and Ajay guided him back down, and Kiera activated the GEFF platform beneath the mattress. Morgan felt the subtle tug of the magnetic forcefield on his flight suit. He arced an arm toward his face and wiped at his eyes, hoping to push away the cloudy haze. The movement caused a sharp pain to shoot down his arm. "Ah, damn. That hurt like a mother."

"Take it easy, Skywalker," Ajay said. "Remember, you do have the bends."

A wave of dizziness swept over Morgan. "Oh, yeah," he said sarcastically. "Thanks for reminding me."

His vision continued to improve, and now he could see Kiera sitting next to him on the bunk and Ajay standing beside her. Their expressions were grim. Putting two and two together, Morgan said, "Something's wrong with the ship."

"Not exactly," Kiera said.

"Where's Shilling?"

"He's ... um ... resting," said Ajay.

"Well, something's the matter. You guys look like you're headed for the gallows." Morgan sat up. The room began to spin. He clamped his eyes shut and gripped the edges of the bunk platform.

"We have a bit of a situation," Kiera said. "We need your help."

"What kind of situation?"

"BLUMOs," said Ajay.

Morgan opened his eyes. "Did they attack again?"

Both Kiera and Ajay nodded. Their expressions were pained, the kind worn by bearers of bad news. And both seemed reluctant to speak.

"I'm not a porcelain doll, people. Give it to me straight. What's going on?"

Ajay darted a look to Kiera as he answered. "The fleet's gone. The BLUMOs have us surrounded."

Morgan occupied his seat on the flight deck with Kiera and Ajay following close behind. When they were all buckled in at their stations, Kiera
kicked off the briefing.

"They've formed a ball around us," she said. She pulled up an image
from the ship's radar, showing the electromagnetic mass around the ship,
and sent it to the other stations' monitors.

Morgan looked out the flight deck windows. "At least we can see them
this time. How far out are they?"

"Approximately a quarter kilometer. Maya's aware of the situation.
They received the fleet sensor alerts, and I sent them a brief sitrep. They
sent us their interpretation of the BLUMOs' actions and some
recommendations. You should go through the files."

"Give me the highlights."

"They think the BLUMOs scanned Major Carillo."

Morgan frowned. "Scan? That didn't look like a *scan* to me."

Kiera summarized the BLUMO analysis linking the encounters
experienced by Nick Reed and Carillo. When she reached the part about
the Callistons, Morgan interrupted. "They think we're Callistons?"

"It sounds nuts, I know, but the report is compelling."

"And there's more," Ajay said. "Let's play him the VLF audio."

"VLF?" Morgan asked.

As Ajay typed in a string of commands, Kiera said, "Yeah, this one was
a stretch for me, but damn if they weren't right."

"Right about what?"

"On a hunch, Mayaguana suggested we turn on our VLF receiver to
see if the BLUMOs were trying to talk to us," Ajay said. "You know, the
whole *Cetus Prime* thing about Nick Reed building a VLF antenna."

Morgan blinked several times as he processed this. Then he understood.
Nick had used the antenna to attract the UMOs.

Ajay handed him a headset. "Listen to this."

Morgan donned the headset and closed his eyes.

The recording began with a series of eerie, high-pitched whines. They reminded Morgan of the sound of race cars zooming past microphones. And then, from among the whines, another sound arose.

Morgan opened his eyes and removed his headset. "That sounds just like a whale."

Ajay smiled. "Cool as hell, isn't it? That is, cool as hell if we weren't about to be dinner."

"Bad mojo, Elroy," Kiera said. "Don't say it. Don't even think it. We don't know if that's their plan."

"What makes you think they have a plan?" Morgan asked.

"If you listen to the full VLF recording, you'll hear a second whale sing," Kiera said. "We think the second one's a UMO queen on Callisto answering the BLUMO queen."

"That's right," Ajay said. "We think the BLUMO queen's been told to keep us hemmed in until the other one shows up."

Morgan frowned. "A second queen? From Callisto? Coming here? Those are some pretty big leaps."

"Not when you look at the data," Kiera said.

"All right. Enlighten me."

"Well, first of all," Kiera said, "the BLUMOs haven't done anything since forming the ball around us. They're just flying along, sort of escorting us inside their ball. Second, there've been several exchanges between the whale singers, and the time gap between the songs has been shrinking, suggesting—"

"Okay, I get it." Morgan didn't need any further explanation. Radio signals travel at the speed of light, so if you know how long it took for a transmitted radio signal to be received, you can calculate the distance it's traveled. Singer A belts out a whale song. Some amount of time later, Singer B answers. Presuming there isn't a lot of UMO "think" time going on in between Song A and Song B, a narrowing gap of time between rounds of songs implies the singers are moving closer to one another.

"Another queen's on her way to us," Morgan said, "presumably traveling with another colony of UMOs. But what makes you think they're UMOs from Callisto?"

"We calculated the distance of the first song exchange," Kiera said. "Our VLF antenna isn't directional, so we don't know which direction the second queen's response came from, but we do know our position at the time the BLUMO queen called the other one. With that as a starting point, we used the navigational system to plot a sphere of the right distance around that position."

Morgan darted his eyes from Kiera to the grinning Ajay. "No effing way! The sphere cuts across Callisto?"

Ajay nodded with gusto.

Kiera said, "It's not conclusive. The sphere also bisects two slices of the asteroid belt about 400 million kilometers apart … and the innermost boundary of the sphere comes close to Mars' current position. Plus, we don't know how long they were singing to each other before we started recording, but it *is* awful curious the outer boundary of the sphere touched Callisto."

"And don't forget, we're headed toward Callisto," Ajay added. "And the time gap between songs is narrowing. So, you see, we need your help to get ready."

"Ready for what?" Morgan asked.

"To sing to the Callisto queen … and pray she's not coming to eat," Ajay said.

Kiera glared at him. "What did I tell you about that? So help me, you keep bringing up dinner and I'll make sure she eats you first."

Ajay swiped two fingers across his closed lips.

Kiera returned her attention to Morgan. "We've sent an update to Mayaguana with the recordings. They haven't responded yet, but we'd rather not wait for their answer. I need to start prepping for the EVA." She relayed Mayaguana's plan to deploy the VLF transmitting antenna through the docked Cargo. "They gave us step-by-step instructions. I'm pretty sure we can do it, but we didn't want to start without your buy-in."

"All right, let me read all the files, including the instructions," Morgan said. "But if there's an EVA required, I'll be the one doing it."

"*No bueno*, Skywalker," Ajay said with a shake of his head. "You're grounded for at least another sixteen hours. Flight surgeon's orders. Gotta get your O2 back up. We can't afford to lose you, especially with Major Carillo and Dr. Shilling out of commission."

"And besides," Kiera said, "I'm the smallest. It'll be easier for me to maneuver inside the Cargo than either of you."

"Wait a minute," Morgan said. "What's wrong with Shilling? You said he was resting."

Ajay looked suddenly sheepish. "Uh ... not exactly."

CHAPTER 11

QUEEN ON DECK

ABOARD *SOL SEAKER*
PORT DENARAU, FIJI
SEPTEMBER 4, 2019 (SEPTEMBER 5 ON FIJI)

Jennifer turned the corner and ran through the marina entrance, waving to the security guard as she passed. With only a few hundred yards to go until she reached *Sol Seaker*'s berth, she quickened her pace to a sprint. Impeded by stiff headwinds, she lowered her head and dug deep for the final stretch.

Crossing an imaginary finish line by the ship's gangway, she stopped the timer on her watch and slowed to a walk. She anchored her hands on her hips and proceeded past *Sol Seaker* to the end of the dock, drawing in gulps of salty air.

As she turned to make her way back to the gangway, she spotted one of the ship's stewards waving to her. Jennifer smiled and waved back. The steward's face turned stern, his waving more animated.

He then cupped his hands around his mouth and called to her. "Hurry!"

Jennifer immediately thought of Pebbles. The preceding summer and fall she had experienced a torrent of nightmare-like visions. Fearing a relapse, Jennifer took off running. When she reached the ramp, she pounded up its length and met the steward at the top. He was more out of breath than Jennifer.

"I didn't know … if I should wake … Dr. Cully," he said.

"Is it Pebbles? Is she having a seizure?"

"No. Follow me!"

The steward grabbed her wrist and led her to the ship's bridge. In the sleek cabin full of computer screens, dials and gauges, two other members of the superyacht's crew were watching a television mounted on the wall behind the captain's chair.

The steward pointed at the TV. "You know these people, right?"

On the screen, Jenna Toffy was standing outside a building. The word "LIVE" flashed in the lower right corner, and a picture of the *Rorschach Explorer* appeared in an inset. The audio was muted, but a crawler at the bottom read:

WNN Exclusive: Tragedy Strikes Rorschach Explorer … *astronauts Morgan, Carillo and UMO expert Dr. Shilling incapacitated … probe fleet destroyed …* Rorschach *surrounded by hostile UMOs … Mayaguana has lost communication with the ship … its position and status are unknown …*

"Can you turn up the sound?" Jennifer said.

The steward grabbed the remote. "I overheard you guys talking about your phone call with Mission Control over dinner last night. Thought Dr. Cully might want to know about it right away. Should I wake him?"

"I'll take care of it," Jennifer said. "Let me watch a little first. I want to hear what Toffy has to say."

"Yes, ma'am."

The sound came on, and Toffy's voice broadcast through the bridge.

" … *repeated attempts, there has been no comment from Augustus Amato, flight director Dr. Dante Fulton, or anyone else from A3rospace Industries. The company and its founder have come under blistering criticism for their silence since the first signs of trouble surfaced three days ago.*

"*One of the most vocal critics has been Dr. Richard Collins, chairman of the advocacy group Concerned Scientists for Equal Access to Space. Dr. Collins joins us now to share his view on these sobering developments …* "

Jennifer asked the steward to retrieve her smart tablet from her cabin while she continued to watch the program. When he returned, Jennifer navigated to her go-to news website for more details. The top headline flashed in red: *WNN's Toffy Blows Lid Off Rorschach Explorer Cover-Up.*

She read the opening paragraphs:

Jenna Toffy, WNN ace reporter and host of Expedition to Callisto, *took to the airwaves shortly before noon today to levy charges of cover-up against A3rospace Industries and its founder, Augustus Amato, for their efforts to hide a serious crisis aboard the* Rorschach Explorer.

Aided by an anonymous source with intimate knowledge of the mission, Toffy produced a series of internal documents and communications revealing the depth of the crisis and A3rospace Industries' frantic attempts to provide assistance.

Jennifer's attention was drawn to a boxed quotation. Its headline read *#nothumbsuckerhere is* Rorschach's Last Hope, and the quote itself read as follows:

FE-TRE to MAYA-FLIGHT: TRE nominal but surrounded by large BLUMO colony. Fleet LOS. CDR, CCDR and MSRS incapacitated. FE and MSAJ unharmed. Will review Maya files and implement Maya BLUMO recommendations and med guidance ASAP. FE-TRE out.

Jennifer had seen enough. She thanked the steward and headed for Anlon's cabin. While Pebbles would no doubt bitch about the early wake-up, Anlon would want to reach out to Amato right away.

The pack hunters had closed in for the kill.

CARGO BAY — THE *RORSCHACH EXPLORER*
FLYING THROUGH THE ASTEROID BELT

An uneasy feeling gnawed at Morgan as he cranked open the door to the airlock connecting the main cabin and the cargo bay. It was the kind of feeling that creeps its way into the back of your mind and finds a place to hide — and then, once it realizes it's safe, it begins to reproduce and spread to other parts of the brain. You can try to ignore its whispers but, at some point, you can't help but listen. And once that happens, once the feeling senses it has an audience, the whispers grow louder. Eventually the feeling takes over, shouting down any thought that dares to intercede.

We're doomed. There's no way out. The BLUMOs have control of the ship. Each second that passes, they take us farther from Earth and closer to lethal radiation and more UMOs. There's no way to stop it from happening. We can't break away from their grip. We can't fight them. We can't fool them. We might as well curl up and suck our thumbs.

Morgan wiped sweat from his forehead. "Fuck that."

He beat back the feeling. *No way. Not today. Not ever. There's always a chance, however small. There's always something we can try, however outlandish. Put one foot in front of the other and keep going. Don't give in. Don't give up. You're freaking Skywalker. They're depending on you. Get your shit together and get us out of this mess.*

Morgan finished opening the door and entered the airlock. More thoughts pummeled the feeling. *One step at a time. Build on small victories. String them together into something bigger, something tangible for the crew to latch on to and boost their confidence. Start with the VLF antenna, Skywalker. That's your way out, whether it works or not.*

As he began to crank the handle of the door leading from the airlock into the cargo bay, Morgan realized Dante and Amato's antenna workaround idea was a godsend. It gave the crew something to do, something to accomplish. It would take their minds off the pulsing blue orb and the tug of hopelessness trying to rip them apart. It would bring them back together.

That's our only chance. We have to stay together. First step, get Shilling back in line.

With both ends of the airlock open, Morgan passed into the pressurized cargo bay. One docking platform still held *Recon-3*; Shilling was lashed to the other. He looked like a mummy, for Kiera and Ajay had used a combination of wire cables and duct tape to strap him down.

Shilling glared up at him. "Well, well. If it isn't the legend himself. Did they wake you to do the honors? What's it going to be? Shoot me out into space? Sacrifice me to the BLUMOs? Another injection, this time lethal?"

Morgan slid a pair of wire cutters from his flight suit pocket and held them up for Shilling to see. "Nah, just gonna snip a couple of fingers off."

Shilling rolled his eyes. "Ha ha."

Morgan smiled and rapped the wire cutters against the scientist's forehead. "Got a question for you, Bob. How old are you? Forty-four or forty-five?"

The blow was forceful enough to make Shilling wince. "I'm forty-two. Why?"

Morgan leaned close to Shilling's face and pressed the wire cutters into the scientist's ribs. "That gives you twenty-three years on me, Bob. But I swear to God Almighty, if you *ever* lay your hands on another member of this crew, I'll whup your ass."

Shilling groaned as Morgan twisted the wire cutters into his rib cage.

"And another thing," Morgan continued. "Until I say otherwise, you are prohibited from stepping foot onto the flight deck or entering the engine control room without my permission. Failure to comply will result in confinement to your quarters for the duration of the mission. Are we clear on all that?"

He maintained pressure on the wire cutters as he waited for Shilling's response. But the red-faced scientist merely glowered at him and said nothing.

Morgan pushed the wire cutters deeper still. "The appropriate response is 'Aye, aye, Colonel,' or 'Yes, sir.' I'll even accept a 'Roger that.' Take your pick."

"All right, all right," cried the writhing Shilling.

"That wasn't one of your choices, Bob."

Wild-eyed, Shilling growled, "Fuck you!"

Morgan twisted the wire cutters again. "I can do this all day, my man."

"Stop! You're going to break my ribs!"

"You have the power to make it stop, Bob. Just say the words."

In between gasps, Shilling nodded and said, "Aye, aye."

Morgan released pressure on the wire cutters and stepped back to wipe the sweat coating his forehead. "I'm glad we had this little chat, Bob. I feel better already. Now, let's get you back on your feet."

As soon as he had cut away the tape and wires holding Shilling to the platform, Shilling began to float upward. Morgan pushed him back down and handed him the GEFF smartwatch Kiera had removed when they tied him up.

Shilling activated the device and stood, his fists clenched at his sides.

Morgan smiled as he slid the wire cutters back in his pocket. "Got something to say, Bob?"

Shilling's face twitched. He raised his fist and pounded the platform. "We had one chance, *one*, to get away, and those gutless cowards blew it!"

"Now, come on, Bob. You don't know that."

"Don't I? Are the BLUMOs still out there?"

"Yep. As a matter of fact, we're completely surrounded. Looks like the colony has grown in size a hundredfold. It appears more are on the way."

"Then we're screwed!"

Morgan placed his hand on Shilling's shoulder. "Look, I understand why you tried to make a run for it. I do. Under the circumstances, I would have been tempted to do the same thing. But be real. It might've worked, but it also might have backfired. We might be in the same spot we're in now, or it might have been worse. Point is, we are where we are, and the only thing we can do now is concentrate on making the best of it."

Shilling stepped back. "Have we aborted the mission? Are we headed back to Earth?"

"No and no. At present, we're back on our original course to Call—"

"Are you *loony*?"

"Hold on, Bob, I wasn't finished."

"Damn it, Paul! Don't you get it? We're not going to make it to Callisto. We *have* to turn around and try to go home. It's the only rational option."

Morgan's hand twitched. Oh, how he wanted to wallop the bastard. But there was a lot of work to be done, and Shilling's help was needed.

"Listen," he said. "A lot's happened since Ajay put you to sleep. Even if I wanted to abort and head home, we can't until we shake the BLUMOs. Right now, I have no idea how to do that. And every extra second I spend trying to get you back on track, we fly farther away from Earth, making it less and less likely that we can make it back. So I need you to nut up and—"

A quaking blow hammered into *Rorschach* from behind, sending Morgan and Shilling tumbling over the docking platform. Kiera's voice spilled from the intercom and echoed around the cavernous bay.

"Colonel Morgan, need you on the flight deck! Please hurry! Oh, God, please hurry!"

The two men exchanged a brief glance and then ran to the airlock.

"Close and lock both doors," Morgan said to Shilling. "Then get your ass to the lab."

Morgan braced for the worst. The tremor in Kiera's voice had signaled more than panic — it sounded closer to terror. At any second, he expected the ship to blow apart or electric discharges to begin slicing through the corridor. And up ahead, he could see flashes of white, almost like strobe lights, through the open flight deck door.

Rorschach lurched forward, and Morgan stumbled and fell. The ship bucked from side to side several times as the autopilot thrusters fought to maintain the vessel's orientation. Morgan was about to yell a command to disable the autopilot when the bucking stopped.

By the time he was up and running again, the ship had begun to spin, and he was sent off his feet, tumbling like a shoe in a dryer. He raked his hands against the rotating walls and snagged a handhold. As the spin increased, Morgan began to feel his body pinning against the wall. He toggled off his GEFF magnets and snaked along the wall of the spinning corridor.

At the door to the flight deck, he gripped the door frame. It was difficult to make sense of the twirling scene that met his eyes. The flashes outside the ship were so intense, he could only squint for a second or two at a time, and what little he could make out between the splotches dotting his vision was surreal. Through the cockpit windows, amid a pulsing sea of blue, an intense battle raged. A battle in which *Rorschach* was only a bystander.

Another jolt aft of the ship sent Morgan flying forward. He sailed right over the commander's seat and crashed into the windows. Pressed against the glass, he looked down to see Kiera strapped in, shielding her eyes with her forearm.

"Punch the engines!" he shouted.

"I can't see!" she yelled back.

Ajay's voice sounded from the co-pilot's station. "Roger dodger!"

The sudden acceleration sent Morgan flying aft, and his leg clipped a headrest and sent him twirling. But just before he spun back into the corridor, a hand gripped his arm, arresting his spin.

A voice beside him called out, "Full power, Ajay! Keep feeding 'em!"

Morgan snapped his head toward the voice. Standing in the doorway, one hand clenching its frame, the other one holding him in place, was none other than Major Julia Carillo, bloodstained patient-garments and all.

Several more aft blows buffeted the ship.

Carillo called out, "Don't let the bumps bother you! They're trying to help!" She nodded toward the windows. "That's what they've been hunting!"

As *Rorschach* veered to the right, Morgan took a glimpse at the battle. Thousands upon thousands of lightning bolts leapt from a swarm of BLUMOs. But it wasn't clear what their target was. All Morgan could see were brilliant flashes of white obscured by an oscillating pink cloud.

He grabbed hold of the door frame. "What the hell is that?"

"I don't know," Carillo answered, releasing him. "But she doesn't like it."

"*She?*"

Crooking her thumb, Carillo pointed behind her. A spinning ball of sparkling blue hovered behind her head. In its center was a throbbing white light.

MISSION CONTROL
A3ROSPACE INDUSTRIES COMMAND AND CONTROL CENTER
MAYAGUANA ISLAND, THE BAHAMAS

Amato and Pritchard entered Mission Control through the back door and walked right into the tumult. Some groups of controllers leaned over consoles and engaged in heated debates; others remained at their stations, examining data on their computers or talking with colleagues on their headsets. At the back of the room, several physicists were congregated around a whiteboard filled with equations and diagrams while one of them passionately argued a point. Another group worked their phones to discuss the crisis with peers at NASA, U.S. Space Command and the European Space Agency.

"Do you see Dante?" Amato asked Pritchard. The mission director wasn't at his station, nor could Amato spot him among the personnel scattered around the room.

"No." Pritchard pointed at a group of staff engaged in a heated debate at a console two rows in front of Dante's station. "He was with the INCO team when I left to get you."

Just then, Dante's head appeared above the control stations at the front of the room. Amato pointed. "There he is. Come on."

As they approached Dante, he saw them coming and led them to a quiet spot beneath the control center's wall of display monitors.

"*Rorschach*'s gone," he said.

"What do you mean, *Rorschach*'s gone?" Amato demanded.

"We can't find it. About two hours ago they downlinked a file to us, but it was corrupted. We sent back a message asking them to resend. That was an hour ago, and they haven't responded. A half hour ago, we started pinging all their antennas. No handshakes. No nothing."

"Could it be radio interference?" Amato asked.

"I sure hope so. If it's not, they've either lost power, or … "

"Let's not go there. Keep trying."

FLIGHT DECK – THE *RORSCHACH EXPLORER*
FLYING THROUGH THE ASTEROID BELT

"I can't see! I'm blind!" Kiera screamed.

The sharp cries shook Morgan from his stupor. He pushed away from Carillo and the spinning cluster of blue-white UMOs.

"Don't be afraid, Paul. She wants to help," Carillo said.

Another jolt hit aft of *Rorschach*, but this time Morgan held his grip on the door frame. Over Kiera's screams, he asked Carillo, "You can communicate with them?"

She nodded.

"Then tell them to stop ramming us. Tell them to stop the spin."

Ajay finally turned to see the bloodied astronaut — and the UMOs hovering by her head. "Oh my God! Major! BLUMOs! Right behind you!"

The panic in his voice only fueled Kiera's hysteria. She flailed her arms as if trying to swat away the space bees. "Help me! I can't see them! Where are they? Keep them off me!"

Morgan pushed off and corralled her in his arms. "It's all right, Kiera. Everything's okay. I got ya."

Kiera fought against his hold, smacking his face with her closed fists.

Ajay's shouts weren't helping matters. "Get away, Major! Quick! Before it zaps you!"

Carillo was now facing the hovering BLUMOs, and the white light at the center of the blue tennis-ball-sized cluster was emitting a stream of pulses bright enough to light up the flight deck.

Down the corridor, Morgan saw Shilling emerge from the lab, only to come to an abrupt halt when he saw the glowing cluster. But his shock lasted for only a second before he resumed pushing toward the flight deck, yelling to Carillo, "Get down, get down!"

He launched himself toward her, apparently intending to tackle her to the floor. But he never got close. With a crackling hiss, the BLUMOs fired a bolt of electricity.

"No!" Carillo shouted.

"Dr. Shilling!" Ajay cried out.

The bolt hit Shilling's outstretched hand. Tendrils leapt off the main discharge and spread across his magnetized flight suit. A guttural bark sounded from his open mouth, and his pupils rolled back behind his eyelids. His body spasmed, and he fell to the magnetized floor, where the last of the discharge-tendrils leapt to the metallic walls and shot down the corridor.

The clash of shouts and sounds sent Kiera into a frenzy. She clawed at Morgan's face and neck while screaming in terror.

Morgan shouted at Carillo. "Tell it to leave, Julia! Tell it to get the *fuck* off our ship!"

Carillo closed her eyes. The white light inside the ball of BLUMOs began to pulse again. She shook her head from side to side. The blue lights around the periphery picked up the pace of their spin. She fell to her knees and clasped her hands together.

Finally, the cluster spiraled around her head, shot to the rear of the ship, and disappeared from view.

LOST PALMS OASIS TRAILHEAD
JOSHUA TREE NATIONAL PARK
TWENTYNINE PALMS, CALIFORNIA

Zane Hunter was positively giddy. The night sky was perfectly clear, the temperature a pleasant seventy degrees. Overhead, Saturn neared its upper culmination, with Jupiter early in its descent. As he finished setting up his telescope, his girlfriend, Shelly Barnes, snuck up from behind and wrapped her arms around him.

"Do you think we'll be able to see them?" she asked.

"See what?"

"The *Rorschach Explorer* fleet."

Zane laughed. "No way. But we'll definitely be able to see Jupiter and Callisto."

She perked up at that. "What about Saturn? Will we be able to see its rings?"

"Ask and ye shall receive." Zane carefully panned the telescope to the left and adjusted the altitude. When Saturn and its crystal-clear rings were centered in the viewfinder, he backed away and bowed to her. "Milady."

"Thank you, noble sir." She bowed in return and leaned over to peer at the planet.

Zane stepped back, observed Shelly's shapely backside, then raised his gaze to the twinkling planet up above.

The sudden flash was so bright it seemed to envelop the whole of Saturn. It lasted for nearly two seconds.

Zane staggered back. "Whoa!"

Shelly pulled away from the telescope with a hand over her eye. "Ow!"

Zane rushed to her side. "Are you okay, babe?"

"My eye's killing me. What happened?"

"I don't know. There was, like, a huge burst of light. I've never seen anything like it."

SEPTEMBER 4-5, 2019

Across North America, millions of people had witnessed the sudden flash of light in the night sky. The Internet was abuzz. Had a huge meteor struck Saturn? Did one of its moons explode? Was this the aftermath of an intergalactic supernova?

Though the flash had appeared on the rising side of Saturn, far away from Jupiter and Callisto, there was also plenty of speculation that this was evidence of a fresh UMO attack on the *Rorschach Explorer*. This rumor gained steam when news outlets reported leaks out of NASA and A3I indicating Mission Control had lost contact with the vessel.

The news reached an exhausted Helen Brock shortly after one a.m., four hours after the event, when she was roused from sleep by a barrage of calls from project teams at Goddard and JPL. She was informed that the flash had been composed mostly of visible and ultraviolet light, but that observatories had detected traces of radio, infrared, X-ray and gamma rays in the flash's invisible afterglow.

By three a.m., a consortium of observatories had calculated the epicenter of the flash: an empty sector of space between the orbits of Saturn's two outermost moons, Iapetus and Titan.

And at 4:36 a.m. Eastern, all hell broke loose. Millions of people looking skyward, from the western longitudes of the Americas to the islands of east Asia, saw a celestial fireworks show unlike any in recorded history. Six more flashes sparked the night sky so close to Saturn they seemed to swallow the ringed planet.

Among the observers were Anlon, Pebbles and Jennifer aboard *Sol Seaker*, out on the waters of the Koro Sea near Fiji. As spectacular as the flashes were, the three friends couldn't help but avert their eyes to lonely Jupiter to the right of Saturn. From their perspective on this late summer night, the two planets looked like neighbors. In reality, Saturn was a billion kilometers from Jupiter, but it was hard to look at the flashes and not think of *Rorschach* and the crew's desperate plight.

CHAPTER 12

MIND'S EYE

As *Rorschach*'s orientation steadied and the ship's acceleration abated, Morgan clamped his hands on Kiera's wrists and guided them away from his face. With his head resting against hers, he said, "They're gone, Kiera. It's okay. It's all over."

Ajay unbuckled from his seat and scrambled toward Shilling, nearly toppling Carillo on his way through the flight deck door. He knelt beside Shilling and placed two fingers on the man's neck. "He's not breathing. There's no pulse." He rolled Shilling over and began to perform CPR.

Morgan left Kiera with Carillo, activated GEFF and dashed for the medical bay. He returned with a portable defibrillator and oxygen tank. For the next few minutes, he and Ajay took turns compressing Shilling's chest and administering mouth-to-mouth resuscitation.

"I've got a pulse!" Ajay said at last, his fingers on Shilling's neck. "It's weak, but it's there."

"Move out of the way." Morgan halted compressions and pressed the oxygen mask over Shilling's mouth. He felt for Shilling's pulse. It was shallow and irregular. "Prep the defib."

"Roger."

Morgan unzipped Shilling's flight suit down to his waist, tore open his T-shirt, and prepped the defibrillator paddles. "Make sure his GEFF is off."

Ajay removed Shilling's GEFF watch and deactivated the magnetic forcefield.

Shilling's body began to float upward. Morgan pressed down on the paddles to push the stricken scientist back to the floor, then triggered the defibrillator's shock.

He pulled the paddles away. "Check his pulse again."

Ajay held the scientist down and put two fingers against his neck. "Still there," he said. "Stronger."

"Good. Julia, we're going to float him to the med bay. I need epinephrine ready to go when we get there. We may not need it, but I want it ready just in case."

By now Carillo had led Kiera over to the others. "Will you be okay?" she asked.

"Go," Kiera said.

Carillo propelled herself toward the med bay.

"What can I do?" Kiera asked. She held out her hands and felt around blindly. "I want to help."

Morgan took hold of her hand and guided it to Shilling's wrist. "Walk with us. Feel for his pulse. Tell me if it drops."

"Roger that."

"Okay, Ajay, let him float up. You get his feet, I'll take his shoulders. You ready, Kiera?"

"Yes."

"Ajay?"

"Let's do it."

DR. KIERA WALSH'S CABIN — THE *RORSCHACH EXPLORER*

No matter how many times Kiera blinked, darkness shrouded her vision. And the more she dabbed away the unending stream of fluid leaking from her tear ducts, the faster the fluid returned. Raw and throbbing, her eyes felt like hot coals burning their way into her head.

Curled into a fetal position on her bunk, she squeezed her eyelids tight and whispered, "This can't be happening."

Though she couldn't see Ajay, she could hear him — the creaking of the bench he sat on, the long sighs that rose and fell like waves, the growls of his stomach. He hadn't spoken much since escorting her here, and she considered his silence a blessing. She didn't want his sympathy, nor was she capable of returning it. She just wanted to fall asleep and forget everything that had happened. She wanted to block out the feeling of hopelessness eating away inside.

Was Morgan right? Was her blindness only temporary? She supposed if she'd been able to see the look on his face, take stock of his body language, she might have been more reassured. But his usual steely confidence had seemed absent from his voice alone.

She couldn't blame him. What a disaster — Shilling electrocuted, aliens invading the ship, hordes of UMOs in complete control of the ship's speed and direction. Oh, and not to mention they'd lost all comms with Mayaguana, all their probes were gone, Carillo was talking to balls of light, there was another alien life-form lurking about … and the ship's flight engineer was now completely blind.

Kiera sniffled and wiped away another trickle sliding down her cheek. The bench creaked, and she felt the weight of Ajay's hand on her shoulder. He slid it along her arm until he reached her hand crooked beneath her chin. Wrapping his fingers around hers, he squeezed.

Under any other circumstance, Kiera would have batted his hand away, but now she lacked the strength to fight the gesture. Instead, in the icy darkness, she laced her fingers through his and squeezed back.

Ajay released a deep sigh, his warm breath rippling over their bonded hands.

MEDICAL BAY — THE *RORSCHACH EXPLORER*

Morgan found Carillo seated on the edge of the examining table, staring at the wall, still dressed in her bloodstained clothes.

"I thought you were going to change your dressings."

"Wasn't feeling it," Carillo said, her eyes still fixed on the wall.

Morgan looked past her to Shilling, strapped to another table. "How's he doing?"

"Stable," Carillo said. "His legs twitched a little while ago but he hasn't woken up. How's Kiera?"

"She's shaken up, but she's tough. She'll get it together." Morgan began to gather up items to re-treat and re-dress Carillo's burns.

"What about her vision?"

"Don't know. Time will tell."

Morgan was betting — hoping — Kiera's blindness was a temporary reaction to the brightness of the strobe-like bursts emitted by the alien life-form locked in combat with the BLUMOs. Those bursts had definitely had a sunlight quality, suggesting they contained ultraviolet radiation. If that was the case, and Kiera's eyes hadn't been exposed to the damaging rays for too long, she would probably recover her vision within a day or two. During that time, the best remedies available to soothe her sunburned eyes were cold packs and darkness.

"And Ajay?" Carillo asked.

Morgan snapped a covered tray to the table's edge. "Lie back."

Carillo reclined on the table with her legs draped over the side. Morgan guided her legs up and extended the table's leg panel.

She looked up at him. "Um, hello … ? How is Ajay?"

"He'll be okay."

She frowned. "Your face says otherwise."

What the hell am I supposed to say? Morgan thought. *That he's nearly comatose with shock?* It was amazing that Ajay had held himself together long enough to disable the autopilot thrusters and fire up *Rorschach*'s engines during the alien throwdown. Even more stupefying was how he rushed to Shilling's aid moments after the scientist was stricken, despite the potential risk of getting zapped by the BLUMOs himself. Morgan had heard tales about the uncommon valor exhibited by the least likely of soldiers during the heat of battle, but he'd never personally witnessed such a display until now.

Yet Ajay's courageous acts had come with a price. When the craziness on the flight deck had subsided, and his brain had the chance to soak in everything that had happened, Ajay just … shut down.

Would he rebound?

Morgan planned to give both Kiera and Ajay twenty-four hours to work through the shock, and then he would try to rally them. If they were able to break free from the BLUMOs, it would be a long journey back to Earth, and he would need them both.

"That was a lot for Ajay to take in," he said. "Hell, it was a lot for *me* to take in."

Carillo gripped his hand. "It was a lot for all of us."

"Yeah, well, it's over now … I hope."

"Me too." She let go of Morgan's hand and looked over at Shilling. "They didn't mean to hurt him. I'm sure of it. They were just trying to protect her."

"I do want to talk about your new friends, but we need to take care of your burns first. Can't afford to risk infection. How're you doing pain-wise?"

"I wouldn't say no to a reload."

"Okay, we've got two options. I can inject you with morphine or we've got topical lidocaine. If your pain is primarily coming from the burns, I'd suggest going with the lidocaine. It'll keep your mind clearer than the morphine will."

"Paul, there's not an inch of my body that doesn't hurt, inside or out."

"Got it. Morphine it is."

Morgan uncovered the tray and retrieved a syringe from its strapped-down contents. He slotted its needle into the medication port inserted into the back of Carillo's hand and injected the pain medication.

After a moment, Carillo smiled, and her eyes closed. "Oh, that feels much better."

Morgan exchanged the syringe for a pair of scissors. "So, do you still want to do this yourself, or should I?"

She opened her eyes and laughed. "Go ahead. Everyone else apparently got a peep show the first time around. Might as well make it a clean sweep."

"I'll drape you as best I can, but I don't want to contaminate your wounds."

"Don't worry about it. Modesty is real low on my priority list right now."

Morgan first strapped her hands, feet, head and waist to the table. Otherwise as soon as he cut away her magnetic clothing, she would float in the cabin's weightless atmosphere. Then he used the shears to slice open the center line of her shirt.

"Tell me about the UMOs," he said. "I take it the white light was the *she* you keep mentioning. The BLUMO queen?"

"I don't know if she's the queen, but she definitely seemed to be the one in charge," Carillo said.

"How does she communicate with you?"

"It's weird. It's not like I hear voices in my head or anything like that. I just have thoughts pop in my mind. You know, not my thoughts, but hers."

"What kinds of thoughts?"

"They're simple. Direct."

Morgan gently peeled back the two halves of the rust-stained shirt and pinned the floating pieces of fabric underneath Carillo's arms. There were two bandages near her shoulders and another just below her breasts. Blood had soaked through all three. He removed the first of the bandages.

"What do you mean by simple and direct?"

Carillo described the string of thoughts that had filled her consciousness when the UMOs first woke her. *Get up. Hurry. It's coming.*

Morgan stopped in the middle of cleaning the wound. "They woke you up? How?"

"They zapped me again," she said.

"What? Where?"

"Forehead. Right above my eyes."

Morgan leaned over to examine her forehead. "I don't see any burns. It's not even red."

"It hurt, sort of like a really bad headache, but it didn't last long. When it was over, I opened my eyes and saw them. Then came the thoughts. Her thoughts."

Morgan applied antibiotic ointment to the wound and covered it with a fresh bandage. As he moved on to the next one, he recalled how Nick Reed

had inexplicably awoken from a brain-dead state with the ability to communicate with the UMOs. Had he received a similar UMO wake-up call?

"And you can answer her?" he asked.

"Have to keep my thoughts short and sweet, but yeah."

Morgan recalled a comment Reed had made in one of his *Cetus Prime*
video logs: *I asked them to take us home, but it looks like they thought I
asked them to take us to their leader.*

"She didn't understand you when you told them to leave the ship," he said.

"That's right. How did you know?"

"You were kind of locked in on each other. The white light kept
flickering."

"It's not easy to communicate. I had the same problem when I asked her
to end the ramming and spinning of the ship. She kept answering ... get away.
Then when I tried to tell her to leave, I couldn't get through to her. I kept
thinking ... go away. She kept answering back ... get away."

"How did you finally get the message across?"

"I got angry. Told her they were hurting us."

When Morgan had finished treating and dressing the burns on
Carillo's torso, he cut away her sleeves and followed the same process with
her forearms. Finally he retrieved a fresh tunic from a cabinet, loosened
the straps holding her upper body to the table, and helped her slide on
the new garment. Then he guided her shoulders back down.

"We're in the home stretch," he said.

Carillo looked down at her pants. "Am I wearing anything
underneath?"

"Don't know. Wasn't part of the triage, remember? I passed out in the
airlock."

She pulled her waistband out a small way and peered down. "The
indignity continues."

"Relax. Keep 'em on. I can cut the pant legs to get to the burns. You
can slip on a new pair after we're all done."

"Okay. Deal."

Morgan cut the legs of Carillo's pants from her ankles to upper thighs,
then cleaned and dressed the burn blisters marring her legs at mid-thigh.

As he worked, he told her about the reports from Mayaguana, including their speculation about why the UMOs had zapped her. He also briefed her on Ajay's VLF recordings, Kiera's conclusion about the two queens singing to each other and Shilling's panicked attempt to escape.

"Geez, how long was I out?"

Morgan applied the last of the bandages. "Don't know. I was out, too. I'd say the better part of a day."

He retrieved a fresh pair of pants from the cabinet and handed them to her. While she changed from her tattered pair into the new ones, he removed the tray and turned to stow the leftover supplies.

"So what now?" Carillo asked.

"Good question. If we were free to maneuver, if we had comms, I'd shoot Augie a message and tell him we're scrubbing and coming home."

Her wardrobe change complete, she stepped up beside him. "We don't have comms?"

Morgan shook his head. "We haven't heard from Maya in quite a while. Under the circumstances, you can be sure they wouldn't go silent on us. And I don't think there's a problem with our antennas. I think the BLUMOs are blocking any signals in or out."

"They're still with us?"

"Oh yeah they are. You can't sense them?"

"No, but I haven't really tried."

"Well, we're going to need you to try pretty soon. I'd hoped they'd disperse after the queen left, but they're still out there, an enormous spinning ball of them with us in the middle ... and they're pushing the hell out of us."

Morgan explained that the BLUMOs had accelerated *Rorschach* to a speed that would put them in reach of Callisto's orbit within sixteen days — nearly two and a half months earlier than planned.

"How is that possible?"

Morgan shrugged. "Chalk it up to the freaky deaky bubble they create. And I have a feeling they haven't even broken a sweat. They *sped up* when I turned off the engines."

On the way from the medical bay to the flight deck, Morgan and Carillo detoured to check in on Kiera and Ajay and discovered their cabins were vacant. As they emerged back into the main corridor, they heard sounds of movement emanating from the rear of the ship. They followed the noises and came upon Kiera and Ajay in the storage room, in the process of offloading the supplies from *Cargo-4*. The blindfolded Kiera was on her knees, shifting containers to make space for the ones Ajay carried through the airlock.

Kiera turned her head in their direction. "Is that you, Colonel Morgan?"

Ajay ducked through the airlock carrying a large storage case. He smiled and put the case down. "It's Colonel Morgan *and* Major Carillo."

"What are you two doing?" Morgan asked.

"We're prepping the Cargo for the VLF antenna install," Kiera said.

"I see. How much more to go?"

"Hmmm. There were fifty-six cases when we started, so that leaves … fourteen more to go. Counting the one Ajay just put down."

"You want some help?" Carillo asked.

"No, we're good. Thanks, though."

"All right," Morgan said. "When you two finish up, meet us in the ready room."

"Roger dodger," Ajay said with a quick salute.

As Morgan and Carillo turned to leave, Morgan mumbled, "So much for the need to rally them."

A short while later, Ajay appeared at the door to the ready room. He turned back toward the corridor. "Just a little further, Kiera. Three more steps."

"I'm fine. Go ahead in, I'll be right there," she said.

"Okay." Ajay nodded to Morgan and Carillo and joined them at the conference table.

Kiera's fingers wrapped around the door frame to steady herself, then she stepped into view as her free hand felt for the other side of the door. "Everybody in their usual places?" she asked.

"Yep," Carillo said.

"Good. I don't want to sit on anyone's lap by mistake."

She slid her hand along the wall, following it to the first corner and across the back wall. When she reached the next corner, she turned toward the table, stepped forward, and said, "Moment of truth."

"A little to your—"

"Shhh, Elroy. I'll tell you if I need help," Kiera said.

With her arms extended, she reached for the chair she normally occupied. She hit it with the back of her right hand, and it swiveled away from her grasp. Edging her thighs against the table, she bent down and snagged the back of the chair on her second try. As she lowered herself onto the seat, she said, "Sorry for the circus act. I'll get better at it."

"Hopefully you won't have to," Morgan said.

"I like the way you think, Skywalker." Kiera smiled. "Now, what's the dealio?"

"Well, we've got some decisions to make."

Morgan outlined their current situation. That the ship was still under the control of the BLUMOs, and they were heading for Callisto at a hyper-accelerated rate. That communication with Mayaguana was still out — whether that was temporary or not, he couldn't tell. And that, with their probe fleet gone, they would have to rely on the supplies aboard the ship and those offloaded from the Cargos.

"I'm sure Augie will launch relief supplies once we've reestablished comms, but under the best of circumstances, they won't link up with us anytime soon," he continued. "Which brings me to our most immediate problem. We will be through the asteroid belt in less than a week."

"And we have no Shields," Kiera said.

"That's right. Unless the BLUMOs are capable of blocking Jupiter's radiation, we're going to have problems."

"Can you talk to them, Major?" Ajay asked. "Tell them the radiation will kill us?"

Carillo shrugged. "I don't know if I can summon the queen, but it makes sense to try as soon as we get the VLF antenna set up."

Kiera raised a hand. "Um ... I missed the whole queen-on-the-bridge thing during my meltdown. How do you talk with her?"

Carillo ran through the same explanation she'd given Morgan, and Kiera said, "That's pretty cool. It fits what Dr. Cully said about how swarms communicate ... and what he said about queens."

"Dr. Cully?" Carillo said.

"Yeah, he wrote one of the reports Maya sent us," Kiera said. "He said colonies don't have a leader during a swarm attack. They respond to the actions of the colony members closest to the threat."

"I'm not sure I see the connection."

"Oh, sorry. You mentioned your dialogue with the queen was based on direct, simple exchanges. Dr. Cully said that swarm communications are short and sweet. They have to be, in order to quickly pass information through the colony when dealing with a threat."

"Well, they sure seemed coordinated when they attacked us and our probes," Morgan said.

"I haven't forgotten the pack hunting," Kiera said. "But Dr. Cully seemed to think the BLUMOs have a pack alpha separate from the queen. I mean, think about their attack on the other alien. The queen was with us, far away from the attack."

"True," Morgan said, "and only some of the BLUMOs surrounding us went after the alien. The rest stayed behind us, pushing us."

"What *was* that alien thing anyway?" Ajay asked. "It looked like a big, spidery cloud."

"Julia?" Morgan asked.

"Don't look at me. I have no idea what it was."

"You said the BLUMOs had been hunting it. That they didn't like it."

"That's the vibe I got from the queen, but that's all I sensed." She frowned.

"Everything okay?" Morgan asked. "You look troubled."

"No, I'm fine. I was just thinking about what Kiera said about the queen. That she stayed far away from the attack."

"That's right," Kiera said. "Dr. Cully said queens don't usually take part in swarms. They're too valuable to risk."

"And you think she hid with us?" Carillo asked.

"Uh-huh."

Carillo's eyes widened. "Oh my God. She wasn't trying to tell *us* to get away. She was asking us to help *her* get away." She leapt from her seat.

Morgan called after her. "Where are you going?"

"Aft. She's still aboard, Paul. That's why they're surrounding us, why they're pushing us so hard."

She was gone by the time Morgan processed the implication. When it hit him, he popped out of his seat. "That other alien must be chasing us."

"Um, Colonel?" Ajay said. "May I say something?"

Morgan turned in the doorway. "Make it fast."

"Aren't we forgetting about someone? The other queen? The one coming from Callisto?"

"Jesus, I totally forgot about that. You two go to the lab and see if you can pick up the whale songs again, find out where that other queen is now. I'm going aft with Julia. Let me know as soon as you've got a fix on the Callisto queen."

CHAPTER 13

ICARUS

OFFICE OF THE CHIEF ADMINISTRATOR
NASA HEADQUARTERS
WASHINGTON, D.C.
SEPTEMBER 5, 2019

At 5:15 a.m., Helen Brock gave up on the idea of trying to get back to sleep. She took a quick shower, dressed, hopped in her car, stopped by her local coffee shop for the biggest cup-o-Joe they sold and drove to NASA headquarters.

When she arrived at 6:40 a.m., reporters and camera crews were already setting up on the street outside the building. This came as no surprise, given the scene Brock had come upon in the coffee shop. Normally the shop bustled with music and chatter, even at six a.m. But today, even though the place was packed with customers, everyone was silent, their eyes glued to the early morning news on the shop's television. They seemed caught in a trance as they watched the video loop of the Saturn flashes and listened to experts debate the possible causes.

As she stood now by her office window, she was just thankful no one had recognized her. That would have made for a dicey wait for her coffee. But she knew that had been only a short-term reprieve. The media expected answers from NASA, and she would be the one to provide them.

While much of what she planned to say about the flashes had already been leaked by overly excited employees or theorized by scientists brought in for interviews, Brock knew the press was eager for NASA's official position. And that would be impossible to deliver this morning given the recency of the events and the amount of data that still needed to be collected and analyzed.

Given the rampant speculation spreading across the globe, she knew the media wouldn't want to hear her say the agency needed more time to noodle on data, so the press conference was likely to turn ugly. They would push her to provide definitive answers and to render judgment on the various theories taking hold among experts and the public. Some of those theories dovetailed with Brock's short list of possible explanations, but without more data it would be reckless to discuss them.

The media couldn't appreciate the enormity of NASA's task. Because so many observatories around the globe had trained their telescopes and instruments on Saturn after the first flash, they had been in perfect positions to capture data during the later flurry. While the abundance of data was a blessing, it was also a curse. Most of those observatories were under no obligation to share their data with NASA. As a result, it would take time to determine who had captured what data and then negotiate for access to the information.

A knock sounded on her open office door. Her assistant, Mary Evans, said, "Dr. Brock, the president is on line one."

"Okay, thanks."

Evans left, closing the door on her way out.

Brock sat down at her desk and picked up the phone. This would be her first conversation with President Andrew Jennings since she was installed as NASA's chief administrator. Jennings was in the throes of a withering congressional investigation into the actions he and his administration had taken to suppress Amato's discoveries on Callisto; as such, he considered NASA a hot potato and had backed away from any direct contact with the space agency for fear that members of Congress would claim he was trying to influence the investigation. Calls for impeachment were already at a fever pitch as it was.

"Good morning, Mr. President."

"Morning, Dr. Brock. Understand you've had a long night."

"Yes, sir, it's certainly been one of the longest I can recall."

"I imagine so." Jennings paused for a few seconds, then said, "Look, Dr. Brock, there are a lot of theories being tossed around. I'd like to know NASA's view on the flashes before you speak with the press."

"I understand, Mr. President. I wish I could provide you with a definitive answer, but we don't have enough data to—"

"The Pentagon tells me there were radiation trails after the flashes that led toward Saturn."

"That's correct." A number of observatories had recorded streams of X-ray and gamma rays after the flashes had faded. The streams had arced toward Saturn, but the radiation readings had disappeared once the streams passed behind Dione, an inner moon of Saturn.

"Could the flashes have been a natural phenomenon?"

The short answer was no. The trails showed evidence of non-ballistic maneuvering. "We think it's unlikely, but we can't rule that possibility out."

"Then what? UMOs? Alien spaceships? Another kind of alien life-form?"

All three options sounded preposterous, yet Brock considered all three equally possible. "As I said, we don't have enough data to reach a conclusion."

"I saw some cock-a-doodle on TV who thinks the flashes were a message," Jennings said.

"Yes, sir. As crazy as it sounds, we have a group of NASA physicists exploring that very possibility." Thus far, they had examined the timing of the seven flashes as well as the comparative frequency and location of each burst. "We can't discern a pattern. It doesn't mean there isn't one, but we've only had a few hours to study the data."

"What's your gut tell you, Brock?"

Given the recent departure of the UMOs from Callisto and the non-ballistic maneuvering detected in the radiation trails, it was within reason to speculate a linkage between the flashes and UMOs. However, there had never been a previous example of UMOs emitting X-rays or gamma rays. Plus, the distance between Callisto and the flashes was so vast, it seemed impossible that the Callisto UMOs could have traveled so far in so short a time.

Was it possible there was a colony, or colonies, of UMOs around Saturn? In Brock's opinion, the answer was a resounding yes. Saturn's magnetic field, while not as strong as Jupiter's, was still very powerful. And Dione was similar to Callisto in many ways.

And just last year, Amato's team had observed a bright flash from a dividing ball of UMOs during what appeared to be a mating ritual. Of course, the Saturn flashes were exponentially more intense than the one Amato's CubeSat recorded.

"Sir, if I had to hazard a guess … "

"You do," Jennings said.

"I'd lean toward UMO activity. It's certainly more plausible than another life-form."

"What about alien ships? That seems to be the running favorite on the networks."

Brock could understand why. Everyone knew the UMOs had been de-icing the spaceport on Callisto, and it stood to reason that they were doing so because they expected something, or someone, to land there. And seeing as the *Cetus Prime* crew had already indicated that the Callistons and UMOs shared a special relationship, and the UMOs had remained behind after the Callistons abandoned the facility, it wasn't a stretch to speculate that it was the arrival of the Callistons that the UMOs were preparing for. Augie Amato had surely reached this conclusion as well. That was why he moved up the launch of the *Rorschach* fleet — to travel to Callisto in time to either meet the Callistons or leave a message of greetings for them.

Arguing against the possibility of alien ships as the sources of the flashes, Calliston or otherwise, was the fact that no instruments had detected radiation signatures in the vicinity of the flashes before they occurred. The flashes just appeared spontaneously.

"I know it sounds wishy-washy, Mr. President, but we just don't have enough data yet to say one way or the other."

"All right, Brock, I understand. How far are you planning to go when you speak to the press?"

"I'm going to stick to the facts. There's no benefit in speculating without more data."

"Sounds like a wise strategy. One last question and I'll get out of your hair. Do you think there's a connection between the flashes and the disappearance of Amato's spacecraft?"

This would be a delicate answer, Brock thought.

"On the record? Other than suspicious timing, there's nothing to suggest a connection. The *Rorschach Explorer* was in the asteroid belt when contact was lost. The flashes occurred over a billion kilometers away. The flash trails lead to Saturn. *Rorschach* was headed to Callisto."

"And *off* the record?"

"Between you and me and the fly on the wall, I'd bet everything I own they're *directly* linked."

MAIN CORRIDOR — THE *RORSCHACH EXPLORER*
FLYING THROUGH THE ASTEROID BELT

Carillo sat on the floor at the junction of the main corridor and the perpendicular corridor leading to the crew's cabins. With her eyes closed and hands on her lap, she took several deep breaths and cleared her mind. Morgan, she knew, stood a few feet behind her, scanning both corridors for blue lights.

"*Come,*" she thought. "*I need you.*"

She waited for half a minute. No thoughts pressed into her consciousness, but she did feel her fingers and ears tingle.

Again, she tried to summon the BLUMO queen.

"*Come. Come now.*"

Her concentration was broken by Morgan's voice. "Are you picking up anything?"

Carillo shook her head. "She hasn't answered me yet, but I think she's close by."

"How can you tell?"

"My skin is prickling." Even as she spoke, the tingling sensation intensified, then circled her head. Carillo opened her eyes. "Actually ... I think she's here."

"Where?"

As if on cue, a white ball of light slowly became visible two feet in front of Carillo's face. A swirl of blue lights faded into view around the queen, racing around the white light.

Carillo smiled and projected a new thought. "*Hello.*"

The white light pulsed.

Carillo closed her eyes. "*Danger? Are you in danger? Are we in danger?*"

The blue lights flashed brighter, and a thin bolt of lightning shot forth and hit Carillo in the forehead. She cringed and fell backward.

Morgan caught her. "Break it off, Julia. Right now."

She raised her hand and rubbed the spot where they'd zapped her. "No, it's okay. She was just delivering a message."

"What message?"

"Shhh. I'm getting a vision."

An image formed in Carillo's mind: a glowing, snake-like creature shooting out tendrils of electricity from all down its length. The tendrils looked like electrical fingers trying to snatch at invisible objects. But each time the fingers reached the peak of their projection and began to curl back toward the snake, they pulsed, and a pinkish cloud oozed from their tips. Brilliant sparkles soon began to dot the pink cloud.

The image slowly faded, and Carillo sat back up, pulling away from Morgan's hold.

"We were right, Paul. The other alien is still out there." She described the creature to Morgan. "In a roundabout way, she says we're in danger."

"What can we do?" he asked.

"Let me find out."

She closed her eyes and formed a new thought. "*Help? Can we help?*"

She felt a wave of relief pass through her body.

She projected another thought. "*We can? Is that what you mean? How? How can we help? What can we do?*"

The wave passed through a second time, accompanied by a thought that popped into her mind. "*Help is coming.*"

Carillo opened her eyes and turned to Morgan. "She says help is coming."

"She must mean the Callisto queen."

Carillo posed a new question to the queen. "*Who is coming? More like you?*"

There was no answer at first, but both the blue and white lights began to flicker in unison.

"What's happening?" Morgan asked.

"I don't know."

A grapefruit-sized ball of spinning blue lights appeared farther down the hallway. It slowly drifted toward the smaller ball surrounding the queen.

"Would you look at that!" Morgan said.

The larger ball merged with the queen's ball right in front of Carillo. And the instant the merge was complete, a strange vision filled Carillo's mind. Shivers raced through her body.

"Whoa," she said.

"What's wrong?"

"She showed me who's coming."

"Who?"

Carillo closed her eyes and tried to make sense of the vision. Focusing her thoughts, she asked the queen to repeat the vision.

"*Again. Show me again.*"

A one-word response leapt into her mind.

"*Stand.*"

Carillo uncurled her crossed legs and pushed herself to her feet. She felt Morgan step up beside her and take her hand.

Another spinning ball of BLUMOs appeared down the hallway, this one the size of a beach ball. It, too, moved forward and merged with the queen's cluster. Together they pulsed — and the vision flowed through Carillo's mind again. This time she noticed more details.

"Incredible."

"What? What's incredible?" Morgan asked.

"They're pack hunters, all right. They're leading the creature into a trap. We're the bait."

"Excuse me?"

"They showed me their plan. Pretty soon we're going to turn to starboard toward two asteroids. That's where they've set up their kill zone."

"But — why would they use us as bait? Their queen is with us. Aren't they supposed to protect her?"

"She's not the queen. That's just a ruse to fool the creature." Carillo pointed to the white light. "She's the pack alpha. The queen is the one who's coming. Trust me, you'll see what I mean when we meet up with her."

Ajay appeared from the lab compartment ahead of the junction. But when he saw the blue-white lights by Carillo's head, he froze.

"It's okay," Morgan said. "What's up, Ajay?"

At that moment the ship lurched to the right. GEFF failed to compensate quickly enough to the sudden change in velocity and, despite the neutralizing gravity effect of the BLUMO bubble around the ship, the three crew members toppled to the floor and crashed against the corridor's portside wall.

Ajay rolled over and faced Morgan. "We've got a big problem," Ajay said. "There's something huge coming up on us fast from behind."

Morgan looked at Carillo. "Looks like you read the vision right."

She nodded. "It's okay, Ajay. We know. It's all right."

"No, you don't understand," Ajay said. "We're trapped. Radar shows there's something even bigger coming at us head-on!"

As the ship continued to turn toward the BLUMO trap, Morgan hoisted his body up with the assistance of the corridor railing. As he reached down to help Carillo to her feet, he called to Ajay. "Get Kiera. Bring her to the flight deck."

"Roger dodger." Ajay toggled off his GEFF magnets and, with a push against the wall, he flew through the lab compartment door with the elegance of an Olympic swimmer leaping off the starting stand.

As Morgan and Carillo walked toward the flight deck with their bodies pressed against the wall and the BLUMO alpha and her entourage trailing behind, Morgan asked Carillo to describe the vision the BLUMOs had shared.

"There are millions of UMOs hiding behind the two asteroids," she said. "The BLUMOs with us are going to pass between the asteroids. When the creature flies through the gap, the Callisto UMOs on each side of the gap are going to attack."

"And what happens to us?" Morgan asked.

"What do you mean?"

"Once we fly through the gap, what happens to us?"

Carillo paused and frowned. "I don't know. I don't remember the vision showing that. I can ask."

"No. Don't."

"Why not?"

They entered the flight deck and moved to their stations. As they buckled into their safety harnesses, Morgan shot Carillo a look. The BLUMOs were floating behind her headrest.

"Can they read your mind?" he asked.

"What?"

"The BLUMOs, do you think they can read your mind?"

"How would I know?"

"Have they anticipated a question before you asked them?"

Carillo thought about that for a moment. "No. I don't think so."

"Good, that means we have a chance."

As the ship slowed and resumed a straight-line heading, Ajay and the blindfolded Kiera floated through the doorway, holding hands.

"A chance for what, Colonel?" Kiera asked.

"Both of you, get strapped in," Morgan said.

"What about Dr. Shilling?" asked Ajay.

"We're just going to have to hope the gurney straps hold. No time for anything else."

He began typing in commands at the commander's station while Ajay assisted Kiera into her seat and buckled her in.

"What's up your sleeve, Paul?" asked Carillo.

"I'll tell you in a sec. First, do me a favor and give Kiera and Ajay a rundown on what's going on."

Carillo repeated the basics of the BLUMOs' plan to kill the creature pursuing them. Then she turned back to Morgan. "Now, what are you planning to do?"

"Can you create a diversion for me?" Morgan asked.

"What kind of diversion?"

"Can you engage the alpha in a conversation?"

"About what?"

"Don't care. Something to distract her. Ask her to tell you more about the creature. Ask her where the UMOs behind the asteroids came from. Hell, ask her about the weather on Jupiter. Just keep her engaged for as long as you can."

"Okay, I'll try."

As Carillo swiveled her seat to face the BLUMOs, Morgan said to Ajay, "Take a look at your messages."

"My messages?"

"Yeah. I sent you something."

Ajay activated the crew messaging app on his console and read the message from Morgan. *Going to attempt to break away from BLUMOs as soon as we pass through the gap. Need you to prepare to transmit message to Maya on all bands, I'll have my hands full. Text of message to follow. Acknowledge.*

A smile formed on Ajay's face. He typed a reply. *Roger dodger, Skywalker.*

You'll have to act quick, Morgan typed. *If we break out and they aren't content to let us go, they'll quickly envelop us again. But I'm hoping they're more interested in their prey than they are their bait. Stand by for Maya message text.*

Copy that.

Kiera had apparently heard the flurry of typing. "Anyone gonna clue the blind girl in?" she asked.

"Sorry, no time," Morgan said. "Just hold on tight and wish us luck."

The white light at the center of the BLUMO ball flickered each time Carillo posed her questions, but the alpha didn't respond. She filled her mind with the vision the alpha had shared and asked again.

"*The creature. Why kill?*"

A rush of dread passed through Carillo — and with it came a thought from the alpha. "*Danger.*"

"*Why danger? Does it hurt you?*"

"*They are coming.*"

The answer puzzled Carillo. It was almost as if the BLUMO didn't understand her question. Did the pack leader mean more of the creatures were coming? Was that the danger? Was the sensation of dread intended to convey that the UMOs were capable of killing one of the creatures, but not more?

"More creatures? Are more coming?"

The white light flickered. In the background, Carillo heard Morgan telling Kiera to hold on tight. Carillo reached up and tightened her harness. As the straps pressed against her shoulders and chest, she felt stabs of pain and groaned.

"Julia, are you okay?" Morgan asked.

She loosened the straps. "Pain meds are wearing off."

A thought from the alpha flashed into her mind. *"Hurt. You are hurt."*

"Yes," Carillo responded. *"You hurt me. You hurt others. No more hurting. We are friends."*

The flickering from the alpha spread to the BLUMOs in the surrounding ball. They pulsed in unison, and a gap began to form in the center of the spinning ball. Then the white light moved out through the hole.

"Colonel," Ajay said, "something's happening. The white light is coming out. It's touching Major Carillo."

"Never mind, Ajay. Pay attention to the transmitters. Coming up on the gap in under a minute. Stay focused."

As the alpha bumped up against the wound beneath her breasts, Carillo felt throbs of warmth penetrate her flight suit and soothe the burn. Then the alpha backed away and retreated inside the protective network of her blue escorts.

A new thought pushed into Carillo's mind. It was a repeat of the earlier communication. *"They are coming."*

"I don't understand," Carillo answered.

Morgan's voice overlapped the alpha's reply. "Here we go. Ajay, you ready?"

"Roger."

Carillo spun her seat around to look out the flight deck window. To the left, beyond the sphere of BLUMOs surrounding the ship, was one of the two asteroids. It looked like nothing more than an inky blob that blocked the canvas of stars in the background. To the right, she saw only stars.

And then the first streak of golden light peeked from behind the asteroid, and Morgan began a countdown. "Ten ... nine ... eight ... " One of his hands reached for the thruster panel, the other for the engine controls.

Carillo gripped her armrests, and a rush of panic flowed through her. A bolt from the BLUMO ball struck her in the head. The alpha screamed into her consciousness. "*No! Friends!*"

Another bolt shot out, this one hitting Morgan's shoulder as he reached three in his countdown.

"What's happening?" shouted Kiera.

Morgan doubled over, his arm quivering.

"We're trying to get away," Ajay said. "The BLUMOs just zapped Skywalker and—"

The ship vaulted forward. Kiera apparently hadn't needed to hear more. Fumbling her hand over the auxiliary engine control panel at her station, she'd turned the VLF engines on and set them at full power. As the propulsion system roared to life, she reached for the thruster panel. "How close are we to the asteroids?"

"Stay on course, stay on course!" Ajay said. "We're punching through."

Enormous flashes exploded all around the *Rorschach Explorer*, shooting blinding rays of white through the flight deck windows. Ajay hit the send button before the flashes overwhelmed his vision.

The pack alpha, slow in its interpretation of Kiera's and Ajay's actions, now swirled into a buzzing frenzy and shot bolts of lightning at the heads of all four crewmembers. Before Carillo passed out, she sensed the alpha's thoughts once more. "*Friends! They are coming!*"

Carillo would not know it until she awoke, but the same thoughts penetrated the minds of her shipmates, along with a stream of images.

A planet ... but it wasn't Jupiter.

A moon ... but not Callisto.

A crater with a spaceport ... but it looked nothing like Nuada.

And a spaceship ... unlike anything the four had ever seen.

AUGUSTUS AMATO'S OFFICE
A3ROSPACE INDUSTRIES COMMAND AND CONTROL CENTER
MAYAGUANA ISLAND, THE BAHAMAS

Through bleary eyes, Amato stared at the painting of the *Rorschach Explorer* flying through space. Its engines glowing and hull gleaming, the proud ship angled toward a purple nebula in some far-off region of the universe. The painting was among several *Rorschach* tributes that graced Amato's office walls, showing the ship gliding toward distant galaxies, orbiting strange planets or landing on alien worlds. The artist had successfully projected a sense of wonder — wouldn't it be amazing to visit such places and see such things.

That's how Amato felt, and it was how he wanted other people to feel. Whether through his Gateway to the Stars museum, his Living Universe garden, the *Rorschach Explorer* or other efforts to share his vision with the world, Amato wanted to inspire people to imagine the possibilities and think boldly about how to turn them into realities.

In looking upon this painting now, however, Amato felt like a shyster. He'd oversold the magic of space exploration — to his colleagues, the public and himself — and he'd underplayed the dangers. It wasn't that he hadn't understood the risks. He was, after all, a man who'd spent his entire professional lifetime in the space-exploration business. He'd been a first-hand witness to a number of NASA's tragedies and an inside observer of others.

What had sent him veering off course was his lack of patience with those who placed too much emphasis on the risks. In many ways, Amato believed the entire concept of manned space flight had fallen prey to the management of risk. Bold moves early in the space program, ones that should have catapulted man into deep space within decades, had fallen back to Earth as the worry-mongers grew in number. Year by year, they whittled down the aspirations of manned missions from exploring the solar system to rotations aboard an orbiting laboratory. Not exactly the stuff of Buck Rogers or Captain Kirk.

And now those same worry-mongers were in ascension. Amato's critics were howling at his hubris — none louder than Dr. Richard Collins. The outspoken scientist had even tagged Amato with a new nickname that had caught on in the media. "Icarus Amato," the man who said be damned with risk.

"Only, unlike Icarus," Collins had crowed when he first coined the nickname on Nigel Ewing's show, "Amato didn't try to fly to the Sun himself. Instead, he sent five innocent people to die for him."

Amato was so immersed in his thoughts he didn't hear the commotion in the hallway outside his office until Mark Myers opened the door. Sounds of jubilation followed the smiling Myers into the office.

"We've received a downlink from *Rorschach!*"

Amato rose from his chair and grabbed his cane. But he had walked no more than a dozen steps toward the door before the celebration pouring from Mission Control came to an abrupt halt. He paused and listened to the new sounds. Dante was rattling instructions over the center's intercom and, in the background, Amato could detect fast-paced chatter and a few angry voices.

Resuming his walk, Amato prepared for the worst. Whatever *Rorschach* had downlinked, it was sobering enough to stamp out the euphoria caused by the transmission's arrival. He thought of Icarus again and mumbled an apology to the crew.

"I should have known better."

CHAPTER 14

OVERLOAD

N o one even noticed Amato as he entered Mission Control. The station controllers were either glued to their consoles or engaged in discussions with colleagues. Pritchard sat by the instrumentation and communications officer as the young woman pointed at her display. Dante hovered over a seated group of Whave Technologies' technicians, peering at their data screens. There was a sense of urgency throughout the room, but none of the people looked despondent. This was not a team confronting the aftermath of a disaster, Amato realized. They were responding to a crisis, that much was certain, but their actions and body language said there was hope.

Myers came up beside him. "Do you want me to get Dante for you?"

"No, let's not distract him."

Pritchard spotted Amato and gave a quick wave. Turning to a controller standing nearby, he handed the man a piece of paper and pointed toward Amato. The man dashed over with the note.

"Message from Skywalker."

The man sped back to his station before Amato could thank him.

Amato handed his cane to Myers and gripped the page with both hands.

CDR-TRE to MAYA-FLIGHT: Good news: CCDR has established direct communication with BLUMO pack alpha a la Nick Reed. Bad news: BLUMO pack alpha aboard TRE and in control of flight dynamics and comms. Heading toward Callisto at 7X VLF max. MSRS critically injured by BLUMOs. Cardiac arrest from electric shock. Revived MSRS but vitals shallow. FE blinded by UV exposure during conflict between BLUMOs surrounding TRE and 2nd ... repeat ... 2nd alien life-form. Hoping FE blindness temporary. CDR and MSAJ attempting TRE escape from BLUMO pack. If successful, aborting mission and returning to Earth. If unsuccessful, will attempt to determine alpha intentions and negotiate release. Keep us in your prayers. CDR-TRE out.

The mix of good news and bad was overwhelming. It was heartening to learn Morgan and Carillo were back in action, but troubling to read of Shilling's and Kiera's injuries. The establishment of direct dialogue with the UMOs was a welcome development, but their seizing of *Rorschach* was not. And then there was the mention of a second alien life-form and a conflict between the two alien species. What kind of aliens? What was the nature of the conflict? Why were the BLUMOs heading toward Callisto? Did the conflict have anything to do with the Saturn flashes?

As he grappled with these questions, Dante walked up. The mission director saw the printout in Amato's hands and said, "Good. You've seen it. Give us another ten minutes and Dennis and I will be ready to give you a full debrief."

"Go," Amato said. He pointed at a small conference room toward the back of the center. "I'll wait in briefing room one."

"See you in ten." Dante hustled back to his station.

As Dante and Pritchard entered the conference room, their expressions were focused and their strides determined. Although their faces displayed two days of stubble and their clothes were wrinkled and apparently slept in, it was clear Morgan's update had energized them.

Myers followed them in, carrying a tray of steaming coffee cups. He handed out the cups and departed, promising Amato he'd be right outside if needed.

Pritchard settled into a chair across the table from Amato and sipped his coffee. Dante handed Amato a packet of papers before taking a seat next to Pritchard.

"Don't beat around the bush, gentlemen," Amato said. "What's the situation?"

"On the whole, a lot better than I thought when I first read Skywalker's note," Dante said. "They're alive. The ship's intact. Most of the systems are nominal."

He explained that the downlink had included a slew of diagnostic data files that had provided Mission Control with a detailed look at the ship's condition. Life support was fully functional. The ship had power, though some systems were offline. All the comms antennas were operational except for the X-band antenna damaged in the first BLUMO attack. At the time the diagnostic reports were created, the VLF engines were turned off and the reaction control system was set to manual, but both appeared undamaged.

"That means Skywalker had full maneuverability for the escape attempt," Pritchard said.

"When will we know if it worked?" Amato asked.

"Forty-five minutes to an hour," Dante said. "We pinged them back immediately after the downlink finished, roughly twenty minutes ago."

Amato did the math in his head. It would take the transmission another fifteen to twenty minutes to reach *Rorschach*, depending on their current position. If they still had the ability to communicate, any return message would arrive back at Mayaguana thirty to forty minutes after that.

"I hate to say it, but the odds they escaped seem small to me," he said.

"Agreed," said Pritchard. "But I don't think Paul would have risked it unless he thought he could succeed."

"Why did he do it?" Amato rubbed his head and stared at his coffee cup. "What the hell is going on out there?"

"It's a good question. Dennis and I had a possible scenario in mind before Skywalker's message arrived," Dante said. "And we still felt pretty good about it even after reading what he had to say … until his mention of the second life-form. That kind of muddied the water a bit."

"Let me hear it anyway," Amato said.

"Okay, let's start with the UMOs on Callisto. We agree there was a specific purpose behind the de-icing of the spaceport?"

"We do," Amato said.

"It could be routine maintenance they perform periodically, or a ritual of some kind. Or, as we discussed before launching the fleet, it could be a sign the UMOs are expecting the Callistons to return soon."

Pritchard picked up the thread. "After the UMOs left Callisto and we lost contact with *Rorschach*, we questioned whether there might be yet another explanation, but then came the Saturn flashes and Paul's message."

"That's right," said Dante. "Colonel Morgan's message implies the BLUMOs are committed to taking *Rorschach* to Callisto."

"That does seem clear," Amato said. "If that's the case, though, why try to escape?"

"We think Paul is concerned with radiation once they exit the asteroid belt. Without the Shields, the crew and ship will be vulnerable to Jupiter's magnetic field," Pritchard said.

"Okay. That makes sense. But if Julia can communicate with them, why not just tell them the radiation is harmful?" Amato said.

Dante reminded him of the difficulties Nick Reed had encountered in communicating with the UMOs that led *Cetus Prime* to Callisto. "From Colonel Morgan's ending comment, it seems they're running into the same issue."

"I suppose that's likely. He's probably also concerned about the possibility of another gamma burst."

Dante shook his head. "Skywalker may be concerned, but we're not. We don't think another one is going to happen."

"Why not?"

"The Saturn flashes."

"Explain."

"About an hour before we received Paul's message, Helen Brock called," Pritchard said. "We had a long conversation about the flashes. Her JPL team has made a couple of significant discoveries. Augie, whatever caused those flashes had mass ... and was traveling a tick under the speed of light."

The two men caught Amato up on the work of the JPL team. JPL had examined data from several observatories that had recorded the flash events. At first blush, the data appeared to show spontaneous explosions, as if an asteroid or comet had broken up and its debris had collided with a previously undetected mass between Iapetus and Titan. A shock wave was evident with each flash, and a trail of radiation waves afterward was suggestive of ejected mass.

But on closer examination, the radiation trails revealed shifts in their spectral lines that implied the ejected masses were traveling close to the speed of light — way too fast to be comet or asteroid debris.

Further, the velocity of each radiation trail was nearly identical. If a collection of debris had collided with an asteroid, the debris would have struck the asteroid at different times and in different spots. Some would have been glancing blows, others direct hits. Given these variabilities, it was effectively impossible that the trails of ejected mass would all follow the same path at the same speed.

"You're suggesting the ejected masses were spacecraft," Amato concluded. "The Callistons returning to our solar system."

"Or … a second alien life-form," said Pritchard. "UMOs can maneuver more nimbly than our spacecraft; who's to say another being can't do the same? And how do we know the new aliens mentioned by Morgan weren't in a spacecraft?"

"And keep in mind the masses turned toward Saturn instead of heading toward Callisto," Dante said. "Another factor suggesting these are not the Callistons."

"But Saturn is a billion kilometers from Jupiter. And *Rorschach* is yet another 350 million kilometers away."

"If they're capable of light speed, they could make the trip to the asteroid belt from Saturn in under two hours," Pritchard said.

"You see how Skywalker's mention of the other aliens messes with the possibility the Callistons have returned?" Dante said. "Another example: Did the UMOs depart Callisto to meet the arriving Calliston ships? Or did the UMOs flee Callisto because they detected the other aliens coming? Perhaps the gamma burst that took out *Juno* signaled their approach, or maybe there was another one after that."

"Why would you say that?" Amato asked.

"There were heavy concentrations of X-rays and gamma rays in the radiation trails after the flashes," Pritchard said. "Helen said the concentrations are similar to what one observes near the tail end of afterglows from pulsar and magnetar beams."

Amato reached for his coffee as he absorbed this information. He sipped the bitter concoction and cringed. Putting it back on the table, he said, "In either case, Callistons or some other aliens, you haven't explained the connection with *Rorschach*. Why are the BLUMOs involved? Why have they hunted the ship? Why are they taking it to Callisto?"

"We don't know, plain and simple," Dante said. "But if Skywalker was able to escape, even if just for an hour, we may have a chance to find out. If our uplink gets through, Antonio Wallace gave us an idea for a workaround that might keep us connected with *Rorschach*." Dante smiled. "A bit of tech trickery."

To overcome the radio interference created by the BLUMOs, Antonio had suggested pinging his drone-landers. The landers' computers included anti-jamming hardware and software that Antonio's firm had initially developed for stealth military drones. This meant the landers were capable of detecting and countering enemy instruments attempting to interfere with their communications. As no one had foreseen the potential for intentional efforts to block communications with the drone-landers aboard *Rorschach*, Antonio's software hadn't been activated prior to launch, but it could be activated remotely.

"The ping we sent was followed by an uplink instructing the landers to power up and toggle on the anti-jamming software," Dante said. "If it's effective, we'll be able to track *Rorschach*. If we're lucky, and the crew notices the landers are active, we can use them to send and receive messages."

OFFICE OF THE CHIEF ADMINISTRATOR
NASA HEADQUARTERS
WASHINGTON, D.C.

Helen sat at her desk with coffee cup in hand. In her other hand, she held a printout of a news article skewering Augustus Amato and Dante Fulton. From the moment the media published the leaked messages between

Rorschach and Mayaguana, the two men had shouldered dual burdens: the need to find the ship and restore communications, and the need to temper speculation regarding the crew's fate. And through it all, they faced unrelenting criticism from every direction.

The reporter who wrote the article Brock now scanned had tried to draw NASA into the cesspool of second-guessers pummeling Amato and Dante, but Brock had refused to add to *Rorschach*'s and Mayaguana's burdens. The reporter *was* successful, however, in extracting a handful of biting quotes from anonymous NASA officials who apparently had scores to settle with Amato. Thankfully, the anonymous cowards were in the minority. For although many of the space agency's employees had been bruised by the public animosity directed at NASA in the aftermath of Amato's *Cetus Prime* and UMO revelations, few blamed the billionaire. Most, including Brock, considered Amato and his team heroes. If that hadn't been evident to the outside world before, it surely was now.

In Houston, Greenbelt, Pasadena and places in between, Brock had seen her NASA colleagues rally to assist Mayaguana in rescuing *Rorschach* from whatever plight had befallen the ship. Project managers from across the agency had volunteered to form crisis teams, and there was no shortage of others willing to join up and pitch in. And as much as Brock would have liked to take credit for the groundswell of support, she knew it had been a grassroots campaign — perhaps bolstered by a social media post from Dennis Pritchard after Amato confirmed the leaked messages were authentic: *They risked all for our brothers and sister on Cetus Prime. Will we give all to aid them now? #Bgood2lanother*

Pritchard's hashtag reference to Nick Reed's final words before departing *Cetus Prime* had deeply touched people not only within the agency but around the world. So many people had followed *Rorschach*'s mission and had come to know the crew as humans, not just astronauts. The same had been true for *Cetus Prime*'s crew.

Within a day of Pritchard's post, the families of the two ships' crews galvanized the *Bgood2lanother* movement. They appeared on television wearing photo badges they'd created to honor all eight astronauts. It was styled after the badge Paul Morgan had commissioned to commemorate the *Cetus Prime* crew twenty-five years ago, and was emblazoned with

Bgood2lanother across its midsection. These badges spread like wildfire, and within a day they were attached to the clothing of NASA employees and everyday citizens alike.

Brock turned back toward her desk and spied her own badge beside her laptop. What a difference those families' single symbolic act had made. Overnight, the drumbeat of hope and determination had begun to rise.

She picked up the badge and thought of her friends aboard *Rorschach* and those working the problems in Mayaguana. She prayed NASA's extra help and the world's positive energy would be enough to save them.

"Dr. Brock?"

She looked up from the photo badge to see her assistant, Mary Evans, standing in the doorway, her own badge pinned to her blouse. Brock could tell from the woman's expression that something was amiss. "Yes, Mary, what is it?"

"Dr. Desai is on hold. She says it's urgent."

Reshma Desai was the project manager for NASA's reconstituted *Cetus Prime* mission team at Goddard Space Flight Center. Desai's team, in conjunction with Ed Chen's former *Juno* team at JPL, was engaged in studies of the ship's systems to determine if certain functionality could be restored or additional data extracted.

"Okay, put her through." Moments later, Brock pressed the blinking light on her handset. "Hello, Reshma. What's up?"

"Are you alone?" Desai asked.

"Yes. Why?"

"Can you call me back on Director Toomey's secure line?"

"Yeah. Why? What's the problem?"

"Just call me back. I'm in his office sitting by the phone."

After Desai's abrupt hang-up, Brock scooted her chair along the length of the credenza behind her desk to reach the handset linked to NASA's encrypted phone network. She dialed the extension for the Goddard Center's director, and Desai answered.

"Director Toomey is here with me," she said.

"Hello, Bob," said Brock.

"Hi, Helen, sorry for the cloak and dagger, but we didn't want to risk another leak," Toomey said.

"I understand. What's happened?"

"We've lost communication with *Cetus Prime*," Desai said.

"Okay. Do we know why?"

There was a pause before Desai replied. "We do."

"Is it a temporary issue or something more?"

Another pause. This time, Toomey answered. "From what Reshma showed me, I'd say we won't be hearing from *Cetus Prime* again."

"Why? What's happened?"

"We confirmed it with Ed Chen at JPL," Desai said. "It's LOS."

"Another gamma burst?"

"Oh, it got struck by something all right, but it wasn't a gamma burst," Toomey said.

"I've just now emailed you two encrypted files," Desai said. "Let me know when you've opened the email and I'll read you the cipher code."

Brock hoisted the handset base and swiveled her chair to place it on her desk. Cupping the handset against her ear with her shoulder, she pulled up her email and clicked on the first file. After entering the cipher provided by Desai, the file opened.

It was a grainy and blurred photograph of a section of the alien spaceport snapped by one of *Cetus Prime*'s cameras. Brock tried to make sense of it. "Are those lights or a reflection of the Sun?"

"Callisto's on the dark side of Jupiter right now. It's not the Sun," Desai said.

"And the shadow?"

"It's never been in any of the photos before."

"When was this taken?"

"It was in *Cetus Prime*'s second-to-last downlink before we lost comms."

Between the section of the spaceport framed in the photograph and *Cetus Prime*, a distance of almost three kilometers, a massive shadow covered most of the crater floor. Around it, the rock-ice debris inside Nuada sparkled. In the visible section of the spaceport, one area glowed as if someone was inside with a flashlight or lantern.

"Speculate," Brock said. "Interpret the photo."

The only sound from the other end of the line was the creaking of a chair. Then Desai spoke, her voice as soft as a child's. "Open the other file. It's from the panoramic camera."

"Cipher?"

Desai read off the new code, and Brock opened the file.

She pushed back in her chair and whispered, "Oh my God."

MISSION CONTROL
A3ROSPACE INDUSTRIES COMMAND AND CONTROL CENTER
MAYAGUANA ISLAND, THE BAHAMAS

Helen Brock's first call was to Dante Fulton's cell phone. When he didn't answer, she called Dennis Pritchard. He tracked down Amato and Dante, and together they engaged Brock in an encrypted satellite video conference from the Mission Control briefing room where they had just finished discussing Morgan's message.

When Brock shared the two photographs, the three men approached the wall-mounted monitor and gaped at the pictures. "I've asked JPL for enhanced images," she said, "but I don't think you really need them to figure out what these show."

In the panoramic photo, a black spaceship rested on the crater floor between the spaceport and *Cetus Prime*.

"That is *not* one of the Calliston ships the *Cetus* crew took," Dante said. "That thing must be at least four hundred meters long and just as tall."

Amato turned from the monitor and paced with his hands clasped behind his back. "More puzzles."

"Helen," Pritchard said, "you mentioned *Cetus Prime* is LOS. Could it be radio interference created by the ship, intentionally or inadvertently?"

"No. Unequivocally not."

"How can you be sure?"

"You all might want to sit down for this," Brock said. Amato ceased pacing and faced the feed of Brock sitting in her conference room. Dante and Pritchard slid into seats at the briefing room table. "I'm not joking, Augie. You should sit."

"Very well, Helen. I can see you're serious." Amato pulled out a chair and lowered himself into it.

"There were several data files downlinked after these photos were transmitted. Whatever aliens landed in that ship breached *Cetus Prime*. I don't mean they cranked open an airlock and tiptoed in. I mean they blew open the main cabin near the pallet. It triggered structural failure alarms. Then they moved into the ship and began disabling systems. I don't know if they just pulled power connections or bludgeoned the equipment, but the systems didn't cycle through their shutdown routines. They were hard cut. I don't know what happened after they disabled comms, but I'm certain we're never going to hear from *Cetus Prime* again."

"Jesus. *Rorschach* is being led right to them," Amato murmured.

"What? You've heard from the crew?" Brock asked.

Dante paraphrased the message sent by Morgan and summarized their efforts to reestablish an active comms link. "We haven't received a return ping yet. It's overdue."

"I see." Brock sighed. "Augie, I don't mean to throw fuel on the fire, but … before the aliens blew open the main cabin, they took something."

Pritchard gasped and rose from his chair. "You said they entered by the pallet."

"That's right."

"Oh, Lord, don't tell me. They took *Perseus*."

Brock wiped a tear from her cheek and nodded.

Perseus, a drone armed with EMP grenades, had been the catalyst of the series of events that left *Cetus Prime* crippled near Mars. The military, anxious to test out EMPs as a deterrent to UMOs in Earth's orbit, had commandeered control of the ship from a DoD station in Mission Control at the Goddard Space Flight Center. They ordered the ship's computers to launch two other probes docked on *Cetus Prime*'s pallet, *CPO* and *Andromeda*, to lure the UMOs into a kill zone with the intention of firing *Perseus*' weapons at the aliens. The quick thinking of the ship's commander, Avery Lockett, had averted that outcome by deactivating the ship's power before *Perseus* cut loose the EMPs.

Avery's action hadn't saved the crew, however. The UMOs, stirred up by radiation emitted by the "bait" probes, destroyed *CPO* and *Andromeda* and zeroed in on *Cetus Prime* thereafter. The UMOs destroyed the ship's engines and left it dead in space. If not for the surprise awakening of Nick two days later, along with his sudden ability to communicate with the UMOs, he, Avery and Christine Baker would have perished.

"What would aliens want with *Perseus*?" Amato said.

CHAPTER 15

SYNC UP

jay reached for his throbbing head and rubbed the achy spot above the bridge of his nose. Why did it hurt so much?

He cracked open his eyelids and shut them just as quickly. The light from his station monitors was too strong. Focusing on the sounds around him, he heard the drone of engines, random beeps and someone snoring.

What was going on?

He searched his memory for answers, but found it difficult to concentrate. Strange images kept blocking his attempts at recall.

Lowering his hands to his lap, he felt the fabric of his flight suit. He smoothed his hands over his thighs, then raised them to pat his torso. When he felt the straps of his safety harness, a snippet of a memory popped into his mind. "*Hold on tight.*"

He reached out, and his fingers brushed up against his station keyboard. Another memory wedged its way through the images. "*Here we go. Ajay, you ready?*"

"Roger dodger," Ajay mumbled.

More snippets streamed through gaps between images.

Ajay's eyelids snapped open. "BLUMOs!"

Though the light worsened his headache, he scanned the flight deck for the blue aliens. There were none to be seen. Even through the flight deck windows, the sea of blue that had dominated the view before was gone.

The others were passed out. Morgan and Carillo were slumped over at their stations, and as Ajay swung his head to the left — a motion that brought on a wave of nausea — he saw Kiera's head curled over her armrest, her arms dangling above her head as if she were a ghost trying to scare a haunted house visitor. She was the one snoring.

He turned to study his bank of computer monitors. A quick review provided several insights, none of them good. The comms dashboard on his center screen displayed static patterns for the ship's radio bands. Data below the patterns indicated zero uplinks from Mayaguana had been received. On the screen to the right of the comms display, the ship's radar system showed a large ball-shaped mass behind the ship. Left of center, the last monitor provided data related to *Rorschach*'s flight status. The ship was still headed toward Callisto, and five hours had elapsed since Morgan's attempt to break away from the BLUMOs.

Ajay looked toward his unconscious commander, and another thought darted to the forefront of his mind. "*No! Friends!*"

He clutched his head. The thought was accompanied by a sharp throb and unfamiliar images. No — not all of them were unfamiliar. He recognized one of them.

"Why am I thinking of Saturn?"

He unbuckled from his seat, tapped his GEFF watch to turn off the magnetic forcefield, and glided to Kiera. He nudged her gently and whispered her name, but though her snoring stopped, she didn't wake. He tried again, this time shaking her and calling her name loudly, but still got no response. He tried to wake Morgan and Carillo as well, with the same results.

Finally he powered off *Rorschach*'s engines. There was no point in draining their batteries. The UMOs were still in control of the ship and, until the others woke up, Ajay was just along for the ride. He wondered if the UMOs had been successful in trapping and killing the creature they hunted.

And then he remembered Shilling. He propelled out of the flight deck and down the corridor to the medical bay. To his relief, he found Shilling was alive, though still unconscious. He adjusted the man's straps and floated back out.

In the crew galley, he raided their refrigerated storage for two pouches of water and two chocolate-peanut butter protein bars. Cupping his booty in one arm, he pushed off the wall, angled his body through the galley door and returned to the flight deck.

Strapped back into his seat, he sipped water and munched on one of the bars. According to the flight clock, which displayed the time both in Coordinated Universal Time as well as in Eastern Daylight Time, it was 11:26 p.m. on Mayaguana. That meant it was 11:26 a.m. the following day in his hometown of Namche Bazaar in Nepal. Saturn popped into his mind again as Ajay thought of his father's favorite planet. He wondered if his family was thinking of him and whether his father was still watching the stars at night.

Ajay smiled. The old man had told him before the mission that he would track *Rorschach*'s progress on the A3I website every day and train his telescope on the ship's coordinates every night. "Someone has to keep an eye on you or you will get yourself into trouble!"

Looking around at his unconscious shipmates, Ajay muttered, "Hope you're still watching, Papa. We could use some help."

As he looked over at Kiera, he noticed something he hadn't seen before: two blinking green lights on her station's desktop. Why didn't he see those before? Perhaps her floating hands had blocked his view.

The flight engineer's station had three panel sections below the monitor displays. The digital gauges on the center panel allowed Kiera to monitor the VLF engines. The mini-displays on the right helped her surveil the reaction control system performance and ship's orientation. The left section showed status information for their fleet of probes. And that was the section where the lights were blinking.

But all the probes were gone, except for the docked *Cargo-4*. So why would two lights be blinking? He could understand one, but two? Was it the Recon in the cargo bay? No. He was certain it had been powered off after Carillo finished locking down the CubeSat. In fact, Ajay remembered it was definitely off when he and Kiera tied Shilling to the companion docking station.

His curiosity was strong enough to temporarily push aside the incessant cycle of images that just wouldn't leave his mind — a spaceship, a moon crater, an ice castle and Saturn. He stowed the half-eaten bar in his breast pocket, unstrapped from his seat and floated over to Kiera.

Angling himself past her bobbing arms, he studied the two blinking lights. Inside the rectangular green digital flashes, white labels read "LAND-1" and "LAND-2."

Ajay frowned. "How did they turn on?"

CARGO BAY — THE *RORSCHACH EXPLORER*

With his GEFF toggled on, Ajay knelt by the two landers, or the "squids," as he liked to call the drones. These four-foot-tall, football-shaped domes were adorned with antennas, booms, satellite dishes and cameras, and were anchored to their docks by clamps that pinned their six folded legs. Fully extended, the legs would raise the crest of the black domes by six feet. Dotting each of the folded segments of the legs were rotating thruster vents that looked to Ajay like suckers on squid tentacles.

He watched the solid and flickering lights on their control panels and listened to the churn of their computers. Concentrating on the lander closest to him, he leaned forward to study the abbreviations beneath the active lights on its midsection control panel. He was distracted by a sound.

He looked up to see a camera on the probe rotating. It stopped with a click. Then it moved another quarter turn and made another click. By the time the third turn and click occurred, Ajay realized what was happening. He looked back to the control panel and ran his finger across the labels until he found it: a solid green light above a single white letter 'X'.

He was too late to hop up and stand in the way of the camera's lens when it snapped its fourth and final photo, but it didn't matter. He turned and dashed for the airlock.

As he passed through into the main corridor, he heard Morgan's voice over the intercom. "Where are you, Ajay? Report."

Running at as full a sprint as GEFF would allow, Ajay shouted toward the open flight deck door. "We have comms! We have comms!"

FLIGHT DECK — THE *RORSCHACH EXPLORER*
SEPTEMBER 6, 2019

It took Morgan and Ajay several minutes of cajoling before Carillo and Kiera finally stirred, and a dozen more before the still-blinded Kiera was coherent enough to walk Ajay through how to access the dashboard for *Land-1*'s control program.

"Now tell me what's on the screen," she said.

"Uh, a bunch of menu options."

"One of the options should be either history or activity."

"Yep, I see one called activity," Ajay said. "Should I click that icon?"

Morgan and Carillo stood behind Ajay as he worked at Kiera's station. Kiera was seated at Shilling's station.

"Yes, that's the one," Kiera said. "There should be a collection of folders."

"Right, there are six. Uplinks, downlinks, firmware updates, application updates, diagnostics, and the last one is—"

"Skywalker," Morgan said. He pointed at the screen. "Open it."

Inside the folder was a listing of nine files. The date stamps shown to the right of the file names indicated they'd been uplinked to *Land-1* within the last three hours. All but one were text files. The last was an image file. The oldest of the files was named OPENFIRST.

Ajay opened it.

The text of the file appeared. Ajay read it aloud for Kiera's benefit while Morgan and Carillo read from the screen.

"*MAYA-FLIGHT to CDR-TRE: Received your transmission. Please acknowledge receipt of ours. We have reestablished tracking of TRE through* Land-1 *and* Land-2. *We are aware of your position and heading but are in the dark as to your status. Please advise. There have been MAJOR developments requiring your IMMEDIATE attention ... repeat ... IMMEDIATE attention. Review follow-on files for more details. Everyone at Maya, NASA and just about everywhere else on Earth is thinking of you.*

We are all standing by to assist in whatever way possible. Be strong and be good to one another. MAYA-FLIGHT out."

Morgan wiped his eyes and ordered Ajay to move out of the seat. Turning to Kiera, he asked, "How do I send a message back?"

Kiera smiled. "Easy-peasy."

A few instructions later, Morgan's text reply was on its way to Mayaguana. He then turned to his crew. "Let's get the rest of these files open, find out what's going on and start working on a new plan."

SET OF *EXPEDITION TO CALLISTO*
WORLD NETWORK NEWS STUDIOS
NEW YORK, NEW YORK
SEPTEMBER 6, 2019

Jenna Toffy stood in the glow of a spotlight on a darkened set. She wore a sleeveless pink dress with a #bgood2lanother photo badge pinned above her left breast. Holding a rolled-up script with both hands, she looked into the camera with an expression akin to that of a minister offering condolences.

"Good evening, ladies and gentlemen, and welcome to *Expedition to Callisto*. I'm your host, Jenna Toffy. For twelve weeks on this program, we have provided our viewers the unique opportunity to ride along with the crew of the *Rorschach Explorer* as they attempted to make history.

"During that time, we were afforded exclusive access to the crew and the men and women supporting the mission at A3rospace Industries. That backstage pass allowed us to present you with amazing video footage, compelling interviews and a chance to get to know the people leading *Rorschach*'s grand adventure. An adventure that took the first of several chilling turns last week during this very program.

"For reasons that have yet to be made clear to WNN, Augustus Amato chose to cut our access after last week's episode, leaving us, like you, in the dark to everything that has happened since. Thankfully, there are heroes with intimate knowledge of the events confronting the brave crew of the *Rorschach Explorer* who have come forward to share information

Mr. Amato could have shared but chose to withhold. WNN has reported news of those events as we've learned of them.

"And tonight, on a special edition of *Expedition to Callisto*, we have more breaking news to report. As we have done with all the *Rorschach* news stories, we reached out to A3I for comment. But, as has been the case since last week, they declined our request.

"Before turning to our team of reporters who've been working this latest twist in *Rorschach*'s journey, one final thought. Some have called our reporting irresponsible, claiming we are undermining A3I's efforts to save the crew and sowing fear among the public. To those voices we say: the public has a right to know, whether the news is pretty or not.

"This isn't just a story about desperate attempts to rescue brave astronauts, or a story about how ego and impatience set the stage for a bungled mission. It is a story about human contact with aliens that may forever reshape life on Earth. On all counts, the public has a right to know. On all counts, Augustus Amato should know that."

MISSION CONTROL
A3ROSPACE INDUSTRIES COMMAND AND CONTROL CENTER
MAYAGUANA ISLAND, THE BAHAMAS

A row of camping cots had been set up against the back wall of Mission Control so exhausted off-duty controllers could try to catch whatever sleep they could while their on-duty counterparts manned the center's stations. Though Dante prodded the staff to return to their Mayaguana dormitory rooms when off-duty, no one would leave, especially not now.

After it appeared that Morgan's gamble to break free from the BLU-MOs had failed, and after it seemed Mayaguana's attempt to link with the Whave Technologies' drone-landers had flopped, a cloud of despair had descended upon Mission Control. But then the improbable had occurred. The landers pinged Mayaguana. The hour delay in their response was still unexplained, but nobody cared. They could reestablish contact.

It wasn't until later, when Antonio Wallace arrived at Mayaguana to review the data transmitted by the landers, that he was able to come up with a reason for the communications downtime. The unique, multi-pronged antennas dedicated to lander comms on *Rorschach*'s instrumentation pallet had found it challenging to find a gap in the BLUMO web surrounding the ship.

"The BLUMOs must have changed their configuration, creating the gap we needed," he hypothesized.

The energized mission control team had spent the next hour uplinking messages to and downlinking status information from the landers. But for the following three hours, there was no response from the *Rorschach* crew. Either they hadn't noticed the landers were active, or they were unable to reply. This cratered emotions once again — until someone suggested activating the drones' cameras.

When the downlink with photos arrived another hour later, Mission Control was heartened to discover that not only was the cargo bay intact, but there was evidence of a visitor. The airlock door was open in one photograph, and the partial shadow of a person's body was visible in another. The two together implied the crew was aware the landers had turned on and had come to the bay to investigate.

A tense hour passed after that, with controllers hovering near Whave Technologies' station in the center, waiting for news of a downlink from *Rorschach*. The place went bonkers when Morgan's text file finally arrived.

CDR-TRE to MAYA-FLIGHT: Roger your transmissions. Clever solution. Good work to all! Beers are on us. TRE status: escape attempt failed, BLUMOs still controlling TRE, but alpha is MIA now. No change in crew status other than some whopping headaches. Appreciate everyone's thoughts, prayers and assistance. Will review files and respond ASAP. You be strong, too. No thumb-sucking here or there. That's an order. CDR-TRE out.

Now the center awaited the crew's next transmission. As confident as Morgan's message had been, everyone in Mission Control, including Dante, Pritchard, Antonio and Amato, wondered how the crew would react to the news of the Saturn flashes, the UMO bugout from the Callisto spaceport, the destruction of *Cetus Prime* and photograph of the alien spacecraft in the Nuada crater.

No one was leaving the center. Not now.

CREW READY ROOM —THE *RORSCHACH EXPLORER*
FLYING THROUGH THE ASTEROID BELT

The crew immediately latched on to the Saturn flashes and the photograph of the alien ship in the Nuada crater. They had all experienced the same rotation of unfamiliar images. Carillo explained the images were similar to those communicated by the BLUMO alpha during their exchange of thoughts. "It sounds like the alpha connected with all of us," she said.

"That explains the bolts of electricity," Ajay said. He shared how the alien had shot bolts at Morgan and Carillo. "But I didn't see any lightning hit me. I just remember talking to Kiera and then … nothing."

Kiera nodded. "And I was just listening to Ajay when a thought blocked out what he was saying: 'No! Friends!'"

"I had the same thought!" Ajay said. "What does it mean?"

"That was the alpha communicating," said Carillo. "She said the same thing to me. She must have figured out Paul's plan. I think she was trying to tell us not to try to escape."

"All right, let's try to put the pieces together," Morgan said. "We all received images of Saturn, a crater, an ice-covered structure and a big-ass black ship identical to the one in this picture."

"And we now know about the Saturn flashes," Kiera added.

"I think it's pretty obvious, don't you?" Carillo said. "The Callistons have returned. The BLUMOs are taking us to meet them. That ship is on Callisto. She shared visions of the spacecraft."

Kiera's blindfold had fallen down over her nose. She pushed it up and tightened the knot behind her head. "Is it obvious though? The vision I had of the ship doesn't look anything like the Calliston ships *Cetus Prime* photographed. And the structure isn't the one on Callisto."

"I agree," said Ajay. "And why would the BLUMOs think the Callistons are friends if they demolished *Cetus Prime*?"

Morgan studied the photograph of the ship. "I think it's time to stop guessing and get some answers. Julia, can you summon the alpha again?"

Carillo shrugged. "It worked before. I don't see why it wouldn't work again."

"Uh … aren't you forgetting something?" Kiera said. "She zapped all of us. I'd say she's pretty pissed we tried to escape."

It was a hard point to argue, but Carillo did. "It sounds counterintuitive, but I don't think she was pissed. I think she was scared we might leave."

Kiera rubbed her forehead. "She has a strange way of showing she's scared."

"They don't have another way to get our attention," Carillo said. "And she didn't just zap us, she communicated the images. She was trying to tell us *why* we shouldn't escape."

"True," said Morgan. "And if she was *really* that pissed, she would have killed us and destroyed the ship. But she didn't. The BLUMOs are *very* interested in us meeting that ship. We should try to find out as much as we can about why."

Kiera sat with arms crossed and her forehead wrinkled into a frown. "If we're going to try, and I get the reasons why we would want to try, we need to communicate our concerns about Jupiter's radiation. If we exit the belt and they take us on a course close to Jupiter, we'll cook."

Morgan nodded. "Agreed. Julia?"

"I'll do my best," she said.

FLIGHT DECK — THE *RORSCHACH EXPLORER*
FLYING THROUGH THE ASTEROID BELT

When everyone was buckled into their seats, Morgan sent another text file to Mayaguana.

CDR-TRE to MAYA-FLIGHT: Transmissions reviewed. Additional perspective VERY valuable. Thank you! We believe BLUMOs are leading TRE to the Nuada crater to meet ship in photo. Long story, no time to tell. CCDR to attempt conversation with BLUMO alpha to learn more. Will transmit more info after CCDR convo. CDR-TRE out.

Then he nodded to Carillo. "Ready when you are."

She closed her eyes and focused on projecting her thoughts to the BLUMO alpha. *"Talk? Scared. Please talk."*

While she waited for the tingle she had felt in her earlier summoning, images of her children and husband filled her mind, and frightening moments in her life drifted up. She recalled her mother hugging her, her father's soothing voice. Emotion swelled inside her. She pursed her lips and breathed deeply — a technique she'd used many times as a fighter pilot and astronaut.

She felt a throbbing sensation in her chest. "Something's happening."

The throbbing sensation felt almost like a wave of energy. It was strong ... and oddly comforting.

"I feel something pushing against my chest," Kiera said. "It feels good."

Morgan and Ajay indicated they felt it as well.

And then Kiera gasped just as a new thought entered Carillo's mind. *"Friends. We are friends."*

Carillo opened her eyes — and gasped herself. The glowing golden light now pulsing in front of her was much larger than the other UMOs they'd encountered — closer to softball-sized than golf-ball-sized — and had no UMO escort buzzing around her. This was not the alpha Carillo had communicated with earlier or the BLUMO queen she'd seen in a vision. It was the Callisto queen.

Carillo formed a new thought. *"We are scared. Free us."*

The image of the black ship on Callisto flashed through her mind along with the queen's reply. *"They have come."*

"Stop. Free us." Carillo concentrated her mental energy on creating an image of Jupiter. *"Too close. It will hurt us. We are scared. Let them come here."*

The queen's gold light began to flicker. *"I will tell them."*

"Tell them what?" Ajay asked. "I heard her side of the exchange, but I didn't hear yours."

Carillo swiveled her chair to face him. "I told her if we get too close to Jupiter, it will hurt us. I asked her to stop pushing us."

"I'd like to pose a question to her," Kiera said.

"Go for it."

Kiera frowned as if forcing her mind to formulate a thought. The queen flickered, and her answer followed. *"Help your kind."*

"Whoa, that was bad-ass," Kiera said. "I just talked with a frickin' alien!"

"What did you ask?" Ajay said.

"I asked her *why* they had come."

"Ask her why they want to help us," Ajay said.

"Do it yourself," Kiera said. "It's easy. Just think of your question, but keep it short and sweet. And for heaven's sake, don't say 'Roger dodger' when she answers you."

That got a laugh from everyone.

Ajay closed his eyes and asked his question. "Why help us?" he said.

"Uh, Ajay?" said Kiera. "You think it, you don't say it."

The answer from the queen pushed into their minds. *"Not help you. Help each other."*

"You were saying?" Ajay said to Kiera.

She smiled. "I stand corrected."

Carillo couldn't help but notice how relaxed everyone had become in the presence of the Callisto queen. Everyone, that is, but Morgan. He was intently working his keyboard while studying his monitors.

"Paul," she said, "are you going to join the conversation?"

Morgan turned to her. "We're slowing down, Julia. The UMOs aren't behind us anymore, they're underneath the ship. I don't know how they're doing it, but they're pulling on us somehow."

"That's weird. I don't feel a thing."

"Me neither," said Ajay.

"Make it a threesome," Kiera added. "Er … let me rephrase that."

More laughter ensued.

"Oh, there's no way you're living that one down!" Ajay said.

She grinned. "Hey, what happens in the asteroid belt stays in the asteroid belt. *Capiche?*"

"Fat chance, sista. I've got it on video and audio."

"You what?"

"I'm recording this to send back home."

The banter was interrupted by a thought from the Callisto queen. *"They are coming. They are near."*

CHAPTER 16

BUMPY RIDE

"How the hell did WNN get a copy of the photo?" Dante fumed. "Who told them about *Cetus Prime*?"

"Don't look at me, Dr. Fulton, I'm just the messenger," Mark Myers said.

"Well it pisses me off!" Dante yelled. His voice carried through Mission Control, silencing conversations. "The leaks have to stop! Do you hear me? Whoever is doing this, you have to *stop*!"

Some people nodded. Others glared. A few ignored the mission director and continued their work.

But Norris Preston hopped out of his seat and shouted back, "It's none of *us*, damn it! We're busting our asses, Dante. Most of us haven't showered or slept in three days! Quit pointing fingers!"

"It's NASA. It's gotta be NASA," another controller said.

Other voices joined in.

"Or someone at headquarters."

"Maybe WNN's hacked our network."

"Or they're intercepting our satellite traffic."

Amato looked over the frustrated, angry faces. Some were glaring at him instead of Dante. He stepped up beside his mission director and raised his hand to call for everyone's attention.

"Look, it's a regrettable situation," he said. "One that I'm responsible for creating. If I'd been more open with the press, they wouldn't feel such a strong need to ferret out information."

"Then why won't you talk with them?" Preston demanded. "They're making us sound like buffoons. They're making *you* sound like a madman."

"Watch it, Norris," Dante said.

"No, he makes valid points, Dante," Amato said. "Everyone, gather round."

As the entire staff of the Mission Control came over to him, he opened his collar and loosened his tie halfway down his chest. Then he leaned on his cane and bowed his head. "I am truly sorry for putting you all in this situation. I confess I've been overwhelmed by the totality of what's happened. Every time I've thought of speaking to the press, something else has gone wrong, and I've become so immersed in trying to understand what to make of it all, I've felt reluctant to say anything."

He lifted his head and looked into the eyes of his team members. "I will remedy that now. But I need you to do something for me ... something more, I should say. You've already given so much of yourselves.

"We can't afford to allow outside pressures to distract us. We can't fight with each other or point fingers. Our friends on *Rorschach* are counting on us. To get them home, we need to stay focused. Don't worry about the leaks. Don't worry what outsiders are saying or thinking. I will take care of that. You have my word."

HANGAR-2
A3ROSPACE INDUSTRIES COMMAND AND CONTROL CENTER
MAYAGUANA ISLAND, THE BAHAMAS
SEPTEMBER 7, 2019

On the high-altitude balloon launch apron outside Hangar-2 stood two of Amato's twelve-foot-tall, domed launch delivery vehicles. Inside them, the Shield CubeSats were ready to ascend into orbit as soon as their balloon platforms were attached. The multi-staged LDVs would be carried high into the atmosphere by the balloons and then released. From there, the staged engines would propel the LDVs into low Earth orbit, the shell casing around the CubeSats would fall away, and Kiera's VLF engines would push the Shields through high Earth orbit and onto the *Rorschach Explorer*. If the mission team was lucky, a cluster of UMOs flitting around in Earth's ionosphere would gather behind the engines to feed on their electromagnetic output and boost the spacecraft's velocity.

Milling around the vehicles were more than two hundred reporters, camera operators and sound specialists, all of them waiting for Amato's press conference to begin. Among them were Jenna Toffy and Nigel Ewing — and neither was faring well in the blustery and humid conditions. The ocean winds flowing over the sand dunes surrounding the launch apron twisted their coifs into snarling morasses, and the blazing morning sun melted their makeup and coated their faces with sweat. Production assistants fanned the two anchors while others shielded them with umbrellas.

They were in the midst of delivering live updates when the hangar doors began to slide open. Their camera operators panned to catch the first glimpses inside the bay. The mass of journalists and support personnel pushed forward.

The walls of the bay were lined with more LDVs, six on each side, and standing in two long rows in front of the vessels were dozens of Amato's technicians, all dressed in the same black-and-gold flight suits worn by the *Rorschach* crew. The men and women responsible for assembling and preparing the LDVs for launch looked upon the press with expressions ranging from scorn to resolve.

As the media walked into the bay, the only sounds were their footsteps, the snapping of camera shutters, the whoosh of overhead air conditioning vents and the echo of distant waves. The LDVs sparkled, their domes covered with magic-marker-inscribed well wishes to the *Rorschach* crew from the technicians and the Mission Control team.

But the oohs and ahhs started as soon as the outer hangar doors closed behind the reporters and an inner hangar door began to open at the far end of the bay. For inside the inner hangar, positioned with its starboard side facing the oncoming crowd, towered the fully assembled *RE2*. The gleaming spacecraft filled three quarters of the football-field-sized bay.

Amato stood at a podium set on the bay floor amidships of *RE2*. He was alone. A dozen off-duty personnel from Mission Control were spaced out along the catwalk above and, off to the side, near the elevators leading to the heart of the command center, another forty A3I staff had congregated.

In front of Amato, rows of chairs had been set up for the press. Mark Myers marshaled the journalists into seats while another member of the Mayaguana team directed camera operators and sound crews to a spot to set up their gear. The LDV crews filed in and stood behind the chairs. The inner bay doors closed, and at nine a.m. EDT, Amato began the conference.

"Good morning and welcome," he said. "I will make a brief statement and then take your questions."

As Amato began his statement, radio waves carrying a message from the *Rorschach Explorer* were passed by A3I's tracking and relay satellite to Mayaguana's satellite dishes and then into Mission Control's computer system.

CDR-TRE to MAYA-FLIGHT: TRE all-stop. Communication with UMOs successful. Awaiting arrival of spacecraft photographed in the Nuada crater. Will have video and audio rolling to record the link-up. Wish us luck. CDR-TRE out.

CREW GALLEY — THE *RORSCHACH EXPLORER*
DRIFTING AT ALL-STOP IN THE ASTEROID BELT
SEPTEMBER 7, 2019

In follow-up exchanges with the Callisto queen, the crew had learned the alien spacecraft would not rendezvous with *Rorschach* for several hours, which gave the crew an opportunity to return to their cabins for a few hours of much-needed sleep. Morgan had first tended to Shilling in the med bay. The scientist was still unconscious, but his vital signs had improved, and following the instructions transmitted by the flight surgeon, Morgan had administered additional medication and refreshed Shilling's IVs.

Now, awakening to feel at least somewhat rested, Morgan returned to the med bay, this time to attend to Carillo. He helped with a modest-as-possible sponge bath, changed her burn dressings and gave her another dose of pain medication.

Finally, he tended to himself. He showered, changed into a fresh flight suit, and went to the galley to get something to eat.

Ajay, Kiera and Carillo were already there, and all of them had spiffed up their appearance for the historic meeting as well. Morgan was beyond relieved to discover that Kiera had recovered partial vision, and she was no longer wearing her blindfold. Everything was blurry, she said, but she could detect light, shapes and movement, and it had clearly improved her mood.

Carillo sipped on a pouch of water. "Sure wish we had some more of your mai tais, Paul. I'm nervous as hell."

"It's probably the morphine making you feel that way," he said.

"You're not nervous?"

"Who? Me?" Morgan smiled. "Nah."

"If Skywalker's not nervous, then neither am I," said Ajay.

"Oh, really? Then why is your leg shaking?" Kiera asked.

"My leg's not shaking."

"I wasn't talking to you. I was talking to Skywalker." She turned and smiled at Morgan. "Still can't see for shit, but I can feel vibrations just fine."

Morgan laughed. "Okay, I'm a wee bit nervous."

"A wee bit?"

"All right. I'm petrified. Happy?" He rose from the table and turned to leave the galley.

Carillo said, "Hey, come back here. She didn't mean anything."

He turned around and winked. "I just have to go get something. Be right back."

When he returned, he carried a gallon-sized pouch filled with a goldish fluid.

Carillo's jaw dropped. "You stinker. You've been holding out on us!"

Morgan patted the bottle. "Emergency reserve."

He tugged the pouch's straw to break the seal, then handed it to Carillo. "Make me proud."

As Carillo drew in sips of the giant mai tai, Kiera said, "I can hear you, Major. Leave some for the rest of us!"

Carillo laughed and guided the pouch into Kiera's hands. "Can't wait to tell this story to my children. Humans' first contact with alien humanoids, and here I am making a cocktail out of morphine and mai tais."

After two generous tugs on the straw, Kiera said, "Seriously, we should switch out of the flight suits and meet them in our Hawaiian shirts." As she held out the pouch for Ajay to take, she waggled her free hand, thumb and pinky extended. "*Mahalo*, Elroy."

"*Mahalo*," Ajay said. He accepted the pouch and sipped. Pulling back from the straw, he turned to Morgan. "How are we going to communicate with them?"

Morgan shrugged. "Beats me. Maybe the queen will show up again and act as a translator."

"That makes sense," Kiera said. "And Ajay, just do me a favor. For the love of Pete, don't say live long and prosper."

Ajay was the first one to laugh, but Morgan laughed the hardest.

The pouch made another round trip before it landed back in Ajay's hands. He took a sip and posed another question. "What do you think the queen meant? When I asked her why the Callistons want to help us, she said they want us to help each other."

"I took that to mean they want to help all humans," Carillo said.

"Really?" said Kiera. "I thought she was saying the aliens want to help us, and they want us to help them."

Morgan snagged the pouch from Ajay. "Who says the aliens are Callistons?"

"Excuse me?" Kiera asked.

"We all received the same mental images. And the queen never showed us an image of the aliens."

"True, but, come on, who else could it be?" Kiera said.

"Maybe it's the mai tais talking," Morgan said, holding the pouch aloft before passing it to Carillo, "but Mayaguana said the aliens destroyed *Cetus Prime* — and I'm having a hard time understanding why the Callistons would do that. It's been gathering ice on Callisto for twenty-four years. Why is it all of a sudden a problem?"

"Maybe they didn't know about it until they came back," Ajay said.

Carillo took a sip and handed the pouch to Kiera. "I think Ajay's right. They come back, find one of their ships missing. They see *Cetus Prime* in the same crater and put two and two together. They get pissed and wreck it."

"But if that's what happened, why did the queen say they want to help us?" Kiera asked.

No one had an answer. When Kiera passed the pouch to Ajay, he placed it on the table and looked around at his crewmates. "I felt the queen was sincere. I believe she's telling us the truth."

Morgan smoothed his Fu Manchu with one hand and patted Ajay's shoulder with the other. "I felt *ohana*, too. Let's hope she wasn't bullshitting us." He scooped up the pouch. There was about a third of a gallon left. He walked to the refrigerator, stored it, then turned back to the others. "Okay. Everybody up."

He led them to the med bay, positioned them in a circle around Shilling and ordered them to hold hands. Morgan held one of Shilling's hands and Kiera held the other, including Shilling in the circle.

Morgan then bowed his head. "I don't know who or what you worship and I don't care, but join me in a prayer.

"Of our own free will we chose to embark on this journey. Let us be strong and show whomever we meet the very best of who we can be. Don't let fear take hold of us. Help us to be good to one another and to them. Amen."

With heads bowed, the crew squeezed each other's hands and echoed Morgan's closing.

When they opened their eyes, the Callisto queen was among them. "*They are here.*"

FLIGHT DECK — THE *RORSCHACH EXPLORER*
DRIFTING AT ALL-STOP IN THE ASTEROID BELT

At a distance, the black ship looked like a smooth rock, the kind you might pick up and skip across the still surface of a lake.

"Get the cameras on it, Julia. Activate all our instruments except spectrometers," Morgan said.

"Roger that."

"Ajay, start recording audio on all channels," Morgan said.

"We're moving again. Magnetometer is off the scale," Carillo said.

There were several uncomfortable jerks on *Rorschach*.

"Feels like wind turbulence," Morgan said.

Kiera leaned her face close to her monitors and squinted with one eye. "How cool is that!"

"What?" Morgan asked.

"They're using magnetism to pull us closer to them. It's like they've created an envelope around us. It honest to God looks like a cupped hand pulling on us."

Morgan pulled up the magnetometer's display at his station. Kiera's description was apt. Tentacles of magnetic flow arced around an open gap at the center.

Carillo looked up at the flickering UMO queen hovering above her station. "Ajay, you picking up anything on comms?"

"Definitely on VLF. Just static on UHF and X-band. Retuning HF … uh … yep, looks like we're picking up chirps, too."

"Pipe in the VLF," Morgan said.

"Roger dodger."

The cabin intercom clicked on to reveal a lively conversation ongoing between the queen and ship. Long, lazy wails intermingled with short bursts of clicks.

Ajay looked out the window at the approaching spacecraft. "Damn that's big!"

Morgan was thinking the same. "Julia, give me an infrared reading. How close is that thing?"

"Looks like just under half a kilometer … now four hundred meters … really slowing down now … three fifty."

"Jesus, it's got to be at least fifty times bigger than *Rorschach*," Morgan said.

In the grainy picture Mayaguana had uplinked, the ship looked big … but not *that* big. As it drew closer, more of its features became visible. It wasn't nearly as flat as it had appeared at a distance or in the Mayaguana image. It looked more ovoid in shape, and its surface shimmered as if coated in mirrors.

"Julia, zoom in with Cam-1."

"Roger that."

The Cam-1 video feed popped up on the central monitor of each of their stations. The shimmers confirmed Morgan's suspicion — the ship was coated with a network of whitish UMOs. The camera feed jiggled for a second, blurring the video feed.

"We are at all-stop," Carillo said. "Distance to target holding steady at two hundred meters. Magnetometer readings dropping again."

Looking out the flight deck windows, Morgan saw no external features on the other vessel. No doors, windows, antennas, satellite dishes or lights. The thing looked like a completely smooth, elongated black egg with a tail that came to a fine point.

He cycled back through the video footage of the ship's approach. "Where's its propulsion system?"

"Good question," Carillo said. "The hull's shiny. Could be solar panels, but I don't see anything that could be exhaust vents or thrusters."

"Should we risk the spectrometers?" Kiera asked. "They've gotta be putting out some kind of radiation."

"No, let's maintain a neutral stance for now," Morgan said. "I don't want to do anything to set them or the UMOs off."

The alien conversation coming through the intercom halted, and the crew quieted along with it. For half a minute, they sat in silence and listened to static. Outside *Rorschach*, the only signs of activity came from the sparkles of the lights coating the alien vessel.

"What now?" Ajay whispered.

"Why are you whispering?" Kiera whispered back.

"I don't know," Ajay said, still whispering.

Carillo joined the whisper brigade. "Paul ... " Her eyes were closed. "She's talking to me again." Her face cycled through expressions as she mouthed silent words.

"What's she saying?" Ajay asked.

"Shhh," Kiera admonished. "Don't distract her."

Finally Carillo's eyes fluttered open and she turned to Morgan. "She said, 'Safe. Friend.' She's trying to tell me something else, but I'm having a hard time understanding her."

"How so?" Morgan asked.

"Well, I keep getting these thoughts that say, 'Talk.' I don't know if she wants me to talk with her, or she's telling us to talk to the ship, or the ship wants to talk with us. I'm trying to get her to clarify, but we're going round in circles."

"Holy moly!" Ajay said.

Morgan wheeled to face Ajay. The Nepali had his headphones on and his hand on a dial at the comms station. With his free hand he pressed the headphones tighter to his ears.

"Ajay?" Kiera said.

He pulled his hand away from the headphones and waved it to quiet her. He further adjusted the dial, his hand shaking. Then he removed the headphones and turned to the others.

"You are *not* gonna believe this."

"They're talking to us?" Kiera asked.

"Not they. *He*," Ajay said.

"On VLF?" Morgan asked.

Ajay shook his head. "UHF."

"Is it one of the Callistons or another UMO?" Kiera asked.

Instead of answering, Ajay turned back to the comms station and entered a command. A moment later, a voice sounded from the intercom.

" ... *Rorschach Explorer*, acknowledge. Repeat, *Rorschach Explorer*, acknowledge. Come on, y'all, don't leave me hanging."

Morgan was suddenly overwhelmed with dizziness. Though it had been more than twenty-five years since he had last seen the man, Morgan recognized the voice immediately.

Carillo looked equally dazed. "It can't be," she said. "It just can't be."

Morgan unbuckled and floated over to Ajay. "Let me talk to him."

Ajay handed Morgan the headphones. He slipped them on, moved the microphone bar to his mouth, and drew in a deep breath. Finally he pushed the call button.

As he spoke, his own voice came over the intercom. "*Rorschach Explorer*, acknowledging. Jesus Christ, Nick, is it really you?"

After a few seconds of static, an exuberant voice replied. "Skywalker! Well I'll be damned. I didn't believe the radio intercepts. How you doing, old man?"

Morgan wiped tears from his eyes and pressed the call button again. His voice faltered as he answered. "Missed the hell out of you, buddy … "

"Yeah … me too," Nick said, emotion tinging his voice as well. "Miss everybody back home."

Morgan began to sob as he removed the headphones. He grabbed hold of a surprised Ajay and hugged him.

Carillo floated up beside them, took the headphones and put them on. "Nick? It's Julia Carillo." Tears ran down her cheeks, but she beamed. "It's *so* good to hear your voice. We hoped … but … we … "

She couldn't finish the sentence. She bent over and started to weep. Morgan understood; she and Nick had been part of the same class of NASA astronauts.

Nick's reply was punctuated by snuffles. "Now don't go getting all worked up. You're gonna make me cry, too."

"It's hard not to," Carillo managed. "Are Avery and Christine with you?"

The question stirred Morgan from his embrace with Ajay. He whispered, "You recording this?"

Ajay nodded.

"No, it's just me," Nick said. "They're all right, though. Better than all right. Hello, Dr. Walsh, Mr. Joshi. Y'all look younger than you do on TV."

"You can see us?" Carillo said.

"Sort of … through our mutual friends."

"The UMOs?"

Nick laughed. "Wow, I haven't heard them called that in a blue moon. Yeah, the UMOs. We call them Cytons."

"Got it." Carillo handed Ajay the headset. "Introduce yourself."

Ajay didn't bother putting the headphones on. He just pressed the call button and said, "Hello, Captain Reed. It's Ajay Joshi. I don't know what to say other than it's amazing to meet you."

He passed the headphones back to Carillo, who placed them in Kiera's hands. She put them on and moved the microphone bar to her lips. "Hi. Kiera Walsh here. I can't believe we're talking with you."

"Well, howdy to both of you," Nick said. "I understand your Dr. Shilling got himself zapped."

"How do you know about him?" Kiera asked.

"Little birdie told me. Or should I say a little Cyton? Is he okay?"

Kiera looked to Morgan, who floated forward and took the headset. "He went into cardiac arrest. We revived him, but we're not sure how much damage was done."

"Yeah, they can pack a punch. Don't worry, we'll fix him up."

"We?" Morgan said.

"You didn't think I could fly this bucket-o'-bolts on my own, did you? I mean, I'm a good pilot and all, but I ain't that good!"

Morgan looked at his shipmates. Ajay mouthed, *Callistons!*

"Nick, who are you flying with? The aliens from Callisto?" Morgan asked.

There was a long pause before Nick answered. "Yeah … and a few others."

"Care to elaborate?"

Another pause. "Look, we should continue this in person. There's a lot to talk about. Y'all wanna come on over and meet the Suhkai?"

"The what?"

"Suhkai. The aliens from Callisto. Make sure to bring Shilling. We've got docs aboard. Like I said, we'll fix him up."

Morgan turned to Carillo, Kiera and Ajay. The Callisto queen swirled around them like a firefly. "What do you think? Want to meet Nick Reed and some more aliens?"

Ajay bounced up and down. "Yes! Yes! Let's do it!"

"I'm in," Carillo said.

"It's what we came for, right?" Kiera said. She shrugged. "Just wish I could see better."

"Maybe their doctor can fix your eyes," Ajay said.

"Guess there's only one way to find out."

Morgan pressed the call button. "How do you plan to bring us aboard, Nick? I don't see any docks on your ship."

"Oh, we got docks all right. I designed this bad boy myself. We're gonna bring you over in style. Of course, you're probably not gonna enjoy our decontamination protocol all that much, but it'll be worth it. I promise."

"All right, just tell us what to do."

"First step: buckle up your crew, Skywalker. This might get a little bumpy."

CHAPTER 17

CLEANSING

A s soon as Morgan and his crew were secured in their seats, and cameras recording the docking, the alien ship moved forward to *Rorschach*'s port side.

Morgan radioed Nick. "Hey, not to be a backseat driver, but our airlock's on the starboard side."

"Let me do the driving, old man. You just enjoy the ride," Nick said.

The alien ship halted its advance, and the Cytons coating the ship's hull flew away.

"Where are they going?" Ajay said.

Carillo cycled through *Rorschach*'s camera feeds. She spotted the Cytons beneath *Rorschach*. "Got 'em. They're below us. Check Cam-9. Looks like they're forming into a ball just forward of the cargo bay."

The alien ship drifted upward until the lowest part of its hull was level with *Rorschach*.

Morgan leaned forward and peered up at the ship through the window. "Man, from here that boat looks bigger than an aircraft carrier."

Carillo switched their monitors to a view from one of the cameras atop *Rorschach*'s instrument pallet. Using a joystick, she rotated and focused the camera on the alien ship. "Something's happening portside."

Driven by a telescoping armature, a section of the shell of the alien ship had pushed outward above *Rorschach* like a sliding drawer.

"There's a dock," Morgan said, pointing. "See it? It's on the arm."

Ajay unbuckled and floated to the window for a closer look. "It's right above us."

Nick's voice came over the intercom. "Hey, Paul? You better tell your sightseer to strap back in or he's gonna get some nasty lumps on his head."

"Come on, Elroy, you heard the man," Kiera said. "Get back to your station."

He saluted her and propelled to his seat.

When Ajay had refastened his harness, Morgan said, "Okay, Nick, we're all set. But remember, we've got a casualty in our med bay, so take it easy."

"Copy that. Just to be on the safe side, let's give your casualty some extra padding."

The queen on the flight deck pulsed, then darted out the flight deck door.

Ajay whipped his head around to follow her flight. "What the heck? Where is she going?"

Carillo pulled up the med bay feed. "Check this out." The feed showed hundreds of Cytons coating Shilling from head to toe.

"Nice padding," Ajay said.

A jolt shook *Rorschach*, and its starboard wing began to pitch upward.

"What's going on?" Ajay asked.

"If I had to guess, we're getting rolled by that ball of UMOs that was beneath us," Morgan said.

Carillo switched back to Cam-9. As Morgan predicted, the camera showed the UMOs congregating on the underside of *Rorschach*'s port wing. As they pulsed in unison, they exerted a magnetic pull on the wing, which rotated the ship until *Rorschach*'s starboard side was perpendicular with the docking armature above.

The ship jolted again. Looking out the flight deck window, Morgan saw they were rising toward the armature.

"Julia, activate our docking sensors," he said.

"Roger." Seconds later, Carillo said, "Fifty meters ... thirty-five ... twenty ... Paul, they're off center by three meters on starboard."

Morgan radioed Nick. "Hey, your Cyton buddies are off by three meters starboard."

"Relax, you old coot, they're not gonna crash your ride."

"Ten meters, still off center by two," Carillo said. "Five meters ... off by one."

Another jolt.

"Okay, Skywalker," Nick said, "Cytons are away. The last five meters are on you. Don't ram my dock."

Morgan laughed. "Roger that. By the way, what's the name of your precious bucket-o'-bolts?"

"Hey man, don't go making fun of my baby. It's state-of-the-art greased lightning."

"No doubt. But does she have a name?"

"Well, the Suhkai name for it is unpronounceable. I can't mimic it without a translator."

"Uh-huh," Morgan said. "So you gave her a name yourself. I know you, Nick Reed. You wanted to rename *Cetus Prime* before we even had a launch schedule pinned down. If I recall correctly, you wanted to call it *Wild Thing*."

Nick's laugh echoed through the cabin. "Oh, this one's *much* classier. I call her *Ethel*."

The flight deck erupted in laughter. Morgan held down the call button so Nick could hear the crew's reaction.

"Hey," Nick said, "it's better than *Rorschach Inkblot* or whatever your ship is called."

By now Carillo had activated their docking autopilot. Several thruster bursts later, she reported the docking-clamps' sensors were green.

Morgan relayed the news to Nick.

"Roger that. We are locked on to you," Nick said. "Pressurizing the airlock on our side. Atmo's gonna be a bit thinner and colder than you're used to, just a heads-up. Nothing you can't handle, but it'll take a little time to adapt."

"Copy," Morgan said. "We'll make sure to bundle up."

"Yeah, about that. Don't bother. Y'all are gonna need to strip down to your birthday suits before you open the airlock. The Suhkai are super-sensitive to foreign germs."

"Excuse me?" Kiera said. "Did he just say we have to get naked?"

"I believe he did."

"Why don't we just wear our EMUs?" Ajay suggested.

Morgan floated the suggestion to Nick. "I realize it'll be more impersonal, but we'd feel more comfortable going that route."

"No can do," said Nick. "Too much risk of a germ exchange." He explained that the crew would be provided clothing once they passed through a decontamination chamber and received inoculations. "The injections are more for your benefit than ours. We've got some exotic germs that could be lethal to you in certain circumstances. You don't wanna bring that shit back to Earth. You might wipe out half the population."

The crew's enthusiasm for boarding *Ethel* took a nosedive. The capper was Nick's final clarification. "Oh, and, uh ... there are a couple side effects I should mention ... "

Morgan radioed back. "Oh, that's great. Explosive diarrhea, I'm guessing?"

"No, nothing like that ... of course, that might happen when you try our grub."

"You're not doing all that well at making this feel like an appealing proposition."

"I know, but believe me, it'll be a hundred percent better experience for you than it was for us. We learned all this the hard way."

Morgan lowered his head and nodded. "Yeah, you guys had it rough, I imagine. Sorry about the petty bitching. More sorry about what happened to *Cetus Prime*. We tried to stop Space Command, but we were too late."

"That's okay, Skywalker. It's like another shooting star to us. Gone and forgotten."

"Well, *you're* not forgotten. None of you are. I want you to know that. We've made sure of that," Morgan said.

"So I gather. Been monitoring Earth broadcasts for a while. Y'all have caused quite a stir. Now, enough titter tatter, you coming aboard or what?"

Morgan turned to face his now-on-the-fence shipmates. "You heard the drill. I'm still going. Anyone with me?"

"He never told us what the side effects are," Ajay said.

"Oh yeah." Morgan radioed Nick. "Nick? About those side effects you mentioned ... ?"

"Yeah ... so ... the detox chemicals are gonna make all your hair fall out. I mean *all* of it ... *everywhere*. Most of it'll grow back in about a month … give or take. And the inoculation kinda makes your skin turn a bit blue. That part lasts about a week."

Morgan looked around to gauge the crew's reaction. "Looks like it'll be a delegation of one, Nick. Just me."

"Oh, come on, Skywalker. Tell them to buck up. I want to meet all of you."

"It's not that simple. Julia has some significant burns. I don't think they'll fare well if they're exposed to harsh chemicals."

"Not to worry. The Suhkai will cover the burns with a salve that'll protect them. Plus, once she's through detox, they can heal the burns."

"Hold on a minute, Nick. Let me discuss it with my people."

"Of course."

Morgan started with Carillo. "I can see you're not fired up about this. You want to take a pass?"

"I don't know, Paul. I would very much like to see Nick and give him a great big hug. And if he says they can protect the burns, I believe him. Hell, I'm not even worried about temporarily losing my hair or turning blue. That's a small price to pay to make contact with an alien race. But what concerns me is the inoculation. How do we know it's safe? What if one of us, or all of us, have an allergic reaction to it?"

"Good point," Morgan said. "Let's see what Nick has to say about it."

Nick assured Morgan the risk of a reaction from the inoculation was minimal. "It'll make you sleepy, that's for sure. Maybe give you a little bit of a fever, but that's it."

Morgan clicked off and turned back to Carillo. "I understand where you're coming from, Julia. It's a fair concern, and if you want to sit this one out, it's your call. But I'm going. I *have* to go."

"Yeah, I know you do," she said. "It's okay. I'll stay on *Rorschach* with Bob. There's no way he'd survive what Nick described."

"But didn't Nick say the aliens could help Dr. Shilling?" Ajay asked.

"He did," Morgan said.

"So shouldn't we take him with us?"

"Us?" Morgan said. "Does that mean you're going?"

"Roger dodger. I came all this way to meet some aliens. I'm not backing out now."

"Well that makes two of us." Morgan turned to Kiera. "Kiera, you've been quiet. Do you want to stay on *Rorschach* with Julia and Bob? Might be a good idea given your eyesight's not all the way back."

"Nah, I'm good. I'll go," she said. "I can't say I'm looking forward to the whole detox thing, but I agree with Major Carillo. It's a small price to pay to meet the lizard men and Captain Reed. I do have one small request, though."

"What's that?"

"I'd like five minutes alone with the mai tai pouch before we leave."

Morgan laughed. "Deal."

He radioed Nick with their plan.

But Nick pushed back. "Look, I really want to see Julia. It will bum me out if she doesn't come aboard. We can quarantine Dr. Shilling in the airlock and take him to our med bay right away. The Suhkai will make sure he's in stable condition before he goes through detox and inoculation. You have my word."

"I'm sure your word is golden, Nick," Morgan said, "but we're going to stick with our plan. Just give the three of us about fifteen minutes to get ready. I need to send an update to our Mission Control Center and we need—"

"Paul?" Nick interrupted.

"Yeah?"

"I'd appreciate it if you didn't contact your people just yet."

Morgan frowned. "Why?"

"I'll explain when you come aboard."

"Uh, I'd like an explanation now if you don't mind. They know we were rendezvousing with your ship. They'll be expecting an update."

There was a long pause before Nick replied. "I'm not ready for people to know I've come back yet."

"But—"

"Look, Paul, all things considered, I don't think it's too much to ask. Just respect my wishes until we've had a chance to discuss things. You'll understand my request after we talk. I'll see you after the inoculations."

CREW AIRLOCK — THE *RORSCHACH EXPLORER*
DOCKED WITH SUHKAI SPACECRAFT ETHEL
DRIFTING AT ALL-STOP IN THE ASTEROID BELT

After emerging from the galley with a smile on her face, Kiera joined Morgan and Ajay in the main crew airlock across the corridor from the ready room and just aft of the flight deck.

"You get your fill of liquid courage?" Morgan asked.

"Uh-huh," she said. "Guess what? I can see a little better now, too."

"That's great news," Ajay said.

"It is." She fixed Ajay with a look. "So I'll be able to tell if your eyes drift my way."

Ajay started to protest the insinuation, but Morgan quickly cut in. "Look, I know this is going to be awkward as hell, but we'll get through it. Just be professional and focus on the end game."

Carillo exited the flight deck and walked up to them, the Callisto queen hovering behind her with a handful of Cyton escorts. "Paul, I think we should treat this like an EVA and set up a regular check-in schedule, like every thirty minutes."

"Good idea. We'll have to rely on Nick to give us access to comms, but I'm sure he'll come through. We'll start the cycle once we're done with the detox."

"Sounds good." Carillo hugged each of her shipmates. "You be careful. All of you."

"What's the matter, Major?" Kiera said. "I can't see you very well, but your voice sounds a little spooked."

"I don't like the radio silence request," Carillo said. "I mean, I get that Nick might not want to send everybody on Earth into a tizzy about him being alive. I can see how he might want to make that known himself. But I don't understand why he's not comfortable with us letting Mayaguana know we linked up. We wouldn't even have to mention Nick yet."

"I wouldn't sweat it," Morgan said. "We'll clear it up first thing when we meet with Nick. In fact, why don't you go ahead now and prepare an update that doesn't mention Nick. That way it'll be ready to go as soon as I give you the green light."

After a few last-minute instructions, Morgan cranked open the airlock door, and the three astronauts entered. Carillo shut the door behind them.

Morgan sighed and began to unzip his flight suit. "Okay, crew. Let's make this quick."

As the three astronauts peeled out of their flight suits and underclothing, they kept their eyes fixed on the far end of the airlock and their thoughts focused on the historic meeting that loomed ahead. As such, they paid no heed to the cluster of blue lights that briefly flickered into view behind them.

DECONTAMINATION CHAMBER – SUHKAI SPACECRAFT *ETHEL*
SEPTEMBER 8, 2019

With her eyelids pressed as tight as she could make them, Kiera felt a clump of her hair slide down her nose. The chemical spray stung, but at least it was warm. The naked march from *Rorschach*'s airlock through *Ethel*'s counterpart chamber and into the decontamination room had been so cold it felt like an ice bath. The air had been almost as frigid as the metallic walkway under the soles of her bare feet.

Now, with her arms raised above her head and her legs spread, Kiera stood still as one of the Suhkai continued to "power wash" her body. She was sorely tempted to open her eyes and take another look at the alien, but feared the chemicals still dripping down her forehead would damage her eyes.

Though Kiera had seen the photographs of the spaceport murals many times, and knew from the *Cetus Prime* logs that the humanoid aliens were taller and thicker than Earthlings, the mental image she had formed of the Suhkai significantly underestimated their height and girth.

From the moment the hazmat-suited aliens had entered the decontamination chamber to greet Kiera and her colleagues, even with her vision still somewhat blurred, she had been able to tell they were easily twice as tall as she and that their arms and legs were as thick as an elephant's limbs.

Only these elephants didn't walk on all fours. Just like in the scenes depicted in the Callisto spaceport murals, they walked upright like humans on two legs supported by two boot-covered feet. They carried equipment with two glove-covered hands attached to two arms. In fact, in their hazmat suits and helmets, save for their exaggerated proportions, they looked human. No wonder the Cytons had been confused by Carillo's spacesuit-covered appearance, thought Kiera.

Daring a peek as the Suhkai now sprayed her feet, Kiera cracked open one eye and looked up at the alien, focusing her attention on the visor of its helmet. She couldn't see much of its face through the condensation covering the visor, but she could pick out its dark, reptilian eyes and gray-green skin. Nope. I'm not dreaming. This is really happening. Shutting her eye once more, Kiera recalled more of the brief and surreal first meeting with the Suhkai.

There had been no formal ceremony or greeting, although Morgan had suggested they bow when the Suhkai approached within reach. The Suhkai had either not seen or not understood the gesture, for they remained as still as statues. Morgan had then extended a hand and introduced himself to them. No response. They remained inert while Ajay took over communications from Morgan and spouted some "me human, you Suhkai" gibberish Kiera assumed he'd seen in some movie or TV show.

When the aliens finally did react, it was not to bestow greetings. Instead, one of the Suhkai used its hands to instruct the three naked astronauts to stand farther apart from one another. Another of the aliens had then raised its arms above its head and spread its legs, a gesture Kiera and her crewmates surmised they were supposed to mimic. Then just as quickly as they'd assumed the pose, the decontamination had commenced. Given the aliens' all-business approach, Kiera was left with the impression the Suhkai weren't particularly social beings or they didn't view the meeting as special. They seemed more concerned about cleaning them of "ick" than anything else.

With that thought lingering in her mind, the "power washing" ended and a new spray began.

This one was more of a mist than the pounding spray from before, and the sting of the chemicals was replaced by a pleasant tingling. Kiera felt a foamy sponge-like pad rubbing the top of her now-bald head. With gentle motions, the Suhkai was bathing her. Slowly and deliberately, it moved from head to toe. She found it relaxing until the alien reached her loins. There, the combination of the tingling mist and the Suhkai rubs produced a different reaction.

Thankfully, her arousal was cut short by the sound of Ajay protesting similar attention to his nether region. Morgan began to laugh, distracting Kiera, and soon her Suhkai moved on to less sensitive areas.

When the cleansing was complete, Kiera opened her eyes again and saw a Suhkai at the far end of the room motioning them toward another doorway. They entered a new chamber, filled with thousands of golden Cytons. Another hazmat-suited Suhkai stood in the center of the room and demonstrated the spread-eagle stance required of them.

Once more, Kiera and the others raised their arms and widened their legs. She watched the Cytons divide into groups and swarm around them. As they began to pelt their bodies with bright light, Kiera snapped her eyes shut. Within seconds, she heard Ajay chiding the Cytons for another close encounter with his private areas, rousing another round of laughter from Morgan. When it was all over, Kiera opened her eyes to see a bald Morgan bemoaning the loss of his prized mustache. "Took me years to get it just right," he grumbled.

She also noticed a dark splotch on his butt cheek. Her vision wasn't clear enough to tell any more than that, but she recalled Carillo's teasing during their Hawaiian party. "So it's true!" she said. "You have lightsabers tattooed on your butt!"

Morgan feigned an effort to cover the tattoo. "Hey, keep your eyes off my butt."

"Ha! Now we know the true source of your Skywalker mojo," she said.

All in all, the decontamination process had been as degrading as Kiera had expected, yet it was also the most fun she'd had since the mai tai party. As they lined up in front of two more Suhkai to receive their inoculations, she felt a renewed camaraderie with her shipmates.

She knew she owed much of her improved spirits to the ever-screwball Ajay. Not only did he look ridiculous hairless and naked, he was so in awe of the Suhkai, he kept on throwing up Vulcan-greeting hand signs to the puzzled aliens in between his efforts to shield his genitals from their view.

Keira watched as the Suhkai administered inoculations to Morgan and Ajay. Despite their intimidating height and girth, Kiera found the Suhkai movements measured and graceful in a way that reminded her of whales gliding through water. What was it they called whales on Earth? Gentle giants?

Her thoughts were interrupted by the hand of one of the aliens touching her head. She looked up and smiled. The alien's facial expression inside the helmet changed. Though Kiera couldn't see its mouth, it seemed to her that the alien smiled back.

The Suhkai cupped its palm over her pate and tilted her neck to the side. The hand was so big, Kiera's head was like a kiwi fruit in its palm. She was certain it could have crushed her skull with ease, but its touch was feather light.

The injection burned and made her neck muscles spasm. Within a few breaths, she felt dizzy and nauseated, and seconds after that she slumped to the floor, her head coming to rest on the boot of the Suhkai. The spasms spread to her shoulders and chest.

Gritting her teeth, she groaned in pain. The burning snaked up into her brain and down her spine. Kiera lost control of her arms and legs, and they flopped against the floor, her fingers and toes clenching with cramps. She tried to cry out for Morgan but choked on thick trails of saliva slithering down her throat.

The monstrous hand of the Suhkai closed around her lower leg, lifted her up, and carried her, dangling upside down, from the room. Kiera was powerless to resist.

Through blurry eyes, she tried to look for her shipmates, but she saw nothing but the gray surface of the floor.

The Suhkai stopped. Kiera felt something cold press against the small of her back. It jolted her spine, making her body go limp.

Then darkness washed over her, and she faded into unconsciousness.

FLIGHT DECK — THE *RORSCHACH EXPLORER*
DOCKED WITH SUHKAI SPACECRAFT *ETHEL*
DRIFTING AT ALL-STOP IN THE ASTEROID BELT

Carillo paced back and forth on the flight deck. It had been over an hour since the others boarded *Ethel* and she still hadn't heard from Morgan. While Nick hadn't provided a time estimate for the detox and inoculation procedures, Carillo couldn't imagine they would have taken more than half an hour combined. She'd tried to raise Nick on the radio but had received no answer.

Frustrated, she turned to the Callisto queen for answers. The gold ball of light had been following her around the ship like a shadow ever since the others disembarked. She asked the queen if she knew why it was taking so long and why Nick didn't answer the radio. But the queen didn't seem to receive her thoughts, for the alien exhibited no flickers or pulses when Carillo projected her questions.

With nothing else to do, Carillo decided to check on Shilling. She found him still unconscious, and even though the docking maneuver was complete, he continued to be surrounded by a blanket of pulsing Cytons. She asked the queen about the purpose of the Cytons and their pulsing, but again her question went unanswered.

As she swapped out Shilling's IV bag, Carillo heard a noise from the corridor. She paused to listen more closely. It was the sound of the airlock cranking open.

"What the … "

She finished attaching the bag to the rack by Shilling's gurney and headed for the med bay door. The Callisto queen and her escorts zoomed in front of her. A thought from the queen cut through Carillo's confusion. "*Stay!*"

The warning was delivered with enough force that Carillo stepped back. *"Why?"*

The cranking sound picked up pace.

Carillo called out, "Paul? Is that you? Is everything okay? Ajay? Kiera?" She moved toward the med bay door once again.

The golden queen suddenly flashed a bright white. *"Stay!"*

Carillo shielded her eyes. *"What's happening?"*

Thumps echoed down the corridor. Carillo could feel the vibrations through her boots. *"Move,"* she commanded.

Not only did the queen and her escorts remain hovering in front of Carillo, another dozen Cytons swirled up from Shilling and joined the blockade.

The thuds grew more intense, and a dark shadow obscured the corridor lights.

"Who's there?" Carillo shouted. "Is that you, Nick? Please say something. You're scaring me."

When the enormous lizard head appeared in the doorway, Carillo backed right into Shilling. The Cytons covering him rose up and slithered over her body. She tried to push them away as she pleaded with the queen. "Stop! Why are you—"

The aim of the Suhkai was true. Carillo slumped to the floor.

CHAPTER 18

LYING EYES

RECOVERY ROOM — SUHKAI SPACECRAFT *ETHEL*
IN ORBIT AROUND SATURN MOON DIONE
SEPTEMBER 10, 2019

Morgan awoke to find himself lying inside a glass-encased pod. His head throbbed and his throat was parched. His hands were covered with mitten-like gloves, and he was clad in a one-piece gray garment. He could feel a hood cinched around his face.

Morgan closed his eyes and tried to remember how he had ended up here. He recalled boarding the alien ship and entering the decontamination center … but nothing after that. Had he fainted?

He looked right and left. Though the light overhead was dim, he could tell his pod was in the middle of an otherwise barren room. Laying his head back against the cushioned surface inside the chamber, he pressed his hands against the glass to see if he could open it.

To his surprise, the casing began to retract.

The second it opened, the warmth inside vanished. The room surrounding him was as cold as *Ethel*'s airlock had been, and Morgan's thin garment did little to protect him.

He propped himself up on his elbows and discovered his muscles were unusually stiff. Pulling his legs up, he swung them awkwardly out of the chamber. With a push of his arms, he sat up and raised his arms above his head. After a good stretch, he tugged off the annoying hood — only to be reminded of his newfound baldness. He moved his hand to his mouth, half-hoping his Fu Manchu mustache had miraculously reappeared while he slept. It hadn't.

He lowered his feet to the floor and attempted to stand. But his legs were weak, and he had to grab hold of the pod's frame to avoid falling.

He heard a door open behind him, and then Nick Reed's voice. "Take it easy, Paul. Your body has to get used to our gravity."

Morgan turned to see Nick Reed standing in the doorway. Except this man looked nothing like the Nick Reed that Morgan remembered. Nick had been a tall blond with the sleek body of a surfer. Sure, that had been twenty-five years ago, and it was natural to assume Nick's appearance would have changed as he aged ... but this wasn't about aging. Nick barely looked human.

"It's a shock, I know," Nick said, stepping closer.

"Jesus, Nick, what happened to you?"

Nick was hairless like Morgan, and his skin was mottled with dark splotches. His hands were swollen to twice their normal size, and judging by the size of his boots, the same applied to his feet. His eyes were almost entirely black, and some of his teeth had fallen out. Worst of all, he looked thin and drawn, and was hunched over as if he carried a heavy load. Yet despite the bodily deformities, his face showed little sign of aging — just a few wrinkles around the eyes — and his voice sounded as youthful as ever.

"What can I say? Apparently, I went out for one too many spacewalks." Nick smiled. In a labored motion, he held out his hand. "Don't worry, you won't catch my ugly. Just don't squeeze too hard. Hand's a bit tender."

Morgan shed the mittens and gently took hold of Nick's hand. Unsatisfied with the greeting, he moved in closer and hugged his bent-over friend. "I'm having a hard time believing all of this, but I'm damn happy to see you."

"Same here," Nick said. He patted Morgan's back. "More than you could know."

As he pulled from the embrace, Morgan noticed his own hands were bluish-pink, almost purple. Well, he'd been warned.

"Where have you been, Nick? Where did you go? Where are Avery and Christine?"

"Long story. Are you hungry?"

"Honestly, not really. I feel queasy."

"Yeah, the vaccines will do that. Still, come on, let's at least get out of here before we both freeze."

Nick led him from the room and down a hallway with walls at least twenty feet tall. A lattice of dim, orangish lights formed an arched ceiling. The combination of the hall and ceiling reminded Morgan of a cathedral — an ice-box-cold cathedral.

Nick took small steps, and he winced with each delicate plant of his feet. Morgan's gait wasn't much better. His legs were unsteady and he wobbled on more than one occasion.

"Where are Ajay and Kiera?" he asked. "In these rooms?" He gestured to the doors that lined both sides of the corridor.

Without breaking his stiff stride, Nick said, "Yep, they're still sleeping off their inoculations. Same with Julia and Bob."

Morgan halted. "What?"

Nick stopped and turned back to look at Morgan. "Bob went into cardiac arrest. Julia called us for help. We brought them aboard and took care of him. Took care of both of them."

Morgan squeezed his eyelids shut and shook his head. While he understood what Nick had said, his mind grappled with the news. "When did this happen? How long have I been out?"

Nick shrugged. "It's been a while since I've thought in terms of Earth time. A day? Maybe more."

"You're joking."

Nick shook his head.

"Good God, Nick. Why didn't you tell us the inoculations would knock us out for so long?"

"I thought I did."

"No, you didn't. You made it sound like we'd see you right afterwards. If I'd known that wasn't the case, I would have been more insistent about checking in back home before we came aboard. They must be worried sick about us."

"Not to worry. Julia transmitted a message after she came aboard."

"She did?"

"Yes. Now follow me."

"Hold up. I want to see them," Morgan said. "Right now. All of them."

"Relax, Paul. We'll check on them later. There's no rush. They're all asleep."

As the hunchbacked Nick resumed walking down the hall, Morgan remained in place. What was up with Nick? He'd always been a home-spun, laid-back kind of person, but the "fah-getta-bout-it" vibe of his responses struck Morgan as too casual under the circumstances.

"Nick, listen to me, buddy. I'm worried about them. I'd like to see them now. It'll just take a few minutes." He approached the closest door. "Who's in this one?"

"Later. Come on, we have a lot to talk about."

"Damn it, Nick. If I had any hairs left, they'd be sticking straight out. Why won't you let me see them?"

Nick sighed and walked back to him. "Look, Paul, it's more important that we talk than it is for you to see your crew right now. You're gonna have to trust me on that."

ABOARD *SOL SEAKER*
ANCHORED OFF THE COAST OF KABARA ISLAND
FIJI ARCHIPELAGO
SEPTEMBER 10, 2019

Jennifer Stevens sat on the floor of Anlon and Pebbles' cabin, her back propped against the foot of the bed. As she stared up at the muted televi-sion, she massaged her *bgood2lanother* badge with her thumb.

Perched on the edge of the bed, her legs brushing up against Jennifer's shoulder, Pebbles said, "I don't know, Jen. I've got a bad feeling about this."

"Well, keep it to yourself," Jennifer said. She turned to Anlon, who sat on an easy chair next to the bed. "Any word from Antonio?"

"Yeah." Anlon set down his cell phone. He lowered his head and whispered, "I'm so sorry, Jen."

Jennifer clutched the badge and fought back tears. "What did he say?"

"Maybe we should turn off the television," Anlon said to Pebbles.

As Pebbles reached for the remote, Jennifer stood. "No! Don't you dare."

"Okay, okay, I won't." Pebbles set down the remote and motioned for Jennifer to sit back down.

Instead, Jennifer wheeled toward Anlon. "What did Antonio say?"

"Look, Jen, it's not—"

"Is it true? Are they real?" Jennifer pointed at the television. It was tuned to WNN. The majority of the screen was devoted to a live shot of Hangar-2 in A3I's Mayaguana complex. Reporters milled about in front of *RE2*, many of them with grim expressions. Across the bottom of the screen, a red banner displayed text in white. *Breaking: Augustus Amato to address authenticity of images acquired by WNN.*

Anlon nodded.

"Damn!" Jennifer kicked the mattress and stormed from the room.

Anlon looked at Pebbles. "I'm sorry. I didn't know what to say."

She rose from the bed and reached for his hand. "It's okay. At least she knows before she sees the pictures. Are they as bad as Jenna Toffy hyped?"

"Looks like we're about to find out."

The television had switched to a close-up shot of Jenna Toffy. Pebbles quickly snatched up the remote and unmuted it.

" ... *minutes ago, I met privately with Augustus Amato, and he confirmed to me that the photos obtained by this network are authentic.*"

An off-camera voice, presumably an in-studio WNN anchor, asked, "*Did he say who took the images? Was it one of the astronauts?*"

"*Chet, he told me the images were recorded by one of two drone-landers aboard the* Rorschach Explorer."

The anchor was only four words into his next question when Toffy interrupted him. "*Chet, he's coming to the podium. I've gotta run.*"

The screen switched to a view of Amato walking to the podium in front of *RE2*, aided by his cane and accompanied by Dante Fulton and Dennis Pritchard. The aerospace titan's eyes were riveted on the podium ahead while camera flashes exploded all around him.

The anchor's voice said, "*Well, ladies and gentlemen, before Mr. Amato begins speaking, I'd like to say it was not an easy decision to break this story. We at WNN understand the sensitivities involved for the crew's families and for the millions who have followed the* Rorschach Explorer's *odyssey, but given the gravity of the circumstances we felt an obligation to report on the photographs we obtained. At the conclusion of the press conference, we will release most of the photographs on our website. But out of respect for the* Rorschach *families, we have chosen to refrain from publishing a few of the more sensitive images."*

Jennifer returned to the cabin and sat down next to Pebbles. "Sorry I lost it."

Pebbles laced her fingers through Jennifer's. "No need to apologize."

On screen, Amato began his comments. *"Two days ago, I came before you to speak willingly and candidly about the* Rorschach Explorer, *its crew and the events that have impacted their mission — our mission. I addressed your questions and dispelled irresponsible rumors. In some cases, I corrected misconceptions and, in other cases, I acknowledged our failures. I promised at that time to be more proactive in sharing information and to provide you with greater access. Since making that commitment, we've held another four press briefings and answered every question put to us.*

"In exchange, I made two requests of the press. Work with us to ensure facts are published, not rumors. And allow us the time to assess and respond to unfolding events before rushing to report incomplete or questionable information obtained from unofficial sources.

"This is an extraordinary mission with profound ramifications for the future of space exploration and our relationships with alien life-forms. As such, it deserves news coverage that reflects the serious nature of these noble pursuits.

"Yet I stand here now, reluctantly, forced to respond to another heap of breathless falsehoods and innuendo. Though I tried to convince WNN to hold off on publishing the eight photographs they acquired, the network has declined. I was told I should have known better than to ask. I guess they are right, but it amazes me I needed to ask in the first place.

"As to the facts, here they are: We received our last communication from the Rorschach Explorer *twenty-eight hours ago as they prepared to rendezvous with an alien spacecraft we believe is piloted by the beings who built the Callisto spaceport. We have been unsuccessful in our attempts to generate a response from the crew since then. However, for much of that time we had an active communication link with two drone-landing vehicles stored in* Rorschach's *cargo bay.*

"Concerned about the crew's welfare, we decided to remotely undock one of the landers and fly it through the ship to provide us with photographs to help us understand why the crew wasn't responding. Many of the resulting photographs are blurry, partially obstructed or simply not the views we might have chosen. This is because without the ability to 'live-steer' the lander, we relied on a pre-programmed flight path based on a digital layout of the ship — and when the lander encountered unexpected obstacles that disrupted its flight path, that negatively affected the precision of its cameras.

"But we nevertheless obtained eight good, unobstructed photographs: three of the main corridor, two of the medical bay, two of the laboratory compartment and one of the engine control room. The photographs show extensive damage to equipment and evidence of a violent struggle. That is all we know. At this hour, despite our ongoing efforts to reestablish communications, we still have not received any contact from the crew, and we've lost our connection with the two landers ... "

As Amato continued to speak, Anlon looked back at the text message from Antonio. *The inside of the ship's been torn apart. It's history. No way it can fly. Sure hope WNN doesn't show all the blood on TV.*

HUMAN CREW GALLEY — SUHKAI SPACECRAFT *ETHEL*
IN ORBIT AROUND SATURN MOON DIONE

Morgan hesitantly followed Nick into a car-like pod. Nick spoke a command, and the pod rose inside a tubular track and delivered them to a higher floor. They exited in front of a doorway and, in response to another spoken command, the doors parted. They stepped into a small airlock and the doors closed behind them.

A gush of hot steam filled the room, making Morgan perspire. Then a tone sounded and the doors at the opposite side of the airlock slid open.

They proceeded into a rounded vestibule with eight doorways spaced evenly around its circumference. Morgan was immediately struck by how different this room felt from anywhere else he'd been on the ship. From the dimensions of the walls, to the temperature, to the furnishings he could see through the open doorways … this place actually felt like it was designed for humans — apart from the dim, orange-red lighting, which was no different from that on the rest of the ship.

Nick led Morgan through one of the doorways into a spacious galley with a full kitchen and a long table with ten chairs. "Have a seat."

As Morgan sat, he said, "Ten chairs? You have other crew? I thought you said Avery and Christine weren't with you."

Nick retrieved a few items from a refrigerator. "They're not."

"Then what's with all the chairs? They're too small for the Suhkai."

"You never know when you might have visitors," Nick said. He returned to the table with two soda-can-sized tubes of a clear liquid and two more filled with a gold gel. He sat down and gave one of each to Morgan. "Good old H2O in that one," he said, pointing, "and nectar of the stars in the other."

Morgan lifted the gold gel and examined it. "Nectar of the stars?"

"It's a sugary compound. It's got some trace minerals, protein, but it's mostly carbohydrates." Nick opened his gold tube, sucked on the spout, and swished the gel in his mouth before swallowing. "This is what kept Avery, Christine and me alive for the early part of our journey."

Morgan uncapped his own tube and squeezed a small amount on his tongue. "Tastes like honey."

"Yeah, it is a lot like honey. Kind of ironic — the Cytons forage the raw ingredients, kind of like bees forage pollen." He held the tube toward the ceiling. "Thank the Suhkai for that. They taught the Cytons to do it. The Suhkai are also responsible for these tubes of water. *And the air we're breathing.*"

Morgan uncapped the water and gulped down half the bottle. It was cold and refreshing — and better-tasting than *Rorschach*'s supply.

Nick continued. "The Suhkai have been exploring the galaxy for hundreds of thousands of years. At least, that's my estimate; they don't think in terms of Earth years. Anyway, one of the biggest challenges of deep space travel, as we both know, is supply. Whether you're talking about food and water, air to breathe or energy for propulsion … supply is a tough nut to crack."

"And the Suhkai cracked that nut?"

"Yep. They learned early on that they didn't need to bring all their supplies with them. They realized it was easier to find the necessary building blocks in space and then make and store supplies as they were needed. You follow me?"

"They learned to harvest asteroids."

Nick shook his head. "Not just asteroids. Planets, moons, comets, stars, you name it. They're remarkable scavengers. They had to be. They didn't have a choice."

He explained that the Suhkai home planet, Suhko, had become uninhabitable — that a series of events had altered the planet's orbit into an exaggerated and unstable elliptic. "Everything started to die. Fortunately for them, and for us, they had already developed the technology to fly into space. They had mining operations on three of their moons, but the situation with their planet also affected the stability of the moons, so … they had to push beyond or perish."

"Let me stop you there, Nick," Morgan said. "How far away from Earth is, or was, their home planet?"

"Thousands of light years."

"And there were UMOs — excuse me, Cytons, in their solar system? Did they bring them to ours?"

"Cytons are everywhere, Paul. There's not a star system in our galaxy without them. In fact, the Suhkai believe life wouldn't exist anywhere in the universe without them. They first discovered them in a nebula the Suhkai named Cyto."

Nick explained that the Suhkai belief system was sort of a mix between how humans think of creation and evolution. "The Suhkai don't buy into our Big Bang Theory, in fact they think it's kind of silly, but they do believe organic life began in a similar way as we do — a slurry of organic compounds sparked to life by an electromagnetic charge. In addition, they believe it's the Cytons that provide the electrical stimulation that creates all organic life in the universe — past, present and future. For that reason they view Cytons, in the collective, as God, although the Suhkai don't worship them like a deity. They don't look to Cytons to answer the mysteries of the universe. But they do revere them. It gives the Suhkai peace to be with Cytons, to travel with them, to interact with them. To the Suhkai, to be in the presence of a single Cyton is like having a piece of God by their side."

The reverence with which Nick spoke about the Cytons made goose bumps form on the back of Morgan's neck. At times, Cytons seemed like simple creatures that could be trained like honeybees. At others, they exhibited complex coordination that belied their appearance. They could be helpful one moment, ruthless the next. They demonstrated curiosity and compassion. They protected their own, hunted with precision and killed with ease. And now here was Nick talking of them as the creators of all life.

"And I'll tell you what, Paul, those little space bees saved Avery, Christine and me many times over the past twenty-four years. Many times." Nick lowered his head and closed his eyes as if in prayer.

Morgan watched him in silence, unwilling to disturb his meditation. When Nick finally looked up again, there was a tear on his cheek.

"Where are Avery and Christine, Nick?"

"On a planet we call Tula. It's been our home for the past twelve years. Well, *their* home, mostly. I've been 'on the road' for the past eleven ... as you can probably tell from the way I look."

A dozen questions surged forward in Morgan's mind. He struggled with which to ask first.

Nick examined the spots on his swollen hands. "Sometimes I kind of wish I'd stayed on Tula."

"Why didn't you?"

Nick smiled. "You like to get straight to the point, don't you?"

"Can you blame me?"

"Nah, I guess not. Truth is, it's a complicated answer. One I don't think you can appreciate without more background — and without meeting with our Suhkai and Cyton hosts."

As if on cue, a Cyton floated into the room and hovered between the two men. Nick stared at the alien, and it began to flicker. Morgan received its reply to Nick in his mind. "*Yes. They are ready.*"

"This is Maggie," Nick said. "That's what I call her. She's been with us since we left Callisto. She'll be our translator. Come on, we need to go meet Haula and Zoor."

Two levels up, Morgan followed Nick and Maggie along another tall, cold hallway. As they approached arched double doors at the corridor's end, the doors opened on their own and two Suhkai emerged to greet them.

This was Morgan's first clear look at the aliens. The ones that had tended to him and the others during decontamination had worn protective suits and helmets, and his only other point of reference was the *Cetus Prime* crew's photographs of murals inside the Callisto spaceport.

They were as tall as standing polar bears. Yet instead of a fur-covered body, the Suhkai were covered by a gray-green scaly skin akin to that of an alligator. The connection with reptiles or dinosaurs was further reinforced by their elongated heads, snout-like noses and dark eyes. Yet while their overall appearance was lizard-like, their facial expressions had distinctly human qualities. Morgan could detect smiles from their mouths that caused their brows to furrow and dimples to form on their cheeks.

On their thick but muscular bodies, these two wore sleeveless tunics that extended down to mid-thigh, with a rounded cut-out at the center of their chests to expose a bulged feature of their bodies. These ribbed bulges looked to Morgan like convex stereo-speaker woofers. There were other pad-like bulges on their forearms and thighs, though these were smooth instead of scaly. It might have been a trick of the light, but it seemed to Morgan that the pads were rising and falling in rhythm with one another. He thought of the injuries Carillo had suffered to her arms and legs and wondered if these pads served a special purpose.

Morgan tapped Nick on the shoulder. "Is there some sort of customary greeting? We tried to introduce ourselves in the decontamination chamber but they didn't seem to understand what we were doing."

Nick laughed. "Under normal circumstances, there would be a long ceremony, but they understand our time is limited. Just follow my lead."

"Okay."

Maggie hovered in front of the chest bulge of the Suhkai on the left. She glowed, and the bulge vibrated in response, as did the sloped holes on both sides of the alien's crested head. Maggie then drifted over to the other, and the exchange was repeated.

Nick stepped forward and raised his hand. He cupped the chest bulge of the Suhkai on the left and lowered his head. The alien's bulge vibrated powerfully enough to make Nick's arm tremble.

Nick pulled his hand away when the trembling ceased. "Your turn. Just place your hand on Haula's sonar. Don't squeeze it — it's not a tit. And don't rub it, it's not Buddha's belly. Just place your hand on it like you would on someone's forehead to feel their temperature. He'll pulse magnetic energy. They do it to feel your magnetic field. It's sort of like reading your aura. When he pulses, say hello in your mind. Maggie will translate."

"They don't speak?"

"They do, but not in any tongue you'd understand, and believe me, you don't want them to try speaking in their language. Their screeches are so intense they'll burst your eardrums. Found that out the hard way."

Morgan did as he was told. The alien's bulge felt different than he'd expected. He'd thought it might be supple, but it had a shell-like hardness. He lowered his head and waited, and after a moment the bulge vibrated, sending a sensation down his arm like a stream of water. It spread across his shoulder blade and ascended his spine.

He projected a thought. *"Hello, Haula. I am Paul."*

Maggie's translated response flowed back immediately. *"Untu, Skywalker."*

Morgan pulled his hand back and looked up at Haula. The alien smiled, showing his jagged teeth, and his crest tubes vibrated as if he was laughing.

Morgan turned to Nick. "He called me Skywalker."

"Yeah, you'll find they know a lot about you and your crew. We had plenty of time to catch up on y'all during the last leg of our trip. Now, careful when you touch Zoor. Those bumps across her abdomen *are* tits. Suhkai aren't real keen on humans touching them there. Again, found that out the hard way."

Her sonar felt no different than Haula's, nor did her vibrations. But her greeting was more expansive. *"Untu. We have looked forward to this union on behalf of our dear friend, Nick. He needs your help. We hope you will give it."*

CHAPTER 19

SCATTERED

Shouting hadn't worked. Neither had the slaps across her face. But finally, Shilling's shaking paid off. Carillo began to rouse from unconsciousness.

"Come on, come on! Wake up, Major, wake up!"

Carillo's eyes cracked open, and she moaned.

"That's it, that's it! Listen to my voice, Major. Focus on my voice." Looking toward the ceiling, he said, "Thank God." Then he laid a bag of ice on her forehead and continued to coax her awake.

Carillo moaned again and reached up to her head. In slurred speech, she said, "I feel awful."

"You've got a fever. Here, have some water."

Shilling guided the straw from a water pouch to her cracked lips. She closed her eyes and pushed it away. He brought it to her lips again.

"Just sip a little," he said.

Carillo closed her lips on the straw and took in some water. As she pulled away, a few drops dribbled out and floated away. He positioned the straw at her lips again and encouraged her to drink more.

"It burns," she said.

"I can't help that, but we need to get fluids in you fast. We've got problems. I need your help."

Carillo's head lolled toward Shilling, sending the ice pack off onto the bunk. "What problems?"

"We're dead in space. The engines aren't working. Neither is RCS. All the comms equipment's been smashed. Most of the lab has been destroyed."

She frowned at him. "Bob, you're bald."

"Yes, I know. So are you."

"What?" Carillo reached up and touched her bare scalp. Then she pulled her hand back down, stared at it and looked at Shilling's face. "Bob ... we're both blue."

"Yeah, I noticed. I thought there might be a problem with life support, not enough oxygen, but life support is working fine. Truth is, it's about the only thing working."

Carillo rolled on her side and tried to look around. "Are we still docked?"

"Docked? What are you talking about?"

"The Suhkai ship ... Nick."

"You're hallucinating. Have more water."

Carillo shoved his hand away and tried to sit up, but almost immediately collapsed back on the bed.

Shilling took hold of her arm and pulled her into a sitting position next to him. He handed her the water pouch. "Major, I hate to rush your recovery, but I need you back on your feet. Colonel Morgan, Ajay and Kiera are gone, and all the computers are dead."

"The Suhkai ... " Carillo mumbled. She put a hand on her neck. "Is there a mark on my neck?"

Shilling examined the area. "No. Why?"

"Have you been to the med bay?" Carillo tried to stand, but teetered and fell back onto the bunk.

Shilling helped her to her feet. "I have. And you don't want to go there. Take my word for it."

"Let me guess," Carillo said. "Lots of blood. On the walls, on the floor."

"Floating in the air ... on the gurney ... nasty slick on the corridor floor, too. Leads all the way to the airlock."

"It's from me," Carillo said. "One of the Suhkai shot me in the neck with a dart of some kind."

Shilling frowned. "I think you need to lie back down. Your head's not right."

"My head is fine," she slurred. "What ... what do you remember?"

"If you mean getting poked by Ajay's syringe, I remember that clearly."

"Let me see your hand." She grabbed his right hand.

"Why?"

"There's no burn."

"What?"

"Take off your shirt," Carillo said.

"Excuse me?"

She felt his chest with both hands.

"What are you doing?" Shilling said, pushing her hands away.

"You don't feel bruised?"

"No. Ajay didn't hit me, he just sedated me."

Carillo looked down at her flight suit. She unzipped it down to her crotch and wiggled her arms from the sleeves. Underneath she wore a T-shirt and underpants.

"Look." She held her arms up for Shilling to see. "My burns. They're completely gone."

Shilling made an effort to examine them, but she pulled her arms away, tugged off her T-shirt, and pushed down the legs of the flight suit. As the shirt floated away, she splayed her arms. "See? They're all gone. The Suhkai healed them."

Shilling politely looked away from Carillo's naked torso. "Could you please cover up?"

"Oh, don't be such a priss." Carillo reached down to grab the fallen flight suit. "You don't remember the UMOs shocking you?"

"The UMOs ... shocked me?"

Carillo slipped back into the suit and zipped it up. "Your heart stopped. Paul and Ajay started it up again but you didn't regain consciousness."

Shilling laughed. "I don't believe you."

"Nick said the Suhkai could heal you. And he said they could heal my burns. But we stayed on *Rorschach*. We didn't go with Paul and the others."

"What are you talking about? Who's Nick?"

"Nick ... as in Nick Reed ... flight engineer of *Cetus Prime*. You know, be good to one another and all that."

"You're out of your mind."

"Am I? Then you explain how we ended up here alone. You tell me where the others went. Why we're bald and blue. Explain why the ship is all busted up and my burns are all healed."

Shilling took two steps back and collapsed on Carillo's bunk. With his head clasped between his hands, he whispered, "I can't. None of this makes sense." He looked up at Carillo. "Can we take five? Please? I feel like I've gone down the rabbit hole and woken up in another world."

Watching Shilling's angst was heart-wrenching. Carillo recalled how lost she had felt as Morgan described all that had happened since the attack during her spacewalk. Yet here she was, treating Shilling like a puppy dog. Don't worry about the details. Do this and get fed. It was unfair and selfish. It was the opposite of being good to one another.

Carillo sat down next to Shilling and wrapped her arm around his shoulder. She apologized and recounted the crew's travails as best she knew them … from the moment Shilling was sedated by Ajay until now.

Shilling was stunned to learn how much had happened. He asked many questions — about the UMOs, the gambit to trap and kill the second alien life-form, the Callisto queen, the images implanted in the crew's minds, the Suhkai, the dialogue with Nick Reed, the Cytons, Morgan's decision to go aboard the alien ship and, lastly, the Suhkai attack on her in the med bay.

"After that, I don't know what the fuck happened," Carillo said. "One minute, I'm standing next to you in the med bay. You're lying there unconscious with a carpet of Cytons on top of you. A bunch of them fly up at me like bees after honey and then a lizard head comes into view at the door. It shoots something at me and I reach for my neck. It feels like half of it is gone and then … whammo … you wake me up. I'm all better. All my wounds are gone and we're on a dead ship in the middle of nowhere."

Shilling rose from the bunk, and Carillo watched him pace the cabin. "What do you think has happened to Paul, Kiera and Ajay?"

"I don't know, but based on what the Suhkai did to *Rorschach* — to us — I can't imagine they're sipping mai tais right now."

"No, I imagine not," Shilling said. "So what are we going to do?"

Carillo stood. "First order of business … find out how bad we're wounded."

Carillo stared at the empty slots in the racks of the battery closet in the engine control room. "Damn it! They took most of the batteries! Nick must have helped. He would know where to look, what to pull."

"Do we have backup batteries?" Shilling asked.

"Not enough, and it probably doesn't matter. I'm sure they took our reserves, too. Jesus, what assholes. They left us in a no-win situation."

"What do you mean?"

She pointed to the leftmost rack. "The missing batteries here? They're dedicated to feed the VLF-engine electron guns. And the ones that are supposed to be in that rack" — she pointed to the back wall — "power *Rorschach*'s thrusters, comms and computer systems. Without both sets, we're dead in the water."

"What about those batteries?" Shilling asked. He gestured to the third rack, which still had its batteries.

"Those power life support, environmental controls and GEFF."

"Can we shift some of those to the other slots?"

"Only if we want to sacrifice life support. Besides, it won't do us any good if we can't repair this." She stepped aside and pointed to the smashed console that managed the engines.

"We wouldn't have to shut off life support for long though, would we? All we need is one good push to generate momentum. We shut off life support long enough to get *Rorschach* moving again, then we switch the batteries back over."

Carillo nodded. "It's feasible. *If* we can fix the engine computer." She waved him across the hall. "Come on, let's see what they left us in the storage room."

The storage room proved to be in even worse shape than the battery closet. Every last container had been emptied, their contents pulverized or melted. Most floated in the weightless cabin, while some metallic debris stuck to the GEFF flooring and walls. And just as Carillo expected, their reserve batteries had been taken.

Carillo knelt down and picked through a pile of broken circuit boards. "Well, that does it. We're screwed."

In the dim glow provided by the emergency lighting in the corridor, Shilling stared blankly at the wreckage. "Why would they do this?"

"I don't know," Carillo said. As she stood up to close the door to the storage room, she wobbled and leaned against the corridor wall. "Wow, I feel super weak all of a sudden."

Shilling came alongside and wrapped his arm around her shoulder. "Come on, you need some more water. And something to eat."

As they started up the corridor toward the galley, Carillo stared at the trail of blood leading from the med bay and puzzled over the tragic turn of events. What had happened to Morgan, Kiera and Ajay? Why did Nick and the Suhkai strand her and Shilling? Was it some kind of sick revenge? Payback for *Cetus Prime*'s marooning? No, that didn't make sense. If Nick wanted revenge, it would be Morgan he would maroon, not Carillo and Shilling. Neither of them had been party to the *Cetus Prime* saga. Unless …

She halted outside the galley. "Hold on a sec. Maybe that's it."

Shilling let go of her shoulder and said, "Excuse me?"

"Maybe Nick stranded us to get back at Morgan."

The damage inflicted on *Rorschach* was similar to the damage wreaked upon *Cetus Prime* — according to Mayaguana's description, anyway. In both cases, the attackers had focused their assaults on technology — instruments, engines and communications. And in both cases, there were clear signs of malice. The *Cetus Prime* attackers hadn't just disabled the ship, NASA suspected they demolished it. And whoever had damaged *Rorschach* had apparently been *supremely* pissed.

After retrieving and unwrapping an energy bar, Carillo took a bite and sat down at the galley table. Shilling took a seat across from her and stared off into the distance, apparently deep in his own thoughts.

The obvious suspect was Nick, Carillo decided. Despite his "gone and forgotten" comment and his friendliness over the radio, maybe he wasn't quite ready to forgive. Twenty-five years in space … wandering who knows where with only two other humans for company … yes, Carillo could see how that could twist a person. The *Rorschach* crew had been in space for less than three months and had already battled fatigue, loneliness, stress and each other.

"Imagine twenty-five years of that shit," she mumbled. "No thank you."

"Twenty-five years of what?" Shilling asked.

She raised her arms and waved her hands around. "Space."

"Ah. I agree. No thank you."

She explained her theory to Shilling. When she finished, she frowned. As appealing as the Nick-revenge theory had seemed at first, there were aspects that didn't jibe. This wasn't just a Nick thing. The Suhkai were in on it, and so were the Callisto UMO queen and her followers. What would they have to gain by helping Nick?

She posed these questions to Shilling.

"Maybe Nick convinced them we were threats," he said. "Or ... maybe it was the other way around."

"Other way around? How so?"

Shilling laid out an alternative theory. "You said the BLUMOs connected with your mind, with the others' minds. Maybe they discerned the aim of our mission. They alerted the UMOs on Callisto and, in turn, they alerted the Suhkai. The Suhkai returned to protect the facility ... to prevent us from exploring it."

Shilling's theory had some compelling elements, Carillo thought, but there were problems with it. "If the Suhkai don't want us to explore the spaceport, why didn't they just say so, through Nick or the UMOs? Hell, if they're that concerned about us, why didn't they order the BLUMOs to destroy *Rorschach*? Why go about it this way? I mean, seriously, why bring you and me aboard their ship, put us through decontamination and inoculation, heal us, and then put us back on a crippled *Rorschach*?"

"True. They do seem like bizarre contradictions," Shilling agreed.

"Plus, it doesn't explain their purpose in returning us to *Rorschach* while hanging on to Paul, Kiera and Ajay."

"Maybe they aren't holding them," Shilling said quietly. "I know it's not pleasant to think about, but our crewmates might be dead."

Carillo hadn't allowed herself to consider the possibility but, now that Shilling had voiced it, she acknowledged it was a plausible explanation for their separation from the others. "That still doesn't explain why they left us alive," she said. "Why they put us back on *Rorschach*."

"Well, it doesn't really matter now." Shilling stood and walked to the refrigerator. "They're gone. We're stranded."

Carillo sighed. "Yeah. We're on our own."

"By the way, I've been meaning to ask you something. When I came in here to get you water earlier, I found tubes like this. What is it?" Shilling said. He held up a tube containing a golden liquid. "More of Morgan's mai tais?"

"Probably."

"I didn't realize he'd brought so much aboard."

"He didn't. That's probably the last of it."

"Uh, I don't think so." Shilling swung the door completely open for Carillo to see. The bottom shelf of the cold storage unit was packed with the tubes.

Carillo frowned and joined Shilling at the refrigerator. There were hundreds of them. She picked one up and examined it more closely. It was a different shape from the pouches NASA had supplied A3I for the mission, and the straw design was different too. It had no bar codes, no identifying marks of any kind.

"This isn't from our food supply," she said. "The Suhkai or Nick must have left it when they brought us back to the ship."

"Is it food … or medicine?" Shilling asked. "Maybe something to make the blue go away."

Carillo shrugged. "Who knows? We'll sort it out later. We've got bigger issues to deal with right now."

HOLDING CELL — SUHKAI FACILITY
SATURN MOON DIONE

Ajay rubbed his bare chin and looked out the towering window at the icy crater. Though it looked different than he had expected, he was glad they had made it to Callisto. He couldn't wait for the others to awake so they could all finally meet Nick Reed and interact with more of the Suhkai.

The only thing he wasn't thrilled about was meeting them wearing the garment he'd been dressed in when he awoke from the detox regimen. The Cyton assigned to him had called it a "robe," but it looked and felt more like a muumuu. A little too breezy for his tastes. He'd asked if he could re-board *Rorschach* to fetch his flight suit but, after several confusing exchanges with the Cyton, Ajay learned that *Rorschach* was still docked with Nick's *Ethel* in orbit — and that a smaller vessel had carried him and the others down here to the surface. So it was the muumuu or nothing.

Ajay turned from the window and walked across the stone floor. On his bare feet, the surface was surprisingly warm. He knew that outside it was two hundred degrees below zero, but inside his quarters the temperature was as pleasant as his dorm room on Mayaguana. And the rations were okay too. A Suhkai had laid out food and drink earlier on the table beside his bed. None of it was "Earth food," but the Cyton indicated that Nick had chosen the fare, so presumably this was the most Earth-like food they had. It included a squishy, gray, bread-like loaf that Ajay had initially viewed with skepticism, but which turned out to be both flavorful and filling. He wasn't as enamored with the golden gelatin, which tasted like metal. But it was the berries, despite their unusual shapes and colors, that he liked best. He had devoured most of them earlier and scooped up the last of them now.

The door to his room slid open and Ajay's Cyton floated in, accompanied by a Suhkai. Ajay waved at both of them, his mouth full of berries. The Suhkai waved back, but said nothing, which was fine with Ajay. The last time one of them had spoken to him, the screeching whale song had almost deafened him.

Ajay looked at the Cyton and thought, *"Time for more medicine?"*

The Cyton flickered. *"Yes. Lie down."*

For the third time since his arrival at the Suhkai facility, Ajay lay on the bed and closed his eyes. The medicine, the Cyton had explained, was necessary to help him adapt to the atmosphere in the spaceport. While the injections didn't hurt, they did put him to sleep, and when he awoke, his muscles ached. But those were small inconveniences. He wanted to explore the spaceport and was willing to endure whatever side effects were necessary.

The Suhkai lifted the sleeve of Ajay's robe and pressed the nozzle of the injector against his bicep.

Seconds later, Ajay was out cold.

The sedative was so effective, Ajay was oblivious to the Suhkai lifting him from the bed and carrying him from the room. He didn't see or feel the lizard-man loading him onto a floating gurney and transporting him to a distant part of the facility, where several Suhkai and Cytons had prepared a table for his arrival.

And he didn't see Kiera … unconscious on the table next to his.

SUHKAI READY ROOM – SUHKAI SPACECRAFT *ETHEL*
IN ORBIT AROUND SATURN MOON DIONE

The chamber in which Morgan met with Nick, Haula, Zoor and Maggie reminded him of *Rorschach*'s ready room — with two rather significant exceptions.

The first one, Morgan had expected: the table and chairs were Suhkai-sized. Haula was kind enough to lift and place Morgan on a chair that, though far too big, had at least been modified to accommodate a human. In other words, he was placed on a booster seat. Nick sat across the table from him, similarly boostered, and Haula and Zoor sat at opposite ends of the oval's rounded peaks. Maggie hovered over the table.

The other difference from the *Rorschach* ready room was the large window on the wall behind Haula. It looked upon an icy moon. In the distance, Saturn shone like a beacon in the darkness of space.

Morgan frowned at Nick. "You want to explain why I can see Saturn? We were in the asteroid belt before coming aboard."

"Precautionary measure," Nick said.

"Precaution against what?"

Haula answered through Maggie. "*Zikzaws. They will not venture this far out now. There are few places to hide, and not enough sustenance.*"

"Zick-what?"

"Zikzaws," Nick said. "Creatures like the one your ship's magnetic trail attracted in the asteroid belt. Nasty bastards. You're lucky the Cyton patrol homed in on you before the Zikzaw did, otherwise they wouldn't have been able to save you."

Morgan thought back to the BLUMOs battling with the pink cloud. "What *are* the Zikzaws?"

"Best way I can describe them — massive electromagnetic snakes," Nick said. "To the Suhkai, they're like vultures, though. They'll consume any potent source of magnetized radiation, but it's their love of metallic hydrogen that makes them tenacious adversaries to the Suhkai."

Nick explained the Suhkai had mined Jupiter and Saturn for thousands of years, extracting both liquid metallic hydrogen and liquid metallic helium from their atmospheres. They refined the two superconducting materials into fuel that powered their ships' propulsion systems.

"So the facility on Callisto isn't a spaceport, it's a refinery," Morgan said.

"Correct." Nick pointed to the window. "There's another one down below on Dione."

Morgan recalled Mayaguana's description of the Saturn flashes and how the trails had disappeared behind Dione. The image of the ice castle transmitted by the Callisto queen popped into his mind.

Nick continued. "Anyway, the Zikzaws used to hover around Jupiter and Saturn, just waiting for one of the Suhkai cruisers to come up out of the atmosphere so they could envelop the ship and absorb their mining booty."

"*They became too troublesome,*" Zoor communicated through Maggie. "*Our people left to work at extraction centers in other solar systems free of the Zikzaw scourge.*"

"But you left ships on Callisto," Morgan said. "And a hive of Cytons. Why?"

Haula answered. "*The planets you call Jupiter and Saturn are still very rich sources of raw materials.*"

"Ah. So you didn't abandon the refineries — you just mothballed them."

"*What is mothball?*" Haula asked.

"Sorry. I mean you closed them for a period of time, expecting you might return and open them again."

"That's right," Nick said.

"Is that what's happening now? You're returning to reopen the facilities?"

Nick looked to Haula and then Zoor. In the middle of the table, Maggie flickered at an intense rate, but Morgan received no thoughts from her. Finally the flashes abated, and Nick spoke.

"They came back for me, Christine and Avery," he said. "The Suhkai had no intention of returning here for their own purposes and, honestly, they hoped they could come and go without being noticed. Unfortunately, y'all kind of messed up that plan. Actually, it's partially my fault. I told them there was no way anyone from Earth would ever find *Cetus Prime*."

Early in *Ethel*'s return to Earth's solar system, Nick explained, the Suhkai had messaged ahead to the Cytons on Callisto and Dione to alert them they would be visiting the facilities, and they asked them to prepare for their arrival. It was during the clearing of ice covering the Nuada crater that the Cytons melted away the ice entombing *Cetus Prime*.

"Honest to God, I didn't remember leaving the EVA comms on when I shut her up. It was damn clever of your Ajay to pick up the signals. When we learned y'all found the ship … and the Suhkai refinery … that kind of shocked us all. Still, we thought we were in good shape to beat you to Callisto. Then you go ahead and move up your launch date. Really lit a fire under our butts to track you down *and* slow you down."

As Morgan processed Nick's last comment, he felt his ire spike. *Rorschach*'s harrowing encounters with the BLUMOs were *intentional* efforts to delay them from reaching Callisto?

"You realize those Cytons damn near killed two of my crew," he snapped. "Why didn't you just radio and ask us to hold off? If you knew it was me at the helm, you know I would have respected your wishes."

"Couldn't," Nick said. "Didn't want anyone on Earth to know I was aboard."

"Why?"

"It would only have caused trouble."

"Why would you think that? The world will be *ecstatic* to learn you're alive."

"Come on, Paul. Look at me, for Christ's sake. I'm dying from the long-term effects of radiation exposure. There's nothing the Suhkai or Cytons can do about it anymore. I'm too far gone. And if they can't help me, you can be sure no one on Earth can. What good would it do me to ride in on a spaceship, step off and drop dead on the tarmac? Besides, I never intended to stay. We're just dropping in long enough to pick up what we need."

"Wait — are you telling me you left Avery and Christine on Tula *eleven years* ago just to come back to Earth for supplies? And then what? Turn around and spend another eleven years flying back to them?"

"Yeah, that pretty much sums it up."

"What kind of supplies would be so important that you'd devote twenty-plus years of your life to pick up?"

A thought from Haula entered Morgan's mind. *"Humans."*

Morgan turned to the Suhkai male. "Excuse me?"

"Avery, Christine and Nick desired to start a human colony on Tula. Alone, they could not accomplish this task. They needed more humans to join them."

At times Morgan could be slow on the uptake, but he connected the dots real fast this time. Nick didn't want anyone to know he was coming back ... because he intended to *kidnap humans to seed their colony on Tula.*

Now the size of the *Ethel* made sense. It was a freaking ark!

"You're insane, Nick," he said. "You can't just roll up, snatch a bunch of people and fly off. I can't believe any of you would even consider it."

"It's the only way," Nick said.

"Bull. I am certain thousands of people, *tens* of thousands, would jump at the opportunity if you offered."

Nick laughed. "Really? Imagine the scene, Paul. We land on Earth. I go before the media and announce I'm seeking two hundred people, two-thirds women, to join us on Tula. Primary qualifications needed? Young and fertile. Two hundred people whose primary task for most of the rest of their lives will be to breed ... and breed ... and breed. Starting during the eleven-year trip, continuing once we land on Tula, and on and on until they can't breed anymore.

"I say to the world: 'I need the makeup of the colonists to come from multiple generations, ranging in age from five to thirty-five.' Who's going to offer up their five-year-old daughter for a lifetime of breeding?

"I tell those who want to volunteer: 'Hey, once we leave Earth, there's no turning back. You'll never see Earth again. You don't like

Tula when we get there, too effing bad. Oh, and a good twenty percent of you will probably die during the journey, and another twenty percent won't survive more than a year on Tula.' No one's signing up for that kind of deal."

"Do you hear yourself talking?" Morgan said. "You think enslavement is a better solution?"

A thought from Zoor invaded his thoughts. "*A small price to pay to extend the reach of humans, to create a new civilization.*"

"Small in whose mind, sister?" Morgan said. "To the slaves, it won't seem small. Or to the families of those you snatch."

"*Skywalker, we have colonized planets, moons and asteroids in many solar systems throughout the galaxy. It is a grueling, unforgiving process to establish a foothold on a new world. In order for a colony to survive, the first several generations must be committed to growing the population. The first generation is the most critical. They must do their part, whether they want to or not.*"

The last of the thoughts from Haula sickened Morgan. He turned to Nick. "Avery and Christine are on board with this?"

Nick nodded.

"The radiation sickness has scrambled your brain, my man." Morgan cupped his bald head in his hands. "This is lunacy. You can't do this."

"You're right about that last part, Paul," Nick said. "*I* can't do it. I'm not going to live long enough to see it through. That's why *you're* going to help — for Avery, Christine and me."

"Like hell I am," Morgan said. "I might not be able to stop you, but I damn sure ain't *helping* you."

Haula projected a thought. "*You are angry. Nick told us you would be. It would be wise for you to return to your chamber and reflect on the implications of refusing to assist Nick.*"

Morgan narrowed his eyes at Nick. "And what 'implications' might those be?"

"If you agree to help, we will release your crew and provide them safe passage back to Earth. *After* we have collected the new colonists."

"And if I refuse?"

"Then your ship and crew will disappear just like *Cetus Prime* did. Only this time, there won't be anything left of your ship for anyone to find."

"You'll kill us. Is that it?"

"Not all of you. Ajay and Kiera will take their places as breeders in our colony."

Morgan launched himself across the table. He managed to wrap his hands around Nick's throat before Maggie shocked him into unconsciousness.

CHAPTER 20

DESPERATE MEASURES

The table of the ready room was piled with CubeSat components. Hands on her hips, Julia Carillo leaned over and assessed the collection.

"So, is there enough here? Can we do it?" Shilling asked.

She smiled and nodded. "It won't be pretty, but we'll be able to fly."

Take that, Rawlings, you old fart! Though she would never have admitted it, the aged fellow astronaut's quip about her post-NASA career had hurt her just as much as his barb aimed at Kiera. *She spends her days teaching teenagers to build toy spaceships.*

Those "teenagers" were actually graduate aerospace engineering students at the University of Virginia, where Carillo led the department's advanced design research initiatives. It was a role that had allowed her to bring brilliant young minds together with those from some of the most innovative aerospace companies in the world. And she did, in fact, assist the students in the construction of conceptual designs, ranging from flight control to propulsion to instrumentation. Some might have looked like toys to Rawlings, but many of them pushed the boundaries of current standards in the industry.

Moreover, Carillo had soaked up the cleverness of her students. They were experts in turning less into more. Of all people, Carillo thought, fellow astronauts like Rawlings and Nick Reed should have appreciated that stranded astronauts wouldn't just curl up and suck their thumbs.

As she began sorting through the parts, she looked up at Shilling. "I love it when people underestimate me."

Rorschach's engine and reaction control systems were damaged beyond repair ... as was the radio equipment in the ship's communication center. The drone-landers were also destroyed. But in their haste to render the ship powerless and voiceless, the Suhkai and Nick had overlooked the subtle in favor of demolishing the obvious.

Exhibit number one: while they destroyed all the remaining antennas and instrument receptacles on the damaged *Recon-3* docked in the cargo bay, they didn't touch its VLF engine or thrusters. Carillo guessed the wrecking crew had believed they had already scuttled the battered probe ... which would have been true, were it not for the parts laid out on the table. They hadn't bothered to open the storage bins beside the two docking platforms, and those bins housed the Shield replacement parts the crew had retrieved from *Cargo-2*. Among them were new batteries, UHF radio transmitter-receivers and UHF antennas.

Miss number two: the brute squad had ignored the cargo bay's docking platform controls stowed behind a wall panel. They likely believed the controls were useless with *Recon-3* out of commission but, as long as Carillo could supply the system with power by switching around batteries in the ship's battery closet, she could use the docking system's embedded short-range UHF radio equipment to control *Recon-3*'s engines and thrusters. The same was true for *Cargo-4*, docked on the starboard side of the ship.

And that was miss number three. The aliens hadn't realized that *Cargo-4*, like any probe in close proximity to *Rorschach*, could be controlled from the cargo bay docking system. Or, if they *had* realized it, they were simply confident they'd inflicted enough damage on *Cargo-4* to eliminate any possibility of using it. They'd opened the floor panel concealing the probe's computer brain and battery and had removed and destroyed all the components. They'd probably destroyed the supply vessel's antennas too, but that was okay. The duplicate parts intended for the second Recon-to-Shield refit were compatible replacements for those removed from *Cargo-4*.

The coup de grâce and Nick Reed special: the VLF transmitting antenna was still neatly coiled in a cargo bay storage hold. In all the chaos surrounding the encounters with the BLUMOs, the crew had never found time to retrieve and install it. Carillo savored the irony. A makeshift VLF antenna had saved the *Cetus Prime* crew, including Nick. Now it might save Carillo and Shilling from Nick's treachery.

She now explained her ramshackle solutions to Shilling. "After we install new parts into *Recon-3* and *Cargo-4*, I'll go out for an EVA to attach *Recon-3* to the instrument array and replace *Cargo-4*'s antenna."

She told him she would utilize a combination of the clamps from the docking platform, EMU safety tethers and a portion of the VLF antenna to anchor the Recon. With its new UHF radio equipment in working order and its engine still functional, the probe would provide the ship with propulsion. Aiding in that effort would be *Cargo-4*.

To sync up the direction of the two probes' engine thrust, she would have to secure *Recon-3* with its nose cone pointing toward the port side of the ship, while *Cargo-4*'s nose, docked into the starboard side of the ship, pointed toward *Rorschach*'s port side.

"You mean we'll be flying sideways?"

"Yep, our port side will be the new bow."

"How will we be able to tell which direction we need to head if we can't see where we're going?" Shilling asked. "We don't have a navigation system."

"Hello, trustee of the Green Bank Observatory here. Former astronaut. Aerospace engineering professor. I know how to read the stars. During my EVA, I'll take a peek at our orientation and use the probe thrusters to orient us toward Earth." Though Carillo tried to make it sound easy, she knew it would be tricky to coordinate *Recon-3*'s and *Cargo-4*'s engines and thrusters without the aid of Kiera's fleet management software. "Besides, we only have to get started in the right direction; Mayaguana will take care of the rest."

She explained that without radio equipment to message Mayaguana, their only communications capability would take the form of telemetry transmitted by the two probes' UHF antennas to Mission Control. Each time the probes were powered on or off, their embedded software automatically pinged Mayaguana to report their status.

"Presuming Mission Control receives the transmissions, *Cargo-4*'s docking clamp and airlock sensors will tell them it's still docked with *Rorschach*," Carillo said. "Then they should notice *Recon-3*'s position relative to *Cargo-4* and realize it's also connected to the ship. I have to believe Mayaguana will ping back and request another round of telemetry, which will give them our heading and velocity."

"And they'll course-correct for us," Shilling said.

"That's what I'm counting on. They can activate the fleet management software from Mission Control and remotely guide us home."

HOLDING CELL — SUHKAI REFINERY
SATURN MOON DIONE

Kiera was so sore she couldn't roll over without experiencing shooting pains in her arms, abdomen and pelvis. With each groan of discomfort, the Cyton assigned to monitor her circled above the bed and queried, "*Hurt? Help?*"

"*Of course I'm hurt, bitch. Of course I need help*," Kiera thought. "*You want to help me? Help me escape.*"

But Kiera knew the retort would do no good. She'd given an approximation of the same answer dozens of times already. The ball of light would flicker, but it never replied. It just hovered like a drone conducting surveillance. That was its purpose. The alien was nothing more than the equivalent of a nurse call button.

This time, however, the Cyton replied. "*Why escape?*"

The question almost made Kiera burst out laughing. Let's see ... where to begin ... oh, I know ... how about being carried like a dead, plucked chicken from the inoculation room. No? Not good enough for you? Then how about being held against my will? Or separated from my companions? Better yet, how about the needle marks on my arms and pelvis? The fresh scar beneath my navel or the raw skin between my legs?

She picked her head up off the bed and screamed at the Cyton. "I'm not a fucking barn animal!"

Each time the Suhkai entered the room, they administered an injection. Kiera always resisted, but no amount of biting, kicking or screamed expletives were effective against the Suhkai. The creatures were too big and too strong for five-foot-three, one-hundred-thirty-five-pound Kiera. And each time she woke up, she had more needle marks and her pain was worse.

"Why fight Suhkai? Suhkai help you."

Kiera leapt from the bed, pulled off her gown and pointed to the needle marks, scar and reddened skin. "This is *help*? The Suhkai aren't helping me. They're hurting me!"

"Help make new humans."

Kiera supposed the alien thought this tidbit would ease her suffering, but it only enraged her more. "I don't want to make new humans! I want to go home. You want to help me? Help me escape! Help me find my friends. Help us go home!"

The Cyton did not respond.

Kiera snatched up her gown and pulled it back on. She turned to the bobbing light and asked, "Why? Why are you doing this? Why are you helping them?"

The Cyton was quick to answer. *"Save humans."*

RECOVERY ROOM — SUHKAI SPACECRAFT *ETHEL*
IN ORBIT AROUND SATURN MOON DIONE

Morgan sat on the floor, back against the wall, head lowered. He wanted to believe the conversation with the Suhkai and Nick had been a nightmare, but the welt on the back of his neck from Maggie's shock was evidence to the contrary.

How could Avery, Christine and Nick have come up with such a monstrous plan? How could they not see the evil, the selfishness, inherent in it? Had the long years in space warped their morality?

A thought formed in his mind. *"Necessary."*

He looked up, but could see no Cyton in the room. He stood, thinking the alien might be hovering behind the sleeping pod in the room's center, but still saw no ball of light. Recalling the BLUMOs' ability to camouflage their presence, he said, "Show yourself."

Over several seconds, a large golden ball of light appeared, hovering at arm's length from his face. Unless Cytons could randomly change size, this Cyton was not Maggie. This one was the Callisto queen.

"You can access my thoughts," Morgan said aloud.

"*Yes.*" The Cyton flickered.

"You are the one who was with us before we docked?"

"*Yes.*"

"Then you lied. You're not a friend. You're a fiend." Morgan returned to his sitting position against the wall.

"*Help humans. Help each other.*"

"Now there's a laugh." Morgan stared at the ball of light. "Nick said the Suhkai view your kind as God. You're not like any god we worship on Earth. No, wait a minute. I take that back. At times in our history, there have been cultures that sacrificed other humans. We call them savages now. Barbarians."

The thought that entered Morgan's mind came from a new source. "*This is not sacrifice. It is survival.*"

"Dress it up any way you want, Zoor," Morgan said. "It's wrong. And you, your little balls of light and Nick can go to hell if you think I'm helping you in any way. Besides, you don't need my help. If you've read my mind, you know that already."

In working through the dilemma, Morgan had already reasoned it would be a simple matter for the Suhkai to fly down, scoop up Nick's complement of breeders and zoom back into space without help from Morgan or anyone else. Cytons would disable the unsuspecting satellite eyes and ears orbiting Earth, allowing Suhkai ships to approach the planet undetected. They would target a remote population, one with little or no defenses — say, an isolated island, or a resort catering to young adults and families. If Nick had been monitoring Earth telecommunications for as long as he claimed, Morgan was sure he had already selected his target.

Morgan didn't know whether Cytons could survive in the lower levels of Earth's atmosphere, since they'd never been observed below the ionosphere, but if they could, it would be no challenge for a swarm of them to camouflage and zap two hundred people into unconsciousness in seconds. From there, the Suhkai would storm the area and collect their quarry. When the clueless humans awoke, they would be bald, blue and ready for breeding.

"You misunderstand the assistance Nick seeks. In fact, there is much you do not understand."

Morgan laughed. "Is this the part where you try to convince me of the virtue in enslaving the innocent?"

"Do you know what a magwave is?"

"No, and I don't care."

The Cyton floated over to Morgan. *"You should. Magwaves saved Nick, Christine and Avery. They could save your race, too … or destroy it."*

He pulled up his knees and wrapped his forearms around them. Staring at the ball of light, he said, "Magwave … a magnetic wave."

The ball flickered. Zoor answered. *"Yes, a very powerful magnetic wave. Cytons have used them to travel throughout the universe for longer than your planet has existed."*

The door opened, and in walked Zoor. The ten-foot alien loomed over the seated Morgan, and the Cyton rose and circled the Suhkai female's head. When it attained enough speed to form a solid halo around Zoor's crest, a bright flash lit up the room.

Morgan shielded his eyes.

When he opened them again, the Cyton was gone, and Zoor was seated in front of him, sitting Indian-style. She smiled, and the tubes on the crest of her elongated head vibrated. The voice of a human woman emanated from them. "We have been practicing our human speech together. Hopefully, y'all can understand me."

The twang was evidence of Nick's influence. It was hardly appropriate to laugh, but that's what Morgan did. "They'd love you down South."

This quip seemed to please Zoor. Her mouth and crest tubes vibrated in unison.

Morgan moved his legs to form a similar posture as Zoor's. "So, am I speaking to Zoor? To the Cyton queen from Callisto? Or both of you?"

Zoor reached out her hands. "It is I, Zoor. Can we start anew? Forget what y'all heard from Nick. We are here to help. You do not know it because of your anger, but you need our help."

Morgan's hands remained in his lap. "Can you both still read my mind?"

"Yes."

"Then free my crew. When you do that ... when they are here with me ... we can start anew. We'll all take a stroll to my ship. Y'all can come aboard, we'll undock from Ethel, *and then we can talk about magwaves all you want."*

Zoor retracted her hands. "That is impossible."

"Thought so. We have an expression on Earth. Bullshit walks." Morgan used his fingers to imitate a person walking away.

"It is impossible because your friends are not here."

"Excuse me?"

"Ajay and Kiera are on the moon below, the moon you call Dione. Julia and Bob are aboard your ship. It is far from here."

A thought passed through Morgan's mind before he could stop it. *"Divide and conquer."*

"Yes, that was Nick's intent," Zoor said. "He believed you would find a way to free them if they stayed here. He considers you very resourceful. Very dangerous."

"Does he now? Is that why he sent you two instead of coming here himself?"

"Nick is near death. Very near."

Morgan couldn't decide which was worse: traveling this far to discover Nick was dead, or finding him alive but maniacal and teamed up with aliens who were just as evil.

"We are not evil."

"Then you must come from a pretty fucked-up place."

Zoor reached out again, and this time she gripped Morgan's hands in her gigantic paws. His mind filled with a vision of a black star spinning faster than any Cyton. A fissure ripped across its surface, and a bolt of energy fired out.

Morgan pulled his hands away and looked up at the Suhkai. What she had just shown him was a lethal gamma burst from a magnetar. "We call magwaves by a different name," he said. "Gamma bursts."

She extended her hands once more. Morgan accepted their embrace this time, and a new vision appeared. It showed a smaller Suhkai vessel, one that looked like the one Nick and the others had photographed on Callisto. At its leading edge, a spinning ball of Cytons drew close to a dark but glowing mass. In an acrobatic maneuver worthy of a supersonic jet pilot, the spinning ball turned hard, pulling the spacecraft with it. An instant later, a crack formed in the glowing mass and a bolt shot forth. The spacecraft and Cytons were swept up into it, and they disappeared in a flash of light.

"My God," Morgan said. He recalled Nick Reed's final message extracted from *Cetus Prime*'s logs: *we're off to go where they went with our UMOs leading the way.*

The Cytons knew how to create starquakes … and they had shown the Suhkai how to ride them. That must have appealed to Nick, the California surfer. He, Avery and Christine had ridden a wave to Tula. A magnetic wave.

"Not just one wave," Zoor said. "Many waves. We think of distance differently than Nick, differently than humans. But in human terms, Nick, Christine and Avery traveled over 100 trillion kilometers to reach Tula … with a number of stops on the way. There is an entire network of magnetars spread throughout the galaxy."

A new vision infiltrated Morgan's thoughts. He tried to pull his hands back, but Zoor gripped them tight. He saw the chiseled black mission commander Avery Lockett, and beside him stood Christine Baker, the vibrant, freckled redhead. She smiled as she cupped her arms around two small children. In front of them both sat Nick, with a third child in his lap. Behind them was a sky of lavender and a meadow of green.

"They ask for your help, Skywalker. Not for evil reasons as you suppose, but for good," Zoor said. "Come. It is time for you to see what I mean."

MISSION CONTROL
A3ROSPACE INDUSTRIES COMMAND AND CONTROL CENTER
MAYAGUANA ISLAND, THE BAHAMAS

Dante gazed at the photo-badge while his thumb circled Kiera's smiling face. He closed his eyes and recalled riding a bobbing paddleboard next to her, watching Jupiter rise. That had been only three months ago, but it now seemed an eternity in the past.

Most of the controllers around him were practically catatonic, their lifeless glares riveted to computer consoles devoid of data. Amato and Pritchard were passed out on cots. No one spoke. The only sounds in Mission Control came from Amato's open-mouthed snores.

And 450 million kilometers away, radio signals from *Recon-3* and *Cargo-4* had just begun their lonely, twenty-five-minute journey toward A3rospace Industries' tracking and data relay satellite.

Dante laid his head on the desktop of his station and sighed. In his hand, he clutched the photo-badge.

TULA HABITAT – SUHKAI SPACECRAFT *ETHEL*
IN ORBIT AROUND SATURN MOON DIONE

Zoor led Morgan into an airlock, and the door closed behind them. Immediately Morgan felt a heavy pressure against his chest. Steam filled the chamber, and he struggled to breathe. He had to bend over and grab hold of his knees, sucking in air like he'd just raced up a hill. To his surprise, Zoor struggled even more than he did; she fell to her knees and gasped.

Just as it seemed they both might pass out, Morgan heard a click. The steam began to thin, and the door at the far end of the chamber opened.

As the haze dissipated, Morgan couldn't believe his eyes. Nor could his ears reconcile the sounds. Through the open door, a forest of trees swayed in a light breeze. Bird calls filled the air. It made no sense. If Morgan didn't know better, he would have thought he'd just stepped out of the ship onto an alien planet. Yet this, all of this, this entire place — was *inside* the spaceship *Ethel*. How was such a feat even possible?

Most unbelievable of all was the blond-haired girl in a frilly dress who pushed through some ferns and dashed toward the Suhkai.

"Zoorie!" she cried.

The girl crashed into the alien's shin and squeezed her leg. She smiled up at Morgan and said, "Hi! I'm Annie. You're Nicky's friend Skywalker. Your clothes look funny."

Morgan just stared at the child. He was too stunned to answer.

The ferns rustled once more, and two teenagers appeared — a brown-skinned boy and a blond-haired white girl. The girl was clearly pregnant. *Very* pregnant.

Annie now attached herself to Morgan's leg. "You didn't answer me. Are you Skywalker? Do you come from Earth? We come from Tula. It's far from Earth. You want to see pictures of our home?"

Zoor picked up the girl and held her in her arms. "Skywalker is a little surprised, Annie. I did not tell him he was going to meet you."

The two teenagers came to a stop in front of Morgan and studied him with fascination. The pregnant girl asked, "Where are the others, Zoorie?"

"They will be here soon," the Suhkai said. "Skywalker, let me introduce you to Sarah and John. Sarah is Nick's daughter with Christine. John is Avery's and Christine's son."

Numb, absolutely numb, Morgan swooned. John had to wrap his arm around Morgan's shoulder to prevent him from tipping over.

Annie reached out to Morgan. "I want a hug, too!" The freckled child peeled from the safety of Zoor's arm and wrapped her arms around Morgan's neck.

Zoor said, "And this little ball of energy is Nick's daughter with Sarah. As you can see, Sarah's about to add another member to the growing Reed-Baker-Lockett family. The child will be John and Sarah's first. A boy. Nick and Christine's eldest child, Tina, lives with Avery and her mother on Tula. At last count, with the assistance of my people, the Tula wing of the family numbered five, but the last communication from Avery is several years old. By now Tina, like Sarah, is of age to breed, and there are likely more Tulan children scampering about."

Morgan carried Annie as the group walked deeper into the spaceship-enclosed habitat. To Morgan's slipper-covered feet, the ground felt like real soil. Actual drops of rain fell on his head and shoulders. He looked up through the canopy of trees at a purplish sky where two moons, one faint and small, the other bright and huge, hovered. He smelled flowers and heard the gurgle of a nearby stream.

They followed a path to a clearing in the middle of the forest. Here stood a home. It looked like a ring of silver igloos linked together by passageways. A red-furred creature was curled on the front stoop, but stood at their approach. It looked to Morgan like a squat ostrich with six legs. It sniffed the air, then retracted its long neck and scurried off into the underbrush.

"That's Woof," Annie said. "He's shy."

Morgan's mind grappled with the scene and the implications. Avery, Christine and Nick had settled on Tula and started a human colony. It seemed an impossible outcome to the tragedy that had stranded the three astronauts on Callisto, but unless Morgan was locked in the most surreal dream ever, it was true.

As they entered the home, Morgan set Annie down, and the girl tugged on his pant leg. "We need more friends. More mommies and daddies. Can you help us?"

CHAPTER 21

RIDE OR DIE

O ver a meal of squishy-gray bread, berries and Nick's nectar of the stars, Morgan listened to Sarah, John and Annie recount the oral history of their parents' settlement on Tula. They rejoiced in the beauty of their home world — a world that Annie spoke about with authority though she had yet to visit it. And of course all three children peppered Morgan with questions about their parents and the mystical planet Earth.

Through it all, Annie sat in the lap formed by Zoor, and three Cytons weaved in spirals, trying to avoid the girl's sweeping hands. If they'd been on Earth, Morgan would have thought she was trying to catch fireflies.

Woof eventually worked up the courage to slink into the house. Morgan held out his hand, and a tentacled-covered tongue flicked out and attached to his fingers. Annie laughed. So did Morgan.

Zoor then took over the storytelling, reciting the tale of the three lost astronauts. It was a tale the children had clearly heard hundreds of times, because they interrupted on multiple occasions to interject details the Suhkai omitted — details Nick Reed had ingrained in their memories.

Avery, Christine and Nick had left Callisto in a Suhkai cruiser, Zoor said, with a swarm of Cytons leading the way. Within a few months, the Cytons came upon a dormant magnetar, and these alien seeders of life stimulated a starquake that propelled the cruiser at light speed toward the closest Suhkai-occupied base.

"It was an asteroid," Annie said. "We stopped there on our way here. It has the neatest caves! They shine like a sun!"

Zoor described the asteroid in more detail. Morgan explained that on Earth, such an asteroid was referred to as a *pallasite* — a mix of glittering gems, magnetic basalt and rock. But the conversation about asteroids reminded him of a lingering question, and he asked it.

"Why was a Zikzaw lurking in the asteroid belt?"

"They are parasites," Zoor said. "Any time there is a large cosmic disruption in which large amounts of radiation are expelled, Zikzaws show up to feed on the aftermath."

"But there's not much radiation in the belt. I mean, compared to Jupiter and Saturn, it's a radiation desert," Morgan said.

Annie interrupted again. "This is boring! Tell him about meeting Nicky."

Zoor smiled and continued her story. When the Suhkai on the pallasite met the three astronauts, they offered them sanctuary. "The Suhkai were impressed that they had survived the long journey on one of our ships," Zoor said. "Your friends credited their survival to the Cytons that accompanied them. Through those Cytons, your friends said they were excited to explore the galaxy. They wanted to know if there were other worlds with humans, or worlds capable of supporting human life."

Annie, clearly frustrated with the pace of Zoor's storytelling, asked Morgan, "Have you ever seen a brown dwarf?"

He confessed he had not. In a matter-of-fact tone, Annie informed him that her parents had lived on another asteroid caught in the orbit of a brown dwarf for a period of time.

John said, "Nicky said it was like a desert motel with a convenience store."

Zoor added that the Suhkai don't seek out perfect environments for settlements in the galaxy. "We find what's available, make the best use of it we can, and then reach further."

"I understand. The asteroid was a stepping stone," Morgan said.

"I see your thoughts," Zoor said. "Yes, a stepping stone."

As she described the sub-star that nourished the asteroid with heat and a small amount of light, Morgan began to appreciate Nick's black eyes and the dim orange-red lights that dominated the Suhkai ship's environs.

HOLDING CELL - SUHKAI REFINERY
SATURN MOON DIONE
SEPTEMBER 12, 2019

As the door to Kiera's quarters opened, the Cyton informed her it was time for more medicine. Lying on the bed, Kiera peeked from a half-closed eye and saw the Suhkai enter.

Kiera gritted her teeth, rolled off the bed and made a run for the open doorway.

While the Suhkai were strong and graceful, she'd also noticed they were also as slow as grazing elephants. She easily dodged the lumbering alien and sprinted into the hallway. Her Cyton shot after her in pursuit. "*Stop! Come back!*"

Kiera had to pick a direction and chose to break to the right. She dashed down the hallway. But as she approached an open door on her right, another Suhkai stepped out, blocking her path.

The Cyton zoomed up from behind. "*Don't hurt! Don't hurt!*"

The Suhkai relaxed its stance and stood aside. Kiera passed by so fast she didn't see Ajay step out behind the Suhkai, but she heard him call her name. She turned back only long enough to scream, "Run!"

Her bare feet scraped the stone floors as she rounded a bend. A short wall on her left overlooked an atrium. A short wall for Suhkai, that is — it was almost as tall as the five-foot-three Kiera. She hoisted herself up and peered over. It was a long way down. "Fuck."

She hopped back down and kept running.

Shadows of approaching Suhkai appeared from around a turn ahead. She stopped and spun back around. A swirl of pulsing light was racing toward her — a swarm of Cytons. She heard the thoughts of the Cyton that had been monitoring her. "*Don't run! No escape!*"

Kiera was trapped. Nowhere to run. Nowhere to hide. She frantically assessed her limited options.

Ajay's bony figure came running around the bend.

The Cytons were within two feet of Kiera when she blew Ajay a kiss and leapt over the wall.

CARGO BAY — THE *RORSCHACH EXPLORER*
FLYING THROUGH THE ASTEROID BELT
SEPTEMBER 12, 2019

The *Rorschach Explorer* shuddered when the *Recon* and *Cargo* engines rumbled to life. Julia Carillo, anchored to a safety tether in the open cargo bay, her gloved fingers pinching the docking control system joystick, yelped. Inside the ship, Robert Shilling belted out a lusty cheer.

Carillo had been unable to discern whether they were still in the asteroid belt or not, but she *had* been able to see the gleaming twinkle of Jupiter in one direction and the Sun in the other. Only a couple of weeks had passed since they had looped around to gaze at Earth one last time, so Carillo knew just where to look for it. She played with the Cargo thrusters until the vessel was flying in the general direction of the twinkling star to the right of the Sun.

After descending back to the dock controls, Carillo paused, staring at the stars moving past the open hold, and said a silent prayer for Morgan, Kiera and Ajay. There was nothing else she or Shilling could do for them now but pray.

"You okay in there, Bob?" she asked when she was finished.

In Shilling's first display of levity since the Hawaiian party, he answered, "Roger dodger. Found what's left of the mai tais."

"Copy that," Carillo said. "Save some for me."

TULA HABITAT — SUHKAI SPACECRAFT *ETHEL*
IN ORBIT AROUND SATURN MOON DIONE
SEPTEMBER 12, 2019

Zoor and the children continued to relay the saga of the *Cetus Prime* astronauts. After leaving the brown-dwarf-asteroid, they were led by the Suhkai to a habitable moon in a distant star cluster, but they soon discovered the environment was too harsh for Christine to produce offspring. Through their network of outposts, the Suhkai then identified a more hospitable planet in a star system a few light years farther away. Tula.

This was where Haula and Zoor entered the story. They were tasked by their elders with transporting Nick, Christine and Avery to the new planet. And two years later — a total of twelve years since the astronauts left Callisto — they arrived at Tula. During the trip, Christine had delivered two children, Tina and John. Sarah was born a little over a year after their arrival on the planet, making her the first true Tulan.

When both the meal and the story were completed, Zoor dismissed the children and led Morgan back out into the rainforest.

"So the idea of building a colony originated before they reached Tula," Morgan said.

"Yes. Your friends made an agreement with the first Suhkai they met. In exchange for our help in searching for human worlds, they agreed to spread life like Cytons and Suhkai."

Droplets pelted Morgan's face as he looked up at Zoor. "How did they go from building their family on Tula to splitting up and sending Nick to fetch more humans from Earth?"

Zoor extended her palm above Morgan's head to shield him from the rain as they walked. "Once it became sufficiently clear to us that Tula would sustain humans — this was shortly after Sarah was born — we told them the reason the Cytons from Callisto had brought them to meet the Suhkai."

This admission caused Morgan to halt. His mind drifted back to the *Cetus Prime* video log in which Nick explained why he believed the Cytons were flying the ship toward Callisto instead of Earth. Nick had said, "*I asked them to take us home, but it looks like they thought I asked them to take us to their leader.*"

In a later log, Nick clarified that the crew believed the Cytons' leaders were the aliens who built the spaceport on Callisto — the "beekeepers." They'd arrived at this conclusion because of the large Cyton hive they discovered inside the structure. And when the three astronauts left the moon in a Suhkai cruiser to go in search of the beekeepers, Nick's final log said they felt it was a better option than starving to death on Callisto.

But now that Morgan thought of that comment, he realized it wasn't true. He recalled the water and nectar Nick had plied him with earlier; Nick had told Morgan they had survived on that very nourishment during their journey to meet the Suhkai. Presumably that meant there had been supplies of both in the spaceport and aboard the cruiser.

The implication: the Cytons had deceived the astronauts in order to lure them onto the Suhkai ship. They led them to believe they would starve to death if they didn't take the ship. The Cytons didn't reveal the stores of nectar and water until *after* they left Callisto.

"Deceived is too strong a word," Zoor said.

"You're wrong. It's the perfect word."

"Regardless, the Cytons had good reason."

"And what would that be?"

They reached the airlock and stepped inside. "I will show you."

A blast of frigid air filled the chamber, and the droplets of water on Morgan's face, hands and clothes turned to ice. He shivered and brushed the crystals off.

The opposite airlock doors opened, and Zoor led him to another room across the hall. A large disc in the center of the floor was matched by a disc of equal size on the ceiling.

"Watch," Zoor said.

Between the two discs, a three-dimensional image appeared: a spinning black star. As in Zoor's earlier vision, a fissure ripped across the star's surface and a bolt of energy fired out. A second later, the twirling star shot forth another gamma burst. Still more followed after that.

The star dissolved and a depiction of Jupiter formed in its place. The gas giant's clouds churned like cream stirred into coffee, then the swirls began to ripple as if a blast of wind had disturbed their lazy curls around the planet. The ripples soon turned into shockwaves — and with a blinding flash, Jupiter was no more.

In that moment, Morgan understood why the Cytons had led Nick and the others to the Suhkai ... and why Nick was hellbent on taking two hundred humans to Tula.

"How long does Earth have?" he asked.

"Who is to say? An Earth day? A year? A few thousand years?"

Morgan thought of the gamma burst that had crippled *Juno*.

"Yes, it was a weak magwave from the same star that will one day destroy Jupiter and Earth," Zoor said.

"And the Cytons were aware of this star and what it would do twenty-four years ago when they encountered *Cetus Prime*?" Morgan asked.

"Yes."

Zoor told Morgan the Cytons use their ability to detect rising magnetic tensions in dormant magnetars to help them determine which are stable enough to stimulate magwaves for space travel purposes and which ones are too volatile. "This star has been unstable for four thousand Earth years."

Four thousand years? A curious number. "So that's why your people left our solar system," Morgan said. "The Cytons told you the magnetar was going to blow. It had nothing to do with the Zikzaws."

"That is not entirely true, but neither is it entirely inaccurate. Recall that I said Zikzaws are drawn to cosmic disruptions."

Morgan put the pieces together. Four thousand years ago, the Cytons had detected a burst from the unstable magnetar, but so had the Zikzaws. They gathered in the asteroid belt near Jupiter to partake in the radiation feast that would result from the planet's destruction and, in so doing, they took notice of the Suhkai miners. While the Zikzaws waited for the big show to start, they sated their appetites on the Suhkai cruisers hauling liquid metallic hydrogen and helium collected from Jupiter's lower atmosphere. The threat of the magnetar, coupled with the presence of the Zikzaws, was too much for the Suhkai. They closed up shop and left.

"Have the Zikzaws lingered in the asteroid belt ever since they arrived?"

"No."

"So their return is not a good sign."

"Perceptive once again, Skywalker."

"How do the Cytons know the magnetar's beams will hit Jupiter and Earth?" Morgan asked. "Couldn't starquakes rip open fissures that direct the beams elsewhere?"

"Yes, that is possible," Zoor said. "Many of the magwaves the star has produced in the past have not crossed Jupiter's orbital path, but many have. The question is: are you willing to bet your planet's survival, your species' existence, on the chance the beams will miss Jupiter and Earth when the magnetar *fully* awakes, when its beams reach full intensity?"

"I see your point."

"I thought you might. Come. Follow me."

CARGO BAY — THE *RORSCHACH EXPLORER*
FLYING THROUGH THE ASTEROID BELT

Carillo checked the digital display of her spacesuit's life support module. "I'm heading inside now. Getting low on O2."

"Roger," Shilling said. "Do you need any help?"

"No, I'm fine. I'll join you on the flight deck after I repressurize."

Carillo powered off the probe engines but left their radios active. She spent the required interval to rebalance her oxygen inside the airlock, then removed her EMU and propelled to the battery closet. They had an additional problem to deal with, one she hadn't shared with Shilling.

The ship's batteries were rechargeable, but they still needed a power source in order to stimulate the recharge. And while the Recon and Cargo had solar panels to accomplish this task, *Rorschach* did not. The ship normally relied on channeling a portion of the energy created by the ship's VLF engines back to the closet for recharging purposes, which meant the batteries would run out at some point unless Carillo came up with a way to restart the ship's engines.

They could get by for a while by limiting life support to certain sections of the ship and turning off just about everything else to lessen the battery drain. In addition, she could swap out the Cargo's battery after it was recharged and use the probe's solar panels to recharge depleted batteries from *Rorschach*. But the ship required far more battery power to operate than the probes did, and she wouldn't be able to swap out batteries fast enough to offset the drain. If she tried to duplicate the effort by swapping out the Recon's recharged battery, she would have to perform additional EVAs, which meant depleting their reserve O2 tanks, not to mention additional radiation exposure. And it still wouldn't be enough. At best, after all that effort, she'd only be buying them some time.

The only real solution was to reactivate one or more of *Rorschach*'s engines. If she couldn't do that, they would lose life support long before they reached Earth. Even if Mayaguana and NASA sent relief probes with fresh batteries, more oxygen and parts to repair the ship's critical systems, the help would arrive too late.

As Carillo stared into the darkened closet, a light glowed from behind her. At first she thought Shilling had arrived with a flashlight … until she noticed the tint of blue. A thought filled her mind. "*Help. We will help. We are friends.*"

HUMAN BREEDING WARD – SUHKAI SPACECRAFT *ETHEL* IN ORBIT AROUND SATURN MOON DIONE

Zoor led Morgan to one of the car-pod elevators, where they descended to a floor that looked like an empty hospital ward. Glass walls lined a wide hallway, revealing rooms with rows of sleep-pod like chambers, and other rooms stocked with what looked like medical equipment. Clusters of workspaces that reminded Morgan of nurses' stations were positioned at intervals all down the center of the hallway, which extended for at least two hundred meters.

As they walked down the hall, peering at the rooms and stations, Zoor said, "Your people will rotate blocks of time in deep sleep during the journey to Tula. They will be monitored from these stations by a combination of Suhkai, Cytons and humans. When they are awake, they will live in one of three Tula habitat levels on this ship — habitats like the one where Sarah, John and Annie live now.

"Children who are not yet of breeding age will be educated and cared for by a select group of Suhkai, Cytons and humans. When their bodies are capable of procreation, they will join the community of breeders. As Nick indicated, all colonists will devote most of their waking energy toward procreation, but they will also devote time to learning and refining the skills necessary to build and maintain their colony on Tula. Suhkai, Cytons and humans will lead this instruction.

"From our experience colonizing new worlds, we know not all humans will survive the journey, nor will all breeders be successful. Still, we estimate that when we arrive at Tula eleven years from now, we will have over five hundred humans. If they adapt well to the planet, the population should triple within ten years, and humanity will have a chance to survive."

Zoor made the plan sound reasonable and well-thought-out. Except for the body-snatching part. Morgan said as much to Zoor. "Why not recruit humans willing to make the journey?"

"If you see a boulder about to crush someone, do you push them out of the way as fast as possible, or do you stop to explain why you are about to push them?" Zoor asked. "Take too long to explain and they are crushed. Push them out of the way without warning and they may be angry at first, but when the boulder lands where they once stood, the anger will quickly fade and they will thank you."

"I appreciate the analogy, but it oversimplifies the situation here," Morgan said. "You're not talking about just pushing someone away from a falling boulder. You're pushing them into a hole from which they can never escape. Given a choice, they may prefer to die from the boulder than spend the rest of their lives in the hole. And if they aren't given that choice, their anger will never fade, they'll never thank you, and they won't breed."

"They will breed. We do not need their cooperation to ensure this."

Morgan halted in the hallway and shook his head. How could beings who had exhibited such altruism toward Nick, Avery and Christine believe in such an approach?

Zoor turned to him. "Space is no different than your oceans, forests or deserts. Every being, everywhere, is in a constant struggle for survival. Eat or be eaten. Kill or be killed. Breed or die off."

"I get that, but—"

"I have spent many Earth years learning about your planet from Nick, Avery and Christine. You routinely take plants and animals from their habitats and move them elsewhere, do you not?"

"Yes, but—"

"In your history, you have displaced groups of humans many times ... often by force, often without explanation. Sometimes for good reasons — natural disasters, disease or conflicts that ravage lands of the innocent. Other times not — conquest, greed or hatred. How is this any different?"

Morgan clenched his jaw. "Like I said before, you can spin it any way you want, but it's still wrong. It's *enslavement*. We've had plenty of experience with the concept in our history. If you listened closely enough to Nick, Avery and Christine, you'd know that humans won't tolerate it."

Zoor's crest tubes began to vibrate as if she was preparing a rebuttal, but Morgan held up his hand. "As I've already said, there's nothing I can do to stop you. I know that. So I'm begging you, Zoor. I'm begging the Cyton queen inside your head right now. Don't do this. Allow me to talk with my fellow humans on Earth and explain the situation. I'm confident volunteers will step forward ... many more volunteers than are necessary to fill a thousand arks like this one. It won't be the ideal mix you seek — no human parents will surrender their young children — but the people who go will be committed, not conscripted, breeders. I have to believe the odds of their survival will be stronger because of it."

LOWER-LEVEL HALLWAY — SUHKAI REFINERY
SATURN MOON DIONE

If Kiera had died in the plunge, she would have been at peace knowing she had saved herself from a lifetime of exploitation. But a swarm of Cytons had enveloped her before she collided with the stone floor below.

As the Cytons carried her shooting along a lower hallway, the ball's magnetic energy prevented her from speaking or even moving. In her thoughts, she pleaded, *"Leave me alone. Let me die!"*

With her eyes closed, she was unaware of the sea of blue surrounding her as a return thought entered her mind. *"We will help. We are friends."*

HUMAN BREEDING WARD – SUHKAI SPACECRAFT *ETHEL* IN ORBIT AROUND SATURN MOON DIONE

"Your solution will not work," Zoor said. "Many humans will die because of it. Nick understands this. Why can't you?"

"Because I refuse to believe it," Morgan said.

"Think, Skywalker. Use your mind. If you tell your people there is a magwave coming that will end your world, it will cause panic. If you say only two hundred can leave for Tula, there will be fighting. Many will die. Your approach risks thousands, possibly millions."

"Then I won't tell them about the magwaves. I'll present it as an exploration mission, a chance to settle on a new world."

Zoor looked down at Morgan and blew an exasperated grunt through her crest tubes. It was powerful enough to knock Morgan against the glass wall directly behind him. "You humans are as stupid as you are stubborn. You do not listen to voices of experience. Such a mission as you describe will not produce enough humans to establish a new society on Tula. The people who go must not think of it as an adventure or relaxing voyage. They must think of it as humans' last chance, possibly their only chance, of survival."

"Why only two hundred?" Morgan countered. "Why not send the ark back after the first volunteers arrive and keep making round trips for as long as the ark can fly, or for as long as Earth still exists?"

The suggestion drew another angry snort from Zoor. "If the first colonists know and believe that others will follow, they will not feel the same pressure to breed. When the next ark arrives, twenty-two Earth years later, only a small fraction of the first colony will still be alive and the second colony will number far too little for humans to survive, for they will relax on the journey, too. Trust me, Skywalker. The Suhkai have seen enough colonies fail to know this will happen."

"Then why not build more arks? Send a thousand people, or two thousand. If you won't build them yourselves, then show us how to do it and *we* will build them."

"In the time it would take us to show you how to build our vessels, how to travel vast distances, how to utilize our technologies, this ark will have already reached Tula. By the time you actually built the ships and began the journey to transport one thousand humans, the Tula population will have surpassed two thousand.

"In the meantime, your people would expend enormous resources. There would be great strife. People would say, 'Why do we waste so much for so few to survive when so many more starve now.' The tensions would worsen as time dragged on. You know this to be true.

"And there would be corruption. In the end, if the ships were successfully built, it would not be the young and fertile who traveled to Tula, but the well-connected. Or worse, wars would break out to possess our technology and ships. Many would die, and the ships and technology would be lost in the fight or diverted for other purposes."

Morgan hated to admit it, but Zoor's scenario was likely. Yet if the aliens had such a dim assessment of humans, why had they been so willing to help Nick, Avery and Christine? He thought, *"If we suck so much, why do you want to save us?"*

"Enough talk, Skywalker. It is time to make your decision. Either take Nick's place and shepherd the colonists during the return trip to Tula, or we will rule over them ourselves and you and your crew will be sacrificed."

Morgan stared Zoor in the eye and shook his head. "I can't, I won't, do it your way, Zoor."

"Fool! Our way is the only way!" The alien pounded her fist through the nearest glass wall. As shards of glass landed around Morgan, a new thought entered his mind. It wasn't his own, and it wasn't from Zoor.

"You lie!"

The hallway began to gleam with a new light. A blue light. A blue light three times larger than any Cyton Morgan had seen. *"You lie to all!"*

Morgan watched the blue light flicker as it approached Zoor. The Suhkai began to tremble. Morgan felt the sensation of static electricity all over his body. In a blinding flash, the Callisto queen shot out from inside Zoor's head. The Suhkai fell, knocking into Morgan on her way to the floor. As he tried to wedge his body from beneath the dazed Suhkai, he looked up to see the blue Cyton hovering over Zoor.

"Tell him!"

The Callisto queen flickered and Morgan's thoughts filled with Zoor's answer. *"No! It is not necessary."*

"You lie! Tell him!" The blue Cyton zapped Zoor's chest bulge and sent another bolt at the Callisto queen. The queen's golden light faltered and she backed away.

As Morgan crawled out of the line of fire, he stared at the blue Cyton and thought back to an earlier comment made by Carillo when she realized she was communicating with the BLUMO pack alpha, not the BLUMO queen. *The queen is the one who's coming. Trust me, you'll see what I mean when we meet up with her.* And then it dawned on him they'd never encountered the BLUMO queen ... until now. Morgan spoke to her. *"Can you understand me? Are you receiving my thoughts?"*

"Yes. We are friends."

Zoor regained her feet and issued a screeching command to the Callisto queen. The golden ball of light blasted a bolt of electricity at the blue Cyton. The heat from the lightning was intense enough to burn Morgan's exposed skin. He curled into a ball and covered his face with his hands.

Morgan didn't see the BLUMO queen's response, but he felt it: a VLF radio wave blast so intense that it not only disintegrated the Callisto queen and killed Zoor, it shook *Ethel* from bow to stern.

That was when Morgan passed out, his eardrums obliterated.

Later, he would learn from Anlon Cully how lucky he had been to survive. VLF radio waves produced during a sperm whale song, Anlon told him, are powerful enough to stop the heart of a human floating within touch of the great beast.

CHAPTER 22

A NEW DAY

Dante Fulton, asleep and drooling on his console, shook awake in response to the screams of Norris Preston. The backup mission director sounded like he was hyperventilating. "Downlink! Downlink! Downlink!"

Thirty-six heads, including Dante's, Amato's and Pritchard's, snapped to attention.

Preston's cracking voice echoed over Mission Control's intercom. "We have pings from *Cargo-4*! *Recon-3*!"

Thirty-six bodies raced for stations around Mission Control. Four hundred million kilometers away, the party was just beginning.

SUHKAI CRUISER LINK-UP WITH THE *RORSCHACH EXPLORER*
ASTEROID BELT
SEPTEMBER 13, 2019

Two hours. That's how long it takes Cytons, unaided by the push from a magwave, to travel 1.2 billion kilometers … the same time and distance it took them to lead a Suhkai cruiser carrying Kiera and Ajay to link up with the *Rorschach Explorer*. When the alien cruiser pulled alongside

Amato's stricken vessel, no radio was necessary. For both vessels were surrounded by spheres of blue light.

In the Suhkai cockpit, Kiera closed her eyes and thought, *"Need a lift?"*

Through *Rorschach*'s BLUMOs, Dr. Robert Shilling answered. *"Roger that. What took you so long?"*

"Sorry. Elroy had to stop at the gift shop on the way out," Kiera said. *"You coming aboard or what?"*

Shilling mentally grumbled something about the need to depressurize.

Ajay responded, *"Depressurize, schmecompressize. Just put on your EMUs and let the BLUMOs do the walking. Oh, and can you pack up flight suits for us … and one for Skywalker, too. Suhkai clothes are a little drafty."*

Thirty minutes later, after Major Julia Carillo had shut down the last of *Rorschach Explorer*'s systems, she pushed herself out into space through the outer airlock door. The blue bubble surrounding her guided her into the airlock of the Suhkai cruiser, where Shilling was already awaiting her arrival.

As soon as the Suhkai pilots had closed the outer airlock door, Kiera summoned the BLUMOs surrounding both ships. *"Find Skywalker."*

HUMAN MEDICAL WARD — SUHKAI SPACECRAFT *ETHEL*
IN ORBIT AROUND SATURN MOON DIONE
SEPTEMBER 12, 2019

When Morgan came to, he was lying on a table in what looked like a hospital room. His hands were bandaged and his ears were ringing. The memories from the Cyton-Suhkai confrontation in the breeding ward flowed into his mind, as did the stinging sensation of the burns on his face and hands.

"We have treated your burns. They will heal before you leave."

Morgan recognized the voice invading his thoughts. It was Haula. He raised his head and looked around. To his right he spied the Suhkai male. The BLUMO queen hovered in midair next to him. Morgan's head began to spin. He lowered it back to the table and asked, "What the hell happened?"

"*We are friends.*"

He craned his neck to look at the flickering ball of blue light. "So you keep saying." He turned to Haula. "Where am I? Where's Zoor?"

"*Zoor is no more,*" Haula answered.

"*We are friends,*" interjected the BLUMO queen. "*We help humans.*"

"You want to be friends? Then convince Nick and Haula here to let me and my people go."

"*Preparations are already underway,*" came Haula's response.

Morgan's head snapped up. "You're serious?"

The BLUMO queen began to pulse, and Morgan's mind filled with visions of Kiera and Ajay in the cockpit of a spaceship piloted by two Suhkai. Another vision showed Carillo and Shilling inside the *Rorschach Explorer.* They all wore smiles.

"Is this some kind of trick?" Morgan asked Haula.

"*No. Humans free,*" the BLUMO queen assured him. "*Suhkai obey me.*"

"Just like that?" Morgan said. He pushed up into a sitting position and once again turned toward Haula. "I don't understand. Don't get me wrong, I'm happy about it, but I don't understand what's happened."

Haula extended his hand. "*There will be time for explanations later. Please rise. Nick awaits you. His time has come.*"

THE REED-BAKER-LOCKETT HOME
TULA HABITAT — SUHKAI SPACECRAFT *ETHEL*

When Morgan, Haula and the BLUMO queen entered the bedroom, the three children were seated on the bed next to Nick, their hands touching him. Maggie hovered over Nick's chest, throbbing light as if mimicking a heartbeat.

Haula projected a thought to Morgan. "*His body is no more. Maggie has kept his mind alive long enough to say goodbye to you and the children. She will translate.*"

As Morgan approached, the children let go of Nick and began to move off the bed. Morgan urged them to stay. "Don't go. Be with him."

They resumed their places and Annie said, "Skywalker's here, Nicky. He's come to say goodbye."

Morgan sat down next to Annie and wrapped his arm around her. Maggie began to flicker, and Nick greeted Morgan. "*Hey there, old man.*"

"Hey, buddy." Morgan choked up.

"*Understand there's a new sheriff in town.*"

Morgan wiped tears from his eyes and turned to look at the BLUMO queen. "Looks that way."

"*She says you're calling the shots now.*"

With his eyes still locked on the blue Cyton, Morgan said, "That's news to me."

"*Well, that's the deal. You made quite an impression on her. She trusts you.*"

Morgan returned his gaze to Nick's lifeless body. "I'm not sure how or why."

"*Apparently you have a blue aura.*"

Sarah intervened. "Cytons, like the Suhkai, can detect our magnetic energy. Yours is blue."

"Blue means you are strong and love helping people," Annie said. "Mine is yellow. I shine like a sun."

"*Yes you do, my sweet,*" Nick said through Maggie.

"What exactly does calling the shots mean, Nick?" Morgan asked.

"*Means you're now responsible for dealing with the magnetar, and for making sure this boat gets to Tula with my family and enough humans to build a lasting presence. I still think the Suhkai approach is the only way to do it, but, at this point, neither I nor the Suhkai are in a position to dictate how you do it. The responsibility has been stripped from us and vested in you. And you better not screw up. I'm counting on you. So are Avery, Christine and the children. Not to mention the human race.*"

Morgan turned to seek confirmation from Haula. The Suhkai responded. "*We are duty-bound to honor the wishes of the spreaders-of-life. This queen now rules your solar system. She has spoken, and we will obey.*"

While Morgan absorbed the import of Nick's and Haula's comments, Nick communicated again. "*Three last requests, Paul.*"

"Yes, Nick, I'm listening."

"*First, don't be all mad at me or Christine or Avery for what we had in mind. I know you don't approve of it, but we were trying to do the right thing. Honest. And don't get all down on the Suhkai. They didn't have to help us, but they did. They don't have to help you, but they will. Lastly, please forgive me for what I put you and your crew through. I took no pleasure from it. I just felt I had no choice.*"

Under the circumstances, it was hard to be mad at Nick, though it wasn't easy to forgive him. "I understand, Nick. And don't worry. I'll do my best to make sure things work out right."

"*I know you will. You're Skywalker, after all.*" Maggie's throbbing slowed. "*Now, where are my little ones?*"

"We're here, Nicky," John said.

"*Good. Now hold your hands out to Maggie, just like I showed you. Don't be afraid. Feel my energy.*" The three children cupped their hands around the Cyton. "*Goodbye, my sweets. I don't want to leave you, but it's time. Remember I love you, and take good care of one another.*"

Maggie glowed brightly enough to swallow the children's hands in an orb of light. When it faded, the Cyton was gone. Morgan watched as the youngsters' hands remained cupped in the air. Their eyes were closed, and peaceful expressions graced their faces. It was as if Maggie had injected Nick's spirit into them as she passed away along with her companion.

TULA HABITAT — SUHKAI SPACECRAFT *ETHEL*

When the airlock door opened, Kiera was the first to step into the Tula habitat. Ajay followed shortly thereafter, his mouth hanging open. Behind him, Carillo waved to the waiting Morgan, while Shilling, engrossed in a thought exchange with the BLUMO queen, came through the door last. There were long hugs and plenty of smiles as the crew reunited with Morgan.

As Morgan separated from an embrace with Carillo, Ajay asked, "What is this place?"

"Another world," said Morgan. "Come on, follow me. I'm sure you have a million questions and so do I, but I want to show you something first."

The BLUMO queen departed as Morgan led his team into the rainforest. Soon they emerged into the clearing where, fifty meters away, the silver domes of the Reed-Baker-Lockett home sparkled under the glow of an artificial sun.

"Wicked!" Ajay said.

"What is it?" Kiera asked.

"Nick Reed's home," said Morgan.

Annie edged into view through the open front door. Sarah and John appeared behind her. "And those children are Nick's family. Well, part of his family. Well, part of Christine's and Avery's, too. The strapping lad is John. The young lady is Sarah, and the little drop of sunshine is Annie. They're anxious to meet you but, before we go to them, there's something you should know. Nick passed away earlier today, so they're hurting a bit. They could use some friendly faces and some TLC."

"Say no more," said Carillo. "I could use some too."

She started walking toward the house with her arms extended toward the children. Shilling followed close behind. As the two astronaut parents neared the front stoop, Woof poked his head out from a nearby bush. The sudden appearance of the creature's ostrich-like head startled Ajay. "What the heck is that?"

"The family pet," said Morgan. "Come on, I'll introduce you."

With Kiera and Ajay following his lead, Morgan walked slowly to the bush, and they all crouched down. He extended his hand to Woof, and the creature sniffed the air. Apparently satisfied that no predators were around, Woof scampered out and licked Morgan's hand.

Morgan encouraged Ajay to hold out his hand. "Careful, though. He'll bite it off if you make a wrong move."

"Huh?" Ajay yanked his hand back.

"I kid, I kid."

A short while later, the *Rorschach* crew and the Reed-Baker-Lockett children gathered in the family dining room for a meal and a trading of stories. The questions and answers flowing back and forth were disjointed at first, but Morgan stepped in to bring order to the dialogue.

He asked the children to begin by telling his crew the tale of the *Cetus Prime* astronauts, beginning with their departure from Callisto and ending with their settling on Tula. The story they shared was more about their parents' adventures than a detailing of facts, so Morgan interjected at various points to explain the who, what, where, why and how parts. Annie was as impatient with his interruptions as she'd been with Zoor's.

Morgan then directed the path of the conversation to cover the Suhkai, Cytons' and Zikzaws' roles in the tale, including a discussion of the magnetar and the reason for Nick's return. During the conversation, Annie hopped from lap to lap until tiring of the dialogue and falling asleep nestled up to her mother, Sarah.

John and Sarah interrupted here and there to elaborate on certain points and correct Morgan on others. Morgan shaded some of the more unseemly details in an effort to avoid speaking badly of Nick in front of the children. The crew seemed to read between the lines. When they shared their own tales, they also tiptoed around certain elements.

When Ajay, the last to share his part of the story, finished speaking, there was a lull in the conversation. Sarah yawned and whispered something to John. He nodded and turned to Morgan. "When will you be leaving?"

"I'm not sure. Why?"

"We want to visit more, but we're exhausted." John stood and picked up the sleeping Annie from Sarah's lap. With a little help from Shilling, the pregnant Sarah rose up as well. The *Rorschach* crew left their seats and gathered around the two teenagers. Careful to avoid waking Annie, they exchanged hugs.

"Please don't go without saying goodbye," Sarah said to Morgan.

He kissed her on the forehead. "Wouldn't dream of it."

"Will you take us to Earth with you, please?" Sarah pleaded. "Annie will be so disappointed if she doesn't get a chance to see and play with other children. She's never seen one. Neither have I or John."

Morgan hugged her again. "I will come back for you in a day or two. I promise you'll see so many children, it'll make Woof's legs pop off."

Sarah smiled, arched up on her toes and pecked Morgan on the cheek. She turned to the others. "Thank you for coming. Thank you for helping us."

Carillo hugged her and said, "I think we're the ones who should be doing the thanking."

After the children departed, the *Rorschach* crew cleaned up and left the house to walk around the meadow behind the home. Woof joined them but then scampered off behind another stand of trees. When they caught up to him, they discovered another home tucked among the trees. Looking across the meadow, they saw similar nooks with other homes.

As they wandered along, Shilling asked, "So I understand that the BLUMOs came to our rescue, Paul, but I'm not clear on why they did."

"I'm not a hundred percent clear myself." Morgan stopped by the edge of a small pond and turned to the group. "While you were all on your way back to *Ethel*, I had a long conversation with Haula, the head Suhkai aboard, and the BLUMO queen. I think I understand most of what they communicated, but there are still some parts that are hazy.

"First of all, most of the BLUMOs that came aboard *Rorschach* during Julia's spacewalk never left. They cloaked themselves and observed, reporting back their observations to the queen. Hence the chirps, quivers and hisses Ajay picked up on the radio afterward. Once the queen developed an opinion of us, that's when she instructed the alpha to connect with Julia."

There was never a moment after that, Morgan told them, when they weren't accompanied by a cloaked BLUMO. When he, Kiera and Ajay went aboard *Ethel*, a cluster of BLUMOs followed them. The same happened later when the Suhkai brought Carillo and Shilling aboard. All the while, those BLUMOs were communicating back to the queen about what was transpiring. When the queen reached the point where she'd learned enough, she intervened.

"But *why* did she intervene?" asked Carillo.

Morgan bent down and dipped his hand in the pond. As he pulled it out, a few jellyfish-like creatures floated to the surface. Woof came up beside him and stepped into the pond. Soon it was floating across the surface like a swan with an ostrich head. "This is where things get a bit complicated, relationship-wise, between different colonies of Cytons and between Cytons and Suhkai."

He related Nick's description of the reverence with which the Suhkai view Cytons, how they see the balls of light as the saviors of their race and the spreaders of life, and how, over hundreds of thousands of years, as the Suhkai expanded their presence in the galaxy, they formed symbiotic bonds with millions of individual Cyton colonies.

"And that's the sticky part. The Suhkai are so spread out now, there is no central command structure of their civilization. Their population spans thousands of light years' worth of distance. The Cytons are spread across even more of the galaxy. In fact, the Suhkai believe they exist beyond the Milky Way. And just like honeybees on Earth, there is no central queen bee that lords over all bees. Each Cyton colony is distinct. Do they collaborate with other colonies? Yes. Do they compete or fight with other colonies? That too."

"I see," said Shilling. "So the BLUMOs cooperated with the Callisto UMOs to a point."

"Exactly. As I understand it from Haula, most of the Cyton colonies in our solar system originated from the hive the Suhkai brought with them thousands of years ago — the one on Callisto. So there's somewhat of an allegiance between the outlying colonies and the Callisto hive, but not to the point of outright deference." Morgan turned to Kiera and Ajay. "Case in point. You know those whale songs going back and forth between the BLUMOs and Callisto? We were wrong about the gist of their conversation. From what I was told, they weren't coordinating a handoff of *Rorschach*. The BLUMO queen was questioning the *purpose* of the handoff and alerting the Callisto queen that there was a Zikzaw lurking about. Their conversation turned into a fight about who was responsible for dealing with the Zikzaw, and then a discussion of a joint effort to kill it."

Shilling sat down on a rock and shook his head. "These are such sophisticated beings. I'm having a hard time believing they're so sentient. None of the UMOs around Earth ever demonstrated anything close to these kinds of interactions and coordination."

"Well, I might be wrong, but I think it comes down to environment." Morgan lowered himself onto the rock next to Shilling. "The harsher the living conditions, the more the Cytons rely on each other and work together. The BLUMOs are tough and clever because they've had to be in order to survive in the belt. They've developed a collective intelligence and honed cooperative tactics."

Kiera sat on the grass and stretched out her legs. "I see what you're saying. Around Earth, food is abundant, and there are no Zikzaws or other big-time threats, so there isn't the same pull for colonies to bond together. As a result they're simpler, more individualistic in their behaviors."

"Kind of like the colony that followed us from Earth," Ajay said.

Woof exited the pond and shook his fur dry, spraying water on the crew.

As Carillo wiped droplets off her flight suit, she said, "That's all very interesting, Paul, but it doesn't answer my question. Why did the BLUMO queen get involved?"

"Short answer — disgust, bitterness," Morgan said. "She couldn't take the hypocrisy of the Suhkai and the complicity of the Callisto hive queen. The magnetar didn't wake up on its own four thousand years ago. The Suhkai *stirred it awake* in the process of creating a magwave to transport hydrogen and helium they'd mined from Jupiter. The Cytons had apparently warned them against trying it, telling them it was too unstable, but the Suhkai ignored them. The BLUMO queen was here when it all went down. Her colony was the one the Suhkai dispatched to deal with the Zikzaws way back then. She considered the Suhkai cowards for leaving.

"So when the Callisto queen alerted her the Suhkai were coming back, it evidently surprised the BLUMO queen. At first she thought the Suhkai were returning to finally deal with the magnetar. You know, clean up their mess. But then the Callisto queen tasked her with intercepting us, and eventually the BLUMO queen figured out the Suhkai were sneaking back to collect humans to seed a new colony on Tula instead of confronting the real issue. That pissed her off. Especially when another Zikzaw showed up. By the way, you want to hear something amazing? The BLUMO queen didn't know humans existed until they found our fleet and started tracking us."

Ajay was examining a piece of fruit he had pulled from the branch of a nearby tree. He turned to look at Morgan. "You're kidding. How could they not know about us?"

Kiera picked at blades of grass. "Not my monkeys, not my circus."

Shilling nodded. "That's probably exactly right. The colonies I've studied around Earth tend to stay away from one another, stick to their own territories. It's probably true of all colonies."

"But *Cetus Prime* … it passed through the belt," Ajay protested.

"With an escort of Cytons from Mars, remember?" Shilling said.

"That's right," Kiera said. "And keep in mind how big the belt is. They may never have crossed paths with the BLUMOs."

Carillo knelt beside Woof and petted his head. "It would certainly explain why they dissected our fleet. They couldn't figure out what to make of us."

"Or what to make of you in your spacesuit," Morgan added.

Kiera brushed grass from her hands. "Or why our UMOs didn't respond to them."

There was a pause in the conversation as the five astronauts absorbed the totality of the information. Drops of rain began to fall. Kiera tilted her head up and let it splash her face. "Oh my God. That feels so good. I never thought I'd ever say it, but man do I miss rain."

"And sunrises," said Shilling. "And my family."

"Ditto," Carillo said.

"Don't forget sunsets," Ajay chipped in.

"Or margaritas," added Morgan.

"Mmmm … how about a big juicy burger," Kiera said.

As more rain fell, they continued to rattle off additional items on their list of missed joys and comforts until Carillo said, "Okay, I think we've firmly established we want to go home. So what's the plan, Paul?"

"Short-term or long-term?"

"Both."

"Well, I've already arranged for the Suhkai to take us to Earth on the cruiser that brought you guys back … with a BLUMO escort, of course. Sounds like it'll be a quick trip, less than a few hours, but first I have some negotiating to do with our hosts about the long-term plan. So I'd say we'll be heading out in less than a day. You guys should get some rest in the meantime." Morgan nodded in the direction of an igloo-house across the meadow. "I've been told we can use one of the homes. The Suhkai will prep whichever one you all choose."

Delighted faces soaked in the news along with the light rain. Carillo said, "Sounds good. By the way, we brought you a flight suit and your boots. The Suhkai are holding them for you."

"Excellent." Morgan wiggled his feet. "I'm kinda tired of the slippers."

"What about Mayaguana?" Kiera asked. "Dante, Mr. Amato and the rest must be beside themselves. Not to mention our families."

"Yeah, you're right, Kiera. We'll give Maya a heads-up before I huddle with the queen and Haula."

"Speaking of which, what's the long-term plan?" Shilling asked.

"Well, we should talk about that. Believe it or not, the BLUMO queen has put me in charge of this boat and the Suhkai crew. She's left the next steps in my hands … *our* hands. To me, it's a no-brainer to send *Ethel* back to Tula with a colony of humans, *willing* humans, people who know what they're signing up for and what's expected of them. Agreed?"

Amid the unanimous bobbing of heads, Shilling asked, "How do you plan to recruit them?"

Morgan shrugged. "Above my pay grade. When we get back, we'll discuss it with Augie, Dennis Pritchard, Helen Brock. Discreetly call in some experts, see what they recommend."

Shilling frowned. "When you say *discreetly*, you mean to say we're not going to tell people about the magnetar?"

"That's another one I'm struggling with, Bob," Morgan said. "I don't want to panic people, but I don't want to lie to them either. So if we're going to talk about it, we've got to find a way to have the conversation without freaking everybody out. I mean, from what the Suhkai shared with me, it could be thousands of years before it finally erupts. Kinda feel that argues in favor of easing into the conversation, but even if we do that, there's no way we'll be able to control people's reactions to the news. Yet we're going to need help to stabilize the magnetar, so we're going to have to clue in some big-brained scientists. And once we —"

Carillo raised her hand. "Whoa there! You hinted at this earlier. We can stabilize it?"

"Well, not alone. Evidently the Cytons and Suhkai have done it before, but it's a dicey deal from what they tell me. No guarantees and all that. It could backfire and the star could blow up. Truth is, we need to get a closer look at it, study it and figure out a plan. The BLUMO queen has committed her colony to help us, and she's commanded the Suhkai to assist. They'll be calling in some help from outside the solar system."

"And where is this magnetar?" Kiera asked.

"Ballpark ... two light years away."

"So it could blow before anyone gets there," Ajay said.

Morgan nodded.

"Geez, that's not a comforting thought," Carillo said.

"No, it isn't, but those are the cards we've been dealt, so those are the cards we'll play with. But I'm also going to ask for additional cards."

He told the crew he would push for an agreement to have *Ethel* make round trips to Tula until it could no longer fly. And he would demand the Suhkai take a contingent of human engineers in the first colony to study the ship during the journey and design other boats that could be added to the caravan over time. "They may not be as grand as this boat, but if we can send four or five at a time, then we can transport more people to Tula."

Ajay's eyes got big. "Or other places in the galaxy."

"You read my mind, Elroy," said Morgan. "I'm also gonna demand the Suhkai hand over the Callisto and Dione facilities so we can establish permanent bases for human space exploration, including a commitment to staff the facilities with Suhkai and a full complement of their cruisers. They don't have to stay in perpetuity, just long enough to show us how to operate the facilities, adapt them for human use, mine Jupiter and Saturn and build the propulsion system that powers their cruisers. Who knows how long it will take us to get up to speed, but once we do, we'll be in a position to start spreading humanity across the galaxy."

"Sounds awful ambitious, Paul," said Shilling.

"Reach for the stars, my man. Reach for the stars."

CHAPTER 23

COMING IN HOT

When Brock's assistant, Mary Evans, knocked on the open door of her office, her eyes were moist with tears.

Brock leaned her hip against the desk to steady herself, anguish clawing at her insides. Oh, God, she thought. Please don't say they're dead.

Evans tried to speak, but the words wouldn't come. Tears leaked down her cheeks.

And then cheers erupted from down the hall.

Brock looked up and locked eyes with Evans. The assistant nodded and broke into a smile, tears still streaming down her face.

"They found them?" Brock asked.

Evans nodded.

"They're alive?"

Evans crossed the office and took Brock by the hand. She managed two words. "Come see."

Down the corridor they ran. As they drew near to Brock's conference room, the celebration from inside reached ear-splitting levels. At the doorway, Evans stood aside and let go of Brock's hand. Everyone was so wrapped up in the moment, no one noticed Brock enter.

The wall-mounted monitor, used for videoconferences with NASA's other centers, was currently showing five split screens. Four of them showed similar scenes of celebration underway. The labels beneath them read A3I-Mayaguana, NASA-JPL, NASA-Goddard and NASA-Houston.

On one, Amato was weeping and Dante was hugging members of Mission Control. Similar scenes graced the feeds from the NASA centers.

But Brock's eyes were glued to the fifth screen, the still image in the center. There, with smiling faces and arms wrapped around each other, were the five crewmembers of the *Rorschach Explorer*, blue, bald and bedraggled. A caption at the bottom read: *CDR-TRE to MAYA-FLIGHT: Need a very ... repeat ... very ... discreet landing zone in eighteen hours, six minutes and twenty seconds. Please advise ASAP. Coming in hot. CDR-TRE out.*

"My God," Brock said. "How is that possible?"

Somehow Amato picked her out amid all the commotion. He looked into the camera on his end and wiped away tears. "I don't know, Helen, but isn't it wonderful?"

LATE ISLAND
TONGA ISLAND ARCHIPELAGO
KORO SEA
SEPTEMBER 14-15, 2019

Sol Seaker pounded through South Pacific swales as it raced toward Late Island. At top speed, the watercraft could travel at seventy-four kilometers per hour. However, in the heavy seas, it managed only fifty. As a result, Anlon, Pebbles and Jennifer arrived at the remote, uninhabited island sixteen hours after Anlon received Amato's call.

But they still made it there before the trail of light descended through the black of night and disappeared into the maw of Late's namesake volcanic crater.

The three companions dove into the island's offshore waters, waded onto its pristine beaches, and trudged up the volcano's eighteen-hundred-foot walls aided by flashlights. At sunrise, Jennifer Stevens, the most athletic of the three, crested the volcano's summit.

She wore her *Rorschach Explorer* wetsuit in honor of the occasion. The sight that met her was one she would never forget.

Climbing up the slope of the vegetation-covered caldera was the crew of the *Rorschach Explorer*.

Jennifer's knees wobbled so much she had to sit. She screamed at the sky, "In your face, Jenna Toffy!"

Pebbles reached the summit just as Jennifer hoisted the last of the crew atop the crumbly caldera. She nearly fell over when she saw the blue astronauts. Eyeing the lot of them suspiciously, she said, "See … this is what happens when you steal aliens' everlasting gobstoppers!"

Anlon didn't quite make it to the top. A hundred feet below the caldera summit, he lowered himself onto a rock and watched the celebration above with a huge smile on his face.

Amato's private jet flew straight to Fiji, stopping to refuel only once. From there its passengers — Amato, Dante and Pritchard — switched over to a Fiji-based seaplane, arranged for by Mark Myers, which took them to Late Island. The plane touched down on the waters surrounding the island at noon, four hours after the *Rorschach* crew boarded *Sol Seaker*.

Anlon dispatched his yacht's dinghy to retrieve the three men. As the dinghy pulled alongside the seaplane's open door. Pebbles spied Amato and shouted, "Ahoy, matey!"

Amato recalled Pebbles' greeting from their first meeting over a year ago. He cupped his hands and shouted back, "Permission to come aboard?"

"Permission granted," Pebbles answered.

A short while later, the dinghy docked in its hold at *Sol Seaker's* stern. As it was secured to its moorings, the crew of the *Rorschach Explorer* descended from mid-deck to meet the disembarking passengers. Anlon and Jennifer watched the reunion from the yacht's upper deck.

Amato buried his head in Skywalker's chest and wept. To the shock of the others, Dante embraced Kiera so passionately, they fell overboard into the water. Pritchard raced up the superyacht's steps and tackled Carillo, Shilling and Ajay.

Morgan whispered into Amato's ear. "Got a surprise for you."

From the pocket of his flight suit, he pulled out a photograph and handed it to Amato. It showed the three *Cetus Prime* astronauts and their first-born children in the Tulan meadow.

Amato gaped at it, then looked up at *Rorschach's* commander.

Morgan nodded and pointed at each of the children, naming them as he moved his finger. He then pulled out a second photo. "This is what John and Sarah look like all grown up. And this little scamp is Annie. She can really talk your ear off."

Amato took the photo and lowered himself onto a step. "They're alive? You've seen them?"

"These three, yes. They'll be here soon. They have to go through the blue wash like us so they don't get or give any ick."

"What about Avery, Christine and Nick?"

"Nick didn't make it, I'm sorry to say. It was a tough end for him, but he was damn heroic to the last. I'll tell you all about it, but this isn't the time."

"Of course," Amato said. "And Avery and Christine?"

"As far as I know, they're still alive. A very, very long way from here."

Tears in his eyes, Amato beamed at the photos as if the family was kin.

Owing to the sixteen-hour time difference between Fiji and America's east coast, the first photograph of the reunion to hit the Internet was posted at 9:36 p.m. EDT the day before the *Rorschach* crew returned to Earth.

It showed the nineteen people aboard *Sol Seaker*, including the ship's hands, huddled together at the stern, with the Koro Sea in the background.

Augustus Amato had ordered the addition of a caption at the bottom: *See what happens when we believe in one another.*

LAUNCH APRON
A3ROSPACE INDUSTRIES COMMAND AND CONTROL CENTER
SEPTEMBER 20, 2019

Five days later, a Suhkai cruiser landed on the launch apron at A3I's May-aguana complex, and Augustus Amato invited the one hundred forty-six employees staffing the center to join him on the tarmac to marvel at it. Cell phone cameras snapped group photos and selfies. Others recorded videos or live-streamed the festivities. The media was on hand, too, but segregated behind a rope line in Hangar-1.

The ship, donated by the Suhkai to Amato to compensate for the damage inflicted on the *Rorschach Explorer*, would play a pivotal role in the months to come. It would shuttle representatives from Earth to *Ethel* to meet with the Suhkai and BLUMO queen and begin the hard work of selecting the first group of humans to join the Reed-Baker-Lockett colony on Tula. It would ferry the first astronauts from the world's space agencies to begin rotations on the Suhkai base on Callisto. And it would lead a team of Earth's foremost scientists to the Suhkai base on Dione to engage in studies of the unstable magnetar, with the aim of preventing its eruption.

But today, the Suhkai vessel would perform the most important of its tasks.

A boarding ramp was wheeled into place at the ship's airlock, and a red carpet was unrolled from the base of the ramp to a group of waiting guests. The airlock door opened, and a military honor guard began its silent march down the red carpet and into the alien ship. Moments later they reemerged carrying a cylindrical container draped with an American flag. Following behind them were four blue and bald people. First came Sarah Baker-Reed, then John Baker-Lockett, and finally Paul Morgan carrying Annie Reed.

The waiting guests — the extended families of the *Cetus Prime* astronauts — wept as the last remains of Captain Nick Reed were escorted down the carpet. Their tears reflected a mix of emotions. For while there was sadness at Nick's loss, there was also joy in the greeting of the crew's Tulan offspring, the relief that comes from closure, and prideful respect for the burdens and sacrifices borne by Nick, Avery and Christine.

Behind the astronauts' families were the rest of the crew of the *Rorschach Explorer* and their families, as well as the surviving members of the *Cetus Prime* mission control team. The honor guard briefly halted in front of Nick Reed's eighty-eight-year-old mother. Steadied by Nick's brothers, Michelle Reed leaned over and kissed the flag-covered casket. She whispered words of love, telling her son she was proud of him and that now it was time for him to rest.

As the honor guard recommenced its march to a waiting hearse, the sea of family and friends parted to make way, each of them touching the casket as it passed by. The immediate family members broke away to embrace the Tulan children.

Paul Morgan stepped aside and went to join his crew.

Julia Carillo, standing with her husband and two children, saw him coming. "I hear from Ajay we have confirmation of your body art."

Morgan laughed and clutched his chest. "How could you do me like that, Elroy? After all we've been through."

Flanked by his parents, Ajay moved an imaginary zipper across his mouth. "I said nothing."

"Uh-huh."

Standing nearby, Kiera Walsh held hands with Dante Fulton, both of them talking with Robert Shilling. Shilling had his arm wrapped around his wife's waist, and his two shy children hid behind his legs.

"So, what's next for you?" Kiera asked.

Shilling squeezed his wife closer. "We've got some catching up to do. After that, it's back to the NASA grind. Might even write a book about our trip."

Kiera cringed. "Be kind to me in it, please." She turned to Shilling's wife. "I was kind of a B-I-T-you-know-what for most of it."

"I don't know what you're talking about," Shilling said.

Kiera smiled. "How many mai tais have you had this morning?"

Ajay interrupted to introduce his parents to Dr. Shilling. While his father quizzed the researcher about UMOs, Ajay motioned Kiera and Dante to join him a discreet distance away from the Shillings and Joshis.

"I thought of some new names last night," he whispered. "How about Rory if it's a boy? You know, for the *Rorschach Explorer*, or Cali — for Callisto — if it's a girl?"

Kiera shook her head and patted her tummy. "You're going to make the next nine months weird, aren't you?"

"Roger dodger." Ajay smiled. Turning serious, he cupped his hand around his mouth and softly said, "If you don't like Rory, how about Tiberius?"

"What? I'm not naming our child Tiberius!"

"Hey, it's my child too," Ajay whispered.

Kiera leaned in and whispered back, "Look, when Dante and I get back from our vacation, you and I will talk names. Until then, zip it."

Morgan overheard the exchange and chuckled.

He spotted Amato standing alone by the Suhkai cruiser, looking up at the spacecraft like a child on Christmas morning. Morgan walked over and joined him. "Pretty impressive, huh?"

Amato nodded. "Buck Rogers would be jealous."

"I was talking with Haula yesterday. He said he's certain they can modify their propulsion system for *RE2*. We'll have to redesign the cargo bay to make room for the fuel cells, but Dante said he's got some options already on the drawing board."

"Wouldn't that be something." Amato waved his cane like a magic wand. "From here to Saturn in the time it takes me to drive from Orlando to West Palm."

They walked back through the hangar, waving and smiling for the media as they passed, and upstairs to Amato's office. When they were seated at Amato's conference table, Morgan looked up at one of the *Rorschach Explorer* paintings. "It was a helluva ship, Augie. It endured a lot of abuse but never quit on us."

"I'm thankful for that, but I'm also angry at myself for putting you and the crew through that abuse. I should never have pushed up the launch. I won't make that mistake again. I promise you."

Morgan shrugged. "I wouldn't beat yourself up over it. If we'd launched on schedule, things would have turned out a whole lot worse. Nick would have already come and gone in *Ethel*. We would never have met the Suhkai. They would have scuttled their refineries on Callisto and Dione. Hell, we wouldn't have known about the Dione facility at all. We would be clueless about the magnetar, about Tula, the children. We wouldn't know what happened to Avery, Christine and Nick. And to top it off, I wouldn't have gotten to know what I look like blue and bald. All in all, things worked out okay."

Both men shared a good laugh.

Amato then said soberly, "Do you think it's possible, Paul? Can we prevent it from happening?"

"I don't know, but I know I'm going to give it my all. With help from the BLUMO Cytons and the Suhkai, we'll have as good a chance as we possibly could … so long as we don't dally and don't let fear paralyze us."

"Are you sure you're up for it? Two years there, two years back … and who knows how long while you're there. Under the best of circumstances, you'll be seventy by the time you return."

"Beats flipping burgers for tourists. Besides, Dennis has the tougher job ahead. He's gonna have his hands full running the colonization selection committee."

"He'll do a splendid job," Amato said. "He's a master politician."

"Yeah, well, he's gonna need every last bit of his patience dealing with the Suhkai. They're very opinionated."

A knock sounded on the door, and Mark Myers poked his head in. "It's time, Mr. Amato."

"Very well, let's get it over with."

Myers walked in and placed a folded black-and-gold flight suit on the table in front of Amato.

"Excited?" Morgan said.

"Scared to death."

"Ah, don't worry, Augie. I asked them to take it easy on you during the ascent."

"Will you come with me?" Amato asked. "I'd feel a lot less nervous with Skywalker by my side."

"Thought you'd never ask." Morgan smiled. "One round trip around Jupiter, coming up."

EPILOGUE

Paul Morgan stood over the hot grill and tended to the patties. A few yards away, a barefoot Annie burst through the lush foliage giggling and screaming as the two children of his next-door neighbor chased her. Her feet were caked with red clay.

Next to him sat Sarah on a chaise lounge, an infant in her arms, and Ajay was explaining the baby's heritage to Morgan's brother, Jason. "So you see, she's the first Tulan to be born on Earth to a mother who was the first Tulan to be created by Earth parents."

With everybody's skin back to normal, and hair regrowing, the backyard barbecue had the feel of a family picnic.

Earlier, before firing up the grill, Morgan had gathered the Tulan children on the Kauai beach down the road from his home, and they'd filmed a video message to Avery and Christine. Ajay had sent it via his laptop to Mayaguana, where Norris Preston relayed it, by way of A3I's satellite, to *Ethel* parked on Callisto, where the Suhkai, in turn, aimed the ship's antenna toward Tula and broadcast the file. It would take eleven years to reach Avery and Christine. And a mere nine months after that, *Ethel* would arrive bearing their children, the children's new guardian Ajay, and a village of human colonists.

It made Morgan sad to realize he'd never see their reply, or live long enough to know whether *Ethel* made it to Tula. But he would be at peace as he went on to do battle with a magnetar. He hadn't brought his astronauts home as he'd hoped, but he felt comfort in knowing that the effort to find them had not come up empty.

Roger that.

Kiera sat on the sofa opposite Jenna Toffy and adjusted the bow on her maternity dress as the two chatted about the *Rorschach Explorer*'s harrowing adventures.

For many of the viewers tuning in to watch the interview, Kiera was a heroic figure. She had been painted as a lightweight prior to — and during — the mission, but the details that had emerged in the months after returning to Earth had made it clear that she was anything but. Jenna Toffy asked her if, in retrospect, she had anything to say to her critics.

"You were called a hothead, a thumb-sucker, a washout," Toffy said.

"Don't forget a misfit, beaks and talons, and I'm pretty sure at least one person called me a bitch," Kiera said with a smile.

"Yes, I do believe there were some other unflattering names as well. So what would you like to say to those skeptics now?"

"Um, I dunno."

"Oh, come on. By all accounts, you were a remarkable astronaut. Resourceful, brave, determined. These are the words your crewmates used to describe you."

"I wasn't any more remarkable than anyone else aboard."

"Yes, but you weren't the wreck-waiting-to-happen many people said you'd be."

Kiera shook her head. "That's not true. I screamed like a frightened child when we were caught up in the battle between the BLUMOs and

Zikzaw. I curled up into a fetal position multiple times. And I jumped off a ledge to try and kill myself."

"But stacked up against all you accomplished, all you endured, those moments of weakness don't make you a wreck."

"You're right, Jenna. They make me human."

For information about other books by K. Patrick Donoghue, including *Dynewave*, book 3 in the Rorschach Explorer Missions series, visit the author's website at <u>kpatrickdonoghue.com</u>.

PARASAUR ILLUSTRATION

GLOSSARY OF TERMS

A3rospace Industries — the name of Augustus Amato's aerospace engineering firm.

A3I — an acronym for A3rospace Industries.

A3I-TDRS — an acronym for A3rospace Industries' tracking and data relay satellite, the satellite that relays data between the *Rorschach Explorer* and Mission Control on Mayaguana.

Andromeda — the name of an instrumentation probe carried by *Cetus Prime*.

BCON — an acronym for a television network. Stands for Be Controversial.

BLUMO — blue-colored UMOs (unidentified magnetic objects, electromagnetic aliens that appear as balls of light). UMOs, in the whole, are also referred to as space bees and Cytons in the story.

Callisto — a moon of Jupiter where Augustus Amato and his team discovered the long-lost spacecraft, *Cetus Prime*, and an alien structure in a crater named Nuada.

Callistons — lizard-like humanoid aliens, also referred to in the story as the Suhkai, the beekeepers and lizard-men.

Cam-1, et al — the names of various cameras on the *Rorschach Explorer* and its accompanying fleet of probes.

CAPCOM — an old NASA acronym that stands for capsule communicator, the liaison between the crew aboard a spacecraft and mission control.

Cargo, *Cargo-1,* **et al** – A3rospace Industries' name for delivery-truck sized supply probes traveling along with the *Rorschach Explorer.* These vessels house provisions, parts and other supplies intended to support *Rorschach's* mission.

CCDR — an acronym used to identify co-pilot Major Julia Carillo in communications between the *Rorschach Explorer* and Mission Control.

CDR — an acronym used to identify the commander of the *Rorschach Explorer* crew, Colonel Paul Morgan, in communications between the *Rorschach Explorer* and Mission Control.

CPO — an acronym for *Cetus Prime Orbiter,* an instrumentation probe carried by *Cetus Prime.*

CubeSat — a small-sized, unmanned instrumentation probe. In *Magwave,* there are two types of CubeSats, Recons and Shields (see their separate descriptions below).

Cytons — an alternative name for UMOs and BLUMOs.

Dione — a moon of Saturn.

DSN — an acronym for NASA's Deep Space Network, a conglomeration of Earth-based satellites that track and communicate with NASA spacecraft in deep space.

Elroy — the nickname for Ajay Joshi and a 1960s-vintage cartoon character.

EMP — an acronym for electromagnetic pulse.

EMU — a NASA acronym for extravehicular mobility unit, otherwise known as a spacesuit.

Ethel — nickname of a Suhkai spaceship.

FE — an acronym identifying flight engineer Dr. Kiera Walsh in communications between the *Rorschach Explorer* and Mission Control.

Gateway Museum — name of Augustus Amato's space memorabilia museum located at the Orlando headquarters complex of A3rospace Industries.

GEFF — an acronym for the gravity environment forcefield aboard the *Rorschach Explorer.*

GRS — an acronym for a gamma ray spectrometer, an instrument that measures gamma radiation.

HEO — an acronym for high Earth orbit.

HF — an acronym for high frequency radio band, also known as shortwave radio.

Iapetus — a moon of Saturn.

INCO — a NASA acronym for the instruments and control officer station in Mission Control.

JPL — an acronym for NASA's Jet Propulsion Laboratory.

km/h — an acronym for kilometers per hour.

LDV — an acronym for launch delivery vehicle, the name of the spacecraft Augustus Amato uses to carry his CubeSats into Earth's orbit.

Living Universe garden — a sculptured garden at A3rospace Industries' Orlando headquarters complex that displays a fanciful depiction of the solar system.

LOS — an acronym meaning loss of signal. It is commonly used by NASA and others to indicate loss of communication with a probe or other type of spacecraft.

LEO — an acronym for low Earth orbit.

Mayaguana, MAYA, Maya — the various names used to describe Augustus Amato's mission control center and launch facility. It is located on the Bahamian island of Mayaguana on the grounds of a former NASA satellite tracking station.

MAYA-FLIGHT — an acronym used to identify mission director Dr. Dante Fulton in communications between the *Rorschach Explorer* and Mission Control.

Mission Control — the instrumentation and communications nerve center where the *Rorschach Explorer* mission is managed.

MSAJ — an acronym used to identify Mission Specialist Ajay Joshi in communications between the *Rorschach Explorer* and Mission Control.

MSRS — an acronym used to identify Mission Specialist Dr. Richard Shilling in communications between the *Rorschach Explorer* and Mission Control.

Perseus — the name of a weaponry probe armed with electromagnetic pulse missiles carried by *Cetus Prime*.

RCS — an acronym for reaction control system, the system that manages the maneuvering thrusters on the *Rorschach Explorer* and its accompanying probes.

Recon, *Recon-1*, et al — A3rospace Industries' name used to identify a specific type of CubeSat probe traveling along with the *Rorschach Explorer*. Recons are outfitted with instrumentation to scan and monitor for various forms of electromagnetic radiation.

RE2 — an acronym for the second generation *Rorschach Explorer*.

Rorschach Explorer — the name of Augustus Amato's spacecraft of the future, designed to carry humans on deep space missions with the support of a fleet of unmanned probes.

SatFleet — a term used to identify the fleet of probes accompanying the *Rorschach Explorer*.

SHF — an acronym for the super-high-frequency radio waves transmitted over X-band radio equipment.

Shield, *Shield-1*, et al — A3rospace Industries' name used to identify a specific type of CubeSat probe traveling along with the *Rorschach Explorer*. Shields are outfitted with special magnets that provide radiation protection for the *Rorschach Explorer* and its accompanying fleet of probes.

Skywalker — the nickname for Colonel Paul Morgan.

Sol Seaker — the name of Dr. Anlon Cully's superyacht.

Suhkai – lizard-like humanoid aliens, also known as Callistons, the beekeepers and the lizard-men.

Titan — a moon of Saturn.

TRE – an acronym used to identify the *Rorschach Explorer* in communications between the *Rorschach Explorer* and Mission Control.

Tula — name of planet in a far-away solar system.

UHF — an acronym for the ultra-high-frequency radio band and ultra-high-frequency radio waves.

UMOs — an acronym for unidentified magnetic objects, electromagnetic aliens that appear as small white, blue, orange or golden balls of lights. They feed on ions in space, the atmosphere of planets, moons and asteroids and ions ejected by the unique VLF engines that power the *Rorschach Explorer* and its accompanying fleet of unmanned probes. They are also referred to in the story as space bees and Cytons.

VLF — an acronym for the very-low-frequency radio band and very-low-frequency radio waves.

VLF engine — a breakthrough propulsion system designed by Dr. Kiera Walsh that utilizes very-low-frequency radio waves to heat and accelerate electrons and ions inside a plasma chamber, producing a lightning-like output that generates propulsion.

Whave Technologies — the name of Dr. Antonio Wallace's high-tech engineering firm.

WNN — an acronym for the television network known as World Network News.

X-band — the term used to identify the radio band used to transmit and receive super-high- frequency (SHF) radio waves.

XTC — an acronym used to identify the *Expedition to Callisto* television program

Zikzaws — electromagnetic, snake-like creatures that appear in the story.

ABOUT THE AUTHOR

Kevin Patrick Donoghue is the author of the Anlon Cully Chronicles archaeology mystery series, the Rorschach Explorer Missions science fiction series and the Unity of Four medical thriller series. His books include:

THE ANLON CULLY CHRONICLES SERIES:

Book 1: *Shadows of the Stone Benders*
Book 2: *Race for the Flash Stone*
Book 3: *Curse of the Painted Lady*
Book 4: *Priestess of Paracas*

THE RORSCHACH EXPLORER MISSIONS SERIES:

Prequel: *UMO* (novella)
Book 1: *Skywave*
Book 2: *Magwave*
Book 3: *Dynewave*

THE UNITY OF FOUR SERIES:

Book 1: *The GODD Chip*

Ways to stay in touch with the author: follow K. Patrick Donoghue — Novelist on Facebook or join the author's email subscriber list by visiting kpatrickdonoghue.com and clicking on the "Join Email List" link on the main menu.

Made in United States
Orlando, FL
12 July 2024